# OCEANBORNE

BOOKS BY KATHERINE IRONS

*Oceanborne*

*Seaborne*

# OCEANBORNE

## KATHERINE IRONS

*B*
*BRAVA*

KENSINGTON PUBLISHING CORP.
www.kensingtonbooks.com

BRAVA BOOKS are published by

Kensington Publishing Corp.
119 West 40th Street
New York, NY 10018

All Kensington titles, imprints and distributed lines are available at special quantity discounts for bulk purchases for sales promotion, premiums, fund-raising, educational or institutional use.

Special book excerpts or customized printings can also be created to fit specific needs. For details, write or phone the office of the Kensington Special Sales Manager: Kensington Publishing Corp., 119 West 40th Street, New York, NY 10018, Attn. Special Sales Department. Phone: 1-800-221-2647.

Brava and the B logo are Reg. U.S. Pat. & TM Off.

ISBN-13: 978-0-7582-6142-7
ISBN-10: 0-7582-6142-X

First Trade Paperback Printing: October 2011

10  9  8  7  6  5  4  3  2  1

Printed in the United States of America

*For Candace, with love . . .*

# CHAPTER 1

*Present day, off the coast of Greece . . .*

It wasn't a good day to die.

In Orion's opinion, no day was a particularly pleasant one to have the flesh ripped from your bones and be devoured alive by a horde of the Phoenician war god's minions. But apparently, Orion wasn't to be given a choice. It was fight his way out of this quickly-constricting circle of Melqart's shades or start singing his own Atlantean death chant worthy of a soon-to-be deceased prince.

Why hadn't he remained on the island a while longer? Most Atlanteans could leave the embrace of the sea and breathe air for short periods of time, but his gift was the knack for remaining on land for days at a time without succumbing to the constant bombardment of poisonous substances that land walkers had created. But, no, he was impatient, as always—eager to be back with his regiment, anxious to carry the news of the latest outrage to the High Council. And where had it gotten him? Seven fathoms deep, surrounded by foul abominations that existed for one purpose—to rip him into bite-sized morsels, grind his bones between their teeth, and swallow him to the last tasty drop.

Shrieking, two of the androgynous soul-suckers surged from the ranks and closed in on him, one on the left, and the other to his right. These were fully mature shades, over six feet from saw-toothed hind flippers to snub-nosed simian heads, armed with poisonous claws—nine to an appendage—each the size of a Bengal tiger's. They dove at him, ghoulish eyes glowing red in ashen, bansheelike faces, gaping maws filled with jagged teeth that could rip and tear through flesh as easily as a great white shark bit through a seal's belly.

Orion grasped the hilt of his broadsword in both hands, swinging it in a figure-eight pattern, slicing one predator in half on his first downward stroke and taking his remaining opponent as he completed the swing. Cutting the creatures in half was the only way to destroy them, and the water around him hissed with a black, acidic slime that he supposed passed for blood with them. The stench was enough to sicken a moray eel! Zeus' bullocks, but he hated killing shades.

Hissing and moaning, the circle widened, and the crunch of cartilage and internal organs grated on Orion's ears. As usual, the horde let no life force go to waste, quickly cannibalizing what was left of their two comrades. His stomach clenched. He was a warrior, a prince who'd spent a lifetime defending the kingdom. He wasn't easily fazed by bloodshed, but the combination of his hangover and the odor brought bile up in his throat.

What he wouldn't give for one of his brothers at his side! A half-dozen shades would have been child's play for him to deal with, but there were two dozen, perhaps three that he'd counted, and a second sword would have made a big difference. For all their ferocity, the creatures showed little courage. If they couldn't swarm over a victim and conquer easily, they drifted away to seek an easier target. Today, in this spot, he was that vulnerable prey.

By Ares' foreskin! How could he have been so stupid? This wasn't even his fight. He hadn't intended to stumble on the human bodies—or rather the gory remains—of two luckless German tourists on the lonely beach. Had he been hunting Melqart's hordes or suspected they were feeding in the area, he would have had a trusted team of seasoned Atlantean warriors and their combat dolphin partners at his back.

The foul things had withdrawn into the shadows, but he could hear them all around him, hissing and moaning, gathering courage for a second rush. He flexed his shoulders and tried to think of some way to get himself out of this alive. On a scale of one to ten, ten being hopeless, he generously gave himself a twelve.

When he'd spotted the first gleam of teeth and red eyes in the depths, he'd sent out a frantic mental SOS to any friendly beings in the area. Mermen would fight beside him, as would dolphins and the occasional lone whale. Once, an ancient sea turtle had proved a godsend when he was cornered by two hammerhead sharks, but squid and eels would as soon join the shades as come to his assistance. They possessed no sense of fair play, caring only to feed their own bellies. And if he died at the teeth and claws of the horde, there would be scraps enough to satisfy the scavengers.

Attacks by Melqart's hordes were less frequent than they'd been in centuries past. The shades were merciless, and intelligence, if they possessed such, was more a group thought process than an individual one. They often pulled down lone swimmers at night, tearing the bodies apart or simply sucking them dry, leaving the humans to believe that the deaths were caused by sharks or barracuda. The creatures reveled in blood, feeding on the life forces of Atlanteans, humans, and other humanoids. And the energy from each life provided substance to their master Melqart.

Orion should have had reinforcements, but regretfully, he was alone. He'd been on leave and had unwisely spent the last two weeks more than slightly intoxicated in the arms of a particularly well-endowed mermaid of vast imagination and dubious moral character. Mermaids were known for their insatiable sexual appetites, and this particular lady was a legend among her own kind. Orion hoped the energy he'd spent in satisfying her wouldn't be the death of him, but she'd been wet, willing, and as tight as a sword sheath. Two dozen interludes had not been enough, and if his groin ached from the rigorous exercise, he could console himself with knowing that he'd gained a wealth of information about triggering multiple orgasms in females, especially in mermaids.

To his left, somewhere near the misty island, a siren's seductive voice sent a frisson of ice down his spine. It was one thing to contemplate the epic dirge his brother would create in memory of his last battle against hopeless odds, and quite another to hear the proclamation of his demise from one of the pitiless hags who'd lured humans to destruction for eons.

Orion sensed, rather than saw, the circle tighten once more. "By Aphrodite's sweet mound," he swore under his breath. They were coming for him, coming in numbers too great for him to overcome. He flexed his sword arm, moved so that his back was guarded by a massive wall of fallen granite, and uttered an Atlantean war cry. If he had to die here and now, he'd not go gently.

*   *   *

Elena knew that coming too close to the jagged rocks jutting up from the sea might be disastrous. Yet, impulsively, despite the rising wind and the ever-increasing rain, she steered the Zodiac nearer to the island. The small watercraft pitched and bounced in the waves, making her question the wisdom of coming out to the shipwreck at all this afternoon. But it wasn't as if she hadn't been doing this half her life, and she was in a Zodiac. They were supposed to be practically unsinkable, weren't they?

She'd approached the expedition's charter boat captain early this morning and asked him to run her out to the site. She knew the seas were too rough for diving. She simply wanted to make certain that the unidentified boat that had been hanging around didn't carry some amateur archeologist who might take the opportunity of the bad weather to poke around the wreck.

But Anso would have none of it. He'd given her a hound-dog look and shaken his head. "No, no, no. No today. No tomorrow. Bad storm. Big waves. Too danger." His heavily accented English wasn't quite as good as her Greek, but he'd made himself clear enough. Rubbing the great belly that bulged out in a hairy tire over his patched trousers, he'd muttered something to his first mate that sent the little man into spasms.

"No today,"

Petros echoed between gales of laughter. Then, he'd pinched his nose and given a bad imitation of drowning. "*Antolia* old boat. No today."

Knowing her cause was hopeless and unable to convince any of her team to go with her, Elena had set off in the Zodiac alone. The thought of losing yet another day of work due to bad weather was maddening. The university's dive permit was for a limited time, and a storm could easily cover the site in silt, burying several weeks of careful excavation. She'd called in too many favors to acquire this project, and so far, they'd uncovered nothing significant. Still, she couldn't shake the feeling that this was no ordinary Phoenician trading vessel, and that just a few inches or feet away waited a discovery that would add enormously to the pool of knowledge about this ancient race of seafarers.

She'd had the same feeling before, two years ago, when she was an assistant on a Nile River expedition. Her hunch had paid off when she'd insisted on making one last dive, and had discovered the ruins of a previously unknown temple dedicated to Hathor, dating several centuries earlier than the rise of her cult. As an archeologist and scientist, Elena knew she should have disdained hunches as superstition, but like her father before her, she'd learned to heed that inner voice.

A curtain of drenching rain broke over the Zodiac, making it difficult to see. Elena yanked off her glasses and tossed them onto the deck. Every instinct told her to steer away from the island before a rock tore a hole in the inflatable's side or punched through the bottom, but she felt an overwhelming need to go closer. And, if she was honest with herself, she was happiest when she was swept up in the rush, savoring life to the bottom of the cup.

Abruptly, amid the foam and churning water, a man's head broke the surface only a few yards ahead. She stared in astonishment as the swimmer raised one hand over his head, grasping something long and black and shiny. Elena blinked, and peered through the heavy rain, certain her eyes were playing tricks on her.

For an instant, she could have sworn that the drowning man held a glittering bronze-age sword. Then, a wave broke over him, and he was lost from sight. Whoever he was, he was obviously in trouble. No one could survive in these conditions.

"Hold on!" she yelled. "I'm coming!" She gunned the motor, fighting waves and tide, guiding the Zodiac closer to the spot where he'd gone down. Her heart pounded against her ribs. If he didn't come up on his own, he was lost. There was no chance of finding him in the churning water. He might have been caught in an undertow, sucked down to be trapped in the rocks and drowned.

"Where are you, damn it?" she cried into the driving rain. She untied a life ring and waited—breathless—for what seemed an eternity. Then, when she was certain that he was gone, he shot up on the port side. For a moment, their gazes locked. They were so close that she could see the color of his eyes. As green as the sea. Her first thought was that his expression wasn't one of panic or despair. Instead, he looked exhilarated.

"Here!" she shouted, throwing the life ring.

He caught it in the air, slipped it over his head, and pulled himself arm over arm to the side of the pitching Zodiac. She couldn't take her hands off the tiller to assist him into the boat, but he managed it on his own, flinging his body over the side and collapsing face down on the deck. Face down was good, because he was stark naked.

Elena didn't have much time to admire the scenery if she didn't want the Zodiac to run smack into a rock pillar dead ahead but, for the blink of an eye, she had a delicious glimpse of wide muscular shoulders, narrow hips, and powerful thighs and calves. No Greek sword—her eyes must have been playing tricks on her—but the man's taut buttocks made up for it.

Her stowaway pushed himself up on his elbows, shook the long yellow hair out of his eyes, and grinned at her. Her heart missed a beat. He looked like a movie star or a model on the cover of *Italian Vogue*. "Run between those rocks!" He pointed. "You can beach it on the sand!"

She wasn't certain she wanted to attempt it, but it might be their only chance. The storm was growing worse. The waves were higher, the wind whipping up a tempest as jagged lightning split the black clouds overhead. Elena had threaded between the rocks to reach this spot, but with the tide coming in, and the force of the waves, it might be more dangerous to try to turn the Zodiac and head back for open water.

"Are you sure we can make it?" Visibility was fast dwindling, and the raindrops battered her face and body.

He flung her another wicked grin, and the strength went out of her knees. "No, but if you don't, you'd better be a good swimmer," he shouted before moving to the bow to balance the weight. "Cut hard to port!" He pointed at a finger of stone barely visible above the waves.

Elena fought the rudder with all her strength, certain that the Zodiac would be dashed against the rocks. She could hear the roar of the surf ahead, but the channel that opened between the jagged stone outcrops seemed impossibly narrow. "Hold on tight!"

If they survived the rocks, she would have to ride the tops of the waves and slide onto the sand, and she'd have to keep the Zodiac at exactly the right angle or an incoming wave would catch it wrong and the inflatable would pitch pole.

"Now!" he shouted. "Go for it!"

She gunned the throttle, but just when she thought they had a chance a wave bigger than the others crashed over the stern of the Zodiac, filling the raft with six inches of water and temporarily blinding her. The motor sputtered. She choked and spat out a mouthful of water. "Come on! Come on!" she screamed, willing the engine to catch and fire. But her plea was in vain. The motor died, and the next thing Elena knew, the Zodiac went end over end and she was flying through the air.

Icy green water closed over her head. She kicked hard and tried to swim, but the force of the tide was too great. She found herself tossed like a bit of driftwood, slamming against rock and suddenly unable to tell which way was the surface. She held her breath until her lungs burned and dark spots swirled in front of her eyes. Panic seized her as she thought, *This is what it feels like to drown.*

The thunder of the surf muted as the cold sea poured into her mouth and nostrils, and her world went from blue-green to a chaos of black and gray. Time slowed and stretched, colors grew more vivid, and she no longer struggled to breathe. She sighed, relaxing her body, surrendering to the pull of the tide, letting go until a white specter loomed out of the deep. Terror greater than her fear of death surged through her as the ghostly creature stared at her with glittering red eyes and bared teeth.

Pain lanced up Elena's thigh, and she kicked out at another shadow. With a burst of will, she twisted and tried to swim, frantic to escape this new nightmare. But she'd used up the last of her strength, and instead of moving farther away from this new menace, she hung suspended in the cold water, mouth wide in a silent scream, as the nightmare advanced ever closer.

# CHAPTER 2

The arrival of the female in the Zodiac had saved Orion's skin, and he knew it all too well. Atlanteans, out of the sea, slowly grew weak and lethargic. Days—and in some cases mere hours—on land would mean certain death. But for Melqart's shades, only a single ray of sunshine would turn them into an oily column of black smoke. Simply, the creatures boiled alive in seconds. As stupid as they were, the horde had a strong sense of self-preservation, and knew better than to follow him out of the water.

Had he merely surfaced, the shades would have swam up under him and pulled him down, devouring him in the process. The pack had cut him off from the beach, and the nearest outcrop of rock had been too far for him to reach. He'd been into the second chorus of his death chant when he'd heard the sound of a boat motor and had retreated to the nearest bolthole—in this case, a human's watercraft.

He hadn't expected the Zodiac to be manned by a female, a beautiful one at that. But man or woman, old or young, attractive or hideous, he was getting in that boat. The trick was in evading the shades in one piece and casting an illusion once he broke water. It wouldn't do for a human to see him as he really was, wouldn't do at all. And since she hadn't run him down or leaped screaming into the sea, he supposed he'd done a fair job of disguising his appearance to appear human.

What he hadn't counted on was the wave that had drowned the engine or the following one that had sent them sailing back into the drink where the horde was waiting. He landed only a few yards from the beach. It would have been child's play to reach solid land and relative safety ahead of the shades if it hadn't been for the woman.

Humans were the enemy, but this one had risked her life to save him. Had she known what he was, it might have been another story, but he couldn't shrug off the debt he owed her. Since he'd been a small child, a code of honor had been drummed into him. He couldn't let her die.

So, reluctantly, Orion turned his back on the shore and threw himself into the fray once more. Cut and thrust. Slice and hack. Single handed. Not only did he have to cut a path through the shades, he had to do it while retrieving the woman from her would-be executioners and using his powers to keep her from drowning.

The art of giving a human the ability to survive underwater was another arrow in an Atlantean's quiver, one that he was somewhat rusty at. Not magic, exactly, but close enough to amaze the masses. He couldn't wait to brag to Alexandros about this heroic interlude. This tale would make a more exciting song than one where he died in the end. Plus, he'd be there to revel in the glory.

Neither of them reached the beach unscathed. He'd been bitten and clawed in a dozen places. Blood ran from a great gash down his thigh to pool on the sand under his feet, and one of the beasts had taken a chunk out of his left bicep. The woman hung limp and lifeless in his arms. Her eyes were open, the irises rolled up so that the whites showed. Her skin was the color of bleached oyster shell except for the place where a shade had sunk his teeth into her thigh. Blood soaked the leg of her torn jeans and drops of blood dripped onto the sand.

His own wounds were insignificant. They would heal of their own accord, slower than if he were underwater, of course, but fast enough. The woman might not fare as well. She was cold, her breathing so shallow as to be barely perceptible. The rain was still beating down on them, and the wind had teeth. Overhead, thunder rumbled ominously. He decided to carry her into the cave that opened only a short distance above the small stretch of sand.

The cavern mouth was small, a place that might be easily overlooked, but he had noted it when he'd been on the island before. Centuries before, humans had taken shelter here, but they were long gone, their bones turned to dust. The floor was covered with fine gold-colored sand, and the air smelled of salt and sea.

He lay the woman face down, pressed gently but firmly on her back, and watched as what seemed like a beaker of water gushed out of her mouth and nose. Immediately, she began to cough and choke. He gave one more good compression, then turned her over, leaned down, and kissed her mouth.

Her eyelids fluttered, and Orion found himself staring into two hauntingly beautiful dark orbs. A shudder ran through her and she gave a small moan.

He kissed her again, surprised at how warm her lips were and how perfectly they molded to his. Excitement shot through him, and he flushed. This wasn't how it was supposed to be. He was simply repaying a debt, her life for his. It wasn't personal. She was human, for Zeus' sake.

Humans, especially the females, were weak, pitiful things, possessing the sexual lure of a dead mollusk.

But not this one. This woman exuded sensuality with the allure of a mermaid. He had the feeling that he'd moved into a realm where nothing was as he'd expected. He was used to being in control where females were concerned. This wasn't the way things were supposed to be, and he didn't like it one bit.

She choked again, bringing up more water. He pulled her into his arms and held her while she brought up the contents of her stomach, taking care to hold her long, brown hair away from her face. She groaned, sagging against him. He laid her back against the rocks, found a handful of seaweed, and used it to wipe her mouth. A second fistful made a poultice to staunch the ragged cut on her thigh. He pressed his fingers against the bite, closed his eyes, and willed the wound to heal. Again, since he was out of the sea, he didn't have his usual power, but it was sufficient to close the punctures and restore the damaged surrounding tissue.

Her color was beginning to return.

He took a deep breath and conjured the illusion that he was human and decent according to human standards. It was hard to use imagination where air breathers' fashion was concerned, and he was short on time. He covered his loins in the likeness of a pair of stretchy, red swim trunks he'd seen a French tourist wearing on a local beach. The garment was ridiculous, not in his opinion nearly as modest as being naked would have been. The woman's lashes fluttered, and she stirred, commanding Orion's full attention.

He couldn't tear his gaze away from her. He knew this was completely illogical. By Jason's fleece, she had no gills or scales and her slender feet were completely without webbing!

Yet, he found her fascinating . . . intriguing.

Her complexion was a dusky olive, her forehead high, her brows dark and arching. Her face was a perfect oval, her nose straight, chin dimpled, and her mouth was made for kissing. He'd never been good with guessing ages when it came to humans, but he supposed she was thirty, at least, a mere child. But those eyes . . . He wondered if she was a sorceress, some sort of earthy naiad or witchling. Those eyes seemed mysterious, as if they were black bottomless pools containing all the secrets of the world.

She blinked and the corners of her mouth turned up in a faint smile. "What happened?" she whispered.

Orion's throat constricted. This was wrong. All wrong. He shouldn't be here. She shouldn't be here. But he had no more power to walk away and leave her than he had to fly.

"Am I dead?" she asked.

He wondered what she'd seen after the boat had catapulted, throwing them into the sea, and he touched her gently on the forehead, willing her to forget everything that happened after they'd made a run for the beach.

"I hope not." He chuckled, more in an attempt to normalize his feelings than because he was amused. "Because if you are, I must be, too."

She tried to sit up, groaned, and fell back. "The Zodiac?"

"Flipped."

She swallowed. "It's expensive," she rasped. "If I lose the inflatable, it will come out of my stipend."

"Tough break."

"That bad?"

He shrugged. "I've seen worse. On the bottom. The motor might be salvageable, but I doubt it. Those rocks gave it a pretty good scrubbing." Not to mention the shades. He'd seen three of them tearing at it with tooth and claw. He supposed they thought it might be alive. No one had ever accused Melqart's horde of being smart.

She swore. In Greek. Her accent was quite good. And the curse imaginative.

"It could be worse," he reminded her. "We could be shark chum." He brushed a long lock of damp hair off her oval face, and simply touching her sent a rush of excitement through him. "You came close to drowning." He'd tried to speak naturally, but his voice grew husky with emotion.

"And I suppose I have you to thank for saving my life?"

He couldn't suppress a grin. "You could say that." His gaze traveled from her classically beautiful face down over her slim body. She was wearing the remains of a black T-shirt bearing the likeness of the temple of Apollo, and faded jeans. The top barely covered her small but nicely shaped breasts. Her waist was small, her hips wide enough to be womanly. Human or not, witchling or not, she was a package. And he wanted to possess her.

Sex with humans was strictly forbidden by Atlantean law. Not that the law prevented the occasional familiarity with the enemy. It did happen. Sadly, being forbidden added spice to the act. But it had been a long time since he'd risked arrest and severe punishment for sport with an air breather. Centuries. And she hadn't been nearly as attractive.

He knew what Alex would say. Have her and be done with it. Get her out of your system. Orion was breathing hard now, fighting his own nature to keep from taking advantage of her. She was so vulnerable, lying here, half naked, grateful to him for coming to her rescue. Seducing her would be as easy as gathering seaweed at low tide.

Atlanteans males were endowed with super-sexual needs that required regular physical gratification. . . . Fortunately, Atlantean females were equally sensual beings. Adults took their pleasure where they found it without remorse or guilt. Only a few, notably the royal family and some noble lines, were monogamous. His parents had been when his mother was alive, although his father, Poseidon, had acquired many wives and even more concubines since her death. Since his older brother Morgan would inherit the throne, there was little need for Orion to consider marriage to one woman. His conquests had been many, and he prided himself on providing equal satisfaction to his partners.

Bedding this woman seemed a sensible solution to what was fast becoming a painful problem. He could disguise himself as a human by throwing a net of illusion over her, but it was difficult to hide his interest, even with the inferior sexual anatomy of one of her kind.

She pushed herself up to a sitting position, rubbed the place where she'd been bitten, and looked down at her bloodstained jeans. "I must have scraped myself against the rocks, but I don't see where—"

"Probably my blood," he lied. Fabrication was easier than explaining how he'd healed her so quickly. "You were lucky."

"Are you hurt?"

"Nothing more than a skinned knee."

"We were both lucky." She began to squeeze the seawater out of her long brown hair. "Of course, if I'm to be grateful to you, you owe me the same. You were drowning when I snatched you out of the waves."

"Me? Drowning? I was not." About to be devoured alive, maybe, but to suggest that an Atlantean male could drown in the ocean was an insult. His pride prickled. "I was just out for a swim."

She laughed. Her laughter was as enticing as the expression in her eyes. And her mouth . . . He wanted to taste those lips again.

She extended a slender hand. "Elena Carter."

He took it. "Orion." She had a firm grip for a woman, and he found himself reluctant to release her. Instead, he lightly caressed the fleshy mound of her palm with his thumb, reveling in the frisson of excitement it gave him.

He felt his loins tighten, and it took all his will power to keep his abundant attributes from rising to the occasion. He didn't want to frighten her away. Slow and easy, that was best in dealing with human females. They didn't possess the sexual appetite of Atlantean women or the staying power to continue a mutually-satisfying session for hours . . . or, in some cases, days.

"No last name?"

His eyes widened. She had him there. He didn't have a last name. He was Orion, son of Poseidon, prince of Atlantis. What did he need with a second name? Everyone who mattered knew who he was.

"Is it a secret?" She parted the torn material of her jeans, obviously searching for an injury, but her flesh had healed perfectly.

"No." He chuckled. "Xenos. Orion Xenos."

"*Stranger.*"

"Excuse me?"

"The meaning of Xenos is *stranger*, isn't it?"

"I suppose it is. I never really thought about it."

"It fits," she said thoughtfully. "Strange that you'd be out in that water, that I'd rescue you, and we'd both end up . . . What? Shipwrecked? I don't suppose there's a telephone on this island. Or a taverna?" She wiped her mouth. "My friends will suspect the worst when I don't come back."

"No, no taverna, although I could use a shot of ouzo." He shook his head. "There's no one on this island at all."

"That's incorrect."

His eyes narrowed. "I assure you that—"

"You're here and I'm here. That makes two of us, so you can hardly say that the island is deserted."

She started to rise and he offered his hand. She took it as if it were her due, as his mother or sisters might. He could almost say that she was regal, for a human. And the brown eyes that met his showed not the slightest hint of fear. Her hand was warm, her grip strong.

"So, Orion Xenos." She pried her hand loose from his and went to stand near the opening to the cave. "What were you doing here? And where's your boat?"

"Lost it," he said. "I was swimming, and it broke loose from the anchor and the tide took it."

"You lost it." She sounded unconvinced. "You happened to be out for a swim off a deserted island in a storm and lost your boat. Interesting."

"I'm sure you have a much more reasonable excuse for why you were sightseeing in this weather." He went to stand beside her. The rain was coming down in sheets, the wind and waves making it difficult to hear.

She looked up at him. "I'm an archeologist. An underwater archeologist. I'm heading up an expedition and I came out to check on the site. The Greek government frowns on antiquity thieves. I wanted to make certain that no one was attempting to dive our site."

"Your site?" He arched a brow. "You're a foreigner. American? This is Greek territory. It can hardly be *your* site."

She ignored his comment. "My father was British. I was born in Cornwall. I have dual citizenship."

"Wonderful. Another foreigner here to plunder our national treasures."

"Not simply treasures of Greece, but artifacts and knowledge that belong to the whole human race," she corrected him. "And we're a fully accredited expedition, here with the blessing of the government. We haven't come to steal anything, only to preserve what is being lost every day."

"To thieves?"

"Thieves and natural forces."

"So we should be grateful to you."

She shrugged. "Your country simply doesn't have the resources to protect the thousands of sites that are in immediate danger. We're excavating the remains of a Phoenician sailing ship that sunk over three thousand years ago."

"That old?" He tried to look impressed. Among his people, three thousand years might be a single lifetime but, he had to remind himself, he was dealing with a less-developed species of humanoid.

"Possibly. The Phoenicians had regular trade routes that plied the seas from Spain to Africa. We've found shards with the image of the goddess Ashera, and a single gold coin. We think this vessel may have been carrying tribute to her temple near Larnaca."

"Ashera?"

"You Greeks know her as Astarte, goddess of—"

"I'm familiar with Astarte," he said, cutting her off. "I'm not totally ignorant."

*Ashera, my aching loins!* He knew the ship in question. The vessel had gone down in a storm much like this one. She was certainly Phoenician, but the woman's time was off by at least five hundred years, and the tribute carried was for Melqart's temple, not Ashera's. The vessel had remained untouched with good reason. Anything with the stench of the Phoenician god of war was best left alone. Melqart guarded his belongings jealously. Human meddling in his possessions might be what had drawn the shades here and cost the lives of the German tourists.

"So, how has your *excavation* gone so far? Any accidents?"

Elena's demeanor cooled. "What an odd question. Why would you ask such a thing? And, no, there haven't been any *accidents*. I know what I'm doing."

He grimaced. "Obviously. That's why you've wrecked your Zodiac and you're cast ashore on a deserted island with a total stranger whom you suspect may be some sort of antiquities thief."

# CHAPTER 3

"Are you always so frank?" Elena asked. He was right on. She did believe he was lying to her. Orion Xenos's half-baked tale about swimming and losing his boat was pitiful. He was involved in something illegal—she would have bet her 1989 Vespa on it. If Orion wasn't here to steal antiquities, then he was a smuggler.

Yet, she had to admit, she found him charming, and very sexy, despite his poor choice in bathing suits. The red stretchy garment was several sizes too small and left little to the imagination. Of course, endowed as he was, it was hard to picture swim trunks that would hide his male attributes.

"Usually," he said.

"Excuse me?"

"You asked if I always speak my mind, and I usually do."

"Right." She wanted to ask where he'd found the red trunks, since he'd been stark naked when she'd pulled him out of the drink, but there didn't seem to be a way to do so without taking the conversation into areas she'd rather avoid. "A shame your boat wasn't washed up on the beach instead of drifting out to sea. We could have used it."

"Not for a while. That surf is wicked."

A loud clap of thunder caused her to draw back from the mouth of the cave. The rain was coming down in torrents, and the temperature was dropping. Her clothes were still wet, and Elena had a feeling that the shelter was about to become uncomfortable.

"You're shivering," he said.

Elena rubbed her arms. "I'm fine." She suspected that it was more the company than the cold that had her trembling. She'd always had a weakness for bad boys.

To a degree . . . She'd spent her lifetime surrounded by men, first as a child on her father's expeditions and later in her science and higher math classes. Archeology had traditionally been a man's domain, but eager young women had flooded the field in the past few decades. Not, however, in the area of underwater archeology. She'd fielded passes from would-be Romeos since she was thirteen, evading and sometimes relishing brief encounters with college professors, treasure hunters, and boat mechanics.

She liked to think that she was a good judge of men, and although Orion appeared to be a genuine rogue, she didn't think that she had anything to fear from him. Her instincts for self-preservation had developed early, and if all else failed, she could always fall back on her years of training in the oriental arts of self-defense.

"I assure you, I'm a gentleman where the female of the species is concerned."

She glanced sideways at him. He seemed bigger in this closed space, and those muscular arms and wide shoulders were more than a match for his movie-star looks. "It's good to know this isn't where you bury the bodies," she quipped.

Orion laughed. "I've met women archeologists before, but they had chin whiskers and bad breath. Plus, they all confined their digging to above ground."

"It's a family business. My grandfather pioneered underwater research in the Black Sea, and my father followed in his footsteps."

"Your grandfather wasn't Howard Carter by any chance?"

"No, afraid not." Elena shrugged. "Different branch of the family. Although they both were well published in their field." Why had she told him that? Did she think he'd be impressed? And how did she always manage to bring up her father, even with total strangers?

Thinking about him was still painful. She'd been nine years old when he'd died, but he remained with her every day. She favored her mother in appearance, except for the eyes. And it was Randal Carter's eyes that looked back at her every time she glanced in a mirror. Damn but she missed him.

"Your English is excellent," she said to Orion, in an effort to change the subject. "Did you study abroad?"

He nodded. "I've always found language fascinating. You, for instance, are an enigma. Your dialect is upper-class European, but your idioms are American, and you have a trace of a Southern accent."

"Guilty." She chuckled. "Boarding school in Switzerland and London, university and grad school in Texas."

His green eyes twinkled with mischief. They were large, haunting eyes, with an exotic slant to them, almost as if a bloodthirsty Scythian lurked somewhere in the shadowy past of his family tree. "Seems we have a lot in common," he said smoothly.

"You attended the Girl's International School in Geneva?"

"What? You're prejudiced against transvestites?" He chuckled. "No, what I meant was that we both seemed to have benefited from an unorthodox but classical education." He motioned toward the back of the cave. "How familiar are you with this island? This cave houses some of the finest examples of Bronze Age Linear B script that I've ever seen."

Elena regarded him suspiciously. "Painted on the cave walls, I suppose."

"First documented in 1911 by Dr. David Jones, one of your fellow Americans. I can't believe you've never heard of them. Photos of them are illustrated in Branford-Edmonds's text on early Minoan writing."

"No, I've never heard of them."

His gaze met hers, the intensity in his liquid green eyes was almost mesmerizing.

"Is this a variation on " 'Come up to my apartment to see my sketches'?" she quipped, but her resistance to his suggestion was rapidly draining away. She did want to see whatever was painted on these walls.

"You can trust me, Elena," he said. "I'd never harm you."

*I can count on him to protect me*, she thought. She glanced away, her eyelids suddenly heavy. Why did she feel so lightheaded? Yet, her desire to inspect the Linear B script intensified with each breath she took. Suddenly, it was important that she not leave this spot without seeing it.

The cave was small, she told herself. It was not as though she was wandering off into the bowels of Athens with this man. They were already here, and she could see the back wall of the cavern. What did she have to lose?

Orion's strong fingers closed around her hand. "Shall I show you?" he asked. "Do you want to come with me?"

She nodded. She did . . . but . . . another moment and she'd fall asleep on her feet. "What are you . . ." She swayed, lost her balance, and would have fallen if he hadn't caught her. What was wrong with her? Had she struck her head when the Zodiac turned over? Was she suffering from a concussion?

"It's all right," he murmured. "I can show you such wonders."

Where had she heard that line before? She was vaguely aware of Orion picking her up and thought she should have been concerned, but he smelled good and his chest was warm when she laid her head against it. The cave seemed to be moving. She felt as though she'd finished off a full bottle of Achaian wine, but she knew she hadn't had a drop of alcohol today. Could he have drugged her?

"You promised to take care of me," she reminded him sleepily.

"And I always keep my word."

He was carrying her toward the back of the shelter. The ceiling was low here, and the walls close on either side. She tried to force her eyes open to see the Linear B paintings, but she felt so sleepy and it was too dark to see clearly. "Are you a scoundrel, Orion?" she managed.

He kissed the crown of her head. "Don't worry. You're safe with me."

"I never . . ."—she yawned—". . . on the first date."

He chuckled. "I'll keep that in mind . . . if the subject comes up."

Sweet sensations tumbled in the pit of her stomach. If she was drunk, it had been some good stuff. She inhaled deeply, taking in the clean ocean scent of him, trying desperately to stay awake and in charge of the situation.

His lips brushed hers in a tender, teasing kiss that made her breasts tingle and bright ribbons of iridescent desire tighten in her womb. She sighed. If this was ravishment, bring it on. She slipped her arms around his neck. "Promise me you're not . . . a serial killer?"

"You can depend on it." He kissed her again, and this time his mouth lingered on hers and the warm tingling flush washed through to the tips of her toes. His kiss deepened and she opened to take him in. He tasted as good as he smelled, and the sensation of his tongue against hers was so intriguing.

"Orion?" She pulled away and drew in a deep breath.

"It's all right," he said. "Nothing bad will happen."

But as she watched, he reached out and touched the wall. Abruptly, where there had been solid stone, an opening gaped, and Orion ducked his head and stepped through it.

"How?" she began. "What is this?"

"A stairway. Don't be afraid."

Still carrying her, Orion descended the stone steps into total darkness. The air here was damp and heavy with the odors of salt and seaweed. Elena struggled in his arms. "I don't like this," she said. This was the same feeling that she'd had inside the Great Pyramid of Giza. She could feel the weight of the stone closing in around them.

"You will. Trust me."

*Trusting you is what got me here,* she thought, but she didn't have the strength to fight him. Sparks of fear skittered down her spine, and she imagined herself breaking free of his embrace, racing back up the steps to the cave and slamming the door. But, try as she would, she couldn't muster the energy to lift her head. "What have you done to me?"

"It's just an illusion. Don't worry. There are no lasting results, and I've told you, you're safe with me."

"An illusion? A dream? I'm dreaming?"

"Yes," he agreed. "Just a dream."

"I didn't split my skull on a rock?"

"Word of honor."

Down and down they went. She might have drifted off to sleep. She couldn't be certain. But when she opened her eyes again, they were no longer in a cave, but a large hall with marble floors. Glowing lights shaped like conch shells adorned the coral walls. The ceiling was high and glittered with artificial stars set into what appeared to be swirls of sea foam and a suggestion of waves. "What is this?" she whispered. "Where are we?"

"The *Keftiu* built this palace in natural caves under the ocean floor. You know them as Minoans."

He lowered her to her feet, and she found that her strength had returned. She turned full circle, eyes wide in astonishment. Stone benches lined the walls, and above them, painted scenes of the sea stretched the length of the corridor. There were stylized skates and rays, lines of leaping dolphins, dancing crabs, and fish of every size and color. Sea snakes and octopi frolicked in blue water amid a rainbow of ocean kelp and grasses and beautiful ferns.

"It's wonderful!" she exclaimed. "But how is it possible?"

He smiled. "Did you think I was taking you to Hades?" He pointed to a low doorway halfway down the hall, flanked by crimson-and-white striped columns. "Beyond, in that chamber, there are pottery tablets inscribed with early writing. There are some good examples of both Linear A and B writing, as well as crude hieroglyphics."

"All three types together? Have they been translated?"

"Some. Most are poems and prayers, but at least two sections describe healing techniques for setting broken bones and curing illnesses caused by long periods at sea."

"Show me!" she said.

"Nothing I'd like better."

\* \* \*

"You spineless jellyfish! How dare you come into this chamber?" Alexandros leaped across the broad marble table to where his half-brother cowered and put a knife to his throat. "Give me one reason why I shouldn't slit your traitorous throat?"

"Poseidon has pardoned me," Caddoc wailed. "You have no right—"

"To spill blood in your father's throne room," Lady Athena finished. "Put your blade away, prince." She laid a gentle hand on Alexandros's shoulder. "He isn't worth defying the king over."

"Our father," Caddoc blubbered. His eyes were wide with fear, his complexion drained of color. Snot ran from his distended nostrils over his lips and down his chin. "You can't kill me! I'm innocent of treason! I swear on my mother's life."

"Which is another pity." Alex scored the scales on Caddoc's neck, cutting deep enough that blood oozed from the gash. "A pity that she still has a life for you to swear on." But he stepped away, nodded to Athena, and returned to his own place on the right of Poseidon's chair where he sat silent and glaring.

What had possessed his father to forgive Caddoc? Any fool knew that he'd acted on his mother's orders in an attempted military coup to wrest the crown from Poseidon. Halimeda had nearly succeeded in poisoning Poseidon and in having most of the royal family murdered so that her son could assume the throne.

"I'm loyal to . . ." Caddoc began, but fell silent when Alex's hand tightened on the hilt of his sword.

*By Ares' shaft!* Alex swore silently. It would be worth facing Poseidon's ire to rid the kingdom of this piece of sea-slug excretia. Hadn't Caddoc and his cronies ambushed Morgan and Rhiannon on their way back to Atlantis? What had Caddoc's excuse been for that? "It was a slow day, so I thought I'd liven things up by killing my brother and the woman he loved"?

A stir outside the door signaled the arrival of the king. Alex and the others stood as his father, older brother, and four other members of the committee entered the room.

"Lord High Poseidon," announced the herald. "King of Atlantis, ruler of the seven seas, giver of mercy, mighty warrior, wise and merciful—"

"Yes, yes," Poseidon said, waving the man out of his way. "They know who I am. We can dispense with the formalities."

Alex tried not to show his amusement. His father, the king, was nothing if not dramatic. He'd taken the time to deck himself out in full war armor tonight. His graying hair was knotted at the nape of his neck, and a trident crown rested on his regal brow. His kilt was woven of gem-studded silver cloth, and knee-high sandals encrusted in pearls. Poseidon's sword was an equal item of priceless art, forged on the banks of the Ganges in a city whose name was lost in the ages, a sword that he knew all too well how to handle, despite his age.

Morgan filed in behind their father, followed by his aunt, Princess Eudora, her consort, Lord Mikhail, and the others. Morgan, as crown prince, slid in between Alex and their father, and everyone else quickly took their seats on benches around the table.

This was a small state room, less formal than the larger ones, but every bit as ornate with rows of columns, inlaid tiles of silver and gold, and painted wall murals detailing the Great Flood that had once destroyed most of the population both above and below the seas.

Poseidon's ice-blue eyes grew hard as he scowled at Caddoc. "What's wrong with you? You look as if you'd just been swallowed and spit out by a Madagascan squid. You might have the courtesy to pull yourself together when you come to a council meeting."

"Father, I . . ."

Alex raised one golden eyebrow in warning, and his half-brother lowered his head. Damn, but he should have finished the job when he had the chance. With any luck he could have had the body out of the chamber and the blood mopped up before the king arrived. He doubted if Lady Athena or any of the others on the committee would have informed on him. They all knew where Caddoc's loyalties lay.

"Proceed," Poseidon commanded. "I think most of you know why Lord Mikhail called this emergency meeting, but we need to make a decision on this at once."

Alex gave Mikhail his full attention as he filled them in on the latest atrocities committed on the shores of the Aegean and the Mediterranean. "Nineteen confirmed deaths in the last turning of the moon," he said. "Three naiads, two mermaids, a silkie, and the rest human. The air breathers are unaware of all but three attacks, and those were attributed to—"

"Sharks, I suppose," the king supplied.

"Yes, Highness," Lord Mikhail said. "The mermaids were found sucked of their life force, blood, and other fluids, as was the silkie. But the humans and the others were ripped to pieces. Without witnesses, we would never have known what happened to them."

"Melqart's shades." Lady Athena sighed. "They grow bold."

"It's worse than you can imagine," Mikhail continued. "One of the humans was a diver working for an international company seeking to drill gas wells to the west of Crete."

"Gas wells? Why weren't we informed of that before?" Lady Jalini demanded. "We can't afford to have humans exploring the ocean floor—"

"Exactly," Mikhail said. "These attacks come at the worst possible time for us."

Alex glanced at Morgan. His brother had recently taken on the responsibility for concealing Atlantean concerns in the Mediterranean, the Ionian Sea, and the Aegean. The waters there were shallow, and it required a joint effort of hundreds of trained priestesses working together and using their paranormal abilities to conceal palaces and outposts maintained by the kingdom. While the mother city was situated in the depths of the mid-Atlantic, evidence of the culture surrounding Greece and Crete was too great to dismantle. And if the earth dwellers found evidence of Atlantis, who knew how quickly they would search for the heart of the kingdom?

"There's more," Princess Eudora said. "It's my sorry lot to report that at least three Atlanteans are missing and unaccounted for in the area." Her blue eyes filled with tears as she looked at Poseidon. "And one, brother, is our own dear Orion."

"Orion?" Alex sat bolt upright. Orion had been on leave, true enough. But he'd said that he intended to spend his time enjoying the sexual delights of a certain mermaid. "He's not overdue, yet," he said to his father. "He was—"

"Taking pleasure with Sjshsglee," his aunt said.

"Hers was one of the bodies found floating off the ruins of Troy," Mikhail said. "If Prince Orion was with her, we have to suspect the worst."

# CHAPTER 4

Deep beneath the sea floor, off the coast of the ruins of the ancient city of Tyre, the Lady Halimeda raged. "You call this a palace? You're a god and this is how you live?" Halimeda swept the crystal goblets and gold platters inlaid with silver from the wooden table. Glass shattered, and the golden filigree plates crafted in Samarkand when Venice was merely a mudflat, bounced and rolled across the sandstone floor, marring the exquisite patterns and denting the rims.

"Silence, woman!" A thunderous roar echoed through the low, shadowy room. "Will you never cease your endless whining?"

"You promised me riches, wealth beyond my imagination," she howled. "I had more servants as a concubine in Poseidon's seraglio than here."

"You have slaves."

"Monstrosities. Things with two heads and fangs. They disgust me."

"I sent you a new body servant only yesterday. A mermaid."

"She was dead. Useless. Sucked dry of her blood."

"You are too particular." The booming voice became

cajoling. "If you were as powerful a sorceress as you claim, you could have restored her."

Glass crunched under Halimeda's slipper and she swore. "You can't restore them once they're dead."

Melqart laughed, a sound that raised the hairs on the back of Halimeda's neck. "I can."

"Good for you. The rest of us, not being immortal, have to make do." She'd not let him bully her. He'd saved her for his own purpose, not for any altruistic reasons. If he wanted her, she was valuable to him, and it would pay to have him remember that she was no ordinary woman.

Melqart growled. "Do not forget yourself. I could render you as lifeless as that mermaid if you displease me."

"Yes, yes, you've told me that before. But, I'm so bored I may as well be dead. There's no entertainment. No music, no plays, no one to talk to. What good is it to have priceless gowns if there's no one to envy them?"

"You're a witch. You cast spells. Surely you can conjure up an audience or a band of musicians."

" 'Cast spells,' " Halimeda mimicked. "It's not as easy as you think."

"And not as easy to be a god in these godless times when men have forgotten who created them."

"I'm sure."

His voice rose in anger, and something else. . . . Self-pity? "I require adoration. Tribute. Sacrifice."

"And I require food," she snapped. "I'm starving."

The nine-foot granite statue of Melqart shimmered and rocked on its pedestal. "Thankless whore! Who saved your worthless life from death by poison? Your face was rotting off, remember? I gave you back your beauty, a beauty greater than Helen of Troy's, and do you appreciate my mercy?"

"I'm hungry!" she screeched. "I'm in no mood for adoration when my bellybutton ring is scraping my backbone." An ivory spoon lay on the floor and Halimeda kicked it viciously. It struck the wall and bounced back, striking her in the shin. "Ouch." She stomped on it, snapping the delicate handle and continued her tirade until the bowl was crushed as well.

"That was tribute from India," the disembodied voice hissed. "Do you have any idea how many men died to lay it at my altar?"

"Do I care?" She spun around. "Show yourself, Melqart. I dislike carrying on a conversation with a chunk of rock." Her face contorted. "Unless you're afraid to face me."

"You're insane." The image of a man with the head of a bull flickered against a windowless wall. "Do you dare to accuse me, Melqart—God of war, Lord of the Underworld—of cowardice?"

"You promised me that I would live like a queen. Look at this place! It's hardly more than a cave. Cold and dark. I doubt if it's been properly cleaned in a millennia."

The bull snorted and tossed his massive horns. He opened his mouth and glittering rubies, emeralds, and uncut diamonds spilled onto the floor. A cascade of pearls followed the jewels. "Look around you." The voice that issued from the bull's throat was that of a man, but distorted, animalistic. "Gold. Silver. Ivory. What more could you want?"

"Food." She rested her balled fists on her hips. "Can I eat pearls? Precious gems? What good to me are your empty dishes and cups? I thirst! I hunger!"

"Very well." He snapped his fingers and lightning flashed.

Instantly, the banquet table that she had so recently

swept clean groaned under the weight of dishes containing figs and dates and raisins, vegetables, and breads. An entire roast pig nestled on a bed of greens. Olives and pitchers of frothy drinks crowded baskets of fried fish, oysters on the half-shell, steamed crabs, roasted lamb, and sliced beef. Grilled pigeon in gravy, stuffed songbirds, and boiled eels were adorned with steamed shrimp and mussels. Cakes and breads, whole rounds of cheese, and containers of yogurt, and dripping honeycombs lined the long board.

"Well, what do you say to that?" the bull-man demanded.

Halimeda smiled. "It smells wonderful." She reached for a slice of lamb and screamed when her hand passed through the meat and platter as if it were air. "Illusion! Nothing but illusion! Am I to be satisfied with conjurer's tricks?"

The bull wavered and its head morphed into that of an elephant, trunk raised and ivory tusks bloodstained. "How many times must I tell you? You no longer need to eat. You are beyond such humanoid weakness."

Sobbing with frustration, she grabbed for a loaf of wheat bread. She could smell it, imagine the taste on her tongue. But, again, she could grasp nothing. The round loaf was perfect, still piping hot, but it wasn't real. "I want food," she shrieked. "You've deceived me."

The elephant's small eyes darkened to pitch, and the image faded. There was another flash of lightning and in place of the pachyderm, Halimeda saw an enormous black dog with a bronze battle collar crouched a few feet from her. The animal's hackles rose and its teeth bared as it growled, sending a wave of foul breath into the air and making her gag. Slobber dripped from the dog's jaws as it leaped onto the table and tore into the roast pig.

Halimeda forced a bored expression and clapped slowly. "A fine performance, but I'm still without nourishment."

The beast raised its head and stared at her with glowing eyes, and icy fingers of fear clutched at her bowels. Halimeda gritted her teeth and glared back. Her trembling chin firmed. If Melqart thought he could intimidate her with circus animals, he'd have to think again.

"This is not what I was promised," she repeated. "I require live maids to do my hair, live bath attendants, live seamstresses."

"Every servant that I've given you flees from your presence. I can't imagine what a live servant would do," he said.

"I don't care for your choices. You give me mindless demons," she accused, warming to her grievances. "Spineless things that give me nightmares. They all stink of rotting flesh. You haven't kept your bargain."

"Do you believe you've kept your part of the bargain?" Melqart growled. "Where is your son who you promised would pay me homage?" The hound's body vanished, leaving only the head and chewing jaws.

Halimeda waited until she sensed that the god of war had taken refuge in the statue again. Usually, his manifestations didn't last long. "My son will come when I call him," she said. The stone image radiated cold, as if a door to the underworld had opened. She suppressed a shiver.

"Why do Poseidon and his whelps still rule Atlantis?"

"I'm a sorceress, not a magician. These things take time."

She stalked to one side of the chamber and peered into a wide floor-to-ceiling mirror. As usual her image did not reflect. She could see the table, the obscene heaps of imaginary food, but she could not see her own face. "You promised me beauty, but where is it? What proof do I have that you're not lying about that, too?"

"You would see it if you wanted to," he said, suddenly consoling. "You have it in your head that the poison destroyed your loveliness, and you refuse to see your own magnificence. Am I to be blamed for your stubbornness?"

She whirled on the statue and glared into the sightless empty eye sockets. The thought that they had once held jewels flicked through her mind, and she wondered if Melqart was as powerful as he had been in millennia past. "Maybe I'm an illusion, too," she dared. "Maybe this is all a lie, and I died in that dungeon. Perhaps you're nothing more than a bad dream."

"Don't say that! Don't dare to say that!" The statue writhed and twisted into the likeness of a giant moray eel. Its mouth yawned, revealing jagged teeth and a bloody interior. Bits of flesh dribbled between its lips. "I took away your pain, Halimeda, but I can give it again. Would you like to know true suffering?"

She had always known when she'd pressed Poseidon too hard or touched a soft spot, so she quickly altered her demeanor. "Come, my lord, let us not quarrel between ourselves. I don't doubt your courage. And, of course, I know that you truly exist, but I'm cross and weak from lack of food. Provide for me all that you promised and my son will come and bring offerings at your shrine."

"He'd better." Slime dripped from the eel's body as it slowly morphed back into the statue of the bull-headed man. "If your son Prince Caddoc disappoints me, I'll feed him to my shades, and all your pleading for his life will be for naught."

Orion looked down at the woman kneeling at his feet and shuddered as an almost uncontrollable sense of desire possessed him. Her damp hair hung over one shoulder, and tendrils curled at the nape of her neck, making him want to bury his face in the enticing hollow and taste her skin. Her scent drew him like adona fern, firing his imagination.

The thought that he could have her here on this floor made his loins throb. It would be easy. No mortal woman could resist an Atlantean male if he loosed his full aura of sexuality upon her. His people were far advanced over the earth-walkers in many aspects, but their weakness was an enhanced need for sexual stimulation. In the way that bull sperm whales became maddened by the need for mating, so did Atlanteans, both men and women.

But here was forbidden fruit. If he took what could be so easily his, Orion would risk honor, career, and his place in line to the throne. He had no wish to become Poseidon; that task would rightfully go to his brother Morgan, but breaking law and tradition for pure sensual pleasure was crossing the line.

He wanted Elena . . . wanted her with a passion that made his blood run hot and his mind giddy with lecherous possibilities. He wanted to run his hands over her smooth, scale-free body, cup her breasts in his hands and coax the nipples into hard, tight nubs. He could imagine the silken texture of her skin and the soft whimpers she'd make as he drew those sweet nipples between his lips and sucked her breasts until she screamed for release, before he'd roam lower to explore the damp crevices between her thighs. He wanted to feel the soft, dark curls of her woman's mound against his lips and to slide his fingers slowly inside her before . . .

No! He couldn't weaken. Stifling a groan, Orion fought the smoldering arousal that threatened to ignite into a blazing heat. Control . . . he must retain control of his body and will. To do less would be his undoing.

Mating with an unwilling partner was one of the greatest of sins among the Atlanteans, punishable by a particularly unpleasant and lengthy death sentence. Women were equals in every way, other than physical strength, and to take advantage of a weaker opponent was looked upon with disgust. Yet, if she desired him, even if she was a land dweller, could their union be so terrible? And she would want him if he willed it. A touch, a glance, a whispered suggestion would be all that it would take to bring about the ends that he wanted so badly. But that, of course, was cheating.

"It's true," Elena cried. "It *is* here. And here! And here!" She ran trembling fingers over a stone tablet inscribed with hieroglyphics from the time of the New Kingdom. "As sharp and clear as if they had been carved yesterday," she babbled. "See this." She pointed to a line of characters.

> "*The cry of the dove rings out.*
> *Dawn breaks, where doest thou fly?*
> *Stop, sweet bird, why must thou . . .*"

"*Scold me*," he translated.

Elena stared at him in astonishment. "You read hieroglyphics?"

He shrugged. "I was always good with languages."

Confusion flickered in her dark eyes, and he knew she realized that she'd underestimated him. He wasn't what she'd thought. How far off she really was, he suspected she'd never guess. She caught her lower lip between her teeth and turned back to the text.

*"I discovered my . . . my sweetheart—"*

"*My lover,*" he corrected huskily. "*I discovered my lover . . .*"

Elena nodded and continued the translation.

> *"I discovered my lover in his bed,*
> *And my heart overflowed with sweetness."*

Orion nodded. "Close enough." Why hadn't she picked an oil merchant's inventory to translate? Hearing love songs read from such kissable lips was intoxicating. Still on her knees, she was close, too close, close enough for him to feel her breath on his bare thighs.

"But New Kingdom? Why are these tablets here with the Linear B?" she demanded. "The time isn't right. They can't be genuine."

He dropped to his knees beside her. "They're real, all right. But not original poetry. Plagiarized from an earlier civilization."

"No," she insisted. "You're wrong about that. "It's Egyptian. *Love Songs of the New Kingdom.* Do you have any idea how old that is? We're talking 1200, maybe 1500 B.C.E. Fully documented by—"

"Plagiarism," he repeated. "Originally composed by—" He broke off, unwilling to cloud the waters by giving the name of the twelfth-dynasty Atlantean court poet who had written the love song in honor of the king's royal marriage. "An earlier civilization," he finished.

She glanced at him again. "Tell me the truth. They aren't genuine, are they? You're not an antiquities thief; you're a dealer in fakes." She stood and dusted her hands off on her jeans. "If these tablets had been discovered in the early nineteenth century, they'd be the centerpiece in a world-class museum, not left here for any lobster fisherman to discover and cart off."

Elena's tone left no doubt in Orion's mind as to what she thought of him, and he felt a punch of embarrassment in his vitals. His desire deflated as he attempted to defend himself.

"No, I wouldn't do that. These are real. I'm not sure why Jones didn't retrieve them, but the photographs exist. I believe his ill health kept him from returning to the site, and when he died . . ."

She sniffed. "But *you* knew where they were." She shook her head. "I'm not the fool you've obviously taken me for. Your charade is over, Mr. Xenos. You'll be lucky if you're not spending the next ten years in a Greek prison."

Orion raised his hands, palm out, and stepped back. She certainly had a way of throwing cold water on his plans for a romantic afternoon. The woman was a shrew. What he'd seen in her and why he'd bothered to show her these treasures was beyond him.

"You think these are fakes?"

"I do. You probably have a little workshop in Athens where your associates turn out statutes of Athena and—"

"Enough," he said. He went to a shelf and pulled out a rough sandstone slab no larger than his two hands held together. "Look at this. What you call Linear A. It's an account of the king's expedition to—"

She made a sound of disgust. "The more you say, the deeper you dig yourself into the swamp," she said. "Linear A has never been translated, and I doubt that you're the first scholar to do so. And having achieved the feat, you don't tell anyone. You keep this bit of knowledge to yourself. Hardly! These must be fakes." She turned away, unwilling to even examine the precious carving. "I appreciate the opportunity to see this structure, but I think it's time we returned to the beach."

"I doubt if the storm is over yet. It was pretty damp up there."

"I'm tough. Let's go, or shall I find the staircase myself?"

"What would it take for you to believe me?"

Elena shook her head. "Sorry. Once you lose credibility with me, you're done for."

He wasn't ready to give up. If he could take her into the sea, there was another place not far from here where the remains of a wall jutted up from the ocean floor. That wall contained inscriptions in Linear B and in Atlantean. But he wasn't sure that the shades had left. They might be lying in wait off the beach, hoping that he and the woman would leave the relative safety of the land.

But she wasn't done. She had to zing him one more time. "You really disappoint me, Orion," she said. "I knew you were some sort of scoundrel, but I didn't take you for stupid, as well." She pushed past him, moving toward the place where they'd entered the outer hall.

"Wait," he said, trying to hold back his anger.

She stopped, spun back to face him, and gave him a rude gesture involving the movement of a particular finger on her right hand. "Go to hell, Orion!"

That was when he lost control.

# CHAPTER 5

Elena was fast, but Orion was faster. Her pulse raced as she heard his bare feet striking the floor behind her. Her survival instinct went into overdrive, and when he grabbed hold of her, she whirled on him, ready for a fight. If Orion wanted to play rough, she was fully prepared to put him down, driving a fist into his Adam's apple, followed by a sharp knee-thrust to his groin.

But, to her surprise, when his fingers tightened on her arm, the message she received wasn't violence, but something entirely different. Orion's touch wasn't that of an assailant, but of a familiar lover. Odder still, her reaction was a powerful flood of sexual arousal. And when he pulled her into his embrace and covered her mouth with his, she could have sworn she heard violins.

She'd once gotten the best of a mugger on the Paris subway, and she'd been waylaid by two camp cooks on a site near the Aswan Dam. Both times, her self-defense skills were up to the task. She'd walked away unscathed, while the men who'd believed she was an easy target learned a lesson in manners. But this time, with this man, she found herself helpless in the face of his seduction.

"Elena."

Her name on his lips raised goose bumps on her arms as

tension sparked between them, and the raw desire in his green eyes made her breath catch in her throat. Her heightened senses were assaulted on all sides. Not only did she hear the strains of a love song, but the air smelled of mountain waterfalls and tropical flowers.

"Elena."

She gasped, opened her mouth to protest, and tilted her face to receive his kiss.

It was electric.

She'd been kissed before. She'd been kissed by boys since she was nine years old, but she'd never felt the ground shift under her feet or had her insides melt to warm Jell-O. And she'd never felt heat flash through her veins or her bones feel as though they'd turned to liquid.

Orion kissed her lips, her eyelids, and her throat. Giddily, she sagged against him, clasping his face between her hands, and kissing him back with equal abandon. The thought that he was a thief and a scoundrel flicked across her mind, but she was beyond caring. All that was important was touching him . . . having him touch her. Arms and legs entangled, they sank down, not onto the cold stone floor as she expected, but onto a luxurious bed of furs.

*I must be hallucinating*, she thought, but undercurrents of delicious sensations overwhelmed her and shattered her resolve. Romantic images tumbled in her mind: apple orchards in bloom, moonlit beaches, Tuscan ruins, and a covered bridge she'd once walked over in Vermont.

*I must be losing my mind!*

Orion kissed her mouth again, and she melted against him. She parted her lips, taking him in, thrilling to the sensation of tongues caressing, of the taste of him. Vaguely, she was aware of him whispering sweet words in her ear, love words that thrilled her in a language that she'd never heard before. And although she didn't understand a single fragment, tears of joy welled in her eyes.

She nipped at the wide expanse of his muscular bare chest, tonguing his skin, savoring the salty-male taste of him, inhaling his scent. Her breath came in quick gasps, and she could feel an urgent tension building in the pit of her stomach. They didn't speak. What she felt was too great for words.

When Orion slipped a big hand under her tee and gently cupped her breast, she groaned with pleasure. And when he bent to kiss her nipple through the thin material, her cleft grew moist and throbbing. She yanked the top over her head, wanting to feel his mouth on her skin.

This time, his caress was slow and teasing. His lips closed over her swollen nipple and his warm tongue laved and then suckled until her need became an exquisite agony. And all the while, he kept stroking her, tracing the curve of her back and buttocks, rubbing and caressing, bringing her to an intense state of need.

His touch was at once tender and demanding, and she craved it as an addict craves the object of his addiction. She could feel her body responding, her breasts growing taut and sensitive, the heat rising in her core. This was madness. Sobbing with unfulfilled need, she rolled onto her back, pulling him on top of her.

She could feel the hard length of his huge erection pressing against her, and she dug her nails into his back. "Please . . . please . . ." she begged. Her breath came in hard, quick gasps, and the heat of his body burned like a smoldering brand. "Yes. Yes." She sobbed with emotion, and reached up to tighten her arms around his neck.

"Elena . . ." He fumbled with the button on her jeans. He was hard and hot and ready for her, bigger than any man she'd ever known. His erect shaft bulged beneath the red trunks. All she could think of was the feel of his body against hers. She had to have him deep inside her.

"Elena," he whispered. "Do you—"

"Yes, yes," she cried. "Now, I want you now!"

"Not yet." He rolled off her and onto the heaped furs before kissing the hollow of her throat, her mouth, and her breasts again, all the while touching and stroking her body.

She had believed that she was at the peak of her excitement, but Orion Xenos knew a few tricks that she hadn't experienced before. She tangled her fingers in his hair and groaned again as his hot, damp kisses moved slowly down over her breasts and belly to linger and caress her inner thighs. She arched her back and closed her eyes when his seeking tongue probed the folds of her cleft.

She was wet and slippery . . . Muscles in her groin contracted, throbbing with desire, her slick passage opening and closing like a tight fist. Elena moaned as she tossed her head from side to side, losing all reason in this all-consuming drive to have him fill her, to have him drive into her hard, over and over, until she climaxed and found the physical release she needed so desperately. "Now," she pleaded. "I want you now."

"I can't . . ." she whimpered. "I'll . . ."

But then he nuzzled her inner folds apart and thrust his hot tongue inside, she experienced a climax so intense that wave after wave of pleasure rocked her and she cried out. He rose on his knees and gathered her sobbing into his arms. He held her, rocking her against him, cradling her, kissing her hair, her face, her bare shoulders, and murmuring her name over and over.

"I want . . . I want . . ." she whispered. "I want you." She ached for him, needed to feel every inch of him.

"And I want you," he answered, gently pushing her

back against the furs and covering her with his beautiful body. He pressed against her, touching and stroking until she felt the throbbing heat growing once more.

"Now!" she insisted. "Now!" She closed her hand around his shaft, savoring the smooth texture and swollen head of his enormous sex. He groaned, and she felt him nudge her quivering folds.

"Are you certain you want this?" he asked. "Of your free will?"

"Yes," she cried. "I do. I want you." She arched against him and opened for his first thrust.

"Can't reach her? What do you mean they don't know where she is?" Greg Hamilton's voice rose above the drone of the motors. His boyish features hardened as his shoulders tensed and he drew himself upright in the leather seat. "Keep trying and let me know as soon as you reach her." He ended the call and reached for his drink. Finding the glass empty, he called for Michelle to bring him a refill.

"Would you like an early supper?" she asked. "I have a nice prime rib and—"

"Just the Scotch. I'm not in the mood for eating." He turned to the window, curbing his impatience, biting back the retort, *If I'd wanted dinner, I would have said so.* Michelle was too good an employee to piss off because Elena had pulled another of her vanishing tricks. Not only was Michelle a top-notch secretary who could double as a flight attendant when he or his father flew, but she had the tits and ass that would stop a clock.

His father had found her dancing in a strip bar in Austin six years ago and been so impressed that he'd paid for her college degree on the condition that she come to work for him after graduation. Michelle had taken him up on it.

Greg suspected that his father had been extracting perks for some time, though; so, as attractive as he found her, he did nothing about it. He didn't like sloppy seconds.

He accepted the single malt Scotch on ice, thanked her, and sipped it slowly as he stared out at the heavy clouds that enveloped the plane in a gray fog. At least he didn't have to make the effort of being sociable. He was the only passenger in the newest of the company's private jets, flying nonstop from Houston to Athens.

He checked his I-Phone again to see if Elena had e-mailed him or attempted to call. Nothing. *Where the hell had she gotten to, now?* He'd made a point of telling her that he had only twenty-four hours of leisure in Athens before he was expected onboard the ship. He'd thought she was looking forward to an evening of hitting the tavernas and nightspots as much as he was.

It was times like this that he wondered why he hadn't given up on Elena Carter and moved on to one of the many young women of Houston society that his mother was constantly pushing on him. As the only son and heir to the Hamilton enterprises, he was expected to marry and produce at least one legitimate male offspring before he turned forty. Elena definitely wasn't Mom's first choice, but so long as she was Caucasian, educated, and knew a seafood fork from an oyster knife, his father was satisfied.

Greg had been planning on popping the question. He liked to think that he had picked her because it made good business sense. Elena's fluency in languages and her European connections would be of immense help in securing the natural gas leases Hamilton Energy needed to be a player on the world stage. The fact that marrying Elena would send his mother on a three-day bender was a plus. No two women could be so totally different. His mother's career had been finding the right man to provide her with the finer things in life and allow her to maintain a premier position in Houston society.

As far as he was concerned, Elena had the goods. Not only was she hot in bed, she could hold her own at a turkey shoot or at a cocktail party. Although she hadn't inherited a fortune from her father, Elena wasn't impressed with his money or background, and she wouldn't expect him to spend the next twelve months picking out silver patterns and wedding caterers.

Elena lived in her own scholarly world of two-thousand-year-old sunken ships and dusty libraries. Theirs could be a civilized twenty-first century marriage where he could continue to live his life the way he liked, and Elena could keep the home fires burning and raise a handful of red-cheeked cherubs to keep his parents amused and out of his hair.

He drained the last drops of twenty-five year Macallan and thought about having another. Instead, he tried Elena's cell again, but all he got was the same "This number is currently not available." Greg glanced at his watch. There was still time to catch a few hours of sleep before they reached Athens' airspace, but he wasn't in the mood for sleeping. He reached for his laptop and began to go over the last reports on the new drilling site.

Sometime later, Michelle appeared at his seat with a steak, and after the first bite, Greg discovered that he was hungrier than he'd thought. Come to think of it, he had missed lunch and had nothing but coffee and a donut for breakfast. "Could you check the weather for me in Athens again?" he asked.

Michelle, as usual, was all efficient smiles.

Hell, Greg thought. If he couldn't catch up with Elena, maybe he'd take Michelle clubbing tonight. The city had too much to offer, and he didn't want to go alone.

\* \* \*

Orion couldn't do it.

As much as he wanted to take what was offered, to bury himself inside Elena and quench the fierce heat that raced through his body like a fever, the wrong of what he was doing cut him deeper.

With a groan, he clenched his hands into fists, summoned all his strength, and rolled off her. Shaking with emotion, he rose to his feet, and backed away. His breath came in hard quick gasps; pain seared through his veins. She lay there waiting, open, and vulnerable.

Never had Orion had to struggle so to control his own will. Her scent filled his head, the feel of her soft white skin and her womanly curves haunted him. So great was his agony that for an instant he failed to maintain his illusion of being human and felt his true appearance flow over him. That, Elena could never see. It was forbidden for a human to see him as what he really was, an Atlantean, a different species.

"Orion? What's wrong?" Elena asked. She raised her head, hair falling over her beautiful face, and stared at him. "Why . . ."

Her voice shocked him back to reality and he returned to the human image that she expected. But he was too close. He couldn't remain so near to her and not take her in every way.

Backing still farther away, Orion waved his hand and used all of his remaining powers to put her into a deep sleep. With a sigh, her eyelids flickered and closed; she slumped back onto the stone floor, and fell into a deep sleep.

They had lain together on the rock. Seaweed had been absent here in the ruins, and his bed of furs had been only another illusion. Concentrating, Orion willed Elena to forget everything that had happened since they left the cave above . . . to remember nothing of the tablets with the ancient writing or his lovemaking. She would wake with a headache, but with no lasting harm. He couldn't say the same of himself. Never had he felt such searing pain behind his eyes.

But, he had to do this . . . if it killed him. There was no other path. He would never be able to forgive himself if he failed.

If he'd used Elena as he wanted to, as much as he still desired her, he would have committed a terrible sin, an act little better than rape. She was human, a weaker species, and she had no defense against his seduction.

Against his better judgment, he went to her, knelt beside her and cradled her head in his arms. Lust raged in his blood, but when he brushed her lips with his, it was only with tenderness. "Sleep, little one," he murmured.

He got to his feet again and walked to the far end of the corridor where the pillars and roof had fallen, sealing off the rest of the structure. He leaned his head against the gray granite and slowly gained control of his body.

He couldn't leave her here, but neither could he remain on the island. The temptation to have her was too great. No wonder the ancient ones had forbidden sexual congress between Atlanteans and humans. There was no contest; it was all too easy. He would have to find one of his own kind and ease his need.

Certain that Elena would sleep for the next hour, he paced while he regained his composure. Gradually, the pain eased, and reason prevailed. The difficult part would be touching her without succumbing to the madness of lust. *I will do this*, he swore silently as he returned to her side. Gathering her in his arms, he carried her up the stone steps to the cave on the beach.

It was a simple thing, almost child's play, to disguise the entrance once more so that if Elena retained some traces of memory of what had happened, which he greatly doubted, she would find no doorway in the rock. It was easy to create illusion regarding the physical attributes of the ocean floor and beaches. What was difficult was hiding Atlantean roads and cities in shallow seas, but that too could be accomplished if enough trained minds were engaged in the project. So his kind had protected their old places from the earth dwellers for many thousands of years.

Orion laid her on a bed of dried kelp. Outside, the storm was receding. It was still daylight, but the water remained rough and he doubted that Elena would attempt to go back into those waves any time soon. He didn't want to risk transporting her underwater, which meant that he'd have to find a boat. Why did nothing ever go as he planned? He should have been back at his duty station, meeting with his captains, planning action against Melqart and his shades. In his lust to possess Elena he'd nearly forgotten the murdered tourists and the consequences their killings set in motion.

Sharing the same planet with humans and maintaining invisibility required constant vigilance. If the Phoenician war god was hunting these shores, the humans would be alarmed. They would fight back, and if they invaded the seas with their great ships and submarines, the Atlanteans would be in mortal danger. Better to seek out the murderers and deal with them quietly before the alarm was raised.

He was a prince of the kingdom. Rarely did he allow his duty to be overshadowed by a whim. How many times had he warned his brothers against becoming involved with human females? And he had nearly fallen into the same trap.

He was ashamed of himself. He still wanted her, but the madness had passed. He'd not take advantage of someone who'd saved his life. He'd see Elena safely back to land and forget that he'd ever laid eyes on her.

# CHAPTER 6

A movement at the cave's entrance caught Orion's eye. His first instinct was to protect Elena, and he tensed, moving to block her from the intruder's line of vision. Unsure if he should remain in his human guise or change back to his own form, he maintained his illusion and called out, "Come in out of the rain. It's dry in here."

A familiar voice drained the tension from Orion's shoulders. "A woman? We thought you were Melqart fodder and you've been dallying with a human female?"

"Alex!"

His twin strode into the cavern, a round shield slung carelessly over one arm. Rain and seawater dripped off his plumed battle helmet, bronze cuirass, and greaves. He had the look of a man newly come from battle, but his fresh wounds were quickly healing and the gleam in his eyes told Orion that Alexandros was more exhilarated than shaken by whatever had crossed his path.

"You picked a poor time to seek out forbidden company." Alex's keen eye had spotted Elena at once. And then he apparently realized that he hadn't altered his appearance and he studied her more intently. "How far can you trust her?"

"It's all right," Orion said, coming to meet his brother

with open arms. "She's sleeping. And it's not what you think. There's been no *dallying*. I have her to thank for my life."

Alex made a sound of disbelief. "I can't wait to hear the story." And then his expression softened. "The shades have been hunting these waters."

"You're telling me. We tangled. You know about the German couple?"

"No, but others." He clasped Orion in a crushing embrace, and this time, when he spoke, his voice couldn't cover his emotion. "Brother. We believed you were with Sjshsglee."

"I was, but after we parted I ran into some trouble on the way back." Orion quickly explained about his discovery of the dead tourists and his own confrontation with an overwhelming horde.

Alex listened without interrupting, but something in his manner told Orion that something was terribly wrong. As an identical twin, Orion had often known what Alex was going to say almost before he did. He'd sensed trouble when Alex appeared, but this was something he didn't want to hear, because it was bad and hearing Alex's words would make it so.

"What's wrong?" Orion asked. "Not the king?" Their father had narrowly escaped death only recently at the hands of Caddoc and his mother. Only once before had Poseidon, high king of Atlantis, been toppled from his throne by treachery and what had followed had been a terrible civil war as his heirs fought for the crown. It was a tragedy that no Atlantean hoped to see again.

"No, not him. Nor any of our brothers or sisters." Alex's green eyes darkened to emerald and his features hardened. "Your mermaid."

"Sjshsglee?" Orion shook his head. "That's not possible. I left her only . . ." Memories flashed across his mind: her beautiful breasts, drops of water glistening on her blue-green scales . . . the sound of her laughter. A fist tightened in his gut. "You're certain? It couldn't have been another of her kind?"

Alexandros shook his head. "I'm sorry. Her remains were identified by one of her sisters."

Black, smothering fury engulfed him, and Orion swore violently. His fingers tightened into fists. He wanted to smash the rock wall, throw himself on the cave floor and pound the crumbling stone, but he contained the rage, forcing it to a locked compartment inside him. Soon, he would free it, and that anger would lend power to his blood vengeance in combat.

Instead, he pictured Sjshsglee as he had seen her last, lips red and swollen from his kisses, thick-lashed, blue eyes heavy-lidded with passion. She had meant more to him than a sexual playmate; she had been his friend for many centuries. Mermaids in general were vain, selfish creatures who thought of little but their own pleasures and could rarely be trusted, but she had been different. There had always been honesty between them, and he believed that she genuinely cared for him, as much as one of the mer folk could.

"She was a rare beauty with the voice of a fallen angel," Alex said. "Many will miss her sweet songs."

"Shades?"

Alex nodded.

Orion exhaled slowly, trying to reason past the wrath that coursed in his head. "Why bother to kill a mermaid? They're more fish than humanoid . . . of little use to Melqart. Her life force would provide him scant energy."

"You know what shades are like. When the sea runs

with blood, they destroy everything that crosses their path. It's why we feared for you."

"You think I'm so easily disposed of?"

"Apparently not." Alex hugged him again. "I'm glad you're not dead, twin. And since you're not, we could use your help. We're sweeping the area. If any remain, we want to make certain they will hunt here no more."

"The pack that was off this island nearly finished me." He motioned toward Elena. "Luckily, she appeared in a small boat and gave me a way out. She saved my life, and I owe her. But I give you my word I've broken no laws with her—at least no serious ones."

"She didn't see you as you are?"

Orion shook his head. "No. I was going to swim to the mainland and fetch a boat for her. I can't leave her. What if she went into the water?"

"You said you found the bodies of the Germans on this island. Are they still here?"

"I buried them. It's their custom."

"But their families will never know what happened to them."

"No." Orion grimaced. "And now that you've told me of the other killings, I'm certain I did the right thing." Absently, he massaged the back of his head. He'd been out of water far longer than was comfortable. He had the knack of remaining on land for days without suffering serious damage, but not without pain. He'd have a whale-size headache if he didn't immerse his body in salt water soon.

"Why would she"—Alex gestured toward Elena—"go in the water? It's too far for her to swim to the mainland."

"Who knows what she'd do? She's unpredictable." Orion couldn't stop thinking about Sjshsglee. It was hard to think of her dead. The thought that the same thing could happen to Elena gave him a sick feeling. "I can't take the chance she might. I owe her my protection."

Alex looked unconvinced. "So your interest in this human is purely honorable?"

Orion met his brother's shrewd gaze. "I found her attractive, if that's what you mean. But nothing happened."

"Take her to her own kind, if you must. But we have no time for you to locate a boat and bring it back. I'm not alone. I have a patrol with me. We'll provide security, and you can carry her to the mainland yourself."

"Underwater?" Orion looked back at where Elena lay, still in a deep slumber. "I've never transported a human, other than Danu." His older brother, Morgan, had involved the two of them in the rescue of a human youngling, a little girl he'd later adopted as his own daughter.

"I was there, remember," Alex said. "If you could keep Danu from drowning, you can do the same for your female."

Alex's tone didn't sit well with him. "Elena," Orion said. "Her name is Elena."

"Careful. Don't let yourself become attached to her."

"I won't. I told you, I owe her a debt. Would you have me abandon her now?"

"Suit yourself, but I'm in enough trouble with our father for my own transgressions. If you're determined to do this, I'll help you, but we have no time to waste. Just make certain she remembers nothing. I'm not overly fond of humans."

"Nor am I, but she's different."

"Every woman you make love to is different, according to you."

Orion clenched his jaw. "I told you, I didn't share pleasure with her."

"Maybe not, but you'd like to."

To that, Orion had no fit answer. As usual, Alexandros was right, and, as usual, he wanted to knock that smirk off his brother's face. It was the problem with having a twin. Alex knew him all too well, and he'd put into words what Orion hadn't wanted to face.

He did desire Elena.

"Are we going to hunt the horde today or not?"

In answer, Orion let his body shift back to his own natural state, picked up Elena, and carried her toward the crashing surf.

She was dreaming. She knew she was dreaming because she was in Orion's arms, and he was swimming—not on the surface of the water, but far below the surface. Above her, she could see schools of multicolored fish and below a sand and lava studded ocean floor.

She was no stranger to swimming and the sea was her passion, but at this depth, she wore her full diving gear and tanks. She was breathing; she could see bubbles rising from her mouth and nose, but she felt no distress or difficulty. She might have been a fish, so easily did she draw each breath.

Her eyes widened as she took in the wonder of swirling water and the man who held her in his arms. Orion. It was Orion, but yet, in a sense, it wasn't. There was something strange about him, something unusual other than the gleaming Phrygian–style Greek helmet on his head. So, she was either dreaming or she'd smashed her head when the Zodiac turned over in the surf, and she'd suffered brain damage.

If she squinted, Orion looked like Brad Pitt playing the role of Achilles in *Troy*. Although her fellow scholars disdained the film for cheap entertainment, she'd loved it, seen it three times in the theater and owned a DVD of the movie. As a scientist and archeologist, she knew where the history and storyline had separated, but she couldn't help it. Brad Pitt was adorable. As was Orion.

She dreamed as everyone dreamed, but she couldn't remember such a vivid dream, and although she sometimes dreamed of diving, she'd never included Greek warriors in her fantasy. Because Orion wasn't alone. Not far away, she could see other Greek or Macedonian infantrymen swimming on either side of them. The others were far enough away that she lost sight of them, and just when she'd decided that they were a figment of her imagination, another soldier would appear. And the one she saw over and over in the distance seemed to be Orion, so that he was both carrying her and in another place at the same time. Decidedly odd, even for a nightmare.

The other Orion carried an Alexander the Great era sword and a round shield that she might have seen on display in a dozen museums around the world. This was definitely a better class of dream, and if she was permanently disabled by cracking her head on a rock, at least she wasn't counting endless white sheep jumping over a white picket fence.

Orion, the one with his arms around her, glanced down at her. "Elena. You're awake."

"You think so?" she managed. If she was, she was in worse condition than she'd thought. "Where are we?"

"Shh," he said. "Close your eyes and sleep."

"Sleep, hell. I want to see." She struggled to break free of his embrace.

"All right." He released her, and when she started to drift away, he caught her hand. "You're safe with me," he assured her. "Safe with us."

She didn't answer. Coming toward them was the largest turtle that she'd ever seen. Moss and barnacles clung to his green shell and two black eyes stared from a massive head, eyes that seemed filled with both ancient knowledge and sorrow. Silently, the turtle glided by, so close that she could have reached out and touched him.

Some divers claimed that the sea was silent, but Elena had never felt that way. She always heard an inner music, a majestic symphony interspersed with the click of dolphins, the poignant cry of whales, and the rhythm of the tides. She heard it now, and the sheer beauty made her feel small and humble.

"Come," Orion said. "Since you're awake, swim with me."

"But how? Have I drowned? I'm dead, aren't I? Is this some sort of test before I get to the place with the white light and the angel trumpets?"

He laughed.

She looked at him more closely. He wore not only a Greek helmet but a cuirass and greaves, gold arm bands, and a great black sword with a silver hilt, a sword definitely not Greek. It must be a sci-fi movie because she could swear his exposed skin was covered in tiny bluish scales, not repulsive fish scales, but intriguing. She reached out to touch his cheek and found it not cold, but warm and alive.

"Are you all extras in some sort of movie?" But she knew the moment it was out of her mouth that couldn't be the answer. Most filming was done on solid land and that that wasn't . . . Well, even extras needed to breathe. Which meant that this she was definitely dreaming.

"I don't understand," she said to him. If this was a nightmare, it wasn't a scary one, simply odd. She wasn't frightened, and she didn't want to wake up any time soon. There was too much to see.

"You don't need to," he said. "You're safe. I promise."

Which was exactly what Howie McMann had said to her in the choir loft when he'd pulled out his teeny weenie and tried to persuade her that you couldn't get pregnant your first time. She hadn't believed it then, and she wasn't sure that she believed Orion now.

"Can you swim?" he asked. "I don't have much time."

"You mean that I have to wake up?"

A dolphin came out of the darkness followed by a younger one. Elena had always been fond of dolphins, and she'd swum with them in the Caribbean. This one was large, over five hundred pounds if she was an ounce, with a network of scars etched into her head and back. The dolphin stared at her curiously before approaching and nudging her with its nose.

"Are you tired?" Orion asked. "Would you prefer to ride?" He tapped the dolphin's nose several times before swinging up on its back. "Come on," he said. "It's all right. Her name is Nohea, and she's very tame. She won't hurt you." He offered his hand.

It was a dream, and in a dream she could ride a dolphin. In fact, riding a dolphin was a secret wish she'd always harbored. She clasped Orion's strong fingers, and in an instant she was up in front of him and clinging to the big mammal's fin. Almost at once, they were flying through the water, through curtains of kelp and past pillars of stone. Fish and sharks and octopi loomed up and flashed past. The dolphin's skin was smooth and warm and soft. So fast did Nohea swim that Elena was certain she'd fall off, but Orion held her tightly around the waist, his strong body pressed against hers.

She had thought that the depths of the sea must be dark, but not in her dream. Iridescent lights glowed around her: blue and pink and green. The water felt like silk against her skin. Never had she felt so weightless, so free.

The dolphin was swimming toward the surface, or perhaps the water was becoming shallower, because Elena was certain they passed directly under the hull of a large ship. Fish were smaller here and quicker, darting away almost before she could identify them.

"Where are we—" she began, but Orion cut her off by leaning close and whispering in her ear.

"Good-bye, Elena. Forget me. Forget all this."

"But I don't want to—"

In a burst of energy, the dolphin rose and leaped out of the sea. Elena saw the beauty of the night, no longer shrouded in clouds but star studded and moonlit. She felt the salt wind on her cheeks and then an all-encompassing blackness.

The boat was rocking gently on the waves. Elena sighed and turned, shielding her eyes from the rising sun. She was sleepy, so sleepy, and the motion of the sea soothed her like the rocking of a cradle. She gave in to the weariness again, and the next time she woke, the sun was high over the horizon, its rays warm against her face and exposed skin.

Elena sat up and looked around. The small wooden dory was anchored to a post driven into the sea, and to her right, no more than a short distance lay a harbor. People walked on the beach, going about their normal day-to-day activities. Two men were stretching a large net to dry in the sun while another smeared pitch on the hull of an overturned boat. She recognized the town, a small fishing village a few miles from her expedition headquarters. But how had she gotten here?

She began to feel her head, her arms, her legs. She wasn't in pain, but why were her memories so confused? There was a strong breeze but no storm, no choppy surf. And how had she gotten into this fishing boat? She didn't think she'd been drinking. If she'd tied one on, she'd have a hangover, wouldn't she?

She was barefoot, and she wore the tattered remains of the clothes she'd worn when she left the harbor this morning. But, by the position of the sun, it couldn't be later than ten or eleven o'clock, so this couldn't be the same morning she'd taken the Zodiac to check the wreck site. Had she lost an entire day? Or had taking the inflatable out in bad weather been the dream? No, she decided. That was too clear in her mind. She'd definitely gone to make certain that no one was intruding on her dive site.

She inspected the interior of the boat in an attempt to discover some clue to the mystery. The dory was old, obviously handmade, without oars or a motor. It contained nothing but a coil of weathered rope, two scarred bench seats, a section of torn fishing net, and a heap of seaweed. The bottom of the boat was dry and dusty; not a drop of seawater had trickled in. But the seaweed was vividly green and glossy with moisture. Odd. How had that gotten into the boat? If the waves had washed the seaweed into the dory, why wasn't the deck damp?

She reached to pick up a handful of seaweed. It was clean and free of motor oil or the flotsam that drifted onto the shore of a harbor. The seaweed felt as soft as satin, and the brilliant green reminded her of something . . . something she should remember but seemed just out of reach. She lifted it and sniffed, inhaling the sweet, salty odor, savoring the smell. As she did, something heavy fell to the bottom of the boat, something bright and glittering.

# CHAPTER 7

Deep beneath the surface of the Atlantic, Prince Caddoc retreated to his suite of rooms in one of the oldest levels of the king's palace, a section usually reserved for visiting dignitaries from outlying and not very important sea kingdoms. It shamed him to be housed as meanly as any barbarian diplomat, but he knew that he was lucky not to have been banished beyond the city walls to Neptune's villa.

Neither Poseidon nor Queen Korinna had forgiven him for his mother's attempt at overturning the throne. It was only his father's age and softening heart that had won him reprieve from execution or being sealed in an ice tomb for a thousand years.

None of which would have happened had he been treated as he deserved. He was Poseidon's eldest-born son and should have been heir to the crown. It was only his mother's position as concubine and later minor queen that had barred him from his rightful inheritance. All his life, he'd lived in the shadow of his half-brothers and sisters, and the ill will he bore them had been tempered and seared to a white-hot hatred. Gladly would he see all of them devoured in the bowels of a seraphim or ground to dust by the jaws of a pod of killer whales . . . all but one. His sister

Morwena was too tasty a morsel to be wasted. He had other plans for her.

He was contemplating the details of those plans as he stepped into his entrance hall. But immediately, he sensed that all was not well. A feeling of dread swept over him, and the scales rose on the back of his neck. Since his return, he'd had no permanent servants attached to his service, and no naiad would dare to enter his quarters without his permission, even to clean. "Who's there?" he cried. His nostrils flared and he felt an urgent need to void his bladder. Instead, he drew his sword. "Who is it?"

"Where have you been?" Halimeda demanded. "I've been waiting for you for hours. I'm starving."

Caddoc flinched, turned left into his high-ceilinged bed-chamber and saw his mother lying in his great, curtained, shell bed. "What are you doing here?" he demanded. Quickly, he darted to slam and lock the outer door through which he'd just entered. "Are you mad? What if someone should hear you? Are you trying to get me killed?"

"Where were you?"

"Keep your voice down, Mother," he cautioned. "The servants spy on me constantly." His scales thrummed unpleasantly. Finding her here in his bedroom was his worst nightmare. Not only was she under a death sentence if she returned to Atlantis, but he was forbidden to have contact with her on penalty of having his own pardon revoked.

Besides, he'd had plans for the evening with a nymph that didn't include his mother. Now, he'd have to send Zephyr away. It had taken him days and the promise of a pearl necklace to get her to agree to meet him, and he'd already sent the jewelry to her quarters. His bowels knotted. His mother always made him nervous, and now more than ever. He definitely needed to seek out his elimination chamber before he shamed himself even further.

"What kind of greeting is this from my only child?" She languidly pushed aside a hanging and glared at him.

Caddoc felt like a small fish about to be devoured by a hammerhead shark. The cramping in the pit of his stomach intensified.

"Aren't you happy to see me?" His mother slid one long shapely leg out of the bed, and he saw that the soles of her feet were dyed as red as the palms of her hands. As usual, she wore next to nothing, a gown—if it could be called a gown—in the filmy Egyptian style, woven of the thinnest white seaweed and nearly transparent.

Caddoc's mouth tightened. His mother had always been a beautiful woman, stunning, some called her, alluring in the most sexual manner. It was her lush curves, her classic features, waist-length, midnight-black hair, and come-hither eyes that had caused the king to lift her to a position of minor wife, or so Caddoc had always believed. *Well, that and her skill with poison.*

Smirking, Halimeda descended the marble steps and kissed his lips. "Foolish boy, you know you've been desolate without me." Her long fingers threaded through his hair, caught and tugged hard enough to cause him pain in a mock show of affection.

Caddoc wanted to scrub away the cold taste of her, but he knew better. "Of course," he lied. "I've been worried sick. But why aren't you with him?"

"Him?" The corners of Halimeda's mouth turned up in a sly smile, but her eyes remained as hard as obsidian. A scarlet octopus with yellow spots crept from her back onto one shoulder and undulated down her arm. She cooed and caressed it, pressing it to her breast, allowing the thing to attach its suckers to—

Gagging, he looked away.

"Him, who?" his mother asked sweetly.

"Melqart." Caddoc lowered his voice to a whisper. "You've pledged yourself to him, haven't you? It must have been him who saved you from Poseidon's dungeon."

She moistened her upper lip with the tip of pink tongue, and he squirmed inside. She was more beautiful than he remembered. No one could guess her age or that she was the mother of a grown son. Her own poisoning, arrest, and imprisonment seemed to have done her no harm. In fact, she seemed rejuvenated, as exquisite and perfect as any goddess.

"Do you doubt my powers? Do you think any cell could hold me?"

Someone tapped lightly on the door, and he glanced in that direction. It was too early for Zephyr, and he wondered who had come seeking him. "Who is it?" he called.

"Prince Caddoc," came the thick and gargled speech of a naiad serving wench. "I bear a message for your ears alone."

"Go away," he ordered. "I'm busy. Come back later."

"But my lady Zephyr bid me—"

"I said, go away. I can see no one until the next turn of the water clock."

"He's entertaining his mother," Halimeda said.

"Shh," Caddoc snapped.

The maid at the door said no more, and he assumed she'd left.

"Answer me!" Halimeda said. "Do you doubt my powers?"

"I know you are a witch, Mother. You've proved it often enough. But sorceress or not, you are forbidden on pain of death to come to Atlantis. If Poseidon learns—"

"Hold your tongue, you whining coward. Leave your father to me. He's as weak and pliable as you are." She traced his bottom lip with one curved nail, and the octopus stretched out one tentacle to imitate her. "I will deal with Poseidon. I have another task for you."

He moved back, trying not to show his distaste, wishing she was anywhere but here . . . wishing he had gone to the Pacific islands as Tora had urged him. Each day he, Caddoc, felt more in danger here and seemed farther from the throne. He doubted if his father would ever forgive him, let alone name him crown prince over his half-brother Morgan.

So far his mother's plotting had come to nothing, and he was far worse off than before. His estates had been confiscated, his herds of sea horses, and personal fortune, all taken from him and redistributed to the masses. Even his allowance had been cut off. How was he to live in the style he'd been accustomed to?

"Aren't you going to ask me what I want of you?" Halimeda said.

"I'm sure you'll tell me soon enough." He was sick of dancing to her tune. It had been a mistake for him to try to be reconciled with the king, his father. Alexandros would need only the faintest excuse to put a knife in his back. Far better to be a visiting prince off some tropical island surrounded by adoring females than a dead prince here.

"Morgan's wife is with child."

"Rhiannon?"

His mother lunged forward and slapped him sharply on the cheek. "Yes, Rhiannon, you fool! What other wife does your brother have?"

He ducked away, his hand itching to draw the sword and cut off her head, but he knew he wouldn't. She was right. He was a coward. The last time he'd disobeyed her openly, she'd cast a spell over him, paralyzing him, filling his throat with nasty, crawling creatures. He shuddered. "What do you want me to do? Do you want her dead?"

She shrugged. "He'd only marry again. No." She shook her head. "It's better to put an end to the child. Rhiannon is a changling. Lord Melqart has given me a potion that will drive her insane and shrivel her womb. That will end Morgan's line and keep his mad wife from spawning any more half-breed brats."

"Easy enough to do," he reasoned. "I have connections in the kitchens. But if she becomes barren and loses her wits, what's to keep him from taking a second wife?"

Halimeda laughed. "Your noble brother has sworn before witnesses to take no other wife while Rhiannon lives. You know he never wished to be high king. If he loses both the wife that he loves and the children he hopes to father—"

"The twins will become Father's heirs, not me!"

She flung the octopus. It smacked his other cheek and slithered over his head and down the back of his neck. He stood there immobile, quivering with rage while she ranted at him. "Never say that! You will be the next Poseidon! Lord Melqart has given me his word. You were the firstborn. You should have been crown prince from the first moment you drew breath."

"Maybe I would have if your grandfather hadn't been a commoner."

She hissed and extended a hand. Light shot from her fingertips, and he dropped to his knees as blood filled his throat and poured from his mouth and eyes. Searing flame ignited his skin. It peeled and curled as his screams choked in his throat.

Caddoc felt his body slam against a marble pillar. He slid down to the floor and lay there panting as the pain gradually seeped out of his battered flesh. "I'm sorry," he sobbed. "I didn't mean it. I will do what you say . . . anything you say."

"Good." She rested her hands on her hips and sighed.

"Get up! There's nothing wrong with you. At least nothing that a helping of courage wouldn't fix."

Trembling, Caddoc looked down at his hands. He feared there would be only bone and blackened tendons, but to his surprise he found himself whole. He'd suffered nothing but loss of his dignity. Still shaken, he got to his feet. "Tell me what to do, Mother. I am your servant in all things."

She looked down her pretty nose at him. "I should hope you are. I created you, and I can as easily rid myself of your incompetence. I'm young enough to have other sons, bold sons who are worthy to sit on the throne of Atlantis."

His lower lip quivered and he felt the sting of salt tears in his eyes. "Give me another chance. I won't fail you again."

"No, you won't. My patience has run out with you, Caddoc."

"Give me the poison. I'll get it right this time."

"Very well." She settled onto a cushioned bench. "But first, I desire food. Order me a feast from the kitchens, the best they have to offer. I'm starving."

"Whatever you wish, Mother." Zephyr would have to wait. He was no longer in the mood for lovemaking. Halimeda would have to be appeased, and then he'd have to get rid of her before she was discovered. Doing her bidding was a small price to have her back in Melqart's realm and out of Atlantis. And as for Morgan's wife, he owed her for the death of his cousin Jason. She deserved whatever fate his mother had planned for her.

"My dinner!" Halimeda reminded him.

"At once, Mother. What do you desire?"

"Everything. All of it." Drool ran from the corners of her mouth, and she wiped it away with the back of her arm. "And the sooner the better."

"As you say, Madame. Everything." *And the sooner you're away the better for me,* he thought as he pulled a braided rope to summon a servant.

The notion that she might be right this time lightened his mood. After all, the twins were warriors, and warriors died all the time in combat. Once Morgan and his wife were dealt with, his mother might have a plan for Orion and Alexandros. . . . He could picture himself sitting at the right hand of Poseidon, imagining the heralds announcing him as Crown Prince Caddoc.

There would be no need to give trinkets to women then. They would willingly throw themselves at his feet and into his bed. . . . Even Morwena. His half-sister had evaded him before, but this was another game. He smiled at his mother. With Halimeda's help, sweet Morwena might be the prize he'd sought for so long.

Elena stared at the heavy gold ring that had fallen from the seaweed. It was inscribed with strange symbols . . . not Linear B, but definitely writing of some kind. The workmanship was exquisite, but it was very old, certainly Bronze Age, possibly Minoan. This was a true work of art. How it had come to be in the bottom of this boat she couldn't imagine. Excitement made her giddy. She'd seen, even held treasures of the ancient world before, and that wasn't why she was so intrigued. She had the strongest hunch that this ring was familiar.

Her complete blank about where she'd been or with whom the night before was every bit as puzzling. She'd never done drugs, and although she enjoyed a drink or two, it wasn't like her to become inebriated. If she'd been the victim of some creep, it wasn't likely that she'd awaken feeling good with no evidence of having been attacked or robbed.

In any case, she needed to get back to her headquarters. Her position as leader of this undersea expedition was too precarious to risk her reputation with her crew and colleagues. This might be the only chance she'd ever get to prove herself and she wasn't about to waste it. Since she'd been a grad student, she'd struggled to overcome her father's legacy of brilliance gone awry. And nothing would allow her to be tarred by the same brush.

She didn't like to think about what had happened to her father, his obsession with an impossible quest, and his breakdown of health, reputation, and finally family. His fanaticism had cost him his life, and cost her the love and companionship of a beloved parent. But the academic world was full of competition and jealousy. Too many people had been unhappy when she'd been granted the opportunity to lead this project, and they'd be delighted to see her fail.

Clutching the precious ring tightly in her left hand, Elena lowered herself over the edge of the dory and began to swim toward shore. She'd solve the question of the ring later. First things first.

"We were wondering when you'd show up." Stefanos stood in the center of the street with a bottle of wine under his arm. "We found the Zodiac at the dock this morning, but no sign of you, Dr. Elena." He grinned, indicating the middle-aged man on the motorbike just pulling away. "Guess you made a warm date."

"A warm date?" She laughed. "You mean that you think I *had* a *hot date.*"

"Not so good, what I said?"

She smiled at him. "You're getting better." Stefanos's English was excellent, except for American slang. He was technically a grad student here to further his education in underwater archeology, but she suspected that he was a plant, inserted in the dive to make certain that nothing illegal or unethical was done.

She liked Stefanos. He had a sense of humor; he was a hard worker, and he always knew where to find good wine at the best prices. But in her opinion, he was more cop than scientist. Plus, Irene, her other Greek grad student, had passed on the information that Stefano's uncle held a position of importance in the Greek government.

Not that she could blame the authorities. The wholesale looting of national Greek treasures was a disgrace, and had gone on since the reign of Alexander of Macedon. Sad to say, many teams of foreign archeologists had enriched their own countries' museums over the years, and even today, not all teams were entirely above board when it came to full disclosure of information. Her sponsor, The Nautical Archeology Program at Texas A & M, was respected worldwide for the integrity of their scholarship and their digs, but she supposed that all expeditions were suspect until proved otherwise.

In any case, Stefanos had been a real find. It was Stefanos who had found the rambling house in the Old Town that served as both headquarters and residence for her team and procured a dive boat and cook and housekeeper. There, amid the narrow twisting alleys and crumbling Venetian architecture, he'd secured a real gem of a rental. Her room even had a balcony, and if she stood on tippy toes and leaned over the precarious wooden railing, she could catch a glimpse of not only the sea but the massive Venetian fortress that overlooked the harbor.

Stefanos glanced at the departing motor bike. "An old friend?"

"Who? Oh, Karl. No, I just hitched a ride with him."

He lost the amused look on his face. "Be careful, Dr.

Elena. Even on Crete, bad things can happen to good people, especially one such as yourself, a beautiful woman. All strangers are not—"

"He's a priest, Stefanos. Here on vacation from Kansas City." She chuckled. "And we were properly introduced by a taverna owner in Agia Galini." She shook her head. "You worry too much. I can take care of myself."

"You wouldn't be the first foreigner to vanish in Greece."

"I'm here, safe and sound," she said, not wanting to dwell any further on what the hell had happened to her. She'd worry about that later. "The sea would have been too rough to dive today anyway."

"At least you're here in time to enjoy some of Anna's fish stew."

He turned back toward the street that led to their alley, and Elena followed, frowning thoughtfully. If the Zodiac was here, she must have returned to Rethymo yesterday. So why didn't she remember doing so?

"We're not the only ones who were looking for you," Stefanos said over his shoulder. "You have a visitor."

"A visitor? Who?" She couldn't imagine who it might be.

"A fellow American. Greg Hamilton."

"Greg? Oh, no." A ripe Greek oath slipped out before she could stop herself. He'd said something about her meeting him in Athens for a night of club hopping. She'd completely forgotten.

"He's waiting in the lounge for you." Stefanos grinned. "And from the sound of him, he's not too happy with you."

# CHAPTER 8

"Where were you? No one saw you since yesterday morning, and it's after two now, for God's sake!" Greg swore and Anna stuck her head out of the kitchen doorway.

The little woman shook her wooden spoon at him. "Me, I not cook in a house where the name of God is used so."

"Sorry, Ma'am," Greg said. "No offense meant."

Anna, all of five feet and as thin as her own spoon handle, scowled. "Take care for your soul." She glanced at Elena. "Will this American be for dinner?"

"No," Greg said.

Elena shook her head. "No, thank you, Anna. Don't count on me either."

Irene, Stefanos, and Hilary entered the spacious lounge. The two women were discussing the significance of an unusual pattern on a section of pottery that they'd pulled from the wreck on their second day of diving.

"I know you and Stefanos have met," Elena said to Greg. "Were you introduced to my team? Dr. Hilary Walden is on the staff at Texas A & M, and Irene is one of our able Greek grad students."

Irene smiled. "We met earlier."

"She was kind enough to offer me coffee while I waited for you," Greg said. "I told you that I was coming to Athens, Elena. I was counting on spending last night with you."

"Let's go upstairs," she said. "There's no reason to intrude on everyone's dinner." Elena led the way out of the spacious, whitewashed sitting room with its four tall windows, high ceiling, and cool, antique tile floors. Greg followed her down the hall and up a flight of wide stairs.

Over the years, the house had been occupied by many owners, but it retained its Venetian bones, softened by Greek practicality. Her bedroom, on the second floor, was as light and airy as the lounge downstairs. Simple white plaster walls and deep windows with wooden louvers that could be shuttered against the mid-day heat offered a cool tranquility. As usual, stacks of books covered her table and spilled onto the two straight-back chairs. She waved Greg to a lumpy but comfortable loveseat and sat down beside him.

"I was worried about you," he said. "Someone, it must have been Stefanos, said that the weather was too bad for diving, but that you'd taken the Zodiac out and—"

"I'm sorry, Greg. I completely forgot you were coming. Not that I forgot you were coming," she added quickly. "But you didn't know what day you were flying in, and—"

"How can you head up a project like this dive and be so irresponsible? This isn't the first time you've stood me up."

She grimaced. "You're right. It's my fault, and I'm sorry. What more can I say?"

"I've got to be on the ship tomorrow. I'll be tied up there for weeks during the exploration. It was our last chance to have a night together. And you pull a vanishing act. Where the hell were you?"

*Good question*, she thought. *Where the hell was I?* "There's no ring on my finger," she answered defensively. "I don't believe I'm obligated to provide an alibi for my comings and goings."

"We could change that." He reached for her hand. "You just have to say the word."

She let him take her hand, but kept a distance between them. "It would never work. As you say, I'm *irresponsible*."

"I didn't mean that and you know it. You're scatter-brained. Right-brained, left-brained, something like that. You get tied up with your work, and you forget everything else."

She nodded. "True. I've always been like that. It's no excuse, but don't count on my changing."

"You care about me, Elena. You can't say you don't."

"You know I do. We're pretty good in bed."

"More than that." He grinned. "We're hot."

She nodded. "But sometimes, great sex isn't enough. I just don't think it would work logistically. You spend half your life jetting around the world, and I'm usually at one isolated site or another."

"It doesn't have to be that way. We could both make changes in our careers." He leaned closer to kiss her, but she pulled away and rose to her feet.

"We've talked about this before. I don't think I'm cut out to be a wife," she said. "At least not to someone like you."

"What?" He stood up. "My family's money offends you? Or is it the 'save the planet/green world' shit?"

"No." She went to a window and looked out on the street below. Children were chasing a cat, and a stout nun in black walked past with loaves of bread in a wicker basket. "Maybe it is, a little. Not the money. I know how much you've put into H.E. Your dad may have founded

Hamilton Energy, but you've expanded the company light-years: solar, wind, geothermal."

"Natural gas and oil are still our bread and butter. Which is why this new gas field could mean so much."

"Ah, I thought we'd get around to that," she said. "You know how I feel about drilling in this part of the world." Her tone softened. "Does it have to be here, Greg? If anything goes wrong, we could lose pieces of history that can't be replaced."

"It won't happen, not if the exploration is done right. The world needs energy. You know the state of Greek finances. A successful new gas field could mean everything to these people."

"But every foot of the sea floor is littered with artifacts. There's so much we haven't learned yet, and so much that's already been lost."

"Which is why the project needs solid archeologists on-board. You could be one of them. You could give this up. Do something you believe in for a steady income. A good income, Elena, one that would allow you to—"

"You want me to take a job with Hamilton Energy?" She shrugged. "I have a job, a career I love. I'm not leaving this site, leaving everything I've ever worked toward, to take a trumped-up position in an oil company."

"That's exactly what I told Dad you'd say." He came to stand beside her and slipped an arm around her shoulders. "Damn, Elena, do you have to always live like a monk?" He indicated the only ornamentation on the walls, a wood and gilt crucifix over her bed. "This room couldn't be more austere if you had a cell in a monastery."

She laughed and turned toward him. He kissed her, and she laid her head against his shoulder. "Am I forgiven?"

"No. I still want to know where you were for over twenty-four hours."

"Woman of mystery, that's me." She studied the room, trying to see it as Greg did. Compared to the five star hotels he usually stayed in, she supposed it was primitive. But this house provided the finest accommodations she'd ever known on a site. Usually, her bed was a cot or a sleeping bag and the roof over her head was a canvas tent.

"I don't know how you can say that I'm roughing it," she said. "I've even got family pictures." On a round marble table beside the austere single bed stood a double picture frame. One half held a photo of her mother on her wedding day; the other side contained a black-and-white snapshot of her father and a dirty-faced seven-year-old on a camel with the Great Pyramid of Giza in the background.

"And a wardrobe to hold your extensive collection of high fashion."

Elena chuckled as he motioned to a duffle bag on the floor in the corner overflowing with shorts, tees, and jeans. "That's not all I own," she defended, motioning toward a little black dress that hung beside a well-worn sweatshirt that read TEXAS A &. The M had been chewed off by some fuzzy rodent on a dig in Colorado.

She stood on tiptoes and kissed him again. "I am sorry that I ruined your evening. When are they expecting you to meet the ship?"

"Early tomorrow morning. I told them it wasn't possible for me to be there today. They're sending a helicopter for me at eight a.m."

"So we have what's left of today and this evening."

He tightened his arm around her. "I meant what I said, lady. I'd like to make you Mrs. Hamilton, even if you won't accept a job with the company."

"I agreed to dinner, nothing more," she reminded him.

"I like you a lot, but I'm not sure that's enough to talk about getting serious."

"You *like me a lot*? Elena, we've been dating for over a year. And neither of us is getting any younger. Mom and Dad are adamant about being grandparents while they're still young enough to enjoy the little rug rats."

She chuckled. "Thanks for reminding me that Social Security looms." She wasn't twenty anymore, but she was hardly retirement material. She'd be thirty-four . . . no, thirty-five on her next birthday. But she wasn't sure she wanted to think about kids yet. She still had so much she wanted to achieve before she added more responsibilities to her life. And the responsibility for a child was a big one.

*And then there was the matter of if she loved Greg?* He was fun to be with, but love? She wasn't sure she knew what love between a man and woman was. She'd thought her parents loved one another, once. But when her father had lost everything, their marriage had faded. No giant split, no fireworks, just polite silence. And a quiet divorce . . . months before her father was lost at sea.

"No rings, and no 'until death do us part,'" she said. "Couldn't you just settle for dinner and a walk on the beach here in Rethymo?"

"You're a tough nut," Greg said. "But I'll take what I can get. Dinner sounds good. I'd like to wrap my teeth around some authentic Greek shish kebab and aged retsina. I presume you know the cafés in town."

"It's early yet, and it wouldn't hurt you to unwind after your flight from the States. How about a swim? We can borrow Stefanos's Vespa, and there's a lovely sand beach at Agia Galini. Did you bring something to swim in?"

"Don't know. Mom has Pilar pack for me, but my luggage went on to meet the ship on the mainland."

"We'll buy you a pair. There's a shop a few blocks from here."

"What are we waiting for?"

"We'll have to hurry before they close for the afternoon. This is Crete, not Houston. Everyone here goes home for a meal and a civilized nap."

"Lead on, woman. I'm in. Just don't expect me to give up on our making things official between us." He grinned. "Where are you going to get a better offer?"

"Where, indeed?" She laughed. "Successful, handsome, and modest. How could any woman refuse?"

"Seriously," he said. "With the Hamilton fortune and Dad's influence at Texas A & M, you're guaranteed to be able to continue your little expeditions, if that's what you want."

"You're trying to bribe me?"

"Damn it, Elena. I want to marry you. What good is family money if it doesn't get me what I want most?"

"It's one way of looking at it, I suppose."

"It's the only way," he assured her. "So, considering all the perks, will you marry me?"

"I'll think about it," she promised, "but don't get your hopes up. I don't make big decisions lightly."

"Fair enough, but you should know that once I set my mind on having something, I don't stop until I get it."

Caddoc closed the stone door, successfully muffling Halimeda's screams. He hurried down the corridor and took the first flight of stairs leading up and away from his suite. He'd done as his mother asked, ordered a feast to be brought to his rooms. But for some reason, she'd been unable to eat a bite. Why or how such a thing was possible, he didn't want to guess. It smelled of Melqart and sorcery, and he wanted no part of it.

When he'd fled the room, she'd been tearing down the bed hangings and flinging them at him. *As if it were his fault.* Whatever bargain she'd made with the Phoenician god of war, it had nothing to do with him. He didn't know how she'd gotten into his quarters or how she'd get out. So long as he didn't bear the blame, he didn't care.

As he passed through a courtyard and into another maze of hallways, Caddoc caught sight of a familiar face, that of his half-sister Morwena. She wasn't alone; a brat was with her—the changeling that his brother Morgan and wife had adopted as their own child.

"Sister," he called. "I've not seen you since my return to Atlantis. You look well." *Very well, indeed,* he thought. Her lime-green tunic was woven of the thinnest sea grass and concealed little of her ample bosom and womanly curves. The short length and plunging neckline left Morwena's shapely throat, arms, and legs exposed. "And who is this precious little one with you?"

"I'm Danu," the child said. She flashed a dimpled smile as Morwena jerked her back and stepped in front of her.

Cute, Caddoc thought, with promise of becoming a real beauty in a century or two.

"What are you doing here?" Morwena asked suspiciously.

"Poseidon has forgiven me. I'm a prince of the blood. I have every right to—"

"Not if it were up to me!" Morwena's blue eyes narrowed. "You may have wormed your way back into Father's graces, but everyone knows what you did. You'll find small welcome in the city and less from the rest of your family."

"The twins? Bloodthirsty bullies, the both of them." He smiled at the child and crouched down to peer into her face. "And where is your mother? I hear she'd not been feeling well."

"Mama threw up."

"Sshh, Danu," Morwena said. "Don't talk to him."

Caddoc laid a hand on Danu's curly blond head. "Pay no attention to her. I'm your Uncle Caddoc. I'm sorry your mother's ill. Maybe she ate something that didn't agree with her."

"Daddy says there's a baby in her tummy." Danu giggled. "That's silly."

"A baby. Well, congratulations are in order. Pass on my good wishes to Morgan and the mother-to-be, sister."

Morwena started to walk away, but he took hold of the child's shoulder. "Don't hurry off. Danu and I are just getting to know each other."

The next thing Caddoc knew, he was lifted and smashed down against a wall. Groggily, he raised his head, but before he could rise, his brother Orion seized him by the throat and pinned him to the floor, holding him there with one sandal-clad foot.

"Don't ever speak to Danu or Morwena again," Orion said. "If you do, I'll twist off your head and use it as a fishing weight." He twisted to look at his sister. "Are you all right? Did he touch you?"

"No. He didn't. We're fine."

Orion removed his foot and stepped back. "Don't move," he warned, raising one finger.

Danu's eyes widened, and the child began to whimper.

"You're scaring her," Morwena said. "It's all right, baby. They're just playing."

"It's not a nice game," Danu said.

Caddoc felt the rush of blood to his face and throat. He wanted to lunge at Orion and run his sword through him.

He wanted to kill all three of them, but his muscles wouldn't work. He lay there, mortified, unable to move.

His brother turned away from him, ignoring him, letting him know that he considered him no threat at all. "Why did you bring her here?" he asked Morwena. "This part of the palace is too isolated to be safe for either of you. You don't know what slime you might slip on."

Morwena picked up Danu. "We were on our way to the archery range. I thought it would be a shortcut. I didn't expect to meet Caddoc."

"What if it was Tora? You have to use caution. Halimeda is still out there."

"I can take care of myself," she said.

"And Danu?"

"He didn't hurt us. He was just being Caddoc."

"Come. I'll see you to the archery court." Orion glared at him once more. "Remember what I said. Stay away from them. Stay away from Morgan and Princess Rhiannon."

"Your word is not law here," Caddoc spat. "Poseidon still rules in Atlantis."

"He does," Orion agreed. "But if you're dead, and the morning tide washes your body away, it won't matter to you who is king. You'll still be fish bait."

# CHAPTER 9

"We should have killed Caddoc," Alexandros draped one arm over Orion's shoulder. "We'll only have to do it later."

"In cold blood?" Orion grimaced. "I'm a soldier, not an executioner."

"Sometimes, you have to be both."

"I hope not." They'd escorted their sister and niece to the archery range on the palace grounds and left them in the care of several of the king's guards. Their brother Marcos and some of his friends had been practicing their skill with the bow, accompanied by a group of young noblemen and women, and Orion had asked Marcos to watch over the two, much to Morwena's annoyance. Marcos was only fourteen, but he'd proved his skill with a bow and his courage. Orion was certain that Morwena and Danu would be safe enough from Caddoc's scheming today.

"I don't like the way he looks at Morwena," Alexandros muttered, stepping away and dropping his arm.

"Nor do I," Orion agreed. "His mother's depravity runs hot in his veins, and she would swive a naiad if he took her fancy. But we could hardly do away with him in front of Danu for the crime of intimidation."

"The kid's tougher than you give her credit for. She was

with us at the old palace, wasn't she? She saw blood flow and good men die. And it was her wit and nerve that freed the dolphins and kept Halimeda's forces from killing Korinna and the children."

"Still, she's a baby. There's no reason for her to see two of her uncles murder a third."

Alexandros's mouth hardened. "Poor reason for letting that scum live."

"We don't know he meant harm to them today."

"He always means harm." Two scouts passed by accompanied by a trio of harbor seals, and Alexandros smiled and greeted them in the old manner. "Tadeu. Moises. Seal folk. May the tides bring you substance."

The mermen saluted and the seals made acknowledgment in their graceful manner, but only Moises spoke. He was a particularly dashing figure, and his voice was the sweet beguiling melody that the nobility of the mer people cultivated. "Prince Alexandros. Prince Orion. Swim safely."

Alexandros waited until they were out of earshot before continuing the earlier conversation. "You're wrong about Caddoc," he said to Orion. "I think he is dangerous."

"He's too weak witted to be dangerous." Orion gazed after the company of scouts. Tadeu and Moises were not the mermen's given names, of course, but ones assumed to make it easier for military service to the kingdom. Most of their names were impossible for Atlanteans to pronounce and harder to remember, following no known pattern.

Sjshsglee's brother was a scout, but Orion had never met him. He would have liked to ask if either of these men were kin and to offer his condolences, but the mer were a race apart. Dead was dead, and although they possessed a certain general sadness, it wasn't their custom to mourn lost individuals. Sjshsglee's brother, had Orion been able to locate him, would have been offended if he acknowledged his relationship with her or showed remorse at her tragic death.

Most Atlanteans believed that the mer were entirely narcissistic, lacking the emotional development to have deep feelings about others, even their families and friends. Orion had never believed that. He'd seen too many brave mermen and mermaids die to protect each other. Rather, he supposed, their attachment to their own kind was so deep and abiding that it was impossible to either express or talk about a personal loss with an Atlantean. Sjshsglee had been the exception, and he vowed to take personal vengeance on her murderers and the source, Melqart.

"I suppose they were here to report to Mikhail."

Orion nodded. A relative newcomer to the court with a vaguely mysterious background, Lord Mikhail had risen quickly to a position of power under Poseidon. As the consort of Poseidon's sister, Princess Eudora, Mikhail could have lived a life of luxury without turning a hand, but he had quickly shown that he was a brilliant administrator. The king had rewarded his services with even higher offices, and recently Mikhail had assumed a command post in international security.

"I would have liked to question those scouts," Alexandros said.

"And what would you have gotten?" Orion grinned. "Songs? Sarcasm?"

The good thing about the mer was their skill at covert actions. Who could suspect a cute and cuddly seal of spying on a commercial fishing fleet or an oil drilling operation? Even those who knew that mer folk spent part of their lives as seals and could readily cloak themselves in sealskin at will, could rarely tell a disguised mermaid or merman from an actual seal. By Hades' rotten cock, he couldn't say if the seals he'd just seen were real or transformed mermen.

The bad thing about the mer, as Alex knew all too well, was that the mer had no system of nobility and no organized government. They maintained a stoic independence that bordered on fanaticism, so much so that most harbored an all-abiding distaste for Atlantean royalty and the intricate system of administration that had worked so well for the kingdom since the beginning of time. As a rule, mer folks would form no alliance with Atlanteans that could be counted on and wished only to be left alone to sit on rocks, sing their haunting songs, and seduce humans for sexual pleasure.

The mer bore grudges for centuries, seemingly without reason. Many a ship had been lured to destruction and all hands drowned because of a vendetta by some scheming mermaid.

Lord Mikhail possessed the uncanny ability to convince the mer that cooperation with the Atlanteans, the naiads, nymphs, and other sea folk was in the best interest of all. The mermen that Mikhail recruited had proved faithful, so far, but they would answer to none but him.

"Are you listening to me?" Alexandros asked.

"Sorry, I was thinking about—"

"About that woman?"

"No, about the mer."

Alexandros shrugged. "It's a waste of time. They are a totally irrational race, worse even than humans. There's no understanding mer."

"You're probably right."

"I am, and I'm right about our half-brother Caddoc, as well."

"I like him no better than you do," Orion said. "But as

evil as Halimeda was, she had the brains. Without his mother to think for him, Caddoc is an empty shell. Rotten and stinking, but without substance."

"Father doesn't think so."

"Poseidon's wisdom is clouded by his attachment to Halimeda."

"Even after she tried to poison him?"

"He ordered her thrown into prison, instead of executing her," Orion argued. "That tells me he still has feelings for her."

"Which is a polite way of saying that he's ruled by his cock."

"Father's more sentimental than you give him credit for."

Alexandros shrugged, his expression conveying his skepticism.

"It can't be easy to order the death of a wife, even an unfaithful one, or to exile your own son."

"All the same, I think Father will live to regret it."

They crossed another garden complex where schools of blue-and-yellow spotted fish swirled in intricate patterns and entered the great columned portico that led to the smaller palace of their Aunt Eudora. This aunt, a favorite of Orion's, had a deep and abiding love for the sculpture and art of lost civilizations, both those of the earth and those beneath the sea. Her home was filled with such treasures, all carefully researched and catalogued. Scholars from many humanoid species came to study her collection. Lord Mikhail shared her passion for these treasures, a trait that had contributed to their attraction to each other.

Mikhail preferred to hold meetings of state in their private library, away from Poseidon's official gathering places. The majority of the staff and officials were trustworthy, but with so many with access to the public halls and rooms of court, security wasn't always as tight as the ruling family wished. Here, Mikhail and Eudora maintained their own palace guard, a company of hardened Atlantean commoners, mer folk, and highly training fighting dolphins. These veterans of many battles answered only to the princess and her consort, and had pledged their lives and honor to their service.

Orion and Alex had come prepared to report on their search for Melqart's horde and the murder of the two German tourists that had gone unreported. Soon after they'd left Elena sleeping in the boat, they had come upon a pack of the killers not far from the harbor. With Alexandros and a full patrol of armed Atlantean warriors, they had eliminated the shades. The fight had been fierce, and the price high. One of their own had been killed and two critically wounded. Never had Orion seen shades battle with such determination. Usually, when the tide turned against them, they would flee, but not this time. Not until the last monster had been destroyed had the struggle ended.

Both Orion and Alex were certain that the attacks would continue until Melqart, once again, sank into a state of torpor. Orion had seen that happen three times in his life and, each time, while the god of war slept, peace reigned, once for over three hundred years.

"We'd be foolish to believe that the outbreak is over, after your victory," Lord Mikhail pronounced, when Orion had finished. "I received confirmation of yet another kill near Rhodes, a fisherman whose nets became entangled. He went into the water to try to free them and was cut to pieces. There wasn't enough of a body left for the other humans in the boat to retrieve. Hopefully, they will believe that the man was attacked by sharks."

"It's rare for shades to kill in daylight, isn't it?" Lady Jalini put in.

"It is," Orion agreed. "But not unheard of. Prince Morgan's daughter, Danu, was nearly devoured on a sunlit morning off the Maine coast. And I have no way of knowing when the German couple met their deaths. The horde is becoming bolder. Something has enraged Melqart."

Faces around the table acknowledged the gravity of Orion's statement. War had raged for millennia between the Atlanteans and the Phoenician god of war, but incidents were generally isolated. This increased hostility could only mean danger for all who lived beneath the oceans. If the humans invaded the seas, it didn't matter if they came hunting sharks or shades. There was bound to be conflict between the kingdom and those who walked the earth.

"Do you believe that the disturbance of the shipwreck off Crete by humans could have set this off?" Lady Jalini asked. Orion turned his full attention to her. She was tiny and dainty, with a childlike voice, but her keen intellect commanded the respect of generals and princes alike.

"It hasn't helped," Lady Athena answered gravely. "It's common knowledge that the ship is Phoenician and carried priests, sacrificial victims, and items sacred to the cult of Melqart. It was bound from Carthage to a temple, perhaps in Tyre, when it went down under a massive wave during a storm. It sank, rather than overturning, so that the treasures were not strewn across the sea floor. All aboard perished."

"I remember that," Poseidon said. "Wasn't there a curse involved?"

"Set and sealed with the deaths of three white bulls and a dozen virgin priestesses," Lady Athena replied. "It's said that any who venture to that spot will die a particularly unpleasant death."

"We've done what we can," Lady Jalini explained. "The

area around the ship is forbidden to Atlanteans. We've left the site untouched and made the usual attempt to hide it from curious humans, but another storm last winter exposed part of the hull. Now an expedition from an American university is excavating. Melqart can't be pleased about that."

Alexandros rose. "As you say, Lady, he can't be pleased. But the mass killings began before the dives on the wreck began. Whatever his reasons, we can't wait any longer. We have to quell this before it escalates."

"You're urging all-out war?" Lord Mikhail asked.

An older nobleman leaped to his feet. "Prince Alexandros is too quick to rush us into combat. I demand a public full vote in High Council!"

Poseidon brought the chamber to silence with an impatient gesture. "I've heard all I need to. Not a year has passed since Halimeda and her followers attempted a palace coup. I've little doubt that she's in league with Melqart. There's no time for committees and debate. If it's war they want, war they shall have!"

Queen Korinna laid a hand on the king's forearm. "Not yet, I beg you, husband. Wait but a little while. We can ready our warriors, but unless Atlantis itself is assaulted, no good can come of rushing into that which will mean certain death for so many of our people."

"And so many humans," Lady Jalini added.

Alexandros frowned. "When have humans ever cared about us?"

"Not all humans are our enemies," Lady Athena replied. And then to the king, she said, "There is wisdom in what our good queen says, Majesty. Humans multiply much faster than Atlanteans. We cannot afford to lose loyal men and women unless there is no other option."

Poseidon, still standing, glared around the round marble

table. "Orion? What say you? You are a little less blood-thirsty than your twin, if hairs are split. Would you declare war now or wait while women and old men argue?"

Orion glanced at his brother and then back to Lord Mikhail before answering. "It will take a few days to call up the troops. So long as our people are on notice that the hounds are loosed, I see no great harm in waiting to see what Melqart plans next."

"So be it," his father proclaimed. "We'll wait a little longer. But there will be no Council vote on this matter. I'm still high king over Atlantis, and I hold the power to declare war."

"You're postponing the inevitable," Alexandros said, an hour later as they walked toward the stables. "It's that woman, isn't it? You're soft on humans because of her."

Orion whirled on his brother. "She's part of that research expedition, Alex. Elena is diving on Melqart's ship. What do you think will happen to her when he finds out? How good do you think her chances of staying alive will be?"

"None." Alexandros made a slashing motion with his hand. "What do you intend to do? Go to her? Explain the situation? 'Excuse me, Elena, but you're intruding on the territory of a four-thousand-year-old Phoenician god of war—you're attempting to steal his property'?"

"No. Not exactly."

"How about, 'I'm party to all this information because I'm not human? I'm an Atlantean. What? You don't believe me? Would you care to come back to my room and see my scales?' "

"You're not funny, Alex."

"Then what will you tell her?"

"Nothing . . . or a lie. I don't know yet. I do know that

I'm not going to watch her dive and be destroyed by that *thing*."

"You can't go anywhere. We're on full standby. You have a duty to be here with your men. Anything less, and—"

"Report me if you want. But she saved my life. I owe her."

Alex took hold of his arm. "I can cover for you for a day or two, brother, but after that, it's on your head. If we fight, you have to assume your command."

"I can't let her die when I could prevent it."

"Go to her, then. Have her and be done with it. Maybe then you'll remember where your loyalties lie."

# CHAPTER 10

Elena and Greg paused to take in the peaceful sight of the fishing boats bobbing at anchor in the harbor. All of Rethymo seemed enchanted tonight. Moonlight glittered on the water, and the stars seemed close enough to touch. It had been a near perfect afternoon and evening. They'd borrowed Stefanos's motorbike and gone to a semi-secluded sand beach used mostly by locals, rather than the tourists. There, they'd shared a bottle of wine, cheese, olives, and a loaf of bread that she purchased at the local bakery and swam and splashed in the warm, clear water like children.

This evening, they'd strolled through the streets of Rethymo, stopping for shish kebabs and more wine at a taverna so small that the interior held only four tables and the staff were all family. It wasn't until they'd left the taverna and walked down by the water that Elena felt the slightest hint of tension.

"Aren't you going to invite me up to your room?" Greg asked.

"Let's not," she said. "I'm tired. You have to catch a hop early in the morning and I'll have a long day on the dive. Can't we just—"

He caught her arm and pulled her close. When Greg

was about to kiss her, she wanted to respond, but at the last second she turned her head so that his lips brushed her cheek. "What's wrong, baby?"

She pushed free. "I told you. I'm tired." She rubbed her back. "I don't know, maybe I'm coming down with something. I just don't feel like it tonight."

"Something or *someone*?" She started to walk away, but he stepped in front of her, blocking her path. "Where were you last night, Elena? Who was he?"

"Who was who? Don't be a jerk, Greg."

"I'm the jerk? Do you know how difficult it was to re-arrange my schedule to come here and find you still off . . . wherever? I'd planned . . ." He uttered a sound of exasperation. "I don't have time to play games. And since when are you too tired for sex?"

"What is this? High school? You buy me dinner and I have to pay for it by falling into bed with you?"

"Give me a break, Elena. Don't play the innocent virgin with me. It's not the first time, or the tenth that we've been intimate. We're an item, a good one. And if you're cheating on me—"

"Cheating on you?" Her temper flared. "You don't own me. I'm not your wife. We don't have any ties on each other."

"So you admit that you were with someone else?"

"Hell, no." Her breath was coming in tight, quick gulps. The truth was, she might have been with some guy last night. She had no idea who she'd been with, or if she'd been alone. She couldn't remember. But one thing was certain. This evening was over as far as Greg was concerned. "You'd better go," she said, "before we both say things we'll regret."

"Just like that? Without an explanation?"

"I'm sorry if I've ruined your sure thing. But unless you get lucky in town, you're sleeping alone tonight."

"Why? If there's not someone else, then why? Why the sudden cold shoulder? It's a little late in the game—"

"Maybe it was always too late for us." She turned and walked away down the cobblestone street, her cheeks burning. She didn't know why she had suddenly decided that she didn't want to be with Greg tonight. It should have been simple. And fun. He was an experienced lover who rarely failed to satisfy her. All she knew was that, suddenly, it felt wrong.

"Wait!" He ran after her. "Don't go," he said. "I have something for you. I bought it for you last night." He dug in his jacket and produced a black velvet jewelry box.

The enormity of what might be inside that box frightened her. She shook her head. "No. If that's what I think it is, I can't accept. I'm not ready to make that kind of commitment."

"Then call this a gift." He shoved the box into her hands.

"I don't want it. Not now. I need time."

"Keep it. Wear it, or throw it into the sea. I don't give a damn. Hock it if you like, and buy a boat or diving equipment or whatever you need for your expeditions."

"I can't accept a ring from you." She tried to give it back to him, but he stepped away and threw up his hands.

"You'll have to, because I'm not taking it back. Think about what it means—what your life can be with me. I'll call you in a day or two."

"You do that," she muttered, half under her breath. "And just maybe I'll answer."

"I love you, Elena. But I meant what I said. The ring is yours. Do whatever you want with it. Just remember that I care about you, more than anybody else ever could."

A couple passing by, arm in arm, paused to stare, and the woman began to clap. "He loves you," she called in French. "How can you resist him?"

Oblivious to their audience, Greg turned and walked swiftly away, leaving her standing there staring after him and holding the velvet box. "This doesn't mean I've agreed to anything!" she said. "I'm not making a commitment that I'm not ready for."

Greg didn't look back, and she passed the box from hand to hand. Part of her wanted to throw it into the harbor, but part of her couldn't resist looking. "Oh, hell," she muttered and opened the box with trembling hands. The ring was a classic style, a single diamond set in platinum— a single precious stone that glittered in the moonlight and must have gone to three carats. "It doesn't mean a thing," she sobbed. "Nothing." But it did, and she knew it did, and she couldn't stop crying.

"I've had one son shame me by breaking the law," Poseidon thundered. "I'll not be defied a second time."

Orion stared stubbornly into his father's eyes. He'd hoped to slip quietly out of the palace and go to Elena before anyone realized that he was gone, but two of the king's guard had waylaid him on the grand staircase and told him that Poseidon demanded his presence in his private chambers.

"I suppose Caddoc has been carrying tales again," Alex said.

"So it's true," their father said. "You have seduced a human female."

Had he, Orion wondered, or had she seduced him? All he knew was that he couldn't get Elena out of his mind. The thought that she could suffer the same fate as Sjshsglee was intolerable. He had to get to her and keep her from Melqart's ship. Any delay might mean her death.

"It will not happen again," Poseidon said. "You put us all in danger by your recklessness."

"Listen to your father," Queen Korinna said gently. "The law was written for good reason. Humans are not like Atlanteans. They are much less evolved."

Orion turned his gaze on her. "How can you say that, Mother? Haven't you come to love Rhiannon like a daughter? And what of little Danu? Does your grand-daughter's smile not light up your life?"

She nodded. "That's unfair. You can't compare your brother's wife and daughter with some woman with whom you've shared pleasures of the body. Danu and Rhiannon are the exception, and they are no longer human. They are Atlantean, and you shame them and yourself by bringing up the past."

He didn't agree, but he wouldn't argue that point now. Poseidon had the power to have him arrested, to lock him up, and keep him from going to Elena. With great effort, he swallowed his anger and bowed his head to his father. "You are right to remind me of my duty, sire." He shrugged. "She was very beautiful for a human."

"They are most alluring," the king agreed. "I myself have been . . ." He glanced at the queen. "You take after me, I'm afraid," he said, chuckling. "Our actions are often ruled by something other than reason when it comes to the joys of pleasure." His blue eyes took on a glint of gray and his voice hardened. "But I will have none of it, do you understand?"

"I understand, sire."

Poseidon glanced at Alexandros. "If your brother disobeys me on this, I will hold you equally responsible. Is that clear?"

Orion stiffened. His hands tightened into fists at his sides. "That's unfair. Alexandros isn't—"

"Silence!" His father rose from his chair. "I will decide what is fair and what isn't. I know you two. Since you were children, when one of you got into mischief, the other was as much to blame."

"We're not children anymore!" Orion flung back.

"Then don't act like a child! Stay away from humans. Take a wife! Take two, or seek your satisfaction among the women of our kind. This discussion is ended. You will do as you're told, or you will both suffer the consequences."

As Elena lowered herself from the side of the *Antolia* and descended toward the wreck, she felt none of the exhilaration she usually did during a dive. Although the surface had been relatively calm, the water seemed unusually murky. She'd seen no schools of fish, no sea life at all, and that was strange. Even the birds that always followed the ship were absent today.

She was anxious to see if the storm had damaged the hull of the ship. Finding a Phoenician vessel in such a state of preservation was rare, and because the ship had sunk rather than gone down on its side or keel up, there was more of a chance of finding the contents of the hold. Usually, when a ship went down, the cargo was strewn over a large area. In the centuries that had passed since the sinking, there would naturally be loss, but something of significance might still be there waiting.

So far, all she had to show for the university's outlay were shards of pottery and one gold coin. She'd received a letter earlier in the week warning that her donations were down and the department had to cut costs. If she couldn't produce something of value soon, the expedition would be shut down early. What wasn't said, but was understood, was that ultimately, she was responsible. If—after all the money spent and the difficulty of getting permission to conduct a search in Greek waters—the site proved a disappointment, her career would suffer. She'd probably never get the opportunity to lead a dig again.

Stefanos, her dive partner, waved. He was no more than a few feet away, yet she could hardly see him. The deeper they went, the more difficult it was to see, and when Elena reached the bottom, she was standing on sand. She could find no sign of the wreck.

The tide swirled around her, and for an instant, she lost track of direction. In deep water, divers often suffered from a sense of euphoria and lost track of reality. This wasn't what she felt. Every instinct told her that something was wrong—that they shouldn't be here.

Where was the ship? The coordinates had been right. It should have been here, but this seabed seemed scoured as clean as a modern roadway. Where were the coral growths? The rocky outcrop that had jutted up within yards of the wreck? She twisted to locate Stefanos and made out the figure of a diver, but her eyes must be playing tricks on her. This man wasn't wearing dive gear. He was bigger than Stefanos, and . . . She bit down hard on her mouthpiece. For a split second, she thought that his dive suit was blue, rather than black, no . . . blue-green and covered in tiny iridescent scales.

Frightened, she swam as hard as she could—not toward the strange figure but away from it. The water had become so dark that it was impossible to see more than a few inches. And abruptly, she collided with something in black. It seized hold of her shoulders, and she panicked and tried to pull free. Stefanos held her tightly, and brought his face close to hers.

When she recognized him, she stopped struggling. Stefanos. Her dive partner. Relief washed over her, and she signaled for them to go up. She could see that he was alarmed as well. Together, they swam toward the surface.

The sunlight had never felt so good on her face. Stefanos pulled off his mask. "What happened down there? Did you see a shark?"

She nodded. What had she seen? Her heart was beating wildly. What was wrong with her? "Yes," she lied, when she'd removed the apparatus and could speak. "A big one. It came at me."

"We must be in the wrong place." He swam toward the *Antolia,* and she followed, still wanting to get out of the water as quickly as she could, overjoyed that the expedition's boat was still here on the surface waiting for them. After what had just happened below, she wouldn't have been shocked to come up and find herself off some tropical island in the South Pacific.

Hilary and the first mate, Petros, stood by the rail and watched as Stefanos climbed the ladder. Elena went up behind him. The tanks on her back felt as if they weighed a ton.

"That was quick," Hilary said. "You haven't been down long enough to—"

Elena leaned against the gunnel for support. Her knees felt as if they were made of rubber. She thought she might be sick. She'd been diving since she was a child, and she'd never lost her nerve before . . . never started imagining monsters.

"This isn't the spot," Stefanos said, looking around.

"Yes, yes," Petros insisted. "Here is the site. How many times does Anso bring you here. This." He pointed at the water with a blackened and scarred thumb. "Down here is your shipwreck."

"You're wrong," Stefanos argued. "We've missed the site. This bottom isn't the same, and Dr. Elena had a close call with a shark."

"You're white as a sheet," Hilary said, staring at her. "Irene. Bring a blanket for Dr. Carter."

"What happened?" Irene asked, hurrying toward them.

"The wreck isn't down there," Stefanos repeated. "The captain must have come out without his glasses or he had too much ouzo last night."

Petros shook his head. "No. Here. Here is right place. Anso is good captain."

"Well, if this is the site, where the hell is our Phoenician wreck?" Elena asked. *And what did I see down there?*

"I think you two need a little more practice," Orion said to his sister and her friend Leda. "I'm sure she caught a glimpse of me. It nearly scared her to death."

"If she saw you, it was your own fault," Morwena said. "You asked us to make certain the boat anchored in the wrong place. We did that, didn't we? It's not easy to disturb the workings of humans' electronic machines. Especially when they are above the surface of the sea."

"Next time I need a favor, I'll ask priestesses who aren't junior grade."

Morwena scoffed. "And who else would become involved with your schemes when Poseidon threatened to imprison you and Alexandros in pack ice for two hundred years?"

"He didn't threaten to seal us in an ice tomb. He threatened *severe consequences*," Orion corrected.

"He was angry because Caddoc told him that you were having sex with the earth walker," his sister said. "And you know the penalty. He didn't have to say it. You know how he is when you disobey him."

Leda smiled at him. "I don't know why you risk your career to play with humans when there are plenty of Atlantean girls who could make you happy."

Above them, the ship's motors started, and the vessel turned back toward Crete. The ruse had worked. This time. Orion doubted if he could convince Morwena and Leda to do the same thing a second time. He'd have to do something more radical to keep Elena away from Melqart's wreck.

"You're right," he said, returning Leda's smile. "You did what I asked you. We stopped them today. Thank you. Now comes the hard part. Don't be tempted to brag about what we did here."

"We're not stupid," Morwena said. "We know we'd be in trouble for helping you defy Poseidon and break the law."

Orion signaled to Nohea. Within minutes, the big dolphin came, her calf close by her side. Accompanying Nohea were more than a dozen male fighting dolphins, and a patrol of Orion's most trusted men. "Take the princess and Lady Leda back to the summer temple," he said. "Guard them as you would Poseidon."

"Can't we stay here with you?" Leda asked. "We have exams coming up. This is much more interesting. I'd like another look at your human female, although I'm not sure what you see in her."

Morwena seized Nohea's collar and swung up onto her back. "Come on, Leda," she said. "Make him angry, and we'll never get to do anything fun like this again."

The soldiers closed in around the two girls.

"Take the safest route," Orion told the captain. "If you see anything suspicious, don't try to confront the horde. Put as much distance between them and you as possible. If a scale on Morwena's body is disturbed, I'll have your head on a squid pole."

The captain grinned and saluted. He would see the girls safely back to Atlantis and no word of what had taken place today would ever pass his lips. Orion waited until they were gone before making for shore. He wanted to be in the harbor when Elena's boat docked. What he would do when he got there, he didn't know, but he'd think of something. He had to.

# CHAPTER 11

As the captain and first mate brought the *Antolia* into the harbor, Elena went over and over the dive in her mind, trying to decide what had just happened. It was obvious that, regardless of Anso's protests, he'd brought them to the wrong spot. They'd go out again tomorrow. He'd correct his error, and when they went down, the wreck would be waiting for them as before. That was the way it had to be. It couldn't have simply vanished. Even if the storm had heaped sand over the ribs of the sunken vessel, it wouldn't have disappeared completely.

What that didn't answer was why she'd had such a scare. The water conditions had been poor, true, but she'd made many dives when the visibility was that poor. The water at the Nile sites had been so muddy that it had been hard to see her own hands in front of her face. What had she imagined that she'd seen? A fish-man? A creature out of a child's fairy-tale book? She had to have been hallucinating, but she had the strangest feeling that this wasn't the first time her mind had played tricks on her recently. When she tried to remember, the details were hazy. It was frustrating. She wasn't on medication, she'd never done drugs—she hadn't even smoked weed in college. That left an undetected brain tumor and early onset Alzheimer's as possibilities, neither of which made for pleasant contemplation.

There was no history of mental health problems on either side of her family, not unless you counted her father's belief that he'd discovered the lost continent of Atlantis. Elena sighed. Thinking of her father always made her sad. How different her career would have been if he hadn't pursued a dream so stubbornly that it had taken over his life. The myth of Atlantis was nothing more than a tall tale, and he'd had to be in total denial to believe that an entire civilization lay beneath the shallow waters of the Aegean Sea without anyone finding it until the late twentieth century.

Yet, Randal Carter had believed his own fantasy, so much so that he'd brought in scholars and news media from all over the world to validate his discovery. And when his farce had been revealed, when divers and photographers found nothing of interest, let alone underwater roads, temples, and palaces, a lifetime of brilliance had gone up in flames. Her father had faced ridicule and accusations of fraud. He'd been asked to resign his professorship and his works had been pulled from university shelves all over Europe.

She'd been too young at the time to understand what had gone wrong, but she did remember the last conversation she ever had with him, in a park in Edinburgh. "Whatever your mother tells you about me, don't believe it," her father had said. "I'm not crazy. Atlantis is there. I saw it. I touched the marble columns. They were as solid as the cobblestones under your feet."

She'd looked into his eyes, the exact shape and color of her own. "But, Atlantis is a myth. My teachers say so," she'd replied, wanting to believe him, hoping that he'd prove them all wrong.

"Was Troy a myth?" He'd bent and hugged her and his soft beard brushed her face. "I've never lied to you, Elena," he said. "I'm not about to start now. Atlantis was once as real as Paris, and when I have the proof, even your mother will have to believe me."

"And you'll be together again?" she'd asked. "In the same house?"

"As much as you and I would like that, it may not happen," he'd answered. "Not everything can be mended."

"But I can still see you," she'd begged. "I can still come to Turkey to the new site? On my summer break? You promised."

He'd nodded, his eyes sad and bloodshot. "You can still come, and this year you'll have your own tent. You'll be an official expedition member with your own credentials. You have my word on it."

Tears clouded Elena's eyes. She had never gone to Turkey that summer. Two weeks before school ended, her father had chartered a boat and gone searching for his fabled Atlantis again. He'd been lost at sea when his ship foundered in a storm not far from here. His body was never found, and *Carter's folly* had become a catchword in classical archeology circles.

The *Antolia* bumped against her mooring post, pulling Elena back into the present. She felt tears on her cheeks and hastily wiped them away. She glanced around, wondering if any of her crew had noticed, but they all seemed to be watching Stefanos as he pulled the Zodiac alongside the ladder.

"Dr. Elena? Do you want to go ashore now? I'll stay and see that the dive equipment is . . ."

Stefanos was still talking as she followed Hilary and Irene into the inflatable. Once they were seated, Irene took the tiller and guided the Zodiac onto the beach.

"Another day lost," Hilary grumbled. "So far, this summer's been a bust."

"Hopefully, tomorrow will be better," Irene said.

Irene and Hilary had developed a close relationship, despite the differences in their ages and background. It wasn't like Hilary to take so to a student. They'd been spending a lot of time alone together in the last few weeks. Elena wondered if they were romantically involved. Certainly, she'd never seen competent but plodding Hilary Walden so animated. Although why tall, blond, and attractive Irene Georgiou would be attracted to a chubby, sixty-something woman with thick glasses and a stammer, Elena couldn't imagine.

Irene was laughing at something Hilary had said, and Hilary was beaming. Elena didn't feel like accompanying them to the house. She wasn't in the mood for small talk, and she didn't want questions about today's disaster that she didn't have answers to.

She needed to be alone to think. And if she went back to her room, she knew she wouldn't be able to resist taking the antique gold ring out of the wall safe where she'd secured the coin from the wreck site. She'd weigh the gold ring in her hand as she'd done last night. She'd held that and the diamond ring that Greg had given her, one in each hand, wondering at how two such similar items had come into her possession in such a short time . . . and wondering which one she valued most.

"Coming, Elena?" Hilary asked. As usual, the older woman hadn't bothered with sun block, and her already ruddy complexion was the color of a pomegranate. By morning, she'd be blistered or peeling, a perfect match to her flaming purple-red hair styled, as always, in a no-nonsense, ultra-short bowl cut that Elena suspected the woman did herself. "Anna promised us *moussaka* tonight."

"You go on ahead," Elena said. "I have some errands I want to run. I'm not certain how long it will take, so don't hold dinner for me."

"What do you think, Dr. Walden?" Irene teased. "Does she have another hot date tonight?"

"Let's meet with Stefano at eight in the morning," Elena said, ignoring Irene's mention of Greg. "After a good night's sleep, we can plan out what's next." Elena didn't know where she would go, someplace where no one knew her . . . where she could just walk and think.

She hadn't gotten far when a strikingly attractive man stepped out of an alley. No, attractive wasn't the word, more *smoothly dangerous*. Picking up handsome strangers on the street was the last thing on her mind, but if she were up for it, he'd be the one. But, somehow, she had the feeling that she knew him, but she couldn't place from where.

"Dr. Carter. I've been looking for you," he said in perfect English.

Elena looked at him, but kept walking. He was devilishly handsome with a classic Greek face, blond hair, and unusual green eyes. "I'm sorry, you must have me confused with—" she began.

He threw up his hands and flashed a killer smile. "Wait, please, I'm not out trolling for rich American tourists. We've met before, and we share mutual friends."

She stopped and studied him more closely. He was tall and sleekly muscular, dressed in expensive shorts and sandals, a short-sleeve button-up shirt, and his face had a hint of a five o'clock shadow. No jewelry, not even a watch, which was good. The gold chain fashion accessory on European men definitely turned her off. His hair was yellow blond, carelessly styled, but meticulously cut. "Go on," she said.

He lowered his voice and turned, shielding her from passersby. "I heard that you're excavating a shipwreck, very old, promising. But bad weather has delayed your progress."

"I'm not sure what I can do for you, Mr. . . ." She offered a faint smile.

"You don't remember me? I'm crushed. Cairo? Fall of 2006? Professor Abrams's dinner party? I remember you. You made quite an impression." He offered his hand. "Forgive my lack of manners. I'm Orion Xenos."

He did look familiar, but she couldn't quite place him. "You don't look like a scholar, Mr. Xenos."

"Orion, please."

He had the slightest upper-class British accent, although she guessed that he was Greek or Italian. His eyes were quite unusual. Looking into them almost made her dizzy. "I'm sorry, I'm at a loss."

"I've come upon something that I think might be of great interest to you."

Suddenly she felt disoriented, overly warm, and definitely lightheaded. "What business are you in?" she asked suspiciously. "I don't . . ."

"But you'll make an exception," he said. "Please, I've frightened you. That wasn't my intention."

He was going to walk away. Oddly, she didn't want that. Her knees felt weak, but the thought that he'd go and she'd never see him again was disturbing. She found herself falling into those beautiful green eyes. "I don't understand," she said. "What do you want from me?"

"Nothing from you. I want to show you something. It's not far. I'm not going to carry you off and sell you into white slavery. You're perfectly safe." He looked around at the crowded street.

"I don't go off with strangers," she said. "Whatever you're selling, I'm not buying."

"Fair enough," he said. "Because I have nothing to sell. My mother did warn me about bold American women, but you hardly seem the type to attack me without provocation."

She found herself smiling at him, her instincts urging her to trust him. "Maybe I do remember you. Are you one of Dr. Abrams's protégés?"

He shook his head. "I was swimming in relatively shallow water, just beyond the outskirts of town. I saw what appears to be a marble stela with traces of Linear B writing."

"Not surprising off Crete," she said. "I would certainly advise you to report it to the antiquities bureau."

"Not only Linear B but hieroglyphs and a third section of inscription unlike anything I've ever seen before. This could be the equivalent of the Rosetta Stone, and I wanted to give you a chance to inspect it before—"

Her eyes widened. He had to be mistaken or lying. It wasn't possible. She fought to control her excitement. "Why me, Mr. Xenos?"

"I'm too small a fish."

"Excuse me?"

"You're the daughter of Randal Carter. You're respected in your own right. If this tablet is what I think it may be, you deserve the credit."

"I do?" She regarded him with suspicion. "And what's in it for you, if you don't want a finder's fee?"

"I want to be part of your dive for the Phoenician ship. I want a place in your expedition. One successful project will do wonders for my career." He grinned. "And I was very impressed by you at Dr. Abrams's dinner."

She knew it was crazy to agree to go. She should check out his credentials first, phone Dr. Abrams. She should let her colleagues know where she was going and with whom. It was common sense. "I can get the Zodiac from our charter. I'll need my diving equipment."

He shook his head. "You won't need it. It's not that deep. We can free dive. The stela is no more than a hundred feet off the shore, in perhaps twenty-five feet of water."

"Not far from Rethymo, you say?"

"Ten minutes' walk."

She shrugged. He was a rogue, certainly, but he appeared harmless. "Just so you know I never carry credit cards or money."

"I suppose that means that dinner's on me."

What Orion was about to do was wrong. He knew it was wrong, but he fully intended to do it anyway. Elena had to go willingly into the sea with him. He had to gain her trust, and to do that, it was necessary to lie to her. The stela he described did exist. He'd shown it to her in the chambers beneath the cave where they had almost been devoured by shades. It just wasn't here, a hundred feet off the beach. Fortunately, his illusion had worked and she'd forgotten that they'd first met when he'd climbed into her Zodiac and that he'd seduced her.

Or had he? Did oral sex count? That was a good question. He'd given Elena pleasure without taking his own. He'd wanted to make love to her in every way. She was a fire in his blood that he couldn't quench. He couldn't sleep for thinking of her; he remembered her scent, the curve of her mouth, and the feel of her soft skin against his. Once they were in his world, perhaps she might offer herself willingly to him. To take advantage of her would be an act he could never forgive himself for. If only she weren't so tempting . . .

But where to take her that she would be safe while he returned to lead his troops against Melqart's horde? Not to the Shamans Caverns, where Alexandros had taken refuge when Morgan was dying. They had used up their store of good will with the serpent people. And there was no question of taking Elena to Atlantis. Not in direct defiance of the king. Poseidon was capable of casting her out to drown or of having her vanish without a trace. Orion didn't fear his father and he wasn't afraid of his anger, but he wouldn't risk Elena's life by putting her at the king's mercy.

There were many outlying Atlantean colonies and there were kingdoms of other species who made the seas their home. The oceans were vast, and it was possible that he might claim sanctuary for a human female in one of them. But he could not remain with her, and without him, she would be unable to survive underwater. Elena was a creature of sun and solid land, and the tides and whirlpools that he loved were alien places to her. He supposed that he could maroon her on some deserted island in the Indian Ocean or the Pacific, but even if he provided all she needed to live, it would cause her great emotional distress.

That left only one option. He must take her to the fabled land of the fairy folk in the earth's hollow core. There would be kindly companions, the oxygen she needed to breathe, and food that she would find familiar. Melqart's minions could not follow her there, and she would be well cared for until he returned to fetch her.

Leaving his shirt and shoes on a rock, Orion waded into the sea. The salt water welcomed him, flowing around his feet and legs, filling him with a sense of peace and contentment.

Elena stripped off her tee and capris. Under it, she was still wearing the flowered bikini that she'd worn beneath her dive suit. Aphrodite, he thought, not rising from the sea but walking into it. He inhaled deeply and waited, hand outstretched. "Will you come with me?" he asked. "Of your own free will?" It was the question he must ask. No Atlantean or mer could take a human into the sea against their will. Not only was it forbidden, it was impossible.

Her eyes narrowed and she rested one graceful hand on a hip. He swallowed, trying to hide the desire that threatened to overwhelm him.

"You're not going to go weird on me now, are you, Xenos?" she asked.

He forced what he hoped was a charming grin and made a playful reply. "What's wrong? Water too cold for you? Afraid to get your feet wet?"

"The stela had better be there," she warned. "And it had better not be a fake."

"Changed your mind?" He picked up her clothing, but didn't let her see him do it.

"No, I'm coming." She stepped into the waves and foam broke around her knees. "Of my own free will."

"Good enough," he said, catching her hand and diving under. She struggled for only a few seconds before he could pass on to her the ability to breathe as he did under water and put her to sleep. It was tricky. She couldn't see him as he was; he had to maintain the illusion of the human he'd pretended to be when he'd approached her on the street in Rethymo.

"It's all right," he soothed as he gathered her in his arms. "You're safe with me. I will stand between you and harm." He swam swiftly into deeper water, away from the shore and any humans that might have watched them go into the sea and willed her into a deeper sleep.

To put distance between them and the current hunting ground of the shades, Orion would utilize the seraphim. Long ago, these enormous wormlike creatures had moved about the seas of a turbulent and ever-changing earth. But their time had passed, and while the seraphim remained technically alive, they had evolved into sedentary beings, much more like their own ancestors that had been introduced to this planet by star travelers in the dawning of the world.

The great predator birds and their descendents, the dinosaurs had ceased to exist, but the seraphim adapted. They grew so large that they lost the ability to move from place to place. Now they no longer reproduced, but they endured. Tens of thousands of years ago, Atlanteans had discovered that they could cross vast distances of the seas by entering the worms' digestive tracts and being moved along at great speed. The trick was to survive the winding corridors, chutes, and impassable grates without being sucked into the worms' feeding chambers and to find the right exit.

Each worm was different, and Orion and his brothers had spent many years memorizing the passages, traps, and possible destination points before Poseidon had allowed them to venture into the seraphim. Miss a chute or slide down the wrong passage, and you could end up as worm dinner, instantly paralyzed by acidic secretions, slowly and agonizingly consumed. Depart at the wrong stop, and you could end up off Borneo instead of the Pillars of Hercules. Many bold men and women had died over the centuries, but lacking the ability to fly as humans did, this was the fastest way to move from one destination to another. Most of the warrior class and some of the priesthood used this risky form of transportation, but the average Atlantean preferred not to.

The nearest wormhole wasn't far, but farther than Orion wanted to swim with Elena in his arms. If they were attacked by predators, shark, or shades, he wasn't certain he could adequately defend her. Orion had known that would be the case, and he was prepared. He gave a sharp whistle, and in less time than it would take to swim back to shore, two of his finest fighting dolphins, Eryx and his brother Pontus appeared pulling a chariot.

Orion preferred to simply ride astride, but he hadn't known how much of a struggle Elena would put up, or how strong her mental resistance would be. A dolphin-drawn chariot was the next best option, not a chariot with wheels as the ancients had used, although he had seen them displayed on state occasions.

This one was hewn from a giant conch shell and reinforced with scales of the same star metal from which his black sword blade was fashioned. The harnesses were simple affairs of braided sea grass, a loop of which was held between the teeth of each dolphin. Signals were given by voice only. Fighting dolphins were skilled warriors in their own right, not beasts of burden.

Orion stepped into the chariot, still holding a sleeping Elena, and they were off with a speed that constantly amazed him. Usually mammals of good humor and playful dispositions, Eryx and Pontus took their mission seriously. If there was danger that they couldn't outswim, they were quite capable of loosing themselves from the chariot and coming to his defense with ramming force and razor-sharp teeth.

"I needn't remind you that no one must know about the woman, not even my brothers," he reminded the dolphins when they reached the opening to the nearest seraphim, and he quickly redressed her in capris and T-shirt.

A series of clicks and whistles assured him that they would keep his secret. "Return to the palace," he said. "I'll make my own way there. Feed and rest. Tomorrow, we may go into battle."

When they had departed, Orion chose a trident from a cluster of those sunk into the sand. The primitive weapon was useful in opening and closing chute doors and in propelling one's self along without smashing into the slippery walls of the seraphim's digestive track.

Orion looked down at Elena cradled in the crook of his arm and was almost overcome by his desire for her. She was lovely, but it was more than her beauty that captivated him. He lowered his head and kissed her parted lips. She tasted as sweet as he'd remembered, and her mouth fit his as if they were two halves of a whole. "Elena," he whispered hoarsely.

She stirred, opened her eyes, and let out a piercing scream.

# CHAPTER 12

E lena stared at the huge red undulating tentacle looming over Orion's head. She hadn't intended to scream—it wasn't in her nature—but this monstrous thing was at least twenty feet long and thicker than an elephant's trunk. Barbed suction cups lined the weaving tentacle, and as she watched, it reared back and slammed into Orion, knocking her from his arms and sending him flying. She skidded across the rocky sea floor and landed flat on her belly, scraping her hands and knees.

She twisted and pushed herself up on her elbows to see a second tentacle, equally as big, snake from the darkness of what appeared to be the mouth of a cave. She clenched her teeth in shock, certain that she was caught in the worst nightmare of her life.

Orion was already on his feet, and from somewhere, he'd produced a sword of shining black metal. Bloody circles and torn flesh gaped on his arm and shoulder where the thing had struck him. "Elena! To me!" he yelled.

The tentacles lashed back and forth through the air. One appendage swung in a mighty arc at Orion's head and surely would have killed him if it had connected, but he ducked and twisted away out of the thing's reach. Swifter than her eye could follow his movement, Orion brought the great sword up and charged, slicing through the tentacle, and sending a five-foot section drifting away on the tide.

The creature shrieked, and a terrible red-orange head and gaping beaked maw filled the cave entrance. Eight sucker-lined legs thrashed. Blood and black ooze poured from the maimed tentacle. Still frozen in panic, another scream caught in Elena's throat as the giant squid's black bulging eye rolled and focused on her with malevolent purpose.

*Wake up*, she told herself. *It's time to wake up from this dream, this nightmare, whatever the hell it is!*

Sheer terror locked her joints and chilled her flesh. It could only *be* a dream, and yet nothing had ever seemed so real. Still, she found herself unable to move a muscle . . . until the thing turned and propelled itself through the water toward her.

Half on hands and knees, half swimming, she fled toward the only refuge she could imagine—the man with the sword. The beast shot out of the hole, larger and more terrifying than any demon, and bore down on her, legs reaching, uninjured tentacle poised to wrap around her . . . to lift her high and plunge her into that pitiless, tooth-filled mouth.

"Orion! Help me!" she cried. But when she raised her head, he was gone. He'd abandoned her to be devoured alive. The tip of the tentacle slapped against her bare leg, and she screamed again as white-hot fire seared her skin. She kicked and twisted, squirming away, landing on her back. The snakelike tentacle reared back and time stopped.

Elena closed her eyes, wanting to wake in her bed with the sheets damp around her and moonlight spilling through the window onto the worn floorboards, wanting but knowing that it would not be. Impossibly, this nightmare was real, more real than anything she'd ever experienced. She screamed again as death in its most terrible form plunged toward her.

"Where is she? You must know," Princess Rhiannon insisted. "Lady Athena saw the two of you leaving the temple together by a servants' entrance. And neither of you were at the renewal ceremony."

Alexandros glared at her. "Speak up, Leda. Where is Morwena?"

Leda burst into tears. "I don't . . . know," she managed between sobs. "We came back together, and I . . . I left her at the great library. She was supposed to . . . supposed to meet me later, but she never came."

"You were missing for what? A day? A night?" Alexandros said. "And you never thought to report it? Has it failed to sink in that we are on the brink of war, and that Morwena is a princess royal?"

Leda's eyes, already red and swollen from weeping, stared back at the two of them in anguish. "We were back . . . safely. I couldn't think that . . . that anything bad could happen to her. Not in the city."

"Back from where?" Rhiannon asked.

Leda shook her head. "I can't tell," she wailed. "I promised Morwena I wouldn't."

"By Athena's short hairs, you'll tell me or—"

Rhiannon stepped in front of Alexandros. "Do you think to terrify the girl with your threats? Be still, brother, and let me find out what we need to know."

Alexandros's eyes grew cold. "If harm has come to our sister through her foolishness, I will do worse than frighten her."

Rhiannon took hold of Leda's arm and drew her into a small chamber off the temple hallway that led to the storerooms. The compartment was shadowy and cool, the only light coming from the luminous tiles on the floor that formed a scene from the founding of Atlantis. Robes, gilded sandals, and headdresses hung from hooks on two walls, and a small fountain gurgled from a helmeted centaur's head to spill into a shell basin in one corner. Otherwise, the chamber was empty.

Alexandros would have followed them in, but Rhiannon waved him back. "Let me handle this," she said, taking Leda's chin between two fingers and raising it so that their gazes met. "I respect your promise to the princess, your friend, Lady Leda," she said. "But she is missing. Surely you can see that that changes everything. You must tell us whatever you know so that we can find her."

"She had her bow," Leda said. "You know what a crack shot she is. What could happen to her in Atlantis? Everyone loves her here."

"I don't know," Rhiannon said, "but it's obvious that something has detained her. She seems sincere in her wish to become a full priestess with all that entails. She's never neglected her duties to the temple before."

Leda nodded, obviously in great distress.

"So," Rhiannon continued, "you can tell us what you know about her whereabouts and why the two of you were missing yesterday or . . ."

Leda swallowed and began to weep again.

Rhiannon tried to be patient. "Perhaps you would rather explain this to Poseidon."

"It was Prince Orion," Leda whimpered before spilling the whole story of the ship and Orion's wish to protect a human female from Melqart's wrath. "He said it was a matter of life and death. I thought it was most romantic."

Alexandros swore a foul oath. "That woman again." He looked at Rhiannon meaningfully.

"We can't go to the king, can we?" Rhiannon said. She was well aware of her father-in-law's threats. There were many attributes of the king that she found admirable, but his inflexibility regarding humans was not one of them. "He'll arrest Orion if he finds out, won't he?"

"Maybe, and maybe he'll just throw him into prison for a few years until his temper cools. My father can be a tyrant when he's crossed," Alexandros said. "We may have to go to him, but not yet. So far, we've no indication that Morwena's come to harm."

"What do you suggest?" Rhiannon asked.

"I suggest that she"—he indicated Leda—"return to her studies and say nothing unless we call for her again. And you should return to your apartment." He glanced at her midsection. "With the baby coming, you don't need to exert yourself."

"Nonsense. I'm pregnant, not an invalid." Never again, she thought, remembering back to another time and other circumstances. Rhiannon sighed. "Morwena is my dear friend as well as my husband's sister. I've no intentions of going quietly to my room and weaving seaweed baby blankets for the next seven months."

"Ten," he corrected. "Our children remain longer in the womb than humans. It takes twelve moon cycles for an Atlantean babe to be born."

"Whatever." She turned back to Leda. "Do as Prince Alexandros says. Go back to your classes and say nothing. We'll find her."

"But how?" Rhiannon asked after Leda had scurried away. "Where do we start looking?"

"We go to Aunt Eudora and Lord Mikhail. His scouts may have seen Morwena leave the city again, or there might be strangers here we are unaware of."

"But if Orion's off the island of Crete? Would she have gone back to him?"

"I'll search that area next, but he may no longer be there. And the troops will be called up in a matter of hours. He has to be here or be stripped of his command." Alexandros's expression was grim. "And if he fails to show up, my brother will be charged with high treason."

"Let me go!" Morwena said. "My brothers will hunt you down and destroy you." She knew him, Tora, Caddoc's man, and sometime lover, if palace gossip could be believed.

The big Samoan's scarred face split in a grin showing front teeth sharpened to points. He never took his gaze off her, and the flat ruin of a nose, divided down the center by an old wound, and black beady eyes that reminded her of a shark's gave her chills. If he was trying to frighten her, he'd succeeded, but Morwena would die before she'd allow him to know it.

She twisted at the bonds that held her wrists bound together at her back. She was badly bruised and bleeding, but she didn't think any of her injuries were serious. In any case, they would mend soon enough.

One shoulder of her *peplos* had been torn in her struggle so that one breast was fully exposed. A sandal, her diadem, and veil had been lost, as well. Tora had stripped her of her bracelets, and earrings, tearing an earlobe in the process. He'd deliberately attempted to shame her, but his ploy hadn't worked. Rather than cowing her by his crude bullying, he'd made her even more determined to escape and see him punished to the fullest degree.

"Whatever reason you have for taking me, it's not good enough," she said. How long had he held her here? They were somewhere beneath the city, she was certain of that. She could well be in her father's palace. There were so many levels and so many rooms that no one was familiar with them all.

She was sure that they hadn't traveled far enough from the spot where he'd kidnapped her to be away from Atlantis proper. But wherever they were, he'd held her here all night and at least part of the following day in this subterranean room.

What did he want with her? If he'd intended rape or murder, he would have done it already. And despite his leers and posturing, he'd made no sexual advances toward her. She had no idea how long Tora had held her prisoner here. Without a timepiece or waterdial, it was hard to tell. On the surface of the sea, one could see the rising and setting of the sun, but beneath the waves, even though time was still counted by day and night and the turning of the moon, the light remained much the same.

Tora had come upon her unawares on the staircase as she'd left the library the evening before. When she and Leda had returned from their adventure with her brother Orion, she wanted to make up the work that she'd missed. Study for the priesthood took many decades; to reach the level of Lady Athena or some of the other most gifted priestesses, she would have to serve and study for centuries. As part of her training, she was writing a thesis on the three visits of the starships that had occurred more than a hundred generations ago. She'd found an old scroll that she'd never seen before and had asked permission to borrow it.

Excited with her find and wanting a quiet place to read it, she'd shown little of the caution her mother had tried to instill in her. As a princess royal, she should have been accompanied by a token palace guard, but she rarely bothered. And rather than using the main staircase, always crowded with scholars, students, and teachers, she'd left the building as was her habit by a little used passage and doorway that opened into the courtyard of the Three Mermaids.

She'd hurried down a narrow seashell path, lined by tall and swaying columns of blue sea grass, past the lovely statues of the mermaids, and out through a small gate that led to a service alley. As she'd exited the gate, Tora had been waiting for her. He'd stepped from the shadows, locked massive arms around her, and clamped a hand over her mouth. Her bow, which she'd had no chance to draw and nock an arrow in, and the precious scroll had been lost as she'd tried to fight him off.

She'd kicked and tried to bite him, but her blows were as useless as if she had thrown herself against the marble columns. She'd gotten off one muffled scream as he'd thrown her roughly into a dolphin conveyance driven by a servant she didn't recognize. Heavy drapes had covered the windows, so that once she was inside, no one could see them.

Tora had leaped into the vehicle after her, surprisingly agile for a man of his bulk and height, and silenced her cries for help by raising his coral war club over her head. Tora could not speak. Someone or something had cut out his tongue long ago, but he did not need words to convey his meaning. She'd lain there on the floor panting, trying not to cry, trying to figure out what had happened and why.

She still had not figured it out. If Tora had snatched her for some purpose other than his own, Caddoc must be behind it. But why? She was Poseidon's daughter, a princess royal. Her claim to the throne was greater than Caddoc's, but three older brothers, Morgan, Orion, and Alexandros stood before her. Eliminating her would be futile if Caddoc was making another try to overturn Poseidon's reign.

She remembered the way Caddoc had behaved when he'd come upon her and Danu in the palace. He was always rude, but his behavior had been disturbing, even for Caddoc. She wondered if he was losing his mind. With a mother like his, she didn't doubt that it was possible. But Caddoc wasn't stupid. He must know that his place here at court hung by a thread. More than that, his existence hung by a thread. If he had commanded Tora to snatch her and hold her against her will, Alexandros would not wait for a trial. Half-brother or not, he would kill Caddoc.

She had summoned all the skills of illusion she had learned at the temple to try to take control of Tora's mind, but either she was too scared to carry out the process or the magic didn't work on underwater Samoans. They were an ancient race, as were the Atlanteans, but the Samoans who made their home beneath the waves were much more primitive. The only result that she could see was that she'd made his head itchy because he kept scratching his close-cropped skull.

There was a noise at the door. The stone slid open noiselessly, and Morwena turned to see who was there. She expected Caddoc, but instead, it was Lady Halimeda who appeared.

"Greetings," she said. And then to Tora, "You've done well and shall have your reward." She motioned toward the doorway. "Now, leave us."

He inclined his head, picked up his war club, and walked out of the room.

Morwena tried not to stare. It was Caddoc's mother,

and yet, how could it be? This woman seemed years younger and so beautiful that she couldn't be real. Morwena wondered if Halimeda had thrown an illusion over herself.

"Why have you done this?" Morwena asked her. Instantly, pain shot through her midsection and she doubled up, biting her lip to keep from crying aloud.

"Hold your tongue until I ask you to speak," the sorceress said.

"I'm not afraid of you."

"No? Perhaps you should be."

Halimeda extended her hand and flames shot from her fingers and scorched Morwena's face, burning her skin and eyes. Liquid ran from her clenched lids, and blisters rose on her cheeks and forehead. Morwena could not suppress a groan.

"I told you to be still! Shall I cut out your tongue? I've no need of it, and you might find yourself much in common with Tora if I did."

"Why?" Morwena cried. Her face was in agony, and knives were tearing her stomach apart. "Why? What have I ever done to you?"

Halimeda laughed.

"I'd hoped you might be able to tell us something about her absence," Alexandros said. He and Lord Mikhail had drawn apart from Rhiannon and Alexandros's aunt, retreating to the older man's private library.

"I will ask, certainly, but none of my people would have seen hurt come to the Princess Morwena without interfering or coming directly to me. Are you sure she isn't in the palace?"

"If she is, we've not been able to find her," Alexandros answered. "I sent word to Morgan to meet us here. I expect him at any moment."

"Your sister is a young woman and very beautiful, if I may say so without causing offense."

"None taken."

"Have you considered that she may have a lover?"

"Morwena?" He was taken aback by the question, but quickly made the adjustment in his mind. His little sister was beautiful, and somehow, without his realizing it, she'd transformed from a mischievous hoyden to a desirable woman. Atlanteans lived a long time, and their youthful years extended far longer than those of a human, but Morwena was no child. "She's never said anything to any of us, if she has."

Mikhail raised a dark brow. "I know that royalty is a breed apart, but yours is a very different family if you would expect your sister to tell you about her lover." He poured two goblets of wine and handed one to Alexandros. "Let me see what I can find out. Meanwhile, we'll begin a quiet search for her."

"She may be with Orion."

"Ah."

"May I take it that whatever I tell you will remain in confidence?"

Mikhail nodded. "The human female he's involved with. I've already had reports. One of my mermen told me that your brother was seen leaving the sea and taking on human form. He's in Crete, or he was as of last night." He took a sip of the wine. "And you believe that Princess Morwena may be involved?"

"You know Poseidon's position on human contact? And he's already warned Orion."

"It's worse than you know. This woman is one of those

who are excavating Melqart's tribute ship. She's already taken something of value from the wreck."

"Melqart will show her no mercy."

"Or Orion if he finds them together. This is serious business, Prince Alexandros. More so because of the military call up tomorrow."

"You say he left the sea. My brother has the ability to remain on land and breathe air much longer than the rest of us. He may still be there."

"He may. He wasn't seen going back into the water."

"Then I can only hope that wherever he is, he has Morwena with him and that they are both safe."

Mikhail nodded. "Hope is a good thing, my prince. So long as it doesn't cloud reason. Melqart is a worthy foe, but when he turns the full force of his anger on a man, it may take more than a brave heart and a keen sword to best him."

# CHAPTER 13

Something struck Elena hard, whipping her back against the sea floor. She felt the burning lash of the suckers, but the death blow she'd expected didn't come. Instead, when she opened her eyes, a storm of black ink swirled around the thrashing creature. She scrambled up and backed away, bleeding in a dozen places, but more from being scraped by shells than the damage done by the squid's tentacles. Her bones ached and she wanted to run—or swim. Every instinct told her to get away. Get away! But she couldn't tear her gaze from the nightmare.

Her father's words came loud and clearly in her head. "Face whatever frightens you most." And the thought followed that—if she fled from this monster—it would hunt her down and destroy her.

"You bitch!" she screamed. "Why didn't you kill me?" She'd known it was coming for her . . . felt the malice in its cold body. She'd been helpless prey, and still the thing had broken off the attack at the last possible second. And then, almost before the words were out of her mouth, she had her answer.

As the squid thrashed and bucked, there was a gap in the black clouds of ink that surrounded it. There, wrapped in the cephalopod's writhing tentacle, she saw Orion only an arm's length from the snapping head and beak.

"Orion!" she cried. He hadn't left her. She'd been spared, but now, he was going to be devoured before her eyes. "No! No!" Between one heartbeat and another, she realized how much she cared if he lived or died. The urge to protect him overwhelmed her, but she had no weapon, nothing to use against the squid.

Desperate, she shouted and waved her arms. "Here! Here!'

The movement caught the creature's attention and its head swiveled toward her. And as it did, Orion brought the point of his sword up and drove it into the squid's right eye.

The water around Elena vibrated with the force of the monster's unearthly shriek. It snapped at Orion with its beak and beat at him with multiple arms. Ignoring the pain from the rows of suckers, Orion yanked the blade free and when the squid's mouth opened to tear him apart, he stabbed again, deep and hard.

Convulsing, the squid released its grip on Orion, but instead of swimming out of its reach, he flung himself at the great head and put out the remaining eye with a downward stroke. The flailing tentacle brushed him from his perch. Still clutching the hilt of his sword, Orion fell, hit the sand, and rolled.

A fog of ink, acrid and choking, filled Elena's lungs. She struggled to breathe as she rushed to where Orion lay motionless and bleeding. The dying squid swayed and flopped, before sagging back against the entrance to the cave. One tentacle quivered and the ten-foot long arms went limp, one by one.

A large ominous shape surged silently through the murky

water, followed quickly by a second. In what seemed like seconds, a third circled and glided over Elena's head.

*Of course. This is a nightmare,* she thought. *Volcanic eruption coming next.*

"Sharks," Orion said. "We've got to find cover. I can't fight them."

"Where?"

He pointed toward the squid. "Over there. We've got to get inside the tunnel."

"We've got to get past that thing?"

"I'm afraid so."

"All right. Lean on me," she urged.

"Take this." He shoved the sword into her hands. "Don't drop it, no matter what happens."

The weapon was so heavy that she could hardly lift it. There was no way that she could swing it to defend them against sharks or anything else. "Can't we leave it?"

"No! We can't leave it."

He could barely stand. Blood seeped from his wounds. Elena knew the blood would attract the predators. She could hear the sounds of teeth and jaws ripping at the squid's body in the black water.

"You're badly hurt."

"We need to get . . . inside that tunnel. In minutes, this will be a feeding frenzy! More . . . more sharks will come."

Elena's knees locked. "You mean we have to go toward them and not away?" She knew the answer. Safety, or what Orion perceived as safety, lay beyond the giant squid and the swarming sharks. "But . . ."

"Don't think about it. Keep moving," he said.

Elena could feel the strength leaving his body.

"I'll do what I can, but . . . it's hard to concentrate."

"Concentrate on what? That we're going to be shark appetizers?"

"That we're not edible." He leaned his head against hers. "I can't explain. It's all a mind game."

"That makes no sense," she argued. "Maybe we'd better try a new solution."

"The tunnel is the only one," he said. "There's no cover on the sea floor around here."

Not seeing the sharks was worse than seeing them. Her skin literally crawled as they covered the few yards between them and the ravaged squid. Visibility was zero. What light the ink hadn't blotted out was now tinted red with blood, whose blood she wasn't sure. Did a squid have blood? Or had the gathering sharks turned on each other?

When Elena's hand connected with something spongy and sticky, she thought she would scream. At any second, she expected to feel a shark rip into her flesh. Once a section of tentacle drifted past, bumping into her and making her shudder. She could almost feel sorry for the squid. Almost, but not quite. All she could think was how close she and Orion had already come to being the main course of the feast.

Soft mushy things brushed against her ankles. She held her breath, and somehow, impossibly, they passed over the remains of the squid and into the cavern.

"We can't stay here either," Orion said. His voice was growing weaker.

"We have to get you medical attention," she said. Her own injuries were painful, but not as serious as his. He'd lost a lot of blood, and the thought that he could still die made her insides clench. Somehow, Orion had become very dear to her. She wasn't sure how or why. She wasn't even certain where they were or how any of this was possible, but it seemed real, and all she could do was to continue to try to keep them both alive.

"That can wait," he said. "I'll be all right, but you can't let me lose consciousness. Where we're going . . ."

The unfinished part was scarier than what he'd said. "It can't be worse than what's just happened," she said.

He coughed. "It could be, but if it is, it won't be nearly as quick."

"Is this a dream?" she asked him. So many things were going round and round in her head. Crazy memories of a flipped Zodiac, of a cave, and tablets covered with ancient inscriptions. Everything was tied up with this man.

Who and what he was, she didn't know, but she had the feeling that she'd been waiting all her life for him. Every adventure she'd ever experienced palled before what had just happened. "You risked your life for me," she said. "You could have run away, but you fought that squid . . . with a sword. Who the hell uses a sword anymore?"

He made a sound that might have been a chuckle if he hadn't been in so much pain. "You'd . . . you'd be surprised."

"I don't know what's going on here. If I'm crazy or you are . . . if I've been run down by a motorbike and I have a concussion . . . or if I'm already dead. But whatever this is, I've never felt so alive."

"Don't try and sort it out," he said. "Not now. Not yet. We've got to tackle the seraphim first."

"The what?"

"Hard to explain. Let's just say it's our fastest way out of here. I'm taking you to somewhere safe."

"You won't be taking me far if you bleed to death in the next few minutes. You need rest. I need to tie up some of your wounds."

"I'm a quick healer."

They had reached what appeared to be a leather or canvas curtain, illuminated by a glowing arc of light. The walls here were rough and rubbery, and from beyond the portal, she could hear a rushing sound almost like a wind tunnel.

"Give me back the sword," Orion said. "Stand behind me and wrap your arms around my waist. Close your eyes, and don't let go. No matter how frightened you are, hold on to me."

"Okay, you're scaring me now. What is this?"

"Transportation. We're going to leap into a kind of force field. We'll be propelled along at a great speed. But the passages divide, and I have to open the right hatchways at the right time."

"I can open them for you, if you tell me where and when."

"No, you can't. It's a little trickier than that. Trust me, Elena. I won't mess this up. I haven't brought you this far to lose you."

"Are you still a virgin?" Halimeda demanded.

Morwena opened her eyes. "It's none of your business." Pain throbbed in her head and belly. Her scales were flaking away. Blisters rose on her arms and legs, and her face was an agony. So much blood ran in her eyes that Halimeda was only a vague shadow standing over her.

"I asked you a question!"

Morwena's throat tightened until she couldn't breathe. *I'm dying*, she thought. Fear, greater than the pain, clutched at her, but she gritted her teeth and would not answer, although blackness filled her consciousness and her lungs seemed ready to explode.

"Baah." Halimeda turned away in disgust. "What my son sees in you, I don't know. You're as stupid as your father."

The pressure on her throat eased, and it seemed to Morwena that the pain in her body dulled.

"A priestess is supposed to remain pure until she reaches her initiation day, isn't she?" Halimeda asked. "Be stubborn. I have other ways of learning what I want to know." She laughed, a sound that made Morwena grow cold inside. "If you are a virgin, you may make the perfect gift for the one I serve. Would you like that, daughter of Poseidon? It must be a thousand years since he's enjoyed a proper sacrifice."

Morwena wanted to curse her. She wanted to tell Halimeda that her father and brothers would not let her go unavenged, but it took all her strength just to keep from screaming.

"Oh, very well. Be as you were." Halimeda muttered an incantation, and Morwena felt the pain drain away. She could feel her blisters receding, skin healing, flesh becoming whole.

"Don't think you'll ever be as beautiful as me," Halimeda warned. "No one is as beautiful as I am, but you're of no use to me ugly." She clapped her hands and one wall of the cell became a shining glass mirror.

Morwena summoned all her strength to stand, and when she looked, she found that she was restored to health. Her dark hair shone; her eyes were bright, and her cheeks glowed pink. The tiny pattern of scales that covered her arms and legs glistened silver-blue. She raised her head and looked directly into the witch's black eyes. "Why have you done this?" she asked. "What have I ever done to make you hate me?"

Halimeda shrugged. "You're not important enough for me to hate you," she said. "It's Poseidon's pride that I would strike down. He could have made me high queen of Atlantis. If he had, the future would be very different." She stepped past Morwena to admire herself in the mirror. "But he was too stupid. And now he must pay."

Morwena glanced at the mirror again and almost re-coiled from the image reflected there—not hers but Halimeda's. When she looked at the witch directly, she saw perfection. But in the mirror, her father's former concubine was little more than a skeleton draped with bits of hanging skin and scales. Her eyes and mouth were black holes; her magnificent head of raven hair was a thin and tangled mass of putrid flesh, rotting fish, and crawling worms.

Morwena suppressed a shudder. The sight was enough to give her nightmares, if she survived to ever sleep again.

Halimeda preened, turning this way and that, clearly pleased at what she saw in the mirror. "What better way to shame Poseidon than that his precious daughter should be body slave to my son? To serve him . . . in all ways." Which could be interesting, considering Caddoc's creativity and sense of humor. Or . . . She tucked a curl behind her ear. "Perhaps I will send you to Melqart's fires. We shall see." She began to hum a tune that made Morwena's blood turn to ice.

Morwena eyed the door.

"Don't even think of it," Halimeda warned. "And don't suppose that dolphin of yours will come to save you. It's shark bait. I had Tora put a spike through its head outside the library where he found you." She trailed fingers down the triple string of pink pearls she wore around her neck. "It wasn't very clever of you to travel without your body-guards. It proves what a child you still are. Do you believe that you can protect yourself against me and my master?"

*Freyja? Freyja was dead?* Morwena choked back a sob. The dolphin had been more than a companion for the last three decades; she'd been as dear as any sister, faithful and intelligent and brave. If Tora had murdered Freyja, it was one more reason to survive and see him brought to justice. Morwena's throat constricted, this time with emotion.

She'd wondered where Freyja was when Tora seized her. But if he had killed the dolphin, someone would find her body and realize that something was terribly wrong. Freyja's death might mean that her absence would be noted and her family would be searching for her. The penalty for harming or killing a dolphin was as great as that for injuring an Atlantean. It could be an error that Halimeda would live to regret.

"It would be easier on you if you would just tell me what I want to know," Halimeda said. "Are you a virgin or not?"

"No." Whatever else Halimeda had in mind, it couldn't be as bad as ending up on Melqart's menu. "I've played the beast with two backs with half the palace guard," Morwena added for good measure.

"Liar!"

"No, it's true. I have taken my pleasure where I found it. As you say, Halimeda, I'm a princess. I can do what I please."

The witch's eyes grew small and malevolent. "I don't believe you. But I'll give you time to think over the wisdom of attempting to match wits with me." A wave of her hand slammed Morwena against the far wall where a floor-to-ceiling cutout in the stone had been left as a storage area.

Morwena's head smacked against the rough surface, but when she tried to raise her hand to touch the aching spot, she found that she was paralyzed.

"Tora!" Halimeda shouted.

It was then that Morwena noticed the pile of fallen stone blocks. *No,* she thought. *She wouldn't.*

The Samoan returned carrying a container of mortar. He opened his tongueless mouth wide, bared his pointed teeth, and then grinned ghoulishly at Morwena.

"Do it!" Halimeda said.

Morwena closed her eyes, but there was nothing she could do to prevent the sounds of *thud, thud* as Tora slammed the stones into place, and slapped on the coral mixture which would cement them into a sealed chamber. Morwena's heart pounded against her chest. Sweat broke out on her forehead, and she bit down on her bottom lip until it bled, but the wall grew steadily and the light faded.

In minutes, Halimeda's laughter was a dull murmur.

*She won't leave me here to die*, Morwena thought. *I'll be of no use to her if no one knows what happened to me. She's only doing this to frighten me.* And Halimeda had succeeded all too well. Other than the safety of those she loved, this was what she feared most. Of all the horrors that could befall her, being shut away to slowly die of starvation in a closed casket, that was the worst.

"Alexandros!" she cried. "Orion! Morgan! Help me!" But the screams were in her head, and no sound came from her lips . . . no sounds at all.

A hatch opened and Elena and Orion were flung out. They landed in soft sand, but for a moment, Elena lay there trying to catch her breath. The time in the passage had gone on and on. How long she couldn't guess. The force of the energy around them had been fierce, and at times, she was aware of other objects tumbling in space around them. And always, there had been the roar of the wind.

But here, all was quiet. Golden light pulsed and filtered down through pale green water. The sand beneath her hands and knees was sparkling white and so very soft. Everywhere schools of multicolored fish, blue and yellow, green and black, orange and purple swam in and out of tall and graceful shrubs of sea grass. Great silver jellyfish glided through arches of seaweed like immense balloons. Elena saw tiny golden sea horses, sea fans, and pulsing spheres of light tinted pink as bubblegum twirling and spinning through the water.

Columns of bubbles rose from the seabed, and when she looked closely, she saw that scattered everywhere were crystal shells that appeared much like clams or oysters. They opened and closed, and as they opened, sweet strains of music poured out.

"Is this real?" Elena asked.

Orion shoved the point of his sword into the sand and used it to push himself upright. "This isn't where we were supposed to get off."

"But what is it?"

"Sanctuary. No predators may hunt here, and all the fish and creatures that you see are plankton eaters." His jaw firmed. "But we could have done worse. We can rest here for a little while, until my strength returns."

"It's beautiful," she said. "No sharks? No electric eels or giant squid?"

"I promise," he said. "Nothing more dangerous than an oyster."

She stood and looked at him. His wounds had stopped bleeding, but he still needed medical attention and probably sleep. "You were very brave," she said. "I've never seen a man braver."

"Come." He took her hand, and she saw that he was able to swim, if a bit shakily, on his own. "I know a good place." She followed him for a short ways to a spot where the seaweed grew in thick velvety fronds that formed a deep green carpet. Taller plants grew together and intertwined making small, cozy alcoves. "If I fall asleep, wake me," he said. "We have to press on as soon as possible."

Orion stretched out on his side, and she sat beside him

and pulled his head into her lap. "You rest," she urged. "I'll keep watch." Against what, she wasn't certain. He'd told her that no sharks would come here. But it seemed the right thing to say, and it seemed to calm him.

"Just for a little while," he said sleepily. "Just long enough for me to get my strength back."

"Shh. Close your eyes." She stroked his head, running her fingers through his long, thick yellow hair. "It's all right," she soothed. "I'm here."

Slowly, Orion relaxed, and the lines on his face eased and smoothed. His breathing came easier, and to Elena's surprise, his injuries began to knit almost before her eyes. After some time had passed, he had fallen into a deep sleep. She found herself almost unable to keep her eyes open.

With a sigh, she stretched out beside him, and almost instantly, fell asleep. And when she awoke, it took her a little while to orientate herself and remember where she was, or at least where she thought she was. What kind of nightmare was this, where she slept and woke without breaking the dream?

She was reluctant to move. Somehow, lying beside Orion had become nestling against him and placing her head in the crook of his arm. Not wanting to wake him just yet, she rolled carefully onto her back and gazed up at the curved roof of their secluded arbor. Silver starfish, smaller than the palm of her hand, drifted in lazy patterns over her head, moving in and out of the leafy canopy. And interspersed with the starfish, seemingly engaged in the same stately dance, were tiny triangular fish, nearly translucent, with black eyes and gilded tails.

"What is this?" she murmured. "Where on earth?" But she wasn't on earth. Whether she had conceived this world in the throes of a coma or in her own imagination, it was

obvious that she was surrounded by salt water. She knew
it was salt by the faint taste of brine on her lips and
tongue.

Orion stirred and gave a sigh beside her.

She turned on her side and pushed up on her elbow so
that she could look at him. He was still sleeping, taking
slow and steady breaths. All his weariness seemed to have
vanished, and the bruises and cuts were gone as if they had
never been there.

She gazed into his face with wonder, suddenly struck by
his beauty. Had there ever been such a perfect man?
Orion's lashes gleamed as golden as the lock of hair that
fell over his broad forehead. His nose might have been the
model for Michelangelo's David, and his mouth . . .

Hesitantly, she touched his bottom lip and shivered at
the thrill that ran through her. So male . . . so sensual . . .
and yet . . .

The urge to kiss him was overwhelming. She leaned
close and brushed his mouth with hers. He sighed again,
and stirred, but he didn't wake. Emboldened, she moistened his bottom lip with the tip of her tongue.

His eyelids flickered, but he still slept soundly.

"Orion?" She slipped her arms around his neck and
pressed her body against his. "Orion, wake up."

He moaned, deep in his throat, and he shifted. One arm
went around her waist. "Elena," he murmured.

Heat flashed through her as she realized what she
wanted of this man. . . . What she needed . . . what she had
to have or die.

# CHAPTER 14

E lena kissed his mouth, his chin, and his eyelids. "Orion . . . Orion," she whispered. "Are you all right?"

Orion moaned.

"Orion." She took his hand and lifted it to her cheek. She kissed the tops of his fingers, pinched the knuckle of his index finger lightly between her teeth. "Wake up," she urged. "Please wake up."

Need for this woman surged through his body. He sighed and rolled his head, but forced himself to keep his eyes closed. Fortunately, she must have been looking at his face, because if she'd gazed lower, she would have seen just how awake he was.

"Please, Orion," she said. "You have to wake up."

He opened one eye and gave her a lazy grin. "Why? This is just getting interesting."

"You!" She tried to pull away, but he caught her. In one swift movement, he pinned her to the bed of seaweed and stretched over her, bracing his greater weight on one elbow and his knees. She opened her mouth to protest and he kissed her. Their tongues touched, and the kiss deepened. Suddenly, he was caught in the throes of his own passion, and this was no longer a game.

"Do you want this?" he asked her between kisses.

"Yes, yes, I do."

She was so warm and soft, the feel of her skin intoxicating. With each breath he inhaled her scent, and it drove him wild. Her hands moved over his chest, her fingers stroking, and he touched and caressed her in turn. Each kiss seemed to bring them closer and intensify the heat igniting in his groin.

"Elena," he murmured as they struggled to remove what clothing they were wearing without breaking the mood. "My beautiful Elena."

He kissed her neck and pressed his lips into the hollow of her throat, inhaling her woman's scent and reveling in the taste of her sweet, salty skin. Elena chuckled, and the sound of her voice sent shivers through his nerve ends. "Woman . . . woman," he said hoarsely. "Are you a sorceress that you do this to me?"

She nuzzled the crown of his head and murmured softly. He couldn't make out the words, but it didn't matter. What was between them here, in this time and place, needed no words.

She put a hand on his chest, and he felt the heat of her palm and small fingers. Sexual pleasure he knew all too well, but he was unfamiliar with this sensation of yearning to share sensual pleasures only with this one woman. He and Elena were two different species, forbidden to mate by the rules of Atlanteans and humans alike, yet he wanted her as fiercely as if this were his first sexual encounter.

He kissed a line from her throat to the spot between her breasts. Elena sighed and molded her body to his, scorching him with the heat of her life force. Her seeking fingers skimmed the nape of his neck, and the intimate gesture sent small bursts of lightning down his spine and turned his bones to liquid.

"Ah, my sweet Elena," he whispered. He couldn't get

enough of her. The taste of her skin was sweet as honey and so soft that he wanted more. He longed to sample the beads of dew between her thighs, licking and sucking until she screamed with pleasure. He wanted to bury his face in her cleft and tease her hard pearl with his tongue until she opened wide for his throbbing cock.

Thinking about what it would feel like to bury himself to the hilt in her wet sheath inflamed his desire. He was hard as marble, swollen to the bursting point, and when he trailed his hungry mouth still lower it was all he could do not to lose control like some untried boy.

He pressed hot kisses into her woman's mound, inhaling her scent, and she groaned as he sought the treasures below with his tongue and lips. She bucked under his embrace, but she tilted her hips to allow him even deeper access. His heart pounded, and the raw hunger to have all of her tore away his last bonds of restraint.

Bright sensations swirled around him, and he felt the first rush of primal creation. With Atlanteans, the pleasure of sexual intercourse was fierce and long lasting, but the mental enjoyment was an undertow of intense magnitude, so great that lovers forever shared a bond once they had joined.

All his life, he had been taught that this experience was true only with two or more Atlanteans. It shouldn't be happening with Elena. She was human . . . she was less evolved physically, mentally, and spiritually.

It couldn't be . . . and yet it was.

He should have waited, should have prolonged the joy between them, but the madness gripped him. She laughed and opened for him and he plunged deep inside her wet and willing body. Crying out, she rose to meet him, catching his rhythm, meeting his wild desire with equal abandon.

"Deeper," she urged. "I want you! All of you!"

Oceans rose and fell; stars wheeled in a black sky, and the fresh wind of creation blew over a blue and seething planet. Images of smoking volcanoes and cresting tides folded one over another. Tiny pinwheels of life sparked to life, for time out of mind, evolving into ever more complex creatures until great leviathans and predators of sky and depths ruled the seas.

And always, amid the wonders of sight and sound, Orion was acutely aware of this exquisite creature . . . this woman beside him and with him and part of him. "Elena . . . Elena . . ." And when the final wave crested and broke, he found her wrapped in his arms, her arms and legs clasped around him, clinging to him and weeping.

"What's wrong?" he begged her. "Did I hurt you? Did I frighten you?"

She opened her eyes and gazed into his. "Orion . . . I . . . never . . ." She sighed and nestled against him. "You were . . ."

"What? I was what?" He kissed her forehead and eyebrows. He kissed away the tears on her cheeks and threaded his fingers through her dark brown hair. "I wouldn't hurt you for the world, my precious, precious darling. I'm so sorry that—"

"Shhh." She brought her fingers to his lips and silenced him. "I've never, ever imagined . . . I mean . . . I've been with other men, but . . ."

"So you're not hurt? I didn't disappoint you?"

She chuckled and burrowed even closer into his chest. "Wonderful," she whispered. "I don't have words to . . ." She pulled his head down and kissed his lips. "You'll be so puffed up, I won't be able to stand you," she teased.

Orion gave a sigh of relief. "I didn't know. You . . . you're different. I was afraid that I . . ."

She nibbled at his lower lip. "Shh, let me just . . ." She closed her eyes and made a sound that reminded him of contented cat's purr.

He sat up and pulled her into his arms, cradling her against him. "It's never been like that for me before," he admitted. "Not with anyone else. You're special, Elena. More special than you could ever realize."

The intensity of his feeling for her jolted Orion to his core. He'd been with hundreds of women in his lifetime. What made this one so different? Was it because she was human and forbidden? The word *love* rose in his mind and he pushed it firmly away. He was an Atlantean prince. Infatuation was normal for him—but love? Never.

She smiled up at him. "Does that mean we can do it again?"

His gut clenched. One smile from her lips and he felt like a boy in the throes of his first encounter with a woman. What weapon did she possess that she could cut to his heart with a look . . . a word?

He tried to cover the rush of emotion he felt for her . . . emotion tangled with desire. Already he could feel the pounding in his blood. "Yes," he answered lightly. "If you'll give me a few minutes to—"

Elena skimmed a fingertip down Orion's bare chest, lingering on the hard nub of his nipple just long enough to see his throat tighten. "Maybe I can do something to help," she suggested.

A sleepy grin spread across his face, and his beautiful green eyes radiated with an inner flame that made her knees go weak and sucked the oxygen from her lungs.

"What exactly did you have in mind?"

"Just a game I know," she managed. Her pulse skipped and fluttered as she broke off a leafy section of seaweed and tied it around his head, taking care to cover his eyes. "Trust me."

"Elena . . ." Sounding dubious, but amused, Orion sat upright, but made no attempt to remove the blindfold.

"Do as I say, for a change," she coaxed. "You don't always have to be in control, do you?"

"Usually."

"Not this time." She placed her hands on his chest and pushed him firmly onto his back. "You'll like it, I promise."

"I'd better."

Elena felt a sudden rush of blood flush her face and throat—not embarrassment—but proof of a rekindled hunger for this beautiful man stretched out in front of her. She drew in a ragged breath. She wasn't an inexperienced teenager. What was it about Orion that made her giddy as a schoolgirl and gave her goose bumps just by being near him?

He was an incredible lover. No man had ever made her feel so intensely when they were making love. Orion was tender, passionate, imaginative, and immensely exciting. Considering what they'd done, she should have been satiated, contented with the sweet afterglow of utter satisfaction rather than greedy for more. But the thought that they might reach those same heights of rapture again made her reckless.

"I'd better like it," he said.

"Don't you trust me?" Tendrils of yellow-blond hair drifted over his forehead, and she had to stifle the urge to brush them aside and shower kisses across his temple. She'd barely touched him, and already her mouth was dry and she could feel an increased sensitivity in her breasts and an aching in her nipples.

"No," he teased. "I don't trust you."

"Give me your hand," she ordered. Pulling loose another piece of seaweed, she knotted it around his left wrist and tied his arm to a swaying column of sea grass. "Not scared, are you?" She quickly repeated the action with his right wrist.

He smiled, and the sexy way the corners of his mouth turned up gave her shivers. She couldn't help thinking of how Orion's mouth had felt against hers . . . on her breasts and between her legs.

"Terrified."

She stifled a giggle. It was no secret to either of them that Orion could have snapped the seaweed bonds easily, but there was something erotic about the thought of having him in her power and she counted on him going along with her charade. "Now the rules are that you can't move," she explained. "If you do, you lose."

"Do I have to pay a forfeit?"

She nodded. "And I'll make it brutal."

"I'll keep that in mind," he said. "And how do I win?"

"If you lie perfectly still, no matter what happens, then I lose."

"What if an eleven-foot tiger shark comes up and takes a bite out of me?"

"No excuses. If you move, you lose."

"It sounds as if the cards are stacked against me. Are you sure you aren't making this up as you go along?"

She giggled. "Nope. Do you want to play, or not?"

"All right, Diana. Have your way with me. But if the squid comes back to finish—"

She smacked his chest with the palm of her hand. "What did you call me?"

He laughed.

She pulled back her hand. Hitting him, even in teasing, had been like striking an oak tree. Orion's skin was softer than bark, but his taut muscles were every bit as hard and unyielding.

"Diana . . . the huntress," he explained. "Diana of your Greek mythology."

"She was real?"

"Absolutely. I never knew her personally, but I have it straight from a reliable source that she was a take-charge kind of woman."

"I'll take your word for it."

"You're sure you're not worried about that squid?"

"If it comes back, I'll be the first to let you know," she promised. "You can't talk either. If you speak, I'm the winner."

"It sounds to me as if you win, no matter what."

"No more talking," she said. "We start now."

She leaned down to brush a feather-light caress on his right knee. Orion sighed, and she trailed soft kisses higher, dipping to tease his inner thigh. He groaned and she nipped his skin between her teeth. "Not a word," she warned.

Mischievously, she reached down to stroke the length of his shaft. It was warm and smooth, and still thick, despite their recent lovemaking. With her free hand, she cupped his large testicles in her hand, marveling at how heavy they were.

"Woman . . ."

"Shh," she murmured. Touching him like this gave her a feeling of power and sent sparks spiraling through her. Orion was a man like every other man, and yet . . . He was somehow more . . . super vibrant, stronger, exceptionally virile . . . larger than life. Everything about him was an exclamation point, and when she was with him, he made her feel as though every moment was thrilling.

She brushed her fingertips over his taut, smooth skin,

reliving the erotic pleasure he'd given her . . . remembering the way she'd felt when he'd plunged deep inside her.

Trembling, she leaned down to press her lips against his rising tumescence, and he inhaled sharply.

"Elena." Orion's powerful fingers threaded through her hair.

"Do you like it when I do this?" she murmured, flicking her tongue against his cock. "And this?" Lightly, she nipped him, small teasing bites that made him groan and flinch.

"Woman . . . you . . ."

She laughed huskily, caught in her own rush of desire as she savored the feel of his hard body . . . as she let her imagination take wing. "You aren't allowed to talk," she reminded him huskily. "Unless you want to forfeit the game?"

His lips compressed into a tight line, but whether he was attempting to stifle a groan or laughter, she couldn't tell. It didn't matter. She'd set out to seduce him and had succeeded in igniting an inferno in her own body.

"Do it," he said.

"Shhh." She took his length in both hands, stroking and massaging with tremulous fingers, using her tongue and lips to excite him, before slowly taking the swollen head of his penis between her lips and suckling.

Orion groaned and bucked. His lean fingers closed on her breast, and he found her nipple and pinched it. Desire shot through her. "Harder!"

A hot sweet substance filled her mouth and she cried out and fell back. He caught her and cradled her against him. She could feel the force of his climax convulsing his body as he groaned and pulled her tight against him.

"Elena! Elena!"

She was wet and hot and aching. She would die if she

couldn't extinguish this fire throbbing in her loins. He threw her back against the bed of seaweed and plunged his face between her thighs, licking and kissing her, thrusting his hard tongue deep inside until she, too, was swept into the tidal wave of utter abandon before reaching the peak and tumbling over in a thousand shattered bits of utter and complete joy.

Sobbing, she clung to him as he laughed and kissed her and held her so tightly that she could barely breathe. "You cheat," he said hoarsely.

"I did not."

"Did."

"Shall we have a rematch?"

He laughed. "You'll be the death of me, woman, but I can't think of a better way to go."

"Go?" Waves of pleasure still thrummed through her body and she sighed and yawned. "I don't even know where I am now." She chuckled. "Before we were almost devoured by that squid, weren't you taking me somewhere?"

Reality jolted him. He should have been back at his post hours ago. If the troops assembled without him, there would be no hiding his absence from Poseidon. "How long have I slept?" He got to his feet, caught her hand, and pulled her erect. "We have to go, Elena. I have to get you to safety." He had to make certain she was all right before he was free to return to his command.

Confused, she looked at him. "But you said we'd be safe here. Sanctuary, you called it."

"It is, but you can't stay here. I have to go, and you can't breathe underwater without me." He gathered her scattered clothing and handed it to her. Somehow, they had both shed every last garment.

Seeing her beautiful naked body was tempting, but he knew that they had to move quickly. "Hurry. Get dressed," he said as he pulled his tunic over his head and strapped on his cuirass and greaves. "We don't have much time. I'll explain later. For now, you have to trust me."

"What do you mean 'I can't breathe without you'? It's my dream . . . or whatever. I assume we're in the ocean, but I'm having no trouble at all."

"And you won't, so long as we're together. It's complicated." How could he make her understand the ancient truths? He was Atlantean; the ocean was his home. Her place was on dry land, and without his presence, his protection, she would drown in the time it took for a wave to crash on the beach and flow back into the sea.

How he or any Atlantean was able to give the gift of life underwater was a mystery, one that he had always known but never questioned. For Elena, the magic would be beyond understanding.

"I don't understand why we have to leave." She stared up at the swaying trees of verdant green kelp that rose above the sea grass arbor. "This seems like paradise."

"It gave us what we needed . . . the time I needed to recover." He located his sword belt and looked around for his helmet. It was nowhere to be seen. He decided that he must have lost it in the battle with the squid or in transport. "Now, I have to get you to the fairies."

She shook her head. "Fairies don't exist."

He rolled his eyes. Humans! Stubborn and close-minded. For thousands of years humans of every continent and culture lived beside the fairy folk. But after the humans had hunted and persecuted them to near extinction, after they had made life impossible on land for them, they pretended that the little people had never existed. It was ever the habit of the human race to deny what made them uncomfortable.

"They do not exist?" he asked her.

"I'm not a child, Orion. How can you expect me to believe in such superstitious claptrap? What next, trolls?" She thought for a second. "Of course, I can't breathe under water either." She looked at him again. "But I have to maintain there's no such thing as fairies, even in my imagination."

"Take that up with the fairy folk when we get there. For now, we have to go back into the seraphim."

She looked unconvinced. "Not that again!"

"Trust me, Elena. I'll protect you."

She shrugged and gave him her hand. "Do I have a choice?"

"Rhiannon? Are you here?" Lady Athena pushed aside the curtain of pearls and entered her daughter's luxurious private quarters. "Rhiannon? We're home."

Worry pricked at Athena. Where were the four guardsmen who should have been at the gate? And where were the household servants? Rhiannon's husband, Morgan, was crown prince. Never in her lifetime had Athena seen the royal family's section of the palace empty and unguarded.

Athena had the afternoon off from her duties at the temple and had used the free time to take her granddaughter Danu with her to visit the dolphin nursery. The five-year-old loved to see and play with the baby dolphins, and Athena was thrilled to spend time with Danu.

When Athena had come to fetch Danu, Rhiannon had confided that Princess Morwena was nowhere to be found. Morgan's brother Prince Alexandros was secretly conducting a search for her, but neither Alex nor Rhiannon wanted the king or the entire court to know, in case Morwena's absence had something to do with Prince Orion's unexplained absence.

Rhiannon had sent a trusted serving girl to ask Morgan to come to their apartments on an urgent matter. Athena knew that her son-in-law had been meeting with his generals. If his wife called him away, he would know that whatever she wanted was serious. Having Danu out of the home for an hour would give Rhiannon time to talk privately with Morgan without risking the child overhearing their conversation.

Athena suspected that had Morgan known about his beloved sister's absence, that would have superseded even the assembly of his troops. Now Athena was anxious to learn if Morwena had turned up or if Prince Morgan knew where she was.

"Rhiannon!" she called again. Not even a lady-in-waiting appeared. The scales rose on the nape of Athena's neck. If Rhiannon had to leave before Athena and Danu got back, she would have left someone to receive her child and watch over her until she returned. As princess royal, Rhiannon commanded a large staff, something that Rhiannon had yet to come to terms with. Her daughter sometimes complained to her about the strain on private life between her and her husband, but Rhiannon would never send both the soldiers and the servants away.

And it wasn't like Rhiannon to go somewhere without telling Danu ahead of time. The two were extremely close, and Rhiannon took motherhood seriously, calling Danu her special treasure. Danu had been born human and transformed only recently into an Atlantean, as had Rhiannon. Danu's life before she had become a daughter of the sea had been one of neglect and loneliness. Both Morgan and Rhiannon were determined to make up for that cruel beginning. They loved Danu unconditionally, and were extremely protective of her.

"Mama!" Danu cried, running ahead of Athena. She

dashed across the large courtyard into Rhiannon's bed-chamber. "Mama?"

The child's voice took on a frightened tone, and Athena rushed after her.

Rhiannon sat at her loom as she often did, but nothing about her seemed normal. No strands of seaweed shimmered on the framework, and none coiled in the basket or rested in Rhiannon's lap, but she seemed to be weaving nevertheless. Her gaze remained fixed on an invisible rug and her hands went through the motions, in spite of Danu's cries of distress and anxious tugging at her mother's tunic.

"Rhiannon, what's wrong?" Athena demanded. All her instincts told her that something terrible had happened. Rhiannon's beautiful blond hair was snarled, and her *peplos* torn and dirty. "Are you ill?"

Rhiannon's only answer was a flat, nonsensical humming. She continued to sway slowly from side to side and repeat her chilling pantomime. It was then that Athena noticed the bloodstains on the hem of her daughter's garment and pulled Danu away.

"She's hurt," Danu said, reaching out to her mother. "Mama's hurt herself."

Fear skimmed down Athena's spine, and she picked up the little girl and cradled her against her breast, shielding her eyes. She gave a sharp whistle and a mature female dolphin swam into the chamber. "Echo," Athena ordered. "Take Danu into the walled garden and keep her safe." Athena looked down into the child's face. "You go with Echo."

"But, Mama . . ." Danu looked frightened.

"I'll take care of your mother. She'll be fine. She's just . . . tired."

She rubbed her eyes with the backs of her fists, trying to be brave. "Babies in their tummy make mommies tired?"

Athena nodded. She glanced around, saw her own personal dolphin, Melika, in the archway and beckoned to her. "Call a general alarm," Athena said quietly. "And bring servants and a healer from the temple."

Almost at once, Echo returned with Danu clinging like a burr to the gilded harness on the dolphin's back. "Come and see," Echo communicated, through a series of clicks. "In the walled court."

"What is it?"

"Guards sleep," the dolphin chirped. "Maids sleep."

"Are they dead?" Athena asked.

Echo's burst of sound was a clear negative. "Sleep."

Danu was calling out to her mother again.

"You must be brave, Danu," Athena said. "Remember, you are a princess, and princesses don't cry. I'll take care of your mama. Echo, take her into Princess Rhiannon's baths. Protect her with your life."

Echo's reply was an angry chatter of clicks and squeaks. The mammal was clearly offended that Athena thought she needed to remind her of her duty. "Good dolphin," she repeated.

"Yes," Athena said. "Echo is a good dolphin. I meant no disrespect, sister." When child and dolphin had once again left the room, Athena went to her daughter, took her by the shoulders, and gently guided her to the bed. The blood was troubling, but it didn't mean Rhiannon was miscarrying, not yet. There were remedies to help her retain her pregnancy, but Athena had to get her off her feet.

"Octopi are dancing," Rhiannon murmured as she lay back docilely on the cushions. "Do you see them?"

*Madness*, Athena thought. *This is no ordinary illness. It smacks of sorcery.* She pressed a palm to Rhiannon's temple. She wasn't fevered, but her skin was colder than it should have been. "Shh, shh, darling, lie still," she crooned. "I'm here. Everything will be all right now. I'm here."

This was the daughter that she'd had to give up at birth, her only child that she'd feared she'd never know. The fates had been kind, and they had been reunited when Rhiannon had returned to the sea. And although their true relationship was a secret to most Atlanteans, Athena loved her fiercely. She would not lose her again.

"Rhiannon!" Prince Morgan came into the room followed by a half-dozen armed guardsmen. "What's happened? Where is Danu? Is she—"

"Danu is safe with Echo," Athena said, "but I fear for Rhiannon. She's bleeding. I'm afraid something may have gone wrong with the pregnancy, and her behavior is abnormal."

Quickly, as the prince gathered his wife in his arms, Athena told him all that she knew. "Echo said that the princess's guard and servants are sleeping in the walled court, but I couldn't leave her alone to go and see for myself."

"Rhiannon," he said urgently to his wife, but she only stared through him, smiled, and began to hum again. "What can have happened to her?" Morgan asked.

"I don't know. If her attendants can be revived, perhaps they can tell us."

Morgan ordered two of the soldiers to go to investigate before turning again to Athena. "Have you called for a healer?" he asked.

Athena nodded.

"This baby means the world to her," he said. "To both of us."

Due to the long lives of Atlanteans and the serious nature of parenthood, many couples chose not to have children at all. Those who did make that choice cherished

each new life. There were no unwanted babies or neglected children as often happened among the overpopu-
lated air breathers. If an accident befell the mother or
father, there were a hundred willing hands to catch and
cradle the child, regardless of age or class. Thus the loss of
any pregnancy was a tragedy in the kingdom.

As one who would someday be the high king and take
the title of *Poseidon* as the ancient Egyptians had named
each of their kings *pharaoh*, it was expected that Morgan
would naturally take more than one wife and father many
children. The crown of Atlantis had passed down from father to son for millennia and the line must continue.

But Rhiannon had not been born to the sea. She would
have none of the old custom of multiple wives. When she
agreed to become Morgan's bride, she had made it clear to
him that she would not share his love with any woman,
and he had sworn his fidelity to her alone. Thus, this unborn babe might well be born heir to the throne of Poseidon. And if the pregnancy came to grief, it could affect the
line of succession if Rhiannon never quickened again.

"I would give my life for this babe," Morgan said, "but
Rhiannon means more to me." His eyes glistened with
tears as he rocked her against him. "My wife," he murmured softly. "My own sweet wife."

Fresh blood seeped into the mattress, and Athena
grasped both of her daughter's hands. "Let me tend to
her," she urged Morgan. "Go to Danu. She's frightened."
She looked meaningfully at him. "Danu saw Rhiannon in
this condition and saw the stains on her tunic."

Morgan looked into Rhiannon's blank eyes. "Why
doesn't she know me? What's happened to her? What
could cause this?"

"Leave her to me," Athena repeated. "Rhiannon is bone
of my bone. I will not give her or her child up without a

fight, but this is healer's work and no place for a husband."

Rhiannon laughed. "The octopi dance for me," she whispered. "They dance and dance. Don't you see them?"

Morgan laid her head back against the cushions. "Save her for me," he said. "Save them both."

"If I can, I will," Athena promised. She did not tell him that she suspected witchcraft. It would frighten him needlessly. If this was magic, it would take stronger magic to fight it. And it might be that she would have to sacrifice the child for the mother.

The prince rose to his feet. "She is my life," he said. "Without her, I'm nothing."

"Without her, you're still Danu's father," Athena said harshly. "She needs you. Go to your child and be strong for her. And let nothing so foolish slip from your lips again."

# CHAPTER 15

"I've done all you ask, great lord," Halimeda said. "Will you not acknowledge my service?" Her voice echoed down the cavern, coming back to her in waves. "... *All you ask ... All you ask ...*"

The massive stone head stared down at her with sightless eyes. Around her there was no life, no schools of fish, no scuttling crabs or waving sea grass, only cold rock and shadows. Halimeda had walked in the deepest part of the Atlantic, and she had swum beneath the frozen North Sea, but this cold seeped through to her bones. This place exuded a chill of unleashed power and it thrilled her.

Again, she congratulated herself on the wisdom of pledging her allegiance to the Phoenician god of war. Melqart would fulfill her greatest wishes, and he would raise her son to the throne of Atlantis. Any sacrifice was worth the prize. Almost any sacrifice, she hedged in her mind. So long as she retained her place and her beauty, she would be the true ruler of the Atlantean kingdom. She would sit in the place of honor, and her son, Caddoc, would defer to her in all things as he always had. After centuries, she would come into her own, and all who had slighted her would pay with their lives.

"Lord Melqart! Hear me," she cried. "I have cast a spell

on the Atlantean royal princess. Even now, her child writhes in the womb and fights for breath. And the mother walks in madness."

Silence.

"Am I not to be rewarded?" she demanded. "Will you not raise my son to high king as you promised?"

The stones beneath her feet shifted and the walls swayed. From somewhere deep in the mountain, she could smell smoke and sulfur and hear the rumble of an awakening volcano. *He comes*, she thought. *Melqart comes at my bidding.*

"Why do you trouble me with trifles?" The voice did not pour from the stone head or from the cave. It vibrated within her head.

"Trifles? It is no trifle," she flung back peevishly. *How could he not see her genius?* "Show me another sorceress so powerful, one who can make herself invisible and slip into the heart of Poseidon's palace to strike at his daughter-in-law."

"I am displeased!"

"Displeased? How can you be displeased? The princess is a jabbering idiot. She will miscarry her brat—and she will quicken with child no more." Of that, Halimeda was certain. How could Morgan go to the bed of a half-wit who wove without thread and sang foolish songs about dancing octopi? He would be disgusted. Any real man would not go within twenty leagues of such an abomination. And soon, her beauty would fade. Perhaps they would lock Rhiannon away—even wall her up as she had done with Princess Morwena.

The features on the polished stone head, a head as high and wide as a man was tall, began to take on life. The eyes, which had been empty sockets, glowed red, and the monstrous mouth opened. "Hold your tongue, witch, or I'll rip it out!"

"But you don't seem to realize what I've done for you!"

"What you've done for me? You are the one who wants revenge on Poseidon! This nonsense about the princess and her bewitching is all your idea."

Halimeda raised her chin. Like all males, the great one saw only the most direct path. She was his servant, but she would not be bullied. He must see that she was a worthy ally. He must give her the respect she was due. "Ending Prince Morgan's line undermines Poseidon's grip on the crown. A kingship must pass father to son. Morgan has sworn a blood oath not to take another wife so long as Rhiannon lives. If he goes back on his word, the people will not accept him as heir."

"This petty ruler, this Poseidon of whom you go on at great length, he has many other sons, does he not? The twin warrior-heroes Orion and Alexandros? The younger sons by his high queen Korinna? The snot-nosed boys of his minor wives and courtesans—any of which, I remind you, witch, can ascend the throne of Atlantis. And unless he had lost his desire, he has the hammer and anvil to make dozens more."

"The petty princes can be dealt with."

The hooded eyes narrowed. "I suppose you will put them all to knitting booties and teach each prince to sing your stupid octopi song."

"I had to start somewhere. Morgan is crown prince. It was logical to begin with him."

The head remained silent for a long time, so long that Halimeda's stomach began to growl and she remembered how hungry she was. She would have to talk to Lord Melqart about the food. His jest had gone on long enough.

It was time he ended the charade and permitted her to enjoy her meat again.

"I know what you're thinking," the voice inside her whispered. "Do you think you can blaspheme in your mind, and I won't know it?"

Anger made her bold. "How do I blaspheme? Have I insulted you by word or deed? Show me another servant of yours who will tell you the truth."

The head roared to life. The face contorted and leaned from the wall to loom over her. Heat blasted her skin and blistered her eyes and throat. "What truth would you tell me, sorceress?"

Whimpering, she fell to her knees and clapped her hands over her eyes. The pain was excruciating. A thrill ran through her. Yes, the pain was terrible—almost sexual. She had always enjoyed mixing pain with her pleasure, in the correct amounts, of course. She'd even given Poseidon a sharkskin whip to use in their most intimate games.

"Maybe I could find a suitable toy for you," Melqart suggested. "One with barbs of volcanic glass on the tips?"

"No, no, that won't be necessary," she whined.

"I'm waiting."

Halimeda began to wonder if it had been such a good idea to come here, to confront Melqart. How was she to have guessed he would be in this mood? "I have a gift . . . a special gift for you, my lord," she said hesitantly. "A worthy sacrifice for your altar."

"And what makes you think I need you to find sacrifices for me?" he roared.

She shielded her face with her hands. The heat had ruined her nails, and she'd spent hours getting them just right. "And when is the last time you've been offered a royal virgin?"

"Male or female?"

"Female. I can lay an Atlantean princess in your flames. How would you like that? Surely that is a source of power."

"You think I haven't had my share of royal flesh? The kings of Phoenicia regularly offered me their firstborn—and all the princesses I wanted. And the Emperor of Chin once sent me—"

"A long time ago," Halimeda said. "Two thousand years, at least. And since then, what has it been? Drunken Dutch sailors? A half-drowned whore your lazy priests scooped out of an Etruscan ditch and stuffed in a wine cask to keep her flesh from rotting before it reached your temple? You call that a proper sacrifice for a god?"

"That may have happened once, but it wasn't a habit. And I compensated by taking the ship and all aboard, including the misbegotten priests. And one was a virgin, the son of an olive merchant. He was without blemish. Quite satisfactory."

"But fat, very fat. They needed a block and tackle to get him onboard the vessel as I remember."

"I didn't know that. How did you know that?"

"I watched them. Do you think I've spent my entire life in a conch shell? I've served other gods beside you. There used to be more of you. Remember Dionysus?"

"Second rate. Not in my league, witch."

"But very popular in his day."

"You babble on about has-beens," Melqart grumbled.

"I'm just saying."

"Out with it. Saying what?"

She heard the weakness in his voice. He was vulnerable. More than a man, perhaps, but with all the failings of one. "You require proper sacrifice and worship. You need humans, mer folk, and Atlanteans to fear you. When your kind ceases to be remembered by the living, you will fade."

"How dare you!" The ground shook again and from deep beneath the earth she heard the roar of a demonic bull. Stones began to fall from the ceiling of the hall and the floor to crumble under her feet. Steam rose through the cracks, and from somewhere deep, she could hear the bubbling hiss of molten lava.

Halimeda threw herself flat and covered her head with her hands. Melqart's rages were much like Poseidon's. If you could survive the first blast, they would pass.

"What of Thera? And Crete?" he demanded. "Who reached up with a fist and crushed them? Who smashed their toy palaces and cities and let the water flow over their bodies?"

"You, mighty one," she answered meekly. "But, that has been some time ago. I do not see the tribute ships sailing to your shrines or the thousands of followers you had when Phoenicia ruled the seas."

"And Carthage. Don't forget Carthage."

"Struck down by the Romans with younger gods," she reminded him.

"And all this will be solved with the sacrifice of one skinny Atlantean virgin?"

"Not all, but it will be a start. And she isn't skinny. She's quite . . . quite nubile." That was the closest she would come to complimenting Morwena's figure. "Remember, the longest swim begins with a single stroke."

"That isn't the way I heard it."

"Well, you must have misheard. That is a quote from my ancestress Iphigeneia—not Agamemnon's daughter. That chit was named after my ancestress, the famous Atlantean philosopher who married a nobleman, a visitor from the stars and went with him to his own kingdom."

"If she did, he probably intended her as food for his journey home."

"No, it's true. I swear. He adored her."

"Liar. Agamemnon killed Iphigeneia himself as a sacrifice to me."

"I just told you. I speak of an earlier Iphigeneia, the grandmother of my grandmother on my father's side. And, for the record, Agamemnon gave the blood of his daughter to Artemis."

"Who served me. Artemis was nothing before I took her in hand."

"Yes, yes," Halimeda said. "But we know how that turned out for Agamemnon, don't we? So he hardly set an example that other men would wish to follow."

"You claim that humans no longer fear me? No longer tremble and prostrate themselves at my name?"

"Not many," she replied. "Most worship coin or the paper equivalent, rather than musty entities."

"Hmm. I will see this *virgin princess* you boast of, but if she isn't worthy, I'll throw her to my shades. I will have only the finest stock sacrificed on my altar."

"She will please you. You have my word."

The earth stopped shaking. Water and steam stopped pouring through the walls. The ceiling ceased to crumble. She waited, knowing that Melqart knew that she'd gotten the better of him and would change the subject to cover his loss of face.

"Where is this son of whom you brag?" he said finally. "Why doesn't he come to worship at my feet?"

"He will come, Lord Melqart. He will come."

His voice dropped to a rumbling murmur. "You claim to serve me, and yet you allow thieves to steal from me."

"What?" She blinked. *What was he talking about?*

"From me!!!"

So loud and terrifying was the voice in her head that Halimeda fell to her knees and clutched at her skull. The pain was so intense that her vision clouded and her teeth became red-hot spikes. "Have mercy!" she cried.

"Gold from my tribute ship!"

"Long ago," she wailed.

"Not long ago. Now! Only days ago!"

"I didn't know. What would you have me do, lord?" she begged. He had been toying with her all along. He was displeased, and this was no act. She had made things worse by wounding his pride, and he wouldn't forgive her for that. Her life and that of her son hung by a single thread of sea grass.

"Send your son to find the thief and bring her to me!"

"Bring who?" Halimeda asked. She was so frightened that she lost control of her bladder. Urine ran down her legs and snot from her nose. "Who has stolen from your gold?"

"Find the thief!" he thundered. "Find the thief and return my treasure or I will strike your precious son deaf and blind! I will send armies to rip out his throat and tear out his manhood. I will have justice, or you will watch as I destroy Caddoc."

"No, lord. Don't. Please! I have been a faithful servant to you."

"He is mine to do with as I please. You have given his soul to me of your own free will." The entity laughed, long and loud and mocking. "And, Halimeda?"

"Yes, lord, I'm listening."

"If he dies, your beauty dies with him. You will live on, a powerless, toothless, hairless hag, an object of pity. You will beg your bread from door to door and all of Atlantis will know that you were a mother so greedy that you sold your only son for a harlot's price."

*  *  *

Elena allowed Orion to lead her back through the tunnel. She would rather have walked to wherever he wanted to take her than to allow herself to be buffeted and tossed in those dark canyons again, but she was in no condition to argue with him.

*What had just happened?* They had intercourse, certainly. But *making love* didn't encompass the feelings she'd experienced. Her body still vibrated with the sweet sensations, and visions of the sights and sounds she'd perceived remained more real than the sight of this beautiful man beside her. Never had anything come close to the satisfaction she had known, and never had she felt more alive. As dreams went, this had to be the Super Bowl of fantasies.

But something troubled her. If this was her dream or nightmare or coma, which it obviously was, why hadn't Orion told her that he loved her? She wasn't certain what she thought of him—she didn't know him well enough to feel that she was *in love.* But what kind of fantastic dream lover wouldn't declare himself? It would have been perfect if he'd just come out and said he loved her and there was no other woman in the world for him. Straight out of an old romance novel, maybe, but it was what a woman wanted to hear. Even her.

But still . . . Thinking about what they'd done . . . the way his bare skin had felt against hers . . . the way their bodies seemed to fit perfectly together, almost as if they'd been lovers for years. Remembering made her muscles go weak and her heart flutter. Her breasts felt swollen and tender; she could feel the moisture gathering between her thighs. . . .

She wanted to do it again . . . wanted to make love to him . . . wanted to touch him and stroke him . . . wanted to savor the same bitter-sweet ecstasy he had given her. . . .

She was jerked unpleasantly from her musings as a hatch opened and they were sucked into the blast. The force field seemed stronger than before, or maybe it was that she hadn't been expecting it. Her arm scraped along one wall, and she was tossed this way and that.

Abruptly, she was tumbling over and over. She tried to catch her breath, but the pressure in her chest was overwhelming. She opened her mouth to scream, but she had no air left in her lungs. Worse, she had lost her grip on Orion and was torn away from him. He had her by one hand, but she was certain that he couldn't hold on. She slammed against a wall, knocking herself giddy, but then when she thought that she was lost, that the nightmare would devour her, Orion's strong arms closed around her.

They turned and twisted, now upright, now facedown but always moving, swept along in a powerful current, until at last, Elena saw a flash of light, a door swing open, and they splashed into water. They plunged down; her foot touched bottom, and then Orion was swimming up and pulling her with him.

Her head broke the surface and she gasped for breath. She heard Orion coughing and sputtering as well. Her vision was clouded by the water, but she blinked, wiped her eyes, and stared around.

This was no ocean, no endless sea of salt water. They'd landed in what appeared to be a tranquil woodland pond. All around the edges were grassy slopes and beyond that towering trees of every shape and kind. She recognized firs and pines, oaks, beech, dogwoods, and chestnuts. The sky was a brilliant blue without a single cloud. In the distance, Elena could see low grassy hills and snow-capped mountains.

"What . . . what is this place?" she sputtered.

Orion paddled lazily beside her. "I told you. This is Eden, land of the fairy folk."

A few strokes took them to a shallow bank, and they waded out and sank down on the thick grass. Bees buzzed overhead and birds flitted from tree branch to tree branch and sang sweet liquid notes. Blossoms of every color peeped from the grass and filled the air with a riot of perfume. As far as she could see there was no highway, no buildings, no power lines, no bridges or towns, only tranquil nature.

"It's another part of the dream, isn't it?" Fairy folk, her eye! Not even in a dream would she conjure up brownies, elves, leprechauns, or any other of the silly imaginary beings that frequented tall tales and children's stories.

The grass was sweet and soft, and the air smelled fresh and clean. Elena flopped back and looked up at the sky where flocks of geese and ducks rode the air currents. Once, when she was fourteen, her mother and one of her mother's boyfriends had taken her camping in the Canadian Rockies. The mountains there had this untouched and primitive atmosphere.

Jack McGregor had been pleasant, with the good sense not to try to be her *best friend or substitute father*. He'd realized that she'd wanted to be left alone with a book, and she didn't want to see him and her mother all smoochy and acting like sex-crazed teenagers. She hadn't wanted to go, but the trip had been a great success. Jack had promised they'd go again in the fall, but unfortunately, by then, her mother had married someone else. What she remembered about that one trip was the sense of peace she'd discovered in the wilderness.

She felt it here. Wherever her dream had taken her, this was a good place, a safe place where nothing could go wrong.

# CHAPTER 16

O rion stretched and yawned and smiled down at Elena before dropping back to tuck his hands under his neck and join her in staring at the blue canopy overhead. It was a relief to relax his guard and take a moment to catch his breath, and the artificial sky here was magnificent.

He wondered if Elena realized that engineers and scientists had put hundreds of years into perfecting the illusion that Eden was a paradise on earth. And it was; it simply occupied the space in the planet's hollow center. And the same technology that had provided an outer earth appearance had provided the fairies with an oxygen level similar to that which sustained humans. Elena would be able to breathe naturally here.

Orion could feel his body making the adjustments necessary to switch from breathing underwater to dry land. He'd been born with the ability to survive for longer periods than most of his kind among the earth walkers, but he never found it easy or particularly pleasant. The force of gravity was stronger and there was a constant barrage of rays from outside the planet's atmosphere. No wonder humans had such short lives.

He never felt those problems in Eden. Technically, this was land, but it was a different kind of terra firma. Here at the earth's core, many natural laws seemed suspended or, in the case of time, worked opposite to that on the outer rim of the planet. It had been just this irregularity that he'd counted on when he'd left Atlantis and his command to bring Elena here to safety.

In legend and in fact, there had always been tales of humans or Atlanteans who'd fallen in with fairies, lost track of time, and returned to find it was a hundred years later. That may have been true when the fairy folk lived on the earth's surface. Here, time for humans and Atlanteans worked exactly the opposite.

Each hour Orion spent in Eden took him backwards on the Atlantean clock. If he was careful and judged correctly, he could get back to his command a few minutes before he'd left, and no one would ever realize that he'd been away. He was less certain on the subject of time for the fairies themselves. Perhaps they existed, as they always had, devoid of the concept or outside its law.

But for a few short hours, he could be with Elena without feeling guilty for not being somewhere else. When the war with Melqart was over, if he survived, he'd return her to Crete, hopefully close enough to the time that they met there that no one would realize she hadn't returned to her companions. At least he would if he could be assured that Melqart wouldn't find her and destroy her later. There were a lot of *ifs*, but he couldn't think of that now. He would face that problem later.

Orion slipped an arm under Elena's shoulders and pulled her closer. He wanted to make love to her again, but he wanted this time to be special for her, and he had a feeling that she would love the enchanted forest pool. "There's a waterfall at the other end of the pond, through the trees. If you'd care to wash the salt water off . . ." He couldn't imagine wanting to rid himself of the smell or sensation of salt against his skin, but Elena was human, and he supposed she might feel differently.

"That sounds heavenly," she answered. "My hair's a sticky mess."

He nuzzled the back of her neck. "Seems perfect to me." He turned and kissed her. "You seem perfect," he murmured. She did.

He tried to tell himself that his feelings for her were what he usually experienced when he was attracted to a desirable woman, but he knew this was something more. In truth, the intensity of his affection for Elena frightened him. She was human; he was Atlantean. That should have been the end of the subject, but it wasn't, and the reality of that was becoming more evident to him with every hour he spent with her.

His brother Morgan had fallen in love with a human woman. They had faced down Poseidon and all the obstacles that prevented the two races from intermingling. Morgan had been willing to trade his destiny for Rhiannon, and in the end, they'd discovered that she had been born of an Atlantean mother. Orion doubted if he'd be that lucky.

He didn't trust his feelings. How could he? He'd been infatuated with many females over the centuries. In his own way, he'd loved Sjshsglee, and she was a mermaid. That relationship was almost as impossible as this one. And yet, Elena was different. What if she was the one he'd been searching for and he let her go because he wasn't strong enough to fight for her?

"Mmm, you taste good, but . . ." She sighed. "I'd still like to see the waterfall."

*And I'd like to see you naked in the sunlight,* he thought. *Would she be as desirable here as she'd been beneath the sea in my world?*

Directing the sun's rays into the center of the earth wasn't an illusion but a feat of engineering. Atlanteans had designed and implemented the system. Engineering had never been his strong suit, but in theory, the plan involved gathering sunshine from the highest mountain ranges, such as the Andes and the Himalayas, and using crystals to redirect it through underground caverns, light wells, and tunnels to be redistributed here in the core.

The sun and moon here were replicas as was the sky, but very good replicas, powered by materials from a planet outside the earth's solar system and left here by the star travelers long ago. Few of the original fairies found fault with their new kingdom, and the generations that had been born in the last thousand years accepted the oddities of Eden as natural. This was home to them, and it was a far kinder place than the surface had ever been. It was rumored that a few solitary fairies still roamed the quiet corners of Europe and Iceland, but Orion suspected that it was more wishing on the part of humans than fact.

Elena caught his face between her palms and turned his head so that she could look directly into his eyes. "You promised me a waterfall," she reminded.

"I did, didn't I?" He rose, pulled her to her feet, and led the way to a narrow path that followed the shore of the pond and then turned off to follow the rocky stream that fed the larger body of water. Here, the brook rushed merrily, the banks were verdant green moss, and the trees on either side were more evergreen than hardwood. The limbs and boughs of the giant pines and hemlocks intertwined, forming a roofed and shadowy passageway with a thick carpet of pine needles underfoot.

Almost immediately, he could hear the rush of the waterfall ahead. "You'll like this," he promised.

They walked a few more yards and stepped out into a

sparkling glade that formed a perfect setting for a fifty-foot cascade that tumbled into another smaller pool ringed all about with woods' violets, lilies of the valley, and clusters of curious little plants known as jack-in-the-pulpits. The glade was enchanted in more ways than one, and Orion wondered if Elena felt the power radiating from the water as he did.

She clapped her hands in delight and turned in a slow circle. "It's wonderful." It seemed like something out of the old movie *Brigadoon*, a place that time forgot. The warm air was misty and sweet with the fragrant scent of the delicate flowers. "It is Eden, isn't it?" Laughing, she stripped away the rags of her remaining clothing and waded into the pool.

Orion followed. The water was warmer than the air and seemed to possess a particular ability to ease every ache and strain. Water so clear that it seemed translucent rose to his chest; the bottom was blue cobblestone covered over with fine white sand.

When Elena ducked under to wet her hair, he plucked a few leaves from a thornless cactuslike succulent that grew at the water's edge and crushed them between his palms. A thick, juicy, sudsy oil with a delightful smell came from the leaves. "Here," he said, holding out his hand to her. "It's called *oriana*. I've been told women like to bathe and wash their hair with it." He'd also been told that it triggered an intense sexual need in females, but he wasn't certain he needed to share that much information.

"Just women?" she teased. "Are you sure you haven't tried it?" She took the liquid and massaged it into her scalp. "If my hair falls out from this, I'll know who to blame."

"Close your eyes and lie back," he ordered. "Trust me." Not only did this pool have curative powers, but the water was more buoyant than most so that Elena floated almost without effort. "Let me." He used the remaining oil that clung to his hands to work up a lather and rubbed it through her hair.

"Feels good," she murmured. "But, if it works so good on my hair, maybe it would be nice on my skin."

"An experiment?"

She laughed.

Gently, he soaped the back of her neck and shoulders. Elena was floating on her back, and he took particular care with her arms and hands, stroking and massaging each finger before moving on to her throat, breasts, and nipples.

"They must be very dirty," she teased, still keeping her eyes closed tightly.

"Filthy." He splashed clean water over her breasts, washing away the suds, then leaned close and kissed her nipples. They puckered into tight pink rosebuds at his touch, and the taste of her made him hard.

She sighed and lay back in his arms. "I think perhaps my belly . . ."

"Just getting to it." He didn't bother with the oil, but continued kissing a trail down over her flat stomach to the triangle of curls at the apex of her thighs. The tension in his groin was growing and he could feel his blood racing.

"Not that, too?" she teased as he stroked her thighs and the folds that hid her sex.

"I'm afraid so," he said. "A terrible case. He was breathing heavily now, and it wasn't from the gravity or the oxygen. He wanted her badly.

Laughing, she twisted out of his arms and splashed his face. "Not so fast," she said. "My turn."

"But I was just . . ."

"On your back," she insisted. "Wait . . . Which leaves do I pick?"

He pointed to another plant growing out from under the bank.

"Lie back. Close your eyes," Elena said.

"I don't think your legs are clean yet."

"Shh. My turn."

He did as he was told, and she began to shampoo his hair as he had done hers. "I don't think—" he began.

"Hush. Fair is fair."

He quickly came to understand how pleasant a bath could be. Elena had a talent for knowing just where to touch him, and her feather-light caresses, the light scratch of her fingernails, and the feel of her breath against his skin soon had him moaning for relief. And when she pressed her lips to his phallus and began to stroke and caress him, it was almost beyond his ability to control his desire.

"No," she said firmly. "Be patient." And when she used her tongue and teeth on him and finally took him in her mouth, they heated the pool to a boiling point.

Elena supposed that they'd slept before awakening to make wild, passionate love again at the base of the waterfall. A curtain of mist surrounded them, making it all seem ethereal, and the sound of the crashing water nearly drowned their mingled cries of passion. Afterwards, they floated together in the pool, and he kissed her over and over and told her that she was the most beautiful woman he'd ever seen.

All her life, Elena had considered herself a private person. She supposed that she'd withdrawn into herself after her father's death. When he was alive, he was the one she'd always talk to; it was never the same with her mother. She'd share her secrets and her dreams with her father, and he'd always listened. He'd never offered advice the way that most adults did with children, and he'd never pointed out how her plans were unrealistic. And once he was gone, she never opened her heart to anyone in the same way again, not to friends, not to her mother, and certainly not to Greg.

Here, in the aftermath of their lovemaking, Elena found herself telling Orion things she would never have revealed to another soul. It was as if she had always known him, as if they had always been part of each other.

"You can't imagine what it was like," she said as they lay drying on the soft bed of moss beside the pool. "I'm good at what I do, but all my professors could see was that I was Randal Carter's daughter, and assume that I'd destroy my reputation as a scholar in the same way my father did."

"Sometimes it's difficult for us to separate ourselves from a famous father."

"I think I share some of his imagination. I just have to remember to keep it from running away with me."

"Such as?"

She laughed. "Since I was a child, I've dreamed of finding Alexander's tomb. It was believed to be destroyed by Caesar's troops when they burned the Roman and Egyptian fleets, but some scholars disagree. Caesar revered Alexander's memory. The body was said to be preserved in honey and encased in an airtight casket of crystal. The casket and the sarcophagus may lie intact at the bottom of the harbor or be buried somewhere in the Valley of the Kings. I'd like to be the one to find it."

"Alexander's tomb? A long shot."

"I know. I told you that I inherited some of my father's romanticism."

"Still, I suppose it's possible. The sea hides many secrets. Why not Alexander's tomb?"

"Exactly. It's why I've devoted my life to seeking out the bits of history that remain on the ocean floor."

For a long time, they lay there, quietly aware of each other, content simply to soak up the peace of the clearing and the tranquil sounds of birdsongs and the waterfall. Finally, Elena broke the silence by asking, "Are your parents living?"

He pushed up on one elbow and a curtain of his yellow hair fell over one eye and half of his face. "Yes. Most decidedly."

She pushed his hair back so that she could look into his beautiful green eyes. "And do you have a good relationship with them?"

"With my mother. With my father, not so much. He can be touchy, and inflexible. He was born believing that he was king."

"I know the type. He sounds much like my mother. She's Italian, of an old family. She's a gifted musician, and her career has always been the most important thing in her life. I'm an only child, and I'm afraid I come in somewhere after her current flame."

"I'm sorry. I was blessed with two good mothers, the one who gave birth to me, and the woman my father married after she died."

"So your mother's dead. How old were you?"

"Young. An accident."

Elena swallowed against the constriction in her throat. Something in Orion's voice warned her not to pry. "I'm sorry," she said. "It must have been difficult for you."

"It was. But you lost a father. You know what it's like. At least you have your mother."

"She took her responsibility seriously, always saw that I had the best boarding schools." She plucked a strand of grass and snapped it between her fingers. *How to explain*

*Chiara that wouldn't make her sound worse than she was?*
"My father was much older than she was. I am what is
commonly referred to as an *accident*. Mother—Chiara—
was something of a free spirit, but I don't believe she ever
wanted children."

"Did she remarry after your father's death?"

"Before, actually. Chiara's been married more times
than I can remember. All of her husbands were wealthy,
and all hopelessly in love with her. She manages to keep
them in her power even after she leaves them for someone
new." She chuckled. "A talent I've never mastered."

"Have you ever been married?"

Elena laughed. "No, although, I have been asked. I'm
not certain I'm the marrying kind of woman."

Orion lifted her hand to his lips and kissed her. "I
thought every woman was the marrying kind."

"You should know better than that."

Elena started and turned toward to see who had spoken. Her eyes widened in surprise. She blinked, not certain
that she wasn't dreaming. But, of course, she was dreaming, wasn't she?

At the edge of the forest stood a white pony with a long,
flowing mane and tail, and on the pony's back sat a child.
No, Elena corrected herself, not a child, a small woman
dressed all in green, a woman more beautiful than Elena
had ever seen.

Elena scrambled to cover herself with her clothing. Neither she nor Orion had bothered to dress after they'd come
out of the pool, and by the shadows, the afternoon had
grown quite late. He seemed to be completely at ease, despite his state of total nudity.

"Brigantia." Orion smiled and executed a courtly bow.
"I was wondering when you'd discover that you had visitors. Elena, this is Brigantia."

Elena struggled to find her voice. The pony looked at her with large, liquid brown eyes, but the beautiful child-woman with the shoulder-length, red-gold hair and the haughty expression kept her attention firmly fixed on Orion.

"You seem to have made yourselves at home," Brigantia said.

Elena couldn't tear her gaze away from her. She had a high, sweet voice, like that of a five-year-old child, and she couldn't have stood much taller than one of seven or eight. She wore a forest green tunic of velvety material, tight leggings that ended in high leather boots, and on her head perched a Robin Hood hat with a red feather. A child-size bow and a quiver of arrows were slung across the back of the saddle. But, strangely, the pony wore no bridle or halter. Brigantia seemed to guide the animal using only the pressure of her knees.

"We've not seen you for a long time," Brigantia continued, still looking at Orion. "And now, you come seeking refuge for this woman, and bringing danger to our world."

"I was hoping you'd see it differently," he said. "I thought you would gladly give her sanctuary."

"At what cost?" She shrugged. "It's not my decision alone. But for me, you can take her home with you."

"Brigantia! Is this any way to greet our guests?" The boughs parted and a second pony, a black one, pushed through into the clearing. The little rider was also female and equally beautiful with long dark hair. Her clothing was much like that of Brigantia's, but on her head, she wore a circlet of wildflowers. She smiled at Orion. "So it's true. It is you. Welcome, Orion. It's been a long time."

He went down on one knee. "Your Majesty. Elena, may I present to you, Olwen, queen of the fairies."

# CHAPTER 17

"Shouldn't we take her to the temple?" Morgan attempted to grasp his wife's flailing hand, but Rhiannon flinched away from him and screamed.

"No! No!" she cried. "I know what you want. What you all want. You want to murder me." Her mouth twisted, and her eyes bulged. "I don't know you!"

"Rhiannon," Morgan said. "Rhiannon, I'm your husband. I love you. I would never harm you."

She bared her teeth at him, and bloody foam dripped from the corners of her mouth. "You can't trick me! I have no husband!" She wrested a hand from the grip of a young priestess and attempted to claw Morgan with her fingernails.

Athena shook her head and waved Morgan away from the bed. "She's still bleeding. If we try to move her, she could lose the child."

"What's wrong with her?" he demanded. "She's never been like this. She was fine when I left this house to meet with the generals. We'd planned an outing with Danu before I have to leave with the troops."

Ismene took the crown prince's arm and led him from the bedchamber. She was one of the oldest living Atlanteans and one of their greatest healers. A small woman with white hair braided into a crown and a thin diadem of silver around her brow, the priestess retained a timeless beauty and carried herself with the grace of someone much younger. "This is no normal illness," she said quietly. "I fear Rhiannon has been bewitched."

Worry etched lines in Morgan's forehead as he glanced back at his wife. "But who would want to hurt her? Rhiannon has harmed no one. She has no enemies."

"Not *her* they wish to hurt, I think," Ismene said, "but *you.*"

He turned his back to the doorway and began to question the healer further about this possible bewitchment in a hushed voice.

Danu slipped between her father and the doorframe to creep close to her mother's couch. Rhiannon lay on a great round bed carved from a marble block and cushioned with thick stuffing and coverlets of the finest Fijian sea grasses. On the headboard were carved sea horses and starfish and shells so rare that they came only from a single beach in all the oceans. Her usually pale green coverlet was woven of the finest material, its pattern one that Danu loved to trace with her fingertips. Not now. Now the beautiful spread was tangled and stained with her mother's blood.

Her mother was sick, maybe dying. Daddy had told her to stay away, that Mommy didn't know what she was doing and she might hurt her, but Danu knew better. Her mother was a royal princess, and the best mother in the world. She told Danu every day how much she loved her. Mommy would never do anything to harm her. Besides, even if there was danger, Danu didn't care. She wasn't a baby. She was five, and she had fought with the dolphins against the bad men. Her mother needed her, and no one would keep her away.

Danu circled to the far side of the bed, climbed up on it,

and scooted to her mother. Mommy was shouting and waving her arms, trying to get out of bed. Lady Athena saw her and her eyes widened. Danu didn't need her to speak to know what she was thinking. Lady Athena was not only a priestess and a healer, but she was Danu's grandmother. That was a secret, and no one could know but Mommy and Daddy and Danu, and Grandmother.

Grandmother knew lots of things that other people didn't. She and Danu could talk to each other without saying stuff out loud. Danu saw that Grandmother was afraid that Mommy would hurt her, and she was going to chase her away from Mommy. But then Grandmother stopped, stared hard at her, and nodded. Immediately, Danu knew that Grandmother understood.

Danu closed her eyes and concentrated until she saw the sparkling green bubbles all around her. The bubbles began to whirl in a big circle. How warm they were. Danu could hear beautiful music coming from the bubbles. She began to sing, not in Atlantean, but in another language, one she hadn't known that she could speak.

Mommy turned her head, and the bad face melted away. She stopped kicking and trying to hit people and lay still. She smiled at Danu and closed her eyes. Her breathing became soft, and she seemed to go to sleep. Danu rose on her knees and pressed two fingers of each hand to the center of her mother's forehead. It was hard to do what she knew she had to. She continued singing and used all her will to make the bubbles go from her head to her mother's.

"Danu!" Her father came back into the room. He looked angry, but Grandmother put a finger to her lips.

"Let the child be," Grandmother said. "See how Rhiannon has relaxed."

Danu didn't take time to explain, partly because she

knew that she needed to keep touching her mother and rubbing her head, and partly because she didn't know the words to tell Daddy what she was doing. She loved him more than anything, but he didn't always understand the things that Grandmother did.

"But she may—" Daddy said, coming toward the bed.

"Hush," Grandmother said. "Your daughter knows what she's doing."

"But how?" one of the young priestesses asked. She was the one that had been trying to hold Mommy down, but hadn't been doing a very good job of it, because Mommy was strong.

Danu ignored the big girl. She studied in the temple with Grandmother, and her name was Ffraid. She was a lot older than Danu, maybe as old as Morwena, but Danu didn't think she knew so much. She was so scared that Danu couldn't understand what she was thinking, only that Ffraid didn't want to be here.

Danu's head began to hurt, but she could feel the green bubbles slipping through her fingers and into her mother's head. Her mother's mouth stopped frowning and turned up in a sleepy smile, but she didn't wake up. Danu stayed by her side until the last of the bubbles slipped down the invisible slide and pushed back the red cloud that had made Mommy angry.

Finally, Danu withdrew her fingers and yawned. She was sleepy, too. She curled up next to her mother and pulled the clean corner of the coverlet over her. She didn't want to leave Mommy, not even for a minute. She wanted to be next to her, as close as she could.

"What just happened?" Morgan stared disbelievingly at his daughter.

Daddy didn't sound mad at her, and that was good. Danu was so tired that she gave him a sleepy smile, closed her eyes, and let the warm happiness lap over her and her mother.

"The bleeding has stopped, Lady Athena," Ffraid said.

Athena rose from the edge of her daughter's bed. "Rhiannon is resting for now. I think the best thing we can do for her is to let her sleep."

"And the baby?" Morgan asked. He dropped to one knee beside the bed and cradled Rhiannon's hand in his. "Do you think the baby will . . ."

"I don't know," she answered. "I've heard of this, but I've never seen it. Danu is a powerful . . ." She shook her head, unable to put a name to what she'd just seen.

"What is she?" Morgan asked. "Priestess? Witch? Fairy?"

"I don't know," Athena said. "What I do know is that we just witnessed a healing of sorts. Priestesses are born with ability, but most of what they know of the arts is learned. Danu is an innocent. Her ability is natural and must be nurtured."

"Is it something humans possess?" he asked. "Is it because she was born an air-breather?"

"The only records of such ability come down to us from long ago. Those children carried the blood of the star men. Perhaps your daughter does as well."

"It's a blessing, isn't it?" he said. "Wherever her powers come from, they've got to be good. She has to be good."

"A sorceress can cause fire to burn in rock and water. She can turn shells to sting rays and build a palace from a handful of sand." Athena raised one fair eyebrow. "A small palace, you understand, but a palace nevertheless. But it might not be permanent. It could wash away on the first tide. What Danu has is the gift of healing. It might be something much more powerful than a sorceress's abilities. We must wait and see if it develops, or if it goes away as Danu gets older."

"But she can help Rhiannon? She *has* helped Rhiannon," he insisted.

"Yes," Athena agreed. "She has brought her mother peace and sleep. But whether that will last when the tide turns, only Zeus knows."

Five more riders nosed their ponies into the little glade by the waterfall. All the young creatures were female, and most wore the same sort of clothing and boots that Brigantia and Olwen favored, although two of the girls—who rode sidesaddle—were in bright-colored, silk dresses with full ruffled skirts. None of the women stood any taller than Elena's shoulder, and most were shorter, but all were beautiful and perfectly proportioned. The fat little ponies with the long manes and tails ranged from red sorrels to bays and palominos. Not a single shaggy animal wore a bridle or halter, and each one was so fuzzy and adorable that Elena longed to pet them.

Elena reached for Orion's hand. This was getting stranger and stranger by the moment. If she didn't know better, which she did, she might begin to believe that these cheerful illusions were fairies, but fortunately, she was a realist. This was as much a part of her dream as the wind tunnel, the sharks, and the giant squid. Still, Orion was solid, and it made her feel better to hold on to him.

One of the little women, a girl in lavender perched on a bay pony with purple ribbons plaited into its flowing mane, guided her mount within an arm's length of Elena and Orion and smiled at them. "Welcome," she said. "I'm Emer, and it would be my pleasure to make you comfortable. If you would please to come with me . . ."

Elena looked at Orion.

"Go ahead," he urged. "You'll be perfectly safe. You must be hungry."

"And she could stand a change of clothing," Brigantia said. "Hers are a disgrace."

Elena's remaining garments did leave much to be desired, but she glanced at Orion again. "You're coming, aren't you?"

"Not to the court," Emer said. Saucy yellow curls bounced as she spoke. "No males are permitted at Olwen's court."

*How odd*, Elena thought. "Thank you," she murmured. "I'll stay with Orion, in that case. I appreciate your hospitality, but . . ."

"He'll come to no harm either," Emer assured her. "Ours is a peaceful kingdom. We haven't cooked or eaten a guest in weeks." She giggled merrily, letting Elena know that she was teasing. "Don't worry about him. The worst Brigantia will do is make him wear a crown of purple daisies." As if the matter was settled, Emer clapped her hands and someone led a piebald pony out of the woods.

"Go ahead," Orion said. "You do know how to ride, don't you?"

"Of course." Her father had seen that she had lessons. He'd insisted that it was part of a lady's education. "But I've never ridden without a bridle," she admitted.

He grinned at her. "That won't be a problem. These ponies are well trained. You only need to think which way you want to go, and they'll take you there."

"As long as it's where it pleases us for you to go." For an instant, Brigantia's pointed little face seemed to reveal hostility, but then she laughed. "Don't worry. The pony is quite gentle."

"His name is Peaches," Queen Olwen said. "He's a favorite of the children."

Elena looked at Emer and back at Orion. She really was hungry, but she didn't want to be on her own tumbling down this rabbit hole. "Promise me you won't run off and leave me," she said to him. Orion was the only solid thing she had to hold on to.

"Word of honor," he said. "Not without proper warning." He caught her around the waist, lifted her into the air, and set her down on the pony's broad back.

To Elena's surprise, the small saddle seemed to mold itself to her shape, making the seat comfortable. Even the stirrups lengthened to fit her longer legs without any of the little people adjusting them. The piebald pony turned his head and glanced up at her through long thick lashes. For a moment, she had the craziest notion that Peaches was going to speak. But instead, it snorted, and pawed the grass impatiently, as if to say, "Let's go."

"Come along," Emer said.

"Yes, do," cried another girl wearing doublet and hose of canary yellow. "I'm Scota, and I'm a cousin to Queen Olwen." Her dark hair was braided in a single long plait, and on her feet, she wore red boots with yellow heels. She looked Elena up and down, and mischief sparkled in her blue eyes. "You're very tall, aren't you? But I think I can find you something fitting to wear."

"That's kind of you," Elena said, introducing herself to the two. "But there's no need for you to put yourselves out. We won't be staying long." *And*, she thought, *this is a dream. When I wake up, my own clothing will be intact.*

Emer laughed again, a bright peal of sound, and her pony turned back out of the clearing. Scota's mount followed, and the little piebald, Peaches, fell in behind them. Elena looked back over her shoulder at Orion. He grinned at her. *He promised he wouldn't leave me without warning*, she thought. *Why doesn't that make me feel any better?*

The three followed the winding path through the thick forest for what seemed like two or three miles before they reached a river and a stone arched bridge. The ponies broke from a walk to a trot as they reached the crest of the bridge, and Elena sensed that they might be nearing the end of their journey.

"There!" Emer said, pointing toward a grove of massive oaks. "Not far now."

The woodland path became wider. It wound through a field of miniature sunflowers that stretched to the right and left as far as the eye could see. Elena cried out with pleasure as she saw the bees and hummingbirds hovering over the golden blooms. Scota seemed equally delighted. She slid from her pony's back and gathered a handful of flowers, quickly weaving them into a floral crown. Shyly, she held it out to Elena.

"I don't think . . ." Elena began.

"No, don't refuse," Emer cautioned. "It would be an insult." She shrugged prettily. "It's an old custom and will show the others that you are a friend."

Scota watched with huge blue eyes. "Not all humans are so," she said. "If Prince Orion brought you, I'm sure you mean us no harm."

"Our history with humans has been long and bitter-sweet," Emer explained.

"I didn't think . . ." Elena felt tongue-tied. What to call them? Orion might say *fairies*, but it might be a joke, and so far she'd seen nothing magical about these unusual little folk. "I assumed that you were not . . . a violent people," she said, all in a rush to cover her embarrassment.

"It's true that our race is a peaceful one," Emer continued. "But for thousands of years, we were persecuted and hunted by the humans, murdered in our homes, or captured and sold into slavery. Our women and young boys were used in the most shameful ways, and when the women quickened with life, they died in attempting to bring forth a half-human child."

"Too big," Scota said. "My own great-great-grandmother died that way. She was kidnapped and held prisoner for weeks. She finally escaped, but it was too late."

"At least she was with her own people at the end," Emer soothed.

"They say she knew a thousand songs and her hands moved over the harp like the wings of a bird. She died too young." Tears welled in Scota's eyes. "Her name was Blathnat." She mounted her pony again and the three rode on toward the towering forest.

As they neared the wood, Elena stared at the giant oaks. They were of a size and age that had once grown in Sherwood in England. The branches grew thick and twisting like great arms reaching into the sky, and when they entered the wood and the trees arched above them protectively, she felt the same sense of peace and awe that she did in an old house of worship.

"Our court is just ahead," Scota said.

Elena didn't know what to expect. Would they live in some sort of quaint village or in a castle? It seemed impolite to ask, so she said, "Why don't you allow men here?"

Emer's chin firmed. "As we have said, we seek a happy and quiet life. What war was ever started by a woman?"

"But Brigantia, Queen Olwen, and some of the others carried bows and arrow quivers," Elena said. "If you don't make war, do you hunt game with bows and arrows?"

"Yes, in a manner of speaking. We are not meat eaters, but this place is rich with rabbits, squirrels, deer, partridge, and wild boar."

"To keep them in check, as nature intended, we brought predators with us," Scota said. "Wolves, wild cats, bear, and fox. Sometimes, it's necessary to protect ourselves from them, so we have become skilled archers. But no fairy may ever take a human life or one of our own, on pain of banishment to the outer earth."

Scota nodded. "It's in a man's nature to crave violence. Men enjoy fighting. They do it for pleasure. When we came here to this new world, there were many more women than men, because our men had fought so hard and long to drive back the humans. It had become their habit to settle all matters with force."

Emer ducked low under a hanging branch, and Elena took care to do the same. "They had acquired many of the ideas of human males," Emer said. "They started making rules about what women could and could not do, and they tried to take away our vote in council."

"So before things got out of hand, we counted noses, took a vote, and decided to live apart from them," Scota said. "It's worked out surprisingly well for us."

"The men just went away? What about your boy children?"

"They live with us until they reach the age of twelve, and then they go to their fathers," Emer explained. "That's the way it's supposed to work, but time here is different. We don't age, so no child has ever had to leave his mother."

"Not one," Scota agreed.

"I see," Elena said. "But how do you procreate? Without men, there can be no children."

"Oh, we have children, aplenty," Elena replied. "As for the pleasures of love . . ." She shrugged again. "There are ways and ways."

"Look!" Scota pointed out what appeared to be an enormous gilded birdcage hanging in the treetops. "There," she said. "Our city."

Elena looked up and saw another and another. "They're so high," she said. "How do you get up there? Fly?"

Emer laughed. "If we could fly, we wouldn't need ponies, would we?"

# CHAPTER 18

The golden birdcage houses were much larger than they appeared on the outside. Much later, after a climb up a dizzying, spiral staircase, Elena was shown through a series of light and airy rooms hung with gauzy draperies into a beautiful chamber that resembled a tiny Roman bathhouse.

Large faces carved in oak representing the four winds adorned the filigree walls, along with others portraying the Green Man of British folklore; Cernunnos, the Celtic deity of the hunt; and a Norn, lovely Urd of the Swans. The pool was not stone or marble, but rather fashioned of shining silver. The benches were green wicker interlaced with growing ivy, and the light was provided by dozens of shimmering firefly creatures with iridescent feathers.

Elena stared at the little beings, trying to decide if they were birds or insects. They fluttered and bounced around the room, hovering over the water, almost like dancing soap bubbles. Entranced, Elena extended her hand, and one of the living candles settled onto her finger. It weighed no more than a pinch of talcum powder. As hard as she tried, she could see no head, or feet, or wings, but the light was so bright and flashed so fast that it was impossible to get a good look. "What are they?" she asked Scota.

"Some humans call them *fairy lights*," she answered. "Others think they are the *Tuatha De Danann*, but they're a much older race, actually an ancestor of the naiads. We know them as . . ." She paused as if searching for the right word. "*Kysii*. In your language, *stardusti*." Her rosy cheeks colored prettily. "Forgive me, Elena. It's so long since I spoke English."

"You have your own language, then?" Elena asked, still admiring the exquisite kysii. "I think it likes me," she said. A warm glow emitted from the light, a warmth that Elena found quite pleasing and made her want to smile.

"Stardusti are thinking beings, but like bees or ants, it's a collective intelligence. As you can see, they're friendly, and of course, drawn to water. We think they came here before time with the star visitors from far away, but their light is said to have healing powers." She smiled mischievously. "And they never need batteries."

"I can believe it." The stardusti rose off her finger and joined the dance of its companions over the bath.

"While you're bathing, I'll see what we can do about finding you something to wear," Scota said. Emer had left them in the entrance way, promising to join Elena later. Several more small women had followed them into the bath, all whispering and giggling and staring at Elena with open curiosity. Scota had chased them all away, telling them that their guest was shy and didn't need help in washing.

"I really don't need another bath," Elena said, looking at the inviting tub. The water smelled like gardenias, not heavy and cloying, but light and sweet. "We swam in—"

Scota giggled. "In the enchanted pool. I'm sure that was Orion's idea, wasn't it?" When Elena nodded, she laughed again. "And then you shared pleasures of the body, did you not?"

"Yes," Elena admitted, feeling her cheeks grow warm.

"Nothing to be ashamed of. That's the spell of the pool. Those who bathe in it become lusty. Anyone would, fairy, human, or Atlantean. I can't say about mer folk. We've never had any of them here. They don't do well out of salt water, but they're much too self-centered to get along with fairies. I think it's because they're a young race, much like overgrown adolescents." She sighed. "Although I hear they are fantastic lovers, at least the mermaids."

*This dream is becoming stranger and stranger*, Elena thought. "Would Orion have known that? About the *unusual* aspects of the pool?" she asked.

"Oh, yes, he would." Scota giggled. "You know how those Atlanteans are. Very sexual beings. And your prince's talents are . . ." She chuckled. "Legendary. In that regard."

"Atlanteans? You said *Atlanteans* are sexual beings."

"Among other things. Atlanteans are very advanced, much more so in some areas than my kind and certainly more so than humans, but sensuality in ingrained in them. What did you think Orion was?"

Elena looked at Scota. "You mean he's an Atlantean? As in Atlantis?"

Scota smiled and nodded, as if Elena were a prize pupil.

Elena exhaled slowly. At least she knew that she was dreaming. She'd been thinking a lot about her father lately. He was the only one who ever talked about Atlantis. Trust her to dream up a hunk of a lover and make him a fish man. She began to undress, which didn't take long, considering the state of what remained of her capris and shirt. She couldn't wait to see what her little friends would come up with for her to wear. A dress made of sunflowers? Maybe a green Robin Hood hat with a feather.

"Go ahead," Scota said. "Don't be shy. The water's lovely."

"This water's not enchanted, is it?"

Scota laughed. "Not for sensual purposes."

"I think I may need that bath, after all. A dash of cold water might set things right." She was still trying to process what Scota had said about Orion being an Atlantean and having legendary sexual prowess.

The bathing pool was a large one, considering that it was located in a tree house and built for little people— more of a hot tub size. Elena walked down the steps leading into the water, and Scota gathered up her discarded clothing. The temperature wasn't cold, but soothingly warm. The water level rose to Elena's waist, but it felt so soft against her skin that she sank down and let it flow over her breasts and shoulders.

"Wait," Scota said. "This fell out of your pocket. You wouldn't want to lose this, I know."

Elena turned toward the little woman, and Scota dropped the heavy gold ring with the strange engraving— the one Elena had discovered in seaweed in the bottom of the boat—into her outstretched hand.

"It's not possible," Elena said. "How could this be here? I left this . . ." Where? Where had she left it? It certainly hadn't been in her capris' pocket. She couldn't think straight. But what stunned her breathless was remembering something else—where she'd originally seen this ring. She'd been only a child, but the image came back to her as clear and vivid as on the day her father had shown her the detailed drawing in his leather-bound site sketchbook. In the years since his death, Elena had often thought of her father's journal and wished she had it, but it had never been seen since the day he'd vanished.

Salt tears clouded Elena's vision. She'd seen the exact likeness of this ring—a ring he claimed to have found in the lost City of Atlantis.

In a circle of sacred rowan trees, before the *Seven*, the ruling council of the kingdom, Orion pleaded for sanctuary for Elena. Queen Olwen was here, wearing nothing but a crown of ivy, likewise Brigantia, Emer, and five other blessed ones that Orion could not place by name. Two had skin as black as ebony, two bore the tint of dark honey in their complexions, and the last was as green as the ivy that trailed from her brow. Orion was the only male present. He had come naked to the circle of rowan, as well. Here, no pretense was permitted; no fine garments or jewels raised one speaker above another.

"We have heard your argument," Brigantia said. "You would leave your human lover here with us while you do battle with Melqart's army."

"I would," Orion said. "With your permission. I would have her safe from harm under your protection."

"But in caring for this human, we would risk much," Emer interjected.

"Perhaps too much," one of the golden-hued girls, who had not spoken before, added her terse opinion.

Orion nodded. "This is neutral ground. Violence has never come to the earth's core."

"Exactly." Brigantia folded her arms across her chest and raised a firm chin. "And you would thrust us into conflict with the Phoenician Lord of War."

Orion glanced at the queen, carefully keeping his features from revealing the uneasiness he felt. Here, in the rowan circle, all votes were supposed to have equal weight, but as with most royalty, that wasn't exactly the case. Some opinions were more equal than others. If Olwen favored his cause, the ballots would likely be cast in Elena's favor.

He'd not expected the fairies to refuse his request. In truth, he hadn't expected them to know about the coming war between Atlantis and Melqart. "He couldn't send his shades here," Orion said. "They can't live in sunlight, and there's no salt water for them to swim in."

Queen Olwen spread her delicate hands. "But the flesh eaters are not the only arrow in Melqart's quiver," she said. "He holds the might of storm, of earthquake, and it is said that he once brought down a mighty Roman city by poison gas and ash."

"Pompeii. But that was long ago," Orion argued. "Melqart's powers have been weakened by time and the turning of the world."

"Are they weaker?" An ebony beauty rose from her wicker throne.

Queen Olwen nodded. "We see you, noble Gambhira, speak your mind."

Gambhira's huge, sloe eyes glittered as cool and hard as sapphires, and her black hair hung to her knees in ringlets. "How do we know that? How do we know he hasn't simply been sleeping? Once, long ago, our kind aided the humans in a battle against him, and Melqart prevailed. His vengeance is still talked about in the dark hours before dawn. Many of our people perished."

"And the humans we died to defend blamed us," the green beauty said. She was the smallest of all the women, and her voice was high and childlike. Her eyes were silver in color, and her long lashes the same rich brown as her short and curly hair.

"And you are?" Orion asked.

"She is Tailtu of the Spring," Brigantia supplied, before

introducing the others. "I assumed you knew the members of the council."

"Ladies." Orion inclined his head to each in turn as Brigantia said her name. "I am honored to be permitted to address you."

"Enough of your flattery," Brigantia said. "We have come here for one purpose."

Tailtu brought her palms together, steepled her fingers in an attitude of deep thought, and leaned forward in her seat. "Atlantean, tell me true. It is said that this Elena that you bring to us robbed Melqart of his temple treasure, and that he has vowed to destroy her."

Olwen stood. "What of your father, mighty Poseidon? Is it his wish that we shelter this woman from Melqart's wrath? For we owe his line of kings much. We could never have come to this place of new beginnings if not for the nobility of Atlantean kings."

"Do you come in Poseidon's name?" Emer demanded.

Orion shook his head. "No. I don't. This is my doing."

"Why?" Olwen asked.

"It's a matter of honor," he said. "Elena saved my life, and I owe her."

"So you deny that you have a more personal relationship with her?" Brigantia said.

"No." Orion inhaled deeply. He was in deep water here, and he knew it. What he didn't know were his feelings for Elena.

Emer rose to her feet. "We know the two of you are lovers. What we desire to know is if your feelings for her are more than sexual."

"I don't see what bearing my relationship with Elena has on my request for sanctuary for her," he said.

"It means a good deal," Olwen replied softly. "Do not forget that we are all female, and what is most important to a woman is not always of the same importance to one of your gender. I charge you, Orion, look into your heart and tell us. Do you love this human enough to take her as your life companion or not?"

Morwena had lost all track of time. She drifted between consciousness and a deep troubled sleep that seemed to suck her down and hold her in a cold trance. She wanted to be awake, and even the fear of not being able to move didn't keep her from fighting to maintain a clear mind. Most of all, she had to keep reminding herself that Halimeda didn't want her dead. If the witch had, she would be dead already, her body disposed of, and no trace left of her passing. Her father's wife wanted something of her or something of him.

Sealing her in this tomb was mental torture, something Halimeda took joy in. Morwena would rather die than go mad as her tormentors surely were. She would survive, no matter what it took. She wouldn't give the witch the pleasure of getting the best of her.

To pass the time, Morwena went over the prayers and songs she had learned in the temple. She pictured in her mind each step of the rituals that she'd witnessed, and she savored every memory, every smell and color. These memories were as clear salt water to a scorched soul. If she could remember the words and notes of a hymn or the healing properties of different seaweeds, shellfish, and mosses, she didn't need food. Instead, she filled her starving body with wisdom, and she was satisfied.

But not knowing how many turns of the water clock had passed was difficult. She could not sit or lie down; there wasn't room in the enclosed space. She could only stand and sometimes rest her head against the rough stone wall at her back. The paralysis had worn off, but she remained weak and disoriented.

Surely, her family and friends had missed her. Were they searching the palace for her? Did they believe that she'd gone away without telling anyone? But she had when she and Leda had gone to help Orion. Her brother would think she was safe at home. Would Alexandros and the others think she was still with Orion? It was a question that troubled her, and she didn't like to dwell on it.

Often she thought of Freyja, her dolphin. She had been so sweet, so faithful, so brave. How many times had she and Freyja faced danger together, and how many times had she ridden to the far reaches of strange waters on her friend's back? Morwena's heart ached for the dolphin.

Freyja hadn't lived out her lifespan. She was young, only thirty-five, and most of her kind lived to seventy and longer. Morwena had raised other dolphins before Freyja, and she knew that they were mortal creatures. Yet, Atlanteans had continued to give their love freely and share their lives with dolphins for tens of thousands of years, knowing that the bonds of affection would be broken over and over by death.

Morwena could almost hear Freyja's excited clicks, see in her mind's eye the beautiful head and intelligent gaze of her friend. Morwena couldn't believe that Freyja was really dead. It would be like Halimeda to tell her that the dolphin had been murdered just to bring her pain, but if Freyja was alive, she would have found her by now. Dolphins had amazing psychic abilities, abilities that went far beyond those of Atlanteans. And Freyja's absence made Morwena's hope for the dolphin's survival fade. "If they've hurt you, I'll make them pay," Morwena swore. "I will. I promise you, Freyja. They will pay in full measure."

At first, when she heard the muted sound of mortar being chipped away, Morwena thought she was dreaming. She had dreamed of rescue again and again. Now, as the sounds echoed through her prison, she gritted her teeth, and tried not to listen.

"Morwena? Are you alive?"

She shuddered. She knew the voice—her half-brother Caddoc.

"Speak to me, my sweet."

Another stone fell, and light filtered into her tomb. She steeled herself. Whatever had possessed Caddoc to break down the wall, it couldn't be good. Either he was acting on his mother's orders, or . . . Or, what? Why would he dare Halimeda's displeasure? Was it possible that he had some scrap of honor left? That he couldn't be a willing participant in her murder?

"My mother has plans for you, Morwena."

She clenched her hands. If the opportunity came for escape, she must not miss it. But, she was weak, so weak. She could swim. If she couldn't stand, she could swim. But could she swim fast enough to evade Caddoc? Had he come to release her from this cell only to drag her to another?

A larger block tumbled away. Caddoc grinned at her, and the last faint hope that he might have come to help her dried up. She knew that smile from his childhood. She had seen it before he'd pulled the legs off a living octopus or yanked a baby sea horse from a smaller boy's hand.

Caddoc was like his mother in that he enjoyed seeing others in pain. People or sea creatures, it didn't matter. Only dolphins were safe from his mischief. All his life, Caddoc had feared dolphins. Morwena believed it was because they could see past his handsome face and smooth lies to the evil within.

Another stone came loose. Her brother reached in and grabbed her arm. He dragged her free of the stone cavity, and held her up to stare into her face. "Rested, are you, sister? Was it peaceful enough for you in there?"

Without the support of the stone wall, her legs didn't have the strength to hold her upright. She sagged forward and would have fallen, but he caught her again. "Are you grateful, Morwena? How grateful?" He leered at her, grabbed her breast and squeezed it crudely.

She screamed, and when he tried to clamp a hand over her mouth, she bit him until blood ran. He slammed her back against the stones. Pain shot through her head, and the room spun. Her knees buckled. He yanked her hard against him, his fingers digging into her flesh, and slipped hard fingers between her legs.

Morwena groaned. He was strong, so strong. She would have to use all her wits to best him. "No need to be so rough," she said. "Why didn't you tell me you wanted to play?"

He lowered his head and ground his mouth against hers. She swallowed her bile, stretched and strained until her hand closed on the dagger at his belt.

"What—" he shouted.

She was too quick for him. She slipped the knife from his sheath and jabbed up, driving the blade into his midsection. "Take that, you bastard!" She spat the taste of him away and twisted the knife in his side.

Shrieking, Caddoc knocked the weapon from her hand and clutched at his wound. "You stabbed me!" He stared down in disbelief as blood seeped through his fingers.

Morwena turned toward the door and saw that it stood open. She dodged around Caddoc's flailing arms and swam for the portal—straight into the Samoan's arms.

Struggling against him, she screamed again, and her cry echoed down the long corridor.

"Shut her up!" Caddoc called.

Tora laughed and threw her at Caddoc. She continued to scream until her brother wrapped both hands around her throat and squeezed. Terrified, Morwena struck at his face and head with her fists. He tightened his choke hold. Black spots danced before her eyes. She gasped for breath and slammed a knee into his groin.

From far off, Morwena heard the garbled sounds of Tora's laughter. Gagging, Caddoc forced her to her knees. Her lungs burned, and her struggle weakened. He bent her back, squeezing, squeezing.

Morwena's head lolled back, and her eyes rolled up in her head. Caddoc cursed and flung her against the wall. Her head struck a protruding section of stone with a dull thud, and she slid limply down to float above the paving stones.

"Get her up!" Caddoc whined. "We've got to seal her back in the wall before my mother . . ."

Tora reached for Morwena's body, dropped to his knees and gathered her in his arms. Her head fell back at an unnatural angle. A trail of dark blood clouded the water. The Samoan raised his gaze to meet Caddoc's and grimaced.

"What's wrong?" Caddoc asked.

Tora shook his head and released Morwena's corpse.

"She's dead? She can't be dead!" Caddoc stared down at her lifeless form.

Tora shrugged, and turned for the door.

"You can't leave me with her!" Caddoc cried. "What will I tell my mother?"

The big Samoan kept going and didn't look back.

# CHAPTER 19

.

Greg Hamilton was beginning to think that he was more like his father than he'd ever wanted to imagine. How could he have been so stupid as to buy Elena a diamond ring without having her agree to marry him first? And when she tried to give the ring back, why hadn't he taken it?

Walking away from her might be a cavalier thing to do, but it wasn't smart. The diamond had set him back more than twenty-five thousand dollars, and buying it had been impulsive. There'd be no denying it. He'd put the damned thing on the company credit card—a card that his father, the company president, had already threatened to cancel.

What if Elena wouldn't marry him? What if she sold the ring and used the money for this latest stupid project? Never mind that he'd told her to do just that. It was big talk, something to say when she'd shocked him by refusing to commit to his proposal of marriage. And now, here he was on Crete with a night at leisure, and no woman to share it.

He'd told Elena that he had to be on the ship in the morning, but that wasn't exactly the truth. The Greek government was giving them a load of shit about the area they wanted to investigate—so much so that the ship was still anchored in some harbor he couldn't pronounce the name of. Typical red tape of dealing with a third world country. Someone claimed that the company didn't have the proper clearance for the drilling. Probably they'd bribed the wrong official, or hadn't offered him enough. At least his father couldn't blame that on him. That was shit for the company lawyers to sort out.

But here he was with money in his pocket, a hard-on, and a powerful need to get extremely drunk. Who the hell did he know in Crete? Or in Greece for that matter? At home, there were a dozen women he could have called, and the phone book was full of pros. As his father liked to say, pros were safe, at least the high-class ones. They didn't smell, they didn't tell, and they could fuck like hell. In Texas, he'd have had no trouble ordering just what he wanted. But on Crete?

Cheap whores could be found in any taverna, but he'd always been fastidious. He wanted clean and he wanted a woman with whom he could walk into a casino with her on his arm and have heads turn and other men wishing they were Greg Hamilton. Plus, he had to admit, he liked the idea of paying for prime snatch. It was an honest trade. They would do anything he asked, barring sadism, which he'd never been into, and once he walked out the door, she was history.

He supposed he could blame the habit on his father. He'd bought him his first whorehouse experience when he'd turned sixteen. They'd flown west for a little father-son bonding. . . . First elk hunting in Wyoming, which had been a bust. They'd frozen their asses off without seeing an elk worth shooting, had camped in the snow, and drank the worst excuse for coffee he'd ever tasted. The food had been bad, and the whiskey cheap. Luckily, the second part of the trip, the poontang at the Muskrat Ranch in Nevada, had been better. When his father explained that this was his son's first time, the madam had fixed him up with a hot Asian number named Mercedes. Four hours with her had been worth riding over half of Wyoming on a cow-gaited mustang.

He wondered where little Mercedes was now. Tight as his father's accountant, that woman. He thought about going back to Elena's house and trying to talk his way in for the night. Maybe, if he gave her some story about the hotels being full, she'd take pity on him. Once he was in her bedroom, he doubted she would hold out long. A few drinks, a little sweet talk, and he'd be home free.

Greg pulled out his cell and started to punch in Elena's number, but then he hit the power button. Damned if he'd run back to her begging like a dog with his tail between his legs. To hell with Elena Carter. And he'd have the ring back, too. If nothing else, he'd have one of the firm's lawyers write a letter demanding she return it.

He walked a little farther along the street. Eighties' disco music poured from a small club on the corner. His mouth was dry. He wanted to go in, have a few drinks, be with people that appreciated him, but they were all strangers. Foreigners. Probably all Greeks with a scattering of German and Japanese tourists. For all he knew, it might be Bee Gee's night.

And then he remembered someone he did know—someone who was on this godforsaken island. Michelle. Her number was already in his cell. As an employee of the company, she was expected to be on duty 24-7.

She picked up on the second ring.

"Michelle?"

"Oh, hi, Greg."

"What are you doing?"

"Just getting in the shower. I was at the beach all afternoon, and I'm all sun lotion and salt."

"Where are you?"

She named a hotel. Nothing but the best for his father's people, all expenses paid, of course.

"What room number?"

She laughed and answered in a sultry Texas drawl that made him homesick. "Why? Want to join me?"

"I like my water hot."

"So do I, Greg. I like everything hot."

"Order a couple of steaks from room service, and a bottle of decent Scotch."

"Macallan 25? Right?"

"You know what I like."

She laughed again. "I think I do. I think I know exactly what you like."

Athena rose and smiled as Prince Morgan came into the bedroom where his wife and daughter lay in a deep sleep. "The bleeding has stopped," she announced. "And Rhiannon's color is much better."

"Does that mean she won't lose the baby?" Morgan approached the bed.

Athena shook her head. "It's too soon to tell, but it's certainly promising. She seems to be sleeping peacefully, not thrashing around as she was. Did you find the intruders?"

"No, nothing." Morgan brushed the hair away from Rhiannon's face, leaned down and kissed the crown of her head. "No more incidents?"

"None, but both she and Danu seem exhausted."

"I'm still not sure it's right to leave Danu here beside her. What if Rhiannon wakes suddenly and is out of her head again? She could harm Danu seriously." Morgan rested his hand on his sword hilt. "I've informed Poseidon of what's happened. He was furious. You know how he dotes on Danu. The king has put all palace guards on alert. Troops are searching the city."

"Yes, but for whom?" his mother-in-law asked. "How would the guards know if they came upon the guilty culprits? It was no shade who came here and bewitched the princess." It had been on the tip of Athena's tongue to say *my daughter*, but they were not alone. Other healers had come to share in Rhiannon's care, and their relationship wasn't commonly known.

Rhiannon, once known as Claire when she lived a human life, had been born to her as the result of a torrid love affair with Rhiannon's human father. That romance was long over, Richard dead and in his grave, but if it became common knowledge, she, Athena, would have to answer for breaking the law. For many years, she had waited and wondered about her daughter, hoping that someday, she would return to the sea. Now, she had. Rhiannon was a mother herself and wife to the crown prince of Atlantis. No need to remind the king or the people of her human origin. She was an Atlantean now, and Athena was part of her daughter's life and that of her family.

As much as Athena loved little Danu, she longed to be present when this new grandchild was born. She wanted to deliver Rhiannon's baby and to watch the new soul take its first strokes. That someone would try to murder the babe in the womb filled her with anger. She would find out who wished Rhiannon and Morgan's son ill and she would have her revenge. This child, if it lived, would be a boy and direct heir to the throne of the kingdom. And whoever had dared to threaten the dynasty would live to regret their evil.

"I believe it's safe to move the princess to the temple now," Athena said.

"Why shouldn't she remain here with me?" Morgan asked.

"In the temple, Rhiannon will be under the protection of hundreds of minds. No evil will touch her there. Besides, you lead your troops into battle. You won't be here to watch over her."

"And Danu? Who will protect her? I can't leave her in these quarters with only the servants to watch over her." He began to pace back and forth. "I don't want to leave them. I'm not afraid to die, but if I do . . ."

"If you should fall in battle, your wife and children will be honored and cared for. You know what the princess means to me, and what your small daughter means. As for the unborn child, we can only hope for his survival. But he comes of strong parents. It may well be that whatever evil attempted to destroy him, he will overcome it."

"He?" Hope flickered in Morgan's eyes. "It's a son? I have a son?"

"The Creator willing, you will have a son, perhaps many sons."

"If Rhiannon can be healed."

"If Danu can heal her," Athena said softly. "Her gift of healing is the most pure I've ever witnessed in a child. If her desires follow her ability, she belongs in the temple. She will be a great asset to the kingdom."

"Only if it is her wish," Morgan answered. "She is as precious to me as if I fathered her."

"You, of all people should know that a father is more than the sperm donor. A true father is one who loves and nourishes the child."

Morgan nodded. "I'd not force her into any path she doesn't want. It's not easy to become a priestess."

"Yet your sister Morwena seeks it."

He nodded. "No one could force Morwena into anything she didn't want. That one has a strong will."

Athena smiled. "And you don't? I believe Poseidon is fortunate to have such sons and daughters." She glanced at the sleeping Danu. "And such grandchildren. Go and do what you must, Prince Morgan. They will be waiting for you when you return."

"All three? Rhiannon and my son and daughter?"

"I'll use all my skill and wisdom to make it so." She shook her head. "I don't do magic. Well you know it. I but follow the old ways and try to teach the young ones the same."

"You're right. My brothers and father will be waiting. And my generals. Kiss Danu for me, and tell her . . . tell her that I love her and that she's to be a good girl and take care of her mother."

He started for the door, then paused, and looked back. "You've not seen Morwena, have you? She'll have my head if I go off to war without bidding her good-bye."

Athena shook her head. "No, I haven't, but I'm sure that Morwena will come to the inner chambers when she hears that Rhiannon is ill. I'll tell her that you asked for her."

"I hope Morwena hasn't done anything foolish. I wouldn't be surprised to find her among the assembled troops, bow and quiver in hand, ready to do battle with Melqart's shades."

Caddoc carried Morwena's body, wrapped in his cloak, through a shadowy and rarely used passageway in the bowels of the palace until he came to a waste shaft. He laid the bundle on the floor, unwrapped it, and stripped her of the remains of the clothes she'd been wearing. Then, he dropped the naked corpse into the rushing channel that carried the contents of toilets and kitchen matter into the garbage area some distance from the city wall. Sharks and other scavengers gathered there. With luck, his little sister would vanish, hair, skin, and bone, and no one would ever know what had happened to her.

A pity, really, that she'd died so easily. He would have liked to have made some use of her before his mother offered her to Melqart as a sacrifice. What difference did it matter to Melqart if Morwena was virgin or not? It wasn't as if there'd have been an inspection of the merchandise. Caddoc had seen offerings executed before. Usually, it was a shoddy affair, carried out in a hurry so that the priests who served the dark lord could be about their own business.

Caddoc slid the flat stone back in place and examined his cloak for telltale blood. It was a good cloak, fashioned of expensive material. He would have hated to dispose of it, but it seemed fine. Now, he'd have to busy himself elsewhere until his mother got over her pique at finding her little princess gone. If he wasn't here, he wouldn't have questions to answer, and he couldn't be blamed. The fault wasn't his, anyway. Tora should have held on to her.

If Morwena hadn't attacked him viciously, he wouldn't have been so angry, and she might be still alive. But he would shed no tears over the haughty little bitch. *Good riddance,* he thought. Another of Poseidon's useless get out of his way. When he, Caddoc, was king, he'd have as many women as he wanted, all prettier and more willing than Morwena.

Just thinking about what he might have done to her excited him. He'd have to find a substitute soon. But first, he had to put distance between himself and Atlantis. Tora was always going on about how wonderful Samoa was.

Maybe they should go there. The island girls were said to be easy, and who better to fulfill their dreams than an Atlantean prince?

Holding the golden ring tightly in her hand, Elena sank into the tub and closed her eyes and sighed deeply. The gardenia-scented water, strangely buoyant, bubbled around her, warm and relaxing. She could feel the tension seeping out of her body and soothing the turmoil in her mind.

Scota lifted a silvery cord from around her neck. "Perhaps you would like to put your ring on this," she suggested. "That way it won't be lost in the tub."

Elena nodded, opened her eyes, and watched as the dainty little woman threaded the cord through the ring, looped it, and slid it over her head.

"Now, it will be safe," Scota said. "If you want anything, just call. The girls will be happy to serve you in any way you wish." She hesitated. "*Any* way at all."

"No, thank you," Elena replied, rubbing the heavy ring between her fingers. "I don't want to seem rude, but I'd like to be alone, if you don't mind."

"As you please, but they are very skilled at massage."

"No," Elena said. "I'm fine." Only a few of the twinkling stardusti remained to illuminate the tub area, leaving the rest of the room in deep shadows. The flickering lights were almost mesmerizing, and just watching them caused a delicious surge of contentment in her chest.

"I'll tell the girls to wait outside in the passageway. If you change your mind, you have only to call out," Scota said. "You are our honored guest. We want you to be . . ."

"Just the bath."

Scota giggled. "If you wish it. Take as much time as you like."

Elena held her breath, listening, as Scota padded away,

leaving her blessedly alone with her thoughts. Cushions were heaped at one end of the tub, and, still fingering the ring, Elena scooted back to rest her head and neck. Unanswered questions tumbled in her mind. The ring, with its mysterious carvings, seemed to give off pulsing warmth, almost as if it were a source of power. Was it her imagination, or was it possible that this could be the same ring that her father had drawn in his sketch book? And if it was, how had it appeared here in her pocket?

Somehow, she felt that Orion was the key, but that was only a wild hunch. As a scientist, she'd been taught not to make assumptions, but to rely on only that which could be backed up with solid proof. Still, both Orion and this place defied all logic. And the intense attraction he had for her was both magical and an enigma. Orion couldn't exist . . . and yet . . . he was as real as her own right hand.

Everything that had happened to her in the past few days was perplexing and wonderful. And somehow, she felt that if she could understand how the ring had returned to her, the puzzle fragments might come together to make sense. Her gut instinct told her that this ring was an important link to Orion and to her father. And . . . in some crazy way, perhaps the ring was a clue as to what had happened to her father in his last hours.

Weariness made trying to make sense of everything even more difficult. With a sigh, she released the ring and allowed it to dangle securely between her breasts. Closing her eyes, she allowed the warmth of the bath to ease her tension. She might have drifted off, but the next thing she knew, someone was gently massaging her temples.

Elena started awake, opened her mouth to protest, but groaned instead. Whoever her bath attendant was, she had marvelous fingers. Ribbons of pure pleasure unfurled over

Elena's scalp and down the back of her neck. "Umm," she murmured. "That feels wonderful."

"Did you call for us?" came a lilting voice from the corridor. "Is there something more you need?"

"No," Elena answered. The magical fingers had moved up and back, rubbing her scalp in tight, circular motions. She groaned as the invisible attendant concentrated her attention on the nape of Elena's neck and the base of her skull.

Elena had always enjoyed professional massage as a way to relax after a particularly grueling expedition, but when Scota had offered the services of the girls, Elena had assumed that the little woman was referring to something more intimate than a neck rub. But this was fantastic. "You know all the spots," she said.

Orion leaned close and whispered in her ear. "I hope so."

Elena gasped and would have cried out, but he seized her shoulders, twisted her toward him, and stifled her surprise with a demanding kiss. In a heartbeat, without breaking the kiss, he slipped soundlessly into the tub and pulled her into his arms.

She clung to him, inhaling his scent, reveling in the hard body pressed against hers. "I thought you couldn't be here," she managed when their mouths parted, "but I'm glad you are. So glad . . ."

"Shh," he warned. "We can't let them find me." He motioned toward the gently blowing curtains that separated the bathing room from the passageway. "We have to be very quiet."

"But how did you . . ." He cut her off with another kiss, and she was swept up in the fire of his touch. His strong fingers moved over her, touching, stroking, teasing her nipples and sending shivers of desire through her body. The bath, the chamber, the strange land of little people and magical fireflies faded before the intensity of the sensations that rocked her as their kisses deepened and all her inhibitions fell away.

An exquisite sweet heat seared her wherever Orion's skin touched hers. She couldn't get close enough, couldn't get enough of stroking and tasting him, of feeling the excitement of having him in her arms. His rigid erection pulsed heat, driving the fatigue from her muscles, instantly inflaming her with a burning need to have him deep inside her.

When he'd made love to her in the sanctuary, she'd believed that nothing could equal that experience, but here and now, the world fell away and left them as if they were the first man and woman ever to come together.

"We'll have to be very quiet," he whispered, before slanting his mouth over hers and nibbling at her lower lip.

His breath was warm on her face. She was conscious of how fast her heart was racing as she leaned even closer. "What will they do if they catch you here?"

"Try to kill me." A warm hand closed over her breast, and Orion teased her nipple with the ball of his thumb. "I see you're taking good care of my ring."

"Your ring?" Her voice sound breathy in her ears.

"Yours now."

His strong hands moved over her, sending shivers of delight from the crown of her head to her toes. "I don't want you to put yourself in danger for me."

"But you're glad I'm here?"

"Yes."

He chuckled. "Beautiful Elena." Catching the lobe of her left ear between his lips, he bit gently, sending another jolt of electricity through her.

She inhaled sharply and pushed him away so that she could stare directly into his eyes. "Why did you come if you knew you would be in danger?"

"Because I couldn't bear to be away from you." He lowered his head to kiss her throat and the hollow between her breasts. "I kept thinking of what I wanted to do to you . . . to have you do to me." He lifted her breast and suckled at the taut nipple until she wanted to scream with pleasure.

"I want you, too," she whispered into his ear. "But not at the risk of your life."

"I suppose it depends on how good you're going to be to me . . . or how bad."

"Tell me about the ring? Where did it come from? Why . . ." She trailed off as Orion kissed and suckled her other breast. It was hard to think, let along talk rationally, when he was making love to her.

She reached for him, and smiling, he ducked beneath the surface of the water. She gasped as he captured her right foot and nibbled his way slowly up her ankle and calf to the inside of her knee. And each time he brushed her skin with his tongue or nipped at her flesh with his strong teeth, she fought to contain whimpers of raw lust.

He lifted his head above the water. "Shall I kiss you here? Or here?" His teeth closed on her inner thigh and she gasped, digging her fingers into his shoulders, nuzzling his hair, and burying her face in his neck.

She glanced toward the doorway where the gauzy curtains stirred. This was crazy. He shouldn't be here. She shouldn't let him be here. At any second, Scota or one of the others might return and find them together. No amount of physical pleasure was worth Orion's life, but . . . She gritted her teeth to keep from moaning aloud. What he was doing to her felt so good.

And all the while, she had no claim to innocence. Her

own hands were busy, her fingers stroking the contours of his broad chest and massive shoulders, and caressing the thick, muscular column of his beautiful neck. And his un-bound hair was a curtain of liquid gold that brushed and tantalized the surface of her skin until she wanted to bury her face in it and inhale his scent.

It was impossible to remain still under his assault. She squirmed and her breathing became ragged and quick as the aching between her thighs intensified. But Orion showed her no mercy. He kept kissing and licking, and bit-ing, slowly working his way toward the source of her hunger.

"Do it!" she urged him. "I can't wait."

When his mouth touched her pubic bone, she came. In-tense contractions of sweet pleasure rippled through her body and she clamped a hand over her mouth to keep from screaming. But before her climax retreated, Orion began to kiss and touch her slick folds. She shivered as his hard tongue invaded her body, and before she could catch her breath, she dissolved in yet another incredible release.

Laughing softly, he surfaced, rolled onto his back and pulled her on top of him. "Mount me," he urged.

Trembling with desire, tears rolling down her cheeks, she eased onto his swollen erection. He was so big that, for an instant, she thought that she couldn't take all of him, but somehow she did. Once they had come together, her desire kindled afresh. She clamped her legs around him and rode him hard, giving as good as she received. Her ex-citement rose to fever pitch before, finally, she felt him shudder beneath her. She lowered her mouth to his, and for one long moment, they were one.

The wave crested and broke, and she collapsed onto his chest, weeping and laughing, forgetting the need to remain silent. Orion cradled her in his arms and kissed her. He whispered into her ear, and long sweet notes of joy unfurled through her body.

She clung to him. "Don't leave me," she murmured.

"I have to. I have things that must be said . . . must be done. And it's safer for you if you don't remember that I was here."

"You think I could ever forget this?"

He chuckled and kissed her bruised lips. "You will," he promised. Then he pressed his palm to her forehead and she heard a shower of tinkling bells, so faint that she wasn't certain it wasn't her imagination.

"Orion?" She looked around the pool. Had he been here? She'd been so sure that they had made fantastic, glorious love. She could still smell his scent, feel his touch on her skin, and still feel the echo of sensation in her veins.

Or had she dreamed him? Suddenly, she felt sleepy. Her eyelids seemed weighed down. She climbed from the pool, wrapped a towel around herself, and lay down on a soft bed of heaped evergreens. Almost before her head hit the cushions, she heard Scota's voice.

"Your food is ready. It's best if you don't remain too long in the bath. The effects of the water can be overwhelming for someone not used to it."

Elena forced her eyes open. "Could I rest here for just a few minutes?"

"If it pleases you." Scota smiled at her. The little woman touched Elena's forehead. "You seem feverish. I hope we didn't let you stay in the water too long. You must be very tired. It's natural for visitors to be somewhat disoriented. Do you feel unwell?"

"No." Elena shook her head. "Just . . ." *How did she feel?* It seemed that there was something that had occurred in the bath, but . . . She sighed. Maybe Scota was right, and she was disoriented. "Just let me lie here for a while longer," she said.

"Did you find the bath water refreshing?" Scota asked. "Most do."

"Yes . . ."

"Don't be concerned if your mind seems to play tricks on you. Our oxygen content is not quite the same as yours on the surface on the earth. What you breathe here is richer, purer. It can have the same effect as strong wine."

"Oh." Elena smiled. "I thought . . . that is, I think I was dreaming . . ."

Scota chuckled. "The water is most conducive to dreams of a passionate nature."

"But you said that this water was different from the pool where Orion and I . . ."

Scota shrugged and spread her hands. "They are different. The pool makes the swimmer lusty. The bath is said to fire the imagination." She giggled. "The girls will come in to rub you with scented oil and brush your hair. Please accept their assistance. You are such a novelty to us, and they would be quite hurt if you don't allow them to make you comfortable."

"Thank you," Elena said. "You've all been very kind."

After her bath, Elena was escorted to a room high in the trees where trays of fruit and vegetables, bowls of honey and cheese, and a wonderful braided loaf of bread were waiting. There was a bed piled high with pillows, a silken coverlet, and a gown of forest green embroidered in silver thread that fit her perfectly. "How did you find clothes big enough for me?" she asked between bites of bread and honey.

"We had it made while you were bathing," Scota explained. "Is it to your liking?"

"It is," Elena said. The stitching was so fine that she could barely see the thread, and the material was so soft and light that it seemed spun of spider's web. "It's beautiful." The garment was laced up the front with silver cord. One shoulder was bare, and the skirt fell to mid-thigh. There were high leather boots in a paler green, a necklace of green stones, and dangling earrings of silver fashioned into the likeness of acorns. "You've all been very kind, but I'd like to see Orion. I need to talk to him."

"After you've rested," her hostess said. "Please, drink and eat as much as you like. When you wake, I'll take you to him."

"Thank you."

"And do have the nectar," Scota said, indicating a crystal pitcher. "It will restore your strength and ease your aches. Rest now. You're safe here."

Elena picked at a slice of melon and some fat strawberries glistening with dew. She sipped at the nectar and found the drink fantastic. A bit of cheese, another slice of bread and honey, and she found her eyes growing heavy. She would lie down on the bed for just a few minutes, but she wouldn't sleep. She really did want to see Orion. She would just . . .

Almost at once, Elena fell into a deep sleep. How long she slept, she didn't know, but when she woke, it was night and the stardusti fluttered around her bed. She sat upright, rubbed her eyes, and saw that Scota was sitting cross-legged on a silken cushion watching her.

"I didn't mean to sleep so long," Elena said. She felt wonderful. No drowsiness clouded her thoughts. She rose and drew on the silk stockings and the soft leather boots. "I'm ready now, if you would please take me to Orion."

"Of course," the little woman agreed. "You are the nicest human I've ever met." She laughed, a merry bubbling burst of sound. "Of course, you're the only human I've ever met. If more were like you, I think we might still be living in our old homelands."

"I like you, too," Elena said, rising to go to her new friend. "I don't think I've ever met anyone like you either . . . a . . ."

Scota giggled. "You can say it. Fairy. I'm a fairy. We're all fairies."

Elena laughed. "You're a dream is what you are. Fairies don't exist."

"Keep telling yourself that." Scota opened a gate at the outer rim of the room. "It's a long way down," she warned.

"Should I have put on the boots?"

"Oh, you don't have to walk. Follow me." And before Elena could question her, Scota sat down, gave herself a push, and disappeared. Elena came to the gate and looked. A bright silvery slide lay beneath her.

"In for a penny," Elena said. "It's no stranger than the rest of this dream." And she sat on the edge of the slide, caught her breath, and let go. The ride to the bottom of the tree was exhilarating, not frightening at all. When she arrived breathless at the bottom, she was squealing with delight. She popped out of the tunnel or tube or whatever it was and landed in a heap of what looked like over-sized cotton puffs.

Again, Scota was waiting, this time with the ponies. Elena mounted Peaches again, and the two rode away from the city of gilded birdcages and the fluttering lights of the stardusti. They rode out of the forest and into the field of sunflowers, lit now by moonlight. They didn't speak, and the only sound was that of the little ponies' hoof beats on the road.

Orion stood with Brigantia and several other women

that Elena didn't know on the far side of the bridge. "Orion," she called as the pony approached.

Orion's features were in shadow, but she could sense his tension.

"Elena? Are you well?" he asked stiffly.

"Yes, I'm well. What's wrong?" She glanced at Brigantia, but the woman's face was impossible to read.

"We have to leave this place," Orion said. "The fairies have denied you sanctuary. I have to take you back."

"Take me back where?" Elena asked. "I don't understand."

"You may not remain here," Brigantia said. "The two of you must leave, at once."

"You realize that you're putting her life in danger." Orion stared at Brigantia. "You may be sending Elena to her death."

"Then you must do all you can to prevent it, Prince of Atlantis," Brigantia replied. "And if she is lost, the fault will be yours, not ours."

# CHAPTER 20

"I don't understand what's happening," Elena said as Orion took her hand and led her back into the pond. "I've got new leather boots on. The water will ruin them. At least give me time to take them off."

"The water won't hurt your boots or your dress," he said. "They are virtually indestructible. And I can't take the time to explain now. If I did, you still wouldn't understand. The fairies have given us only a few minutes to leave, and we have to go."

"But why?" she asked. "I like it here. You're not getting me back in that wind tunnel thing."

"I'm afraid that's exactly where we're going."

"No." She dug her heels into the sand and tried to pull away. "You have to give me answers. I won't be dragged away like—" She yelled in protest as Orion grabbed her and threw her over his shoulder. "Put me down, you big oaf! Don't think you can bully me!"

She might as well have tried to pit her strength against that of a bull. Orion, usually so gentle with her, so sweet and reasonable, was an immovable object. "Stop it!" she cried. "You can't just drag me away like a cave man!" But he could—and did. In seconds they were in water that rose to his shoulders, and then closed over her head.

The next thing she knew, they were back in the tunnel, only this time, Orion held her tightly against him. She tucked her head into his shoulder, held on with all her might, and closed her eyes. Eventually, the tornado spit them out, and she found herself standing alone on a street corner in Rethymo in the gathering dusk.

Shaken, Elena leaned against the wall of a restaurant. She was lightheaded. Her thoughts tumbled in her head, her eyes couldn't seem to focus. Her mind was a total blank. For the life of her, she couldn't recall her own name or where she was going.

"Are you ill, mademoiselle?" A young man in a waiter's apron stared into her face. "Please, come in. Sit."

"Maybe I should," she managed. He took her arm and led her to a table just inside the doorway.

"Perhaps some wine," he suggested.

"No." Elena shook her head. "Water, please." The older couple at the next table stared at her. "If I could just sit here for a moment," Elena murmured.

"Certainly. Take all the time you want. I'll get your water." He returned in less than a minute with a bottle of spring water, which he deftly opened and poured into a squat, heavy glass. "I am Guillaume, mademoiselle. My aunt owns this restaurant."

Elena looked at him. He was young, perhaps eighteen, and blond. English was not his first language, but he didn't sound as if he were a native of Crete. "You aren't Greek, are you?"

He laughed. "No. I am French, but I'm still the best waiter on the island."

"Perhaps in Rethymo. You still have much to learn." A plump, gray-haired woman appeared beside him. Her expression was concerned but pleasant. "Welcome, mademoiselle, to the Three Fishermen. I am Mama Thea. I hope my nephew is not too forward in snatching you off the street. He takes any excuse to practice his English."

Elena took a sip of the water. She was feeling much better, well enough to feel embarrassment at causing a scene. Her momentary amnesia had passed, and with relief, she remembered who and where she was. "I'm sorry. I didn't mean to . . ." She took a deep breath and offered her hand to the woman. "I'm Elena Carter. I'm here with an archeological team excavating a shipwreck off the coast. I've been out on a boat all day. I think I must have gotten too much sun."

Her memories came flooding back. They'd searched for the shipwreck, and despite the captain's protests that his GPS was working correctly, they hadn't been able to locate the site. Nothing had gone right this week. First the unpleasantness with Greg when he'd shown up with an engagement ring she wasn't sure she wanted, and then more delays on the project. She'd come to Greece with such high hopes, and nothing was working out as she'd planned.

"Exactly so. Our sun is very hot for those not born to it. You are English, perhaps?"

"American," Elena corrected her, "but my father was English. I'm afraid that I'm not hungry, and the last thing I need is wine. I don't want to seem rude after your kindness, but I . . ." She searched in her jacket pocket for her cell. "I seem to have misplaced my phone. If I could just call someone from my team? We're renting a house in the old section of town, and . . ."

"Of course, we will call your friends. I have a daughter not much older than you. What kind of mama would I be if I could not offer a little help to a young woman in distress? If you feel well enough to walk home, my friend Orion would be happy to see you get there safely."

A man moved from the shadows. Elena looked at him.

There was something vaguely familiar about him, but she couldn't place what. She should have remembered him. It was rare to see such a handsome man with such broad shoulders and an engaging smile.

"I would be glad to see the lady home," he said. "If she's willing to allow me."

"You'll be as safe as a nun in church," Mama Thea assured her. "We've known Orion for years. He's one of our best customers."

Guillaume gave his aunt a questioning look.

Orion slapped the young man on the back heartily. "Long enough to see this one learn to carry a tray without spilling *skordalia* into the customers' laps." He extended his hand to Elena. "Orion Xenos at your service."

"Have we already met somewhere before, Mr. Xenos?" she asked. He really did look familiar. How could she have forgotten such a hunk? His eyes were an amazing green, stunning. She stared up into them, wondering if the extraordinary color might be from contacts, but it appeared not. He really had beautiful eyes. She felt a flush of interest that she was afraid might show in her face. Not only drop-dead good looking, but sexy as hell.

"I think not," he said smoothly. "I could never have forgotten you."

She studied him. He was well dressed, trendy. High-end leather sandals, expensive button-up shirt with short sleeves, no jewelry. He had a five o'clock shadow, but his yellow-blond hair was freshly cut and styled. Orion Xenos, whatever he did for a living, did well for himself. She liked his face. It was the kind of face that a woman instinctively trusted—while she lusted after his body. She decided this Orion was all right. Apparently, Mama Thea thought so as well.

Elena remembered walking out of the restaurant on

Orion's arm, strolling down to the water's edge, laughing, talking, and skimming stones across the tops of the waves. There was a period that went all blurry in her mind, and when she was next fully aware of herself and her surroundings, they were a good thirty feet below the surface and swimming out to sea.

More than that, she remembered Orion. This was the man with whom she'd just spent the most vivid days and nights of her life. The fight with the giant squid, the terrifying ride down the wind tunnel, and the out-of-body experiences in the fairy world suddenly surrounded her. She stopped swimming and stared at him.

"What's going on?" she demanded. "What kind of mind games are you playing with me? And what was all that in the restaurant about *we've never met before because I'd remember?*"

He pulled her into his arms, not roughly this time, but tenderly. He leaned down and kissed her, and the sweet sensation of his mouth against hers took her breath away. Heart thudding, she clung to him, as memories of their intense lovemaking swept over her. Desire flared in her and she wanted more, but he gently kissed her again, and then held her at arm's length.

"I'm taking you home to meet my mother," he said. "I know this is a lot to swallow all at once, but I think I love you. No . . ." He took a deep breath. "I do love you, Elena. I want you to know exactly who and what I am, but most important, I want you to be safe."

"Safe from what?" He'd said something similar once before as they'd waded into that strange pond where the two of them had encountered the exquisite little people who claimed to be fairies. It hadn't made sense then, and it made less now. "Why is my life in danger?"

"Because the Phoenician shipwreck you're excavating is

cursed." His solemn green gaze captured hers, and her heart skipped a beat. "You found something at the site, a single artifact buried in the sand."

"Yes, a gold coin."

"The owner wants it back."

"What owner? That ship is thousands of years old. Do you mean the coin doesn't date to the same time period? It definitely could have been Phoenician. Unless it was a forgery. Is that what you're trying to tell me, that the gold was planted there?"

"No, it wasn't planted. And it's authentic." He pulled her against him and hugged her tightly. "Elena, I know this is a lot to take on faith. And telling you the truth isn't easy."

"The truth? You've lied to me? So I do know you?"

"I've lied to you, deceived you, and seduced you. When I want to, I'm a sexy guy. You might say I'm irresistible. But, all that was before. Now, it's different. I want to be honest with you, but there's much that you'll find difficult to accept. You humans—"

"What do you mean? *You humans*? I suppose you're . . ." Suddenly, what the fairy woman had told her made perfect sense. Which meant she had been dreaming . . . was still dreaming. "You . . . you're not human," she stammered. "You're something else?" She felt giddy. It was a lot easier when she simply thought she was in a coma. "You think you're from Atlantis?"

"Not think, Elena. I am from Atlantis. And, I'll prove it to you. I'm taking you there."

"You're taking me to Atlantis," she repeated. "You're telling me this isn't a dream, that everything that has happened in the last few days has been real."

"Not quite everything. I'm not certain what you remember. On land, you shouldn't remember anything of what happens when you're with me under the sea. And neither should you remember me."

"I'm surprised you're admitting that you're a fish," she flung back at him. "Why not a fairy?" Her bewilderment was fast turning to anger. "You lied to me? You made love to me? We made love, and it was good—damned good. And all the time you were lying about everything?"

"Just hear me out."

"Why should I? How do I tell the lies from the truth?" She jerked free of him.

"I won't lie to you again. I promise you that."

"And why is this different from before? Why was it all right then, but not now?" This made even less sense than when she thought she was crazy, yet eerily, there was a solid thread of reason through it all. "What makes you think I want to meet your mother? How do I know that she won't lie to me, as well?"

He ignored her verbal jab. "Elena. What do you think you know about Atlantis?"

"It's a myth that got my father killed."

"And what if I told you that Atlantis is just as real as London, or Paris, or New York City? Just a lot older."

She shook her head. "It's not possible. If it was real, people—human people—would have discovered it. The Mediterranean isn't uninhabited. Archeologists, divers, fishermen, various militaries, they all scan the sea floor. My boyfriend, I should say my ex-boyfriend, because that's what he'll be when I see him next. Greg—his name is Greg Hamilton. He's part of a team investigating natural gas sites. If Atlantis is there, why haven't they found it?"

"It's complicated."

"That's always your answer when you don't want to explain something, isn't it?"

"I'll try to simplify things. We met the day you took the Zodiac out by yourself to check on your wreck site."

"Then why don't I remember that?" she demanded. Oddly, she found herself wanting to believe him. It was impossible, of course. It went right along with fairies and a giant wind tunnel that sucked you along at the speed of light like some revved-up subway system, but deep inside, she wanted to believe that he was more than a liar.

And she didn't want either of them to be a fugitive from a mental asylum. Because, despite everything, she cared for him. A lot. Fish or man with a big imagination, Orion was someone special.

"We can play mind games," he said. "We have the ability to cast illusions, to make humans believe they see what we want them to see. If you thought I'd appeared out of the ocean and that I wasn't human, what would be your reaction?"

"I'd believe you escaped from a mental ward."

"Or you have," he suggested.

She frowned.

"Seriously. If you really thought that I was an extraterrestrial who'd just popped up out of the water into your inflatable raft, what would you do?"

She considered. "I'd be terrified. Probably my first instinct would be to use a spear gun on you."

"Exactly. So, to keep you from being unduly frightened, I made you see me as a human male, not as I really am."

"What? Have you got webbed feet? Gills? Are you some kind of super lizard with a dorsal fin down your spine?"

He was looking at her with such sad eyes that she eased up on the sarcasm. "Orion . . . Is that even your name? Do you have names, or is it just, 'Here, fishy, fishy.' "

"Orion is the name my parents gave me."

"So you just came up out of the waves and picked my boat to hop into?"

He grimaced. "Actually, I was in trouble. Something nasty was trying to eat me. A lot of something nasties. There were more than I could fight off. You came along in your Zodiac at the right time."

"So you jumped into my boat, and what? Hypnotized me into thinking you were human?" A school of bait fish swirled by, pursued by several larger fish.

"Something like that."

"So this isn't what you really look like?"

He shook his head. "I know this is hard for you, Elena, doubly hard because you're a woman of science. I respect that, and I respect your intelligence."

"So much that you had to string me out with a pack of lies about being from Atlantis?"

"Be rational. How long can you hold your breath? A minute? Two? And how long have we been down? You're with me. That's why you aren't drowning. Humans came from the sea, in the dawn of time. Some say we were once the same, humans and Atlanteans, but we've evolved in different ways. We have different strengths and weaknesses."

"Which doesn't explain how you managed to hide ... What? A city? Right under our feet?"

"Atlantis isn't in the Aegean or the Mediterranean. If your father claimed to have found it, what he actually came upon was one of our old palaces or outposts. The city—the kingdom is much larger. I can't tell you where it lies, for obvious reasons, but humans have explored less than two percent of the sea floor. Most of our planet is water, yet your kind knows less about the oceans than the surface of the moon."

"So why hasn't anyone else stumbled on one of these

palaces in the Mediterranean? In the last three thousand years?" She was intrigued by his argument, but she wasn't gullible. He hadn't convinced her yet.

"Illusion again, not just created by an individual, but by hundreds of trained Atlanteans. Explorers see what we want them to see. And remember, the floor of the ocean is constantly rising. Many of our large structures are beneath the floor surface. Keeping traces of our civilization hidden requires enormous energy, and it must go on constantly. If your father did find proof of our culture, it was simply an error on the part of our scientists."

"But why would you go to all the trouble?"

"Because humans and Atlanteans have been enemies for at least five thousand years. Think of it. Every one of your societies has a story about the Great Flood. Even the Eskimos of North America."

"We don't call them Eskimos anymore," she corrected him. "They're 'indigenous peoples' or known by their tribal names."

"Don't be stubborn, Elena. Let your mind open to the possibility that we might exist. I proved that the fairies exist, didn't I?"

She narrowed her gaze. "How do I know that you aren't the result of a brain tumor?"

He shrugged and grinned. "I've been called a lot of things by beautiful women, but never a tumor. I assure you, I'm as real as you. If you cut me, I'll bleed. I could show you, if it would make you feel better." He slipped the sword from his belt sheath and raised it over his left arm.

"No. No more blood. I've seen enough blood. What I want to know is—"

"Shhh!" His eyes widened, and he seized her arm. "Something's happening. Can't you feel it?"

The sand beneath her feet seemed to shudder, and the

earth groaned. The tide seemed to stop flowing, and the fish around them began to swim frantically out toward deeper water.

"Come, Elena," he said. "We've got to get out of here!"

"What is it?"

"Earthquake."

# CHAPTER 21

The rumbling grew louder, and plaster fell from the ceiling. Greg rolled over and blinked, trying to decide if this was a bad dream or if the bed under him was really shaking. His head felt like a bucket of wet cement that had been mixed with pure Scotch, stood in the sun for three days, and started to ferment. Another chunk of the plaster overhead broke loose and fell onto his chest. Greg's stomach heaved and he supported himself with one hand to keep from falling out of bed.

Something soft gave way under his weight. A woman screamed. He stared as Michelle's mascara-smeared face appeared from under the sheets. "What's happening?" she cried.

Greg was up and moving. He was stark naked, but the chair where he'd tossed his pants last night was gone. A gaping hole in the floor testified to the violence of whatever was happening. "Come on!" he yelled. "We've got to get out of here!"

*What was Michelle doing in his bed?* The state of her undress when she tumbled out answered his question. She was wearing his red-and-blue Hamilton-plaid boxers, his tie, and nothing else. Her short blond hair stood up like a rooster's comb, but the rest of her was prime as she struggled to hold up the oversized shorts with one hand and pull on her gold flip-flops with the other.

The plate glass along the outer wall billowed in and then out, before crumbling in jagged sections. Sounds of screaming, cars crashing, and glass breaking poured in the gaps left by the missing windows. Greg smelled smoke, and the building shook again, harder.

"To hell with your shoes!" he said. "Let's get out of here!"

Michelle thrust her left foot into the remaining flip-flop, grabbed his shirt off the foot of the bed, and leaped across a growing fissure in the floor to reach a small, red makeup case.

"Are you nuts?" Greg bellowed.

"I need it!"

He grabbed a handful of her hair. She struggled free and grabbed the case. Greg leaped over the now two-foot wide crack, threw her over his shoulder, jumped back, and carried Michelle, red case and all toward the door.

The hall was filled with panicked guests, all in various states of undress. Two couples were standing near the elevator pounding on the down button. Greg dropped Michelle roughly onto her feet. "You're on your own now, babe," he said.

He ran past the group by the elevator and headed toward the fire door that opened onto the stairs. The smoke was worse here in the corridor, but Michelle was quick. Somehow, she got in front of him and beat him to the stair door and blocked his way. "Get those assholes by the elevator," she shouted. "If they get on, they'll all die."

"You're crazy! Who do you think I am, fuckin' Batman?" *What floor were they on? Third? Fourth? Not too high, but too high off the ground to jump.*

"You're G.R.'s son," Michelle said. "If you leave those

poor bastards to fry, you'll never be able to look yourself in the mirror again!"

Two more people ran up behind him, and Michelle stepped aside to allow them escape down the stairs.

Greg scowled. All he had to do was shove the stupid bitch out of the way. If those idiots didn't know better than to take an elevator when the hotel was coming down around their ears, they deserved to die. Natural selection and all.

Steel and concrete groaned. The noise was deafening. Chunks of wall and ceiling fell and crashed and rolled on the hall carpet. The shaking started again, not as strong, but lasting longer. Greg glanced back at Michelle. Her jaw was set and she stared him straight in the eye. The top of her spiked hair came only to his chin, but she looked formidable.

"I'm getting out of here alive," she warned when the grinding subsided enough for him to hear her, "and I'll tell your father how brave you were when the earthquake hit."

*His dad with his damned medals and Vietnam War stories. Living with his old man would be impossible if he had any excuse to call his son a coward.*

Cursing, Greg turned back toward the crowd at the elevator. Unbelievably, the elevator door slid open. As Greg dashed up, he could see the empty shaft gaping open like a black hole. There was no elevator waiting, but that didn't keep the idiots in the back from shoving the people nearest the door.

A gray-haired woman in a maid's uniform tripped and fell forward. The old man next to her grabbed the back of her blouse, catching her as she teetered over the abyss. Greg shouldered through, seized her by the right arm, and dragged her shrieking and sobbing back into the hallway.

"Get away, all of you!" he ordered. "Take the stairs, unless you don't mind a hundred-foot drop!"

A tall man in a three-piece suit with blood running down his face started to protest in a language Greg couldn't understand. Greg spun him around and half pushed, half threw him in the direction of the fire door. "Get moving!" he shouted. "That way out! Everybody! That way!" More people crowded the passageway. "Take the stairs!" Greg bellowed.

At the fire-escape door, he heard Michelle giving her best flight attendant spiel in a firm but efficient voice. "Keep calm! This way! Keep moving! No need to panic! Walk, don't run! Follow the stairs to the emergency exit!"

Greg's eyes and nose were running. His throat felt like he'd been eating ground glass. Smoke poured up the elevator shaft in black clouds and spewed out into the corridor, but the crowd did exactly as they'd been told. "Anybody else?" he shouted, when he couldn't see any more guests or employees down the hall. "Anybody still in their rooms?"

"All out, sir," a teenage boy in a bellhop's uniform tugged at his elbow. "We checked every room on this floor."

So much plaster dust was in the air that Greg had to find his way back to the stairs by trailing his hand along one wall. The thought that he wouldn't find it made the hair stand up at his nape. He was scared enough to piss himself. *Some hero*, he thought.

"Come on, Greg!" Michelle called. "Hurry! I think the steps are going."

"I'm here. Wait for me!" His breath came in choking gulps.

They were the last ones out, and they took the stairs two at a time. At one point, they found their way partially blocked by fallen debris, but the people ahead of them scrambled over. Greg gave the elderly maid a boost, then helped Michelle to find her footing on the crumbling concrete.

The walls were growing hot, and Greg's eyes were so full of smoke and falling crap that he could hardly see. He was coughing his lungs out, but he kept going. He could feel cool air on his face from the open door below, and nothing was stopping him from reaching it.

They burst out of the emergency exit hand in hand, and threw themselves down on the grass. The evacuees from the hotel were all around them, some standing stupidly and staring, a few sobbing, while others ran away. Greg started to heave and threw up what remained of last night's porterhouse and a gut full of Scotch.

When he managed to get one eye open, he saw Michelle sitting cross-legged a few feet away. Her face and hair were black with smoke and caked with plaster. She'd lost her jacket, and his shirt hung in shreds, but she was laughing like hell.

"Thought you said you weren't Batman," she croaked. "Looked like it to me."

He leaned over and vomited again. When he could talk again, he'd curse her until a fly wouldn't land on her. He groaned and sank down, but she wouldn't leave him in peace. Like a damned greenhead horsefly, she kept pestering him.

"I think . . ." She broke off and coughed, spit, and coughed again. "We need to get out of here."

Through his one open eye, he saw she was still clutching the damned makeup case.

"This hotel is right on the beach," she reminded him.

"So?" It seemed to him that the tremors had almost

stopped. If the ground would stay still and the remains of the hotel didn't fall on him, his stomach might stop turning inside out.

"After an earthquake, there's always a chance of a tsunami." Michelle pulled at his arm. "We need to move."

"A what?" Greg threw up again, but this time there was nothing but bile, and it burned his throat like acid.

"Tidal wave," she said. "Remember Japan? This ground isn't high enough. We could have a fifty-foot wall of water hit us."

That got his attention. "A tidal wave?" He wished he'd had the sense to stay in Texas. They had tornados sometimes, but the ground had the sense to stay in one place and walls of water didn't threaten to drown him. Instantly, he was on his feet and moving away from the sea. He looked around for a vehicle, but the parking lot was on the far side of the hotel and he didn't want to waste time.

Michelle seemed to read his mind. "There!" She pointed to a snub-nosed sedan sitting catty-corner in the middle of a dead-end street.

He couldn't read the Greek lettering painted on the side, but there was a light attached to the roof. "A cop car? Twenty bucks says there's no keys in it."

"Lucky for you my brother taught me the fine art of hotwiring." Michelle ran toward the sedan, makeup case in hand.

There was nothing for him to do but go after her, or sit there looking like an ass. Around them was sheer pandemonium, people screaming, smoke pouring out the hotel windows, dogs running loose, sirens and alarms blaring.

Michelle seemed oblivious to it all. She headed for the police car like a retriever after a downed duck. Greg glanced back over his shoulder at the ocean. It seemed as calm as a millpond, but he remembered those TV news clips from the Christmas tidal wave in Indonesia, and he had no intentions of having his face plastered across the screen as one of the victims.

By the time he reached the car, Michelle was already attacking the ignition with what looked like an oversized nail file. She had the engine running in two minutes flat.

"Move over, and let me drive," he ordered.

"Bullshit. Fasten your seatbelt and hold on." She pointed back the way they'd come.

Greg looked. It was weird. It looked to him as though the surf was moving out, leaving a strip of dark, wet sand a lot wider than it had been the last time he'd looked.

Michelle tossed the red makeup case in the back seat, threw the car into first, and took off over the curb and across an open lot. She hit the accelerator hard. The little sedan bounced and skidded but kept moving forward. Greg had a brief glimpse of a fat man in uniform running after the car and blowing a whistle.

Greg's head hit the ceiling and slammed into the window frame before he got his seatbelt fastened. He had to give it to her: The bitch could drive. Maybe better than him. She took a sharp corner around a building, plowed through another hotel parking lot, and took a narrow road uphill away from the beach. Pedestrians leaped out of her way. Cars honked, and drivers cursed and waved their fists in a universal message of disapproval, but Michelle only pressed harder on the gas pedal.

"What if you're wrong about the tidal wave?" he shouted above the screeching tires.

She laughed. "Then you'll have to call your father and get him to bail us out of a Greek jail for stealing a police car."

"All right. All right," he agreed, getting into the mood. "Bonnie and Clyde. But I've got one question."

She maneuvered the vehicle around a stalled tour bus, took out a sign for a museum, and made it back onto the street without blowing a tire. Part of the sign clung to the undercarriage of the car for a few blocks and then fell away. "Which is?" she asked.

"You seem to have your shit together. Why the damned makeup case? Got money, drugs, or jewelry in it?"

"Nope." She took her eyes off the road long enough to wink at him and raise her left hand. On her third finger was a wide gold band. "Our marriage certificate."

"Marriage certificate? What the hell are you talking about? I wasn't that drunk last night."

"The hell you weren't." She swerved right to miss a donkey, left to avoid an abandoned motor scooter. The little car fishtailed, but kept rolling. "We were married by a Greek Orthodox priest," she said. "In a five-hundred-year-old church overlooking the sea. Saint Philippos."

"A priest? He wouldn't. Foreigners can't get married that easy here. I know very well—"

"You know shit, Greg. You told him I was preggers and that you'd do the legal part later. You also wrote a company check for a large donation to the church. I've got the ring and the good father's signature on our marriage license."

"You can't blackmail me."

"Not trying to. And after last night, I could be carrying your son and heir. You insisted on riding bareback, cowboy. You told me that was the only way for a real man to go—and during my most fertile time of the month, too."

He swore. "You won't get away with it."

"Lots of marriages make do on less." She made a sharp left and the wheels of the car screeched. "We're two of a kind, Greg. We like the high life, and we like getting our way. And we're both Catholic, if I remember correctly.

And the last time I went to Wednesday night mass with your mother, she told me how much it would mean to her if you married in the church. She'll be delighted."

Michelle hit the brakes. The sedan slid to a grinding stop, and she opened the door. "I think we're far enough away now," she said. "No sense in pushing our luck with the local *gendarmes*. It's time to ditch the ride."

He got out of the car, came around to her side, and yanked the red case out of Michelle's hand. "What's to keep me from taking this phony marriage certificate, tearing it up, and leaving you stuck on this island without a way home?"

She smiled up at him. "Not a thing, Greg. Only, that's a copy. I asked you for a hundred dollar bill, right after the ceremony. You gave me two of them, and I tipped the priest's housekeeper a Benjamin Franklin to FedEx the original, to your mom. I thought it would make nice reading with her morning coffee."

"You're a conniving bitch."

She nodded. "I am, but as of last night, I'm your conniving bitch. It's official. I'm Mrs. Gregory Hamilton, Jr. Can't you just wait to get home and start planning our wedding reception?"

Silt swirled up from the sea floor to cloud Orion's vision. Around them, dolphins, rays, and a large octopus fled by. Smaller fish swam in panicked circles as the rumbling of the troubled earth grew louder. Elena clung to Orion's neck. Whatever she felt toward him, what they were facing now wiped the slate clean. What mattered was surviving.

He didn't want to think of attempting to use the nearest seraphim. It was too risky. The primeval worms were as likely to be destroyed by an earthquake as any natural feature or structure. If the earth opened under them, he and Elena could be trapped in the seraphim's intestinal tract and crushed by the weight of their host.

Normally, he could call for help from a dolphin or other large mammal, but not when they were swimming for their lives. A dolphin companion or soldier was different; he could depend on them to come to his aid, but not one of the wild ones. He had to get Elena to safety, and he had to get back to Atlantis before his father realized that he was missing.

The timing still wasn't quite right, despite Orion's time manipulation. Time travel wasn't exactly a science, not for fairies, and certainly not for Atlanteans. He'd managed to return to the evening that he'd originally met Elena in Rethymo, when he'd posed as an antique dealer, but the scenario hadn't gone as it had before. Traveling back in time had disoriented Elena, and he'd had to approach her in the restaurant and use all his skills to convince the proprietor that she'd known him for years.

There had been no earthquake that first night, either. He and Elena had gone into the water, and he'd taken her to the seraphim where they'd stepped into the path of the squid. But, he was certain he would have known if an earthquake had struck near Crete. The fairies would have known as well and said something. That was the trouble with dabbling in time travel. When you retraced your steps, you often found that the path you believed was familiar had changed.

"Are we going to die?" Elena demanded. Her arms were tight around his neck, and she clung to him as he swam.

"Not if I can help it."

"Good. Because if we get out of this alive, I intend to kill you myself."

# CHAPTER 22

Palace guards saluted sharply as Morgan approached the marble columned antechamber that led to Poseidon's private apartments. The king had sent orders for him to come at once on a matter of extreme urgency and to bring no attendants. Morgan returned the salute, speaking to the four soldiers in turn, calling each by name. "Aigeus, is Prince Alexandros here yet?" Morgan asked the last man, a bald-headed veteran with a jagged scar down his face and a crooked grin.

"Yes, sir. Inside."

"Good man. My regards to your father."

"I'll tell him, sir. He'll be pleased you remembered him."

"How could I forget the hero of Madagascar? His exploits are legendary."

"Thank you, Prince Morgan." The man grinned wider, exposing a missing front tooth. "And those exploits grow with every telling."

"Let him brag. He's earned it," Morgan said.

He passed through the archway and found his brother standing at the room's outer wall. This was a marvel of architecture, carved of a single sheet of transparent crystal that permitted the occupants a view into the formal gardens where a rainbow of fish and exotic plant life flourished. It provided an ever-changing kaleidoscope of beauty, a welcome respite from an often harried royal schedule. The garden was protected so that no predators could enter, and the fish grew larger and tamer than most of their species.

Alexandros turned as Morgan entered, smiled, and extended his hand. "Brother."

Morgan gripped Alexandros's hand and the two embraced. "You've heard?" Morgan asked.

"Yes. How are they? Any change?"

"Rhiannon is resting quietly. I don't know what will happen when she wakes, but Danu seems to have a quieting affect on her."

Alex waited, the unspoken question hovering between them.

"It's too soon to tell if we've lost the babe." Morgan's voice cracked. "The high priestess believes it will be a boy."

"Lady Athena is certain it's sorcery?"

Morgan nodded. "There's only one person I can think of who's capable of such treachery."

"Our dear stepmother." Alex's green eyes chilled to the hue of frost. "I told our father that he should have killed Halimeda when he caught her trying to poison him. I offered to do the deed if he didn't want the shame of a public trial."

Morgan glanced away as a shiver rippled through his body. There were dark depths to this brother he loved so dearly. Morgan could kill in the heat of battle or to protect another, but cold-blooded execution was beyond him. Alexandros had been trained as an assassin, and as such, he was one of the kingdom's most valued assets. Sometimes, Morgan feared that Alex didn't hold life as precious as he should.

"You'll be Poseidon one day," Alexandros said. "Would you have the stomach to order the elimination of filth such as Halimeda—a faithless wife who didn't shrink from attacking Rhiannon and your unborn son? Could you do it if you knew that making the wrong decision would mean the deaths of innocents?"

"I believe in law."

Alex shrugged. "But the court is not always as certain as my blade. Had I finished her when she was in prison, she wouldn't have been alive to threaten those you hold dear."

Morgan could see the reason in Alex's words, but it went against his grain to fight wickedness with more of the same. "Isn't there a danger that wielding such power could corrupt a king and turn him into a despot? If he could dispose of his enemies so easily, what would keep him from using those methods on those who displeased him or whose guilt wasn't as readily apparent?"

Alexandros smiled, a thin smile that didn't touch the fierce gleam in his eyes. "'Power corrupts the mighty'? I studied the same philosophers as you, brother, but I seem to have taken a different message. Halimeda and the abomination she serves deserve no mercy from us, because they would offer us none. Are we to battle such evil shackled by rules that we've created, when no such rules compel them? Because we fear misusing power?"

"The kingdom of Atlantis was founded on law and mercy. Those rules have served us well for many thousands of years."

Alexandros shrugged. "Best that you will be Poseidon and not me. I say if we'd killed the bitch when we had her, we wouldn't be fighting the same battle a second time. Only it isn't us fighting it, is it? It's your wife and child."

"Enough! We've no time for your childish squabbles."

Morgan looked up to see his mother in the doorway. She wore full regalia today, including her crown, which meant that she was prepared to take the reins of government in hand . . . which also meant that their father intended to take the battlefield personally. He was struck as he always was by her youth and beauty. Korinna glowed with an inner light that made her look nearly as young as Morwena. "Have either of you seen Orion today? Or Morwena?"

"I saw Orion earlier." Alexandros moved to kiss her cheek. "Are you well, Mother?"

"Morwena?" she repeated.

"I think our sister may be with him," Alex said.

"Your father calls for him."

"He may be with his generals," Morgan suggested.

"How is Rhiannon?"

"Better, I think."

"Come in, and close the door after you."

No guards were permitted in the private apartments of the royal family, but both Alex and Morgan retained their weapons. Usually, Poseidon forbade even his sons to come into his presence armed, but no one made mention of it today. With war imminent, more than one custom was broken for the sake of security. The group within the large chamber was small: Poseidon, Lord Mikhail, Lady Jalini, Zale the vizier, their younger half-brother Paris, Morgan, Alexandros, and their mother the queen.

No formality was demanded among such a select gathering, and Lord Mikhail was the first to speak up. "Highness. Your sister, Princess Eudora, sends her regrets. She would have come at your bidding, but she felt that Lady Athena needed her help with Princess Rhiannon."

"Understandable," Poseidon said. "Although we will

miss her wisdom at this meeting." Morgan noted that their father was dressed for battle, as well, in bronze cuirass and greaves. His helmet lay on a table within arm's reach, and this was no ceremonial prop but scarred battle gear. The king glanced at Zale, met his gaze, and nodded.

The vizier surveyed the assembly. "There's been an earthquake off Crete, and we believe it is Melqart's doing."

"An earthquake?" Lady Jalini repeated. "How bad?"

"The usual," the queen replied. "Structures affected, some injuries to humans and minimal loss of sea life, but we fear the worst is to come."

"My contacts report that the earthquake is only a precursor to a tsunami," Mikhail said. "Loss of human life could be terrible."

"And you think Melqart is at fault?" Morgan asked. "For what purpose?"

"My mermen are convinced that the Phoenician god of war seeks revenge against the humans because some of them desecrated his treasure ship and stole what was his. His priests were overheard saying that their lord seeks blood payment and the return of his possession or he will devastate the area and all life in it."

"This complicates our position." Poseidon rose from his chair. When the others stood as well, he waved them back to their seats. "None of that. We're not here to impress . . ." He frowned. "Where the Hades is your brother Orion?"

"On his way, sire," Alexandros said. "He's been occupied . . . making preparations for the coming battle."

Poseidon's forehead wrinkled as his scowl deepened. "Trust him to be late."

Paris stood beside Morgan, and when it seemed to Morgan that he was about to speak, Morgan elbowed him and shook his head. Paris was young, no longer a teenager, but young. Fresh out of the military academy and coming off his first tour of commanding men, this was his first council. This half-brother was bright and bold, but this was not the time or place for him to venture an opinion in the king's council.

Their father had rewarded Paris's competence by inviting him in, but he'd be all too quick to find fault with anything Paris said. Poseidon was wary of sons that might seek to edge out an aging sire. He might even shame Paris by criticizing him in front of the others and attempting to send him away like some naughty child. And with Paris's temper, it wouldn't do for the two of them to clash. It seemed both he and Alexandros had received a double dose of their father's temperament, and it didn't pay to stand in their way when they lost control.

"The high queen believes we should send aid to the humans," Poseidon continued. "Radical, I know, considering our relationship with them."

"Humanitarian aid is never radical," their mother said with quiet force. "And our people are capable of helping without revealing their identities."

"We'd have to move at once," Zale said. He'd remained on his feet, and now, he leaned on his staff of office. "It would disrupt our plans to attack Melqart's shades along the coasts, and there might not even be a tidal wave. This is risky, in my mind."

"My vote is to go to the humans' assistance," Morgan said, seconding the queen. "It wouldn't be the first time we've done so."

"I agree," Alex said. "Too many bodies in the sea agitates the predators and disturbs the natural balance. If we can save lives, we frustrate Melqart. And if our people are already in the Aegean, they can form ranks quickly."

Morgan glanced at Alexandros. His brother wasn't quite as heartless as he liked to appear. He'd brought Rhiannon to the Shaman's Caves when he, Morgan, was dying, and he'd fought against overwhelming odds to rescue Danu from the horde. For all his killer's instincts, Alex had a soft spot for children, be they human, Atlantean, or dolphin. He couldn't stand by and see any come to harm needlessly.

"I must disagree with the princes," the vizier said. "Coming between the humans and Melqart is dangerous. Better we carry out our plans and let the humans save themselves." He frowned. "You know that I'm not one who regards the loss of life lightly. I think only of the good of the kingdom."

A stone panel slid quietly aside behind and to the left of the throne. Morgan's hand went to his sword hilt, then relaxed as Orion stepped into the room. "Sire." He inclined his head. "Mother."

Queen Korinna favored him with a smile. Orion had always been a favorite of hers. "My son. You are most welcome here."

"I may not be," Orion answered. "I presume you've heard of the earthquake that rocked Crete and the neighboring islands."

"I've informed them," Lord Mikhail said. "The question is whether or not a tidal wave will follow, and if it does—"

"A tsunami is already building in the depths," Orion said. "The dolphins and mammals are evacuating. I've just come from there."

"We must help them," Lady Jalini said.

Orion looked at his father. "Poseidon? The decision is yours."

"Please, for me if for no other reason." Queen Korinna laid a hand on her husband's arm. "You are too great a king to do anything less."

"So be it," Poseidon agreed. "But they must be volunteers, and no one without the highest skills in illusion may go. I won't have the kingdom put in danger to rescue a few tourists."

"I knew that's what you would say," Orion answered. "I've already begun your mission. I brought a human female with me. Had I abandoned her, she might not have survived. She needs care and sanctuary until I can make other arrangements."

Alexandros tensed.

*Oh, shit*, Morgan thought. *My little brother has fallen into the same trap I did—he's entangled with a human.*

"A human woman? Here?" The veins stood out on Poseidon's forehead and his face turned an ominous red. "You brought her here?"

"And he can take her away, once it's safe," the queen soothed.

"She is very susceptible," Orion said. "I assure you that I can cause her to forget everything she sees here."

The queen smiled at her husband. "I know you would have done the same, my lord. Your son Orion is a master of illusion. I know we can trust him to do all with the utmost care for the security of our people."

"Where is she?" Poseidon demanded. "You haven't brought her into this meeting, have you? Is she hiding there behind the drapes?"

"No, my lord," Orion replied obediently. "I left her in the care of the Princess Morwena."

Alexandros's eyes narrowed, and he glanced at Morgan. Morgan shrugged.

"They are in the great library, sire," Orion said. "The

human is a scientist, and she showed great interest in our collection of scrolls. My sister offered to watch over the woman while I came to obey your command."

"Morwena's a fine one to watch over your human," Poseidon said with unconcealed sarcasm. "When has she ever bothered to concern herself with proper behavior for a royal princess? She's as much a scamp as the four of you." He glanced at the queen. "Has any king of Atlantis ever been burdened by such wayward children?"

"They are spirited, my lord," the queen agreed. "A trait they inherit from their father."

"Highness, if you wish us to save as many lives as possible, we must dispatch a force at once," Lord Mikhail said.

"You tend to it," the king said. "And take . . ." He pointed at Paris. "Take that youngster with you. We'll see how well he's earned the grades he achieved at the academy."

"Have we your leave to assist Lord Mikhail?" Orion asked his father. "Morgan, Alexandros, and me?"

"You may go, but you may not stay," Poseidon said. "I need you here. We may need to move swiftly to attack the horde if they take advantage of the tidal wave. You have your own commands."

"Thus speaks Poseidon, high king of Atlantis," Zale declared. "We hear and obey, great lord."

"And may we not live to regret my decision," the king said with a pointed look toward the queen. "For we all know where the suggestion came from and where blame must fall if this turns out badly."

"It will not," she assured him. "And now I will leave you gentlemen to decide how best to proceed," she said. "May the Creator smile on your deeds and reward your valor." And with that, she rose, motioned to Lady Jalini, and the two left the room together.

* * *

In the library, Morwena gathered an armload of scrolls and deposited them on the marble table in front of Elena. "Here are some of our earliest histories," she said. "I can translate if you'd like."

Elena gently unrolled the first scroll. She wasn't certain of what material it was fashioned, and the inscription was unlike anything she'd ever seen. She could hardly tear her eyes away, and yet, she could hardly stop staring at the vast structure that rose around her.

If this was a dream and not Atlantis, she had a better imagination than she'd ever guessed. Instead of an archeologist, she should have become a screen writer. She would have made her fortune.

The princess, Morwena, as Orion had introduced her, seemed a perfectly ordinarily, if exceedingly beautiful and intelligent, young woman, an easygoing girl with a bow and quiver of arrows thrown over one shoulder. She was friendly without being overly false, and she seemed genuinely excited to be given the task of baby-sitting the stranger.

Around them, scholars and students removed scrolls from the compartments on the walls, seemingly studying them and taking notes as might have taken place in any university library. They looked like perfectly ordinary people, not monsters or freaks. Elena saw no obvious gills or webbed feet or fish tails. What were strange were the dolphins that swam through the vast rooms, seemingly as occupied with the pursuit of research and academic tasks as the people.

"We can't stay long," Morwena whispered. "I have a dance class that I'll be thrown out of if I don't attend. I've already missed two sessions and Lady Halcyone is quite strict. But she isn't ill-tempered. I'm certain she'll allow you to watch. We've never had a human visitor, but we often have beings from other . . ." She hesitated. "Other places."

"So . . ." Elena said. "You aren't human, and none of these . . . people." She indicated the occupants of the library. "They are . . . like Orion."

"Yes, Atlanteans," Morwena said.

"And they . . . they look . . . exactly like humans?"

"Not exactly."

"Different."

Morwena nodded.

"A little different, or scary different?" The teaser for an old TV movie flashed across Elena's mind, and she watched the image of something like a walking catfish arise from a pond . . . something *From the Black Lagoon.*

"Different. Not scary to us, certainly. Natural." Morwena sighed. "It must seem strange to you, but I assure you, we're quite peaceful. No one here will take a bite out of you." She chuckled. "Bad joke, I'm sorry."

"It's a great deal to swallow," Elena agreed. She had a suspicion that Orion and his sister might still be hypnotizing her or using *illusion* as Orion had said. She might be seeing what they wanted her to see, but she wasn't ready to take that leap, so she pursued that line of questioning no further.

"This library," Elena said. "It's . . . it's . . . I've never seen anything like it." It was large, larger even than the Museum of Natural History at the Smithsonian in Washington, but much more beautiful. The columns and statues and soaring dome were magnificent. The long tables and benches were apparently fashioned of pink marble, and all was neat and orderly. It was breathtaking, as much so as her first sight of the city Orion had told her was the capital of Atlantis.

She was fast running out of rational explanations for him and this whole under-ocean world. Could it be possible that it was real? That this was Atlantis—that her father had been right and the city was as real as Paris? This was all too confusing . . . and too intriguing. If she was dreaming, she didn't want to wake up. That would mean leaving Orion and his wonderful world behind. And she didn't want to do that, not by half.

Getting here—to this place Orion insisted was Atlantis—had been frightening. Against his better judgment, Orion had relented and led her into another of the strange wind tunnels. When the earthquake had grown worse, he'd called the seraphim transport the best of several bad choices.

The passage had been surprisingly brief, even though Orion claimed that they'd traveled halfway across the Atlantic to reach the kingdom. It had seemed to take only a minute or two. This city was like something out of ancient Greece or an altered Egyptian Alexandria. Everywhere she looked there were columned buildings and wide streets and open parkland, at least what Orion called parkland or public gardens.

Elena had had only a few minutes to recover her wits when Orion had whistled up a passing dolphin that had swum away and returned with his sister Morwena. At first Morwena was all eyes and nearly speechless with wonder at meeting her, but that quickly changed.

"You two will be fast friends," Orion assured them. "And now, if you'll excuse me, I have to be somewhere important."

"Which is?" Elena demanded.

"I'll explain later," he'd replied, and then he was gone, leaving his sister to guide and watch over her.

"I was on my way to the library," Morwena had explained. "That's how I got here so fast. It's only a short way. Would you like to see it?"

Which was how they'd arrived here. But now, apparently, Morwena was about to lead her away to someplace she referred to as the temple where she was a student. Elena wanted to ask Morwena's age, but didn't want to appear rude. She could be anywhere from her late teens to late twenties, and stunning enough to be a world-class model. Since most of what Orion had ever told her had been an untruth, Elena knew she should be skeptical about anyone she met or anything she saw here, but she liked Morwena. And she thought Orion might be right about their becoming friends.

"We'll take a short cut," Orion's sister said, signaling to an attendant to take charge of the scrolls they'd examined. "My dolphin, Freyja, is waiting for us outside the Courtyard of the Three Mermaids. She'll let us ride double. If we hurry, I won't even be the last one to class."

Morwena slung the quiver over her shoulder and picked up her bow. "It's a beautiful courtyard with shell paths and a lovely sculpture."

"I'm going to dance class with a Diana lookalike, riding double on a dolphin." Elena took a deep breath. "Do I have a choice?"

Morwena smiled, a mischievous grin that reminded Elena of Orion's. "We always have a choice," the princess said. "Don't be afraid. Freyja is perfectly safe. And not a soul would harm us in Atlantis."

# CHAPTER 23

In the heart of Melqart's temple, Halimeda watched as he lifted a bronze bowl from the fire and tilted it back and forth. The boiling water splashed over the sides, and she could smell the skin on his hands cooking and see blisters rising. She'd always taken pleasure from the pain of others, and it excited her to imagine what it would feel like if Melqart were Atlantean.

But, he was not. He was not anything that knew physical sensation, not hot or cold, not wet or dry. She wondered if he was lonely, despite the sacrificial brides that had been offered him over the eons. Gods such as Melqart had their limitations. As much as he liked to pretend that he was lusty, she doubted that he'd ever experienced real sexual satisfaction. And as much as he boasted of his limitless power, he had weaknesses. She intended to ferret out those weaknesses and exploit them for her own gain.

Her own needs were much more primitive and easily satisfied. She craved beauty in her face and form, and that she'd been born with. She enjoyed potent wine, fatty meat and fish, preferably raw and still twitching, glittering jewels, and rich clothing. She yearned for constant adoration, bawdy play, and frequent orgasm. Melqart had teased and tantalized her with promises of sexual delights beyond any she could imagine, but so far, he'd given her nothing but a headache. For all the disappointments he'd caused her, she had to admit that Poseidon was a more potent lover who'd rarely failed to please her between the sheets.

When she'd attempted to eliminate Poseidon, she'd traded her position as a queen of Atlantis to be Melqart's handmaiden. Now, she wondered if she'd made a poor choice. True, the king hadn't made her high queen as she desired, but she had gained much from the arrangement, and she'd managed to keep her son on the path to inheriting the throne.

Melqart had done nothing for Caddoc and little for her, other than countering the poison she'd tried to administer to her husband and restoring her natural good looks. Without a doubt, the god of war was not the deity he'd pretended to be, not in any area.

When Melqart wasn't transforming himself into a sperm whale, a man-bull abomination, or a giant toad with drooling mouth and warty skin, he could assume the image of a handsome naked male with awesome equipment. She had yet to see those promising attributes in action. She doubted that he ever made proper use of his multitudes of virgins. In short, until he proved otherwise, she considered the Phoenician god of war to be nothing short of an overblown adolescent with an active imagination.

Sensing that the bloom was off the oyster where she was concerned, Melqart had sought to impress her. He boasted that he could cause the earth to shake and the sea to rise and scour the face of the land empty of life. "These humans who dare to steal from my treasure ship will remember my name!" he'd roared. "And they shall tremble before my image."

Halimeda was dubious. She'd have to see the earthquake and tidal wave to be impressed. Watching humans suffer and die wasn't as much fun as if they had been her personal enemies among the Atlantean royal family. But drowning her rival queens and concubines wasn't an option. They weren't immortal; they could die, but it wasn't as easy as snuffing out the lives of silkies, mermaids, or masses of puny humans. To keep herself from expiring from pure boredom, she'd keep up her own campaign against the house of Poseidon.

Melqart continued to shake the bowl to and fro, and deep in the bowels of the earth, rock groaned and split and lava boiled. "Come forth!" he hissed. "Rise up!"

As Halimeda listened, the groaning became the howling of damned souls and she felt the cave shudder. "This roof isn't going to come down around my ears, is it?" she demanded. "Not much of a spell if you make the earth crack and heave and crush your own high priestess."

"Cease your endless nagging or I will smash you like the centipede you are," he warned. "I am master here. You exist only through my mercy. And no one has appointed you high priestess."

"Consort, then," she suggested. "Your queen, if you will."

"Melqart needs no queen."

She rolled her eyes. He'd come to believe he did, soon enough, and she'd be certain he thought it was his idea. She'd intended to inform him of her plans to snatch Poseidon's daughter as a sacrificial offering. Perhaps the promise of fresh virgin fuel for his fires would ignite the lust Melqart dangled like bait just out of reach.

Soon, this very night, Caddoc and Tora would snatch Morwena and deliver her up trussed like a breakfast squid. Halimeda might even allow Caddoc the credit for bringing Melqart the prize. So far, her son had done little to win Melqart's favor, and they needed his help.

Morgan's wife and unborn child, she would deal with personally. She'd bribed a servant for a few strands of Rhiannon's hair and an intimate article of clothing. Halimeda would need to go to the princess's apartments if she could find her way into the palace unobserved. Such a powerful spell wouldn't work properly at a distance. It was too easy to make a mistake and either kill Rhiannon or send her into a frenzy, rather than driving her permanently insane. And the magic had to be strong enough to destroy the fetus and to wither Rhiannon's womb so that it would quicken with life no more.

White caps flecked the tops of the waves in Melqart's copper bowl. The water swirled and churned in a circular motion until the gleaming bottom of the container was revealed. As Halimeda watched, the bowl cracked and fell in two halves, but the water didn't spill onto the stone floor. Instead, the liquid hovered in the air like a living blob, contracted into a tight mass, and flowed forward in a malevolent wall many times its original size.

Melqart laughed. "Already their buildings crumble and fires gnaw at their cities. When I tire of the humans' screams, I'll send the tidal wave. Would you care to see?"

He seemed in a good mood. It was on the tip of Halimeda's tongue to tell him about Morwena and her suitability for sacrifice, but it might be wiser to remain still until she could produce Poseidon's daughter for his pleasure. Melqart might not be as powerful as he claimed, but it didn't do to anger him unnecessarily. And to promise him a virgin princess and then not deliver might have unpleasant repercussions.

Halimeda believed the Samoan to be worthy of her

trust, but she wasn't convinced that he was infallible. Tora was Caddoc's man, and where her son was concerned, sad to say, her most brilliant plans sometimes went amiss. While her son had inherited her beauty, he hadn't been fortunate enough to get her brains as well. At times, she thought Caddoc bordered on stupid. Luckily, intelligence wasn't required of royalty. What was important was the ability to intimidate one's subjects and to reproduce an heir.

"I'd forgotten how much fun an earthquake can be!" Melqart declared.

He'd sprouted those ridiculous horns again, blue ones that curled outward. Ridiculous appearing, in her opinion. *Make up your mind*, Halimeda thought. Be a bull or a man, but not both at the same time—it was disgusting.

"Are you certain you don't want to see the results?" he asked.

"If you must, omnificent one," Halimeda said. "Show me your handiwork, and then I have an appointment that I must keep—with Prince Morgan's family."

"Now that you've got her here, what do you intend to do with the human?" Alexandros asked his twin. The two had gathered volunteers from the troops and were preparing to travel by seraphim to the earthquake-ravaged coasts. They would be there in less time than it had taken to convince Poseidon that they should go to the humans' aid, but whether they would be there before the tsunami hit was anyone's guess.

"I don't want to talk about Elena," Orion said. "We've not settled things between us yet."

"But you want her?"

"Yes."

Alexandros arched a golden eyebrow. "But you haven't

asked *the question?* Which means you aren't sure." He grimaced. "Take her back to her own kind, brother. Deposit her on some mountaintop far from Melqart, and forget you ever met her."

"I can't." Orion strapped a trident to his back. When it came to seraphim, he preferred his own weapons.

"Can't or won't?"

"I said I didn't want to talk about her."

"Father's not stupid. When he stops to think about it, he'll realize that this woman of yours is more than a victim of the earthquake that you rescued. He'll come down on you hammer and tongs. You know how prejudiced he can be where humans are concerned."

"Drop it, Alex."

Orion's second-in-command approached. "Men are ready, sir."

Orion nodded and tightened the cords that secured his sword sheath. "We'll lead off. Follow, but pace yourselves. It won't do to put too many in the canal at one time. We'll rendezvous off the beach at Rethymo."

"Yes, sir!"

"And warn the men to keep their shields up. There are bound to be people with their little camera phones. Snap. Snap. We want no likenesses identifying us as other than human. I'll have the skin off any man's back who drops his illusion, even for a heartbeat."

The warrior slammed his fist against his chest, acknowledging both the order and the reason behind it. He was a steady man, and Orion trusted him. Every soldier with them had been handpicked. Orion only hoped they arrived in time to save lives. If they didn't, going would be a waste of time, and the king didn't accept excuses.

Orion wished he'd had time to return to Elena and tell her that he had to leave. He couldn't have explained why, but she'd be angry with him for depositing her with Morwena and vanishing. His sister would take good care of Elena. He was certain of that. He only hoped she could maintain her own illusion.

He would have to be the one to take the final step and let Elena see his true appearance. He wanted to take things slowly between them. He thought he loved her—he was certain she was the woman for him. But asking her to give up her human life to be with him and his kind at the bottom of the sea was a giant step. If he asked, and she refused, the consequences for him would be bad. Not simply bad—disastrous. He had no desire to spend the next thousand years entombed in a block of ice.

Alexandros leaned close. "Watch your back, brother."

"You watch it." Orion grinned. "And I'll watch yours."

"Oh, I will," Alexandros replied. "If anything happened to you, I'd be the one stuck with trying to return your woman to land and making sure her memory is wiped as clean as a rain-washed beach."

Morwena led Elena down a series of steps and through a narrow doorway that led from the library into the Court of the Three Mermaids. Morwena hoped that her teacher and friends wouldn't be angry with her for bringing Elena to the dance class at the temple. Most of the others would probably be intrigued, as she was, by Elena's novelty.

Elena was the first human she'd ever spoken to, and to her surprise, Morwena found Orion's guest both intelligent and fascinating. But she knew that many Atlanteans thought little of the earth walkers. Because there had been bad feeling between the species for so many thousands of years, there was a strong prejudice against humans among her people. Someone was bound to complain, and it wouldn't take much effort to submit a request for official censure against both her and Elena.

Not that that bothered Morwena. She usually went her own way, and if she made enemies in the process, so be it. She'd been censured more than once since she'd begun her studies. It was more important that she keep her promise to Orion to protect Elena and to make her feel welcome. Besides, she reasoned, being Poseidon's daughter did have a few perks. It would take something really bad to get her expelled from the temple.

Morwena thought that bringing Elena along would be better than skipping her class in ritual dancing. It was a required course that she had to pass, and she'd already missed two classes this period. Not that Morwena didn't enjoy it—she did. But dancing didn't come naturally to her as it did to Alexandros or to her mother. She always felt that she was one step off the beat. She'd always been more at home on the archery range or riding a half-broken sea horse in the open ocean far from the city walls.

Luckily, the path she'd chosen for her future was wide. The temple had room for men and women of many different talents and skills. Becoming a high-degree priestess took decades and was never an easy life. She had three more grades to complete before she had to decide which area to major in. The problem was, she was interested in so many things. Illusion had always fascinated her, but Lady Athena's gift of healing called to her as well. Morwena had an inborn love of far vision and some natural talent for seeing into the past or the future, but the field was crowded. It would take luck and many years of study to rise high enough to reach a place of prominence in the science.

"I like to come this way," Morwena said to Elena as

they followed the curving shell walk around the three statues through the swaying columns of greenery. "Not so
crowded. And I thought you might like the garden. My
dolphin Freyja is waiting in the alley just beyond that
gate."

Elena stopped to admire the sculptures. The mermaids
were carved of single blocks of white marble, four times
life size. One was captured in the act of throwing a fishing
net, the second played an Irish harp, and the third cradled
an infant and wept for her lost human lover. "How magnificent," Elena said. "They seem almost alive."

"There's a wonderful story about these mermaids.
They're supposed to be three sisters. Orion can tell it better than I can. He's a wonderful storyteller, but I suppose
you already know that about him." Morwena had no
doubts that this woman meant more to her brother than
he'd said.

Elena shook her head. "No, I didn't know that about
him. I do know that he has a huge imagination and a
smooth way with words."

"He took minor orders in the priesthood as a bard. He's
a warrior first and foremost, of course, but he can hold an
audience spellbound. And he has a beautiful singing voice.
Most of our bards sing as well as recite the old tales and
poetry."

Elena stared at her in confusion. "Orion is a priest?"

"Perhaps not the same as in your world. One of my tu-
tors told me that your priests are celibate. Is that true?"

"Some are, but there are different religions. I imagine
it's the same with you."

"Among the Atlanteans, a celibate male . . . or a female
would be an oddity. I've never heard of one." She shrugged.
"We are a sensual race, not so much as the mermaids, but

much more than humans. Love is an art among us, one we all strive to explore as fully as possible."

An alarmed hiss and an angry series of clicks caught Morwena's attention. "Wait here." She motioned to Elena. "I'm not sure what's upsetting Freyja." She slipped her bow from her shoulder, hurried to the high gate, and pushed it open.

"Freyja? What—" Someone grabbed her and slammed her against the stone wall, knocking the breath out of her. The bow fell from her numbed fingers, and she heard Freyja squeal in distress.

"Is something wrong?" Elena followed her through the gateway.

A man grabbed Morwena by the throat. Not any man— Caddoc's crony, the tongue-less Samoan. He had a sack in his hand and tried to pull it over her head. "Freyja!" Morwena cried. "Help me!" She kicked out at Tora and struggled to break free.

With an angry hiss, Freyja swam at the Samoan, butting him hard with her head. Tora twisted and jabbed the dolphin with a long spike. Blood streamed from the wound.

"Stop!" Morwena shouted. "Help me!" Tora's fingers dug into her throat and she struggled to pry them away. He shoved her hard against the wall again. Her head hit the stone, nearly knocking her senseless. The Samoan thrust his face inches from hers. He was so close that she could smell his foul breath. His small eyes burned with menace.

"Why are you doing this?" she demanded. "Let me go!"

Tora backhanded her. He raised the sack again, and tried to cover her face with it, but she'd brought a knee up, hitting him hard in the testicles. He grunted, took a step back, and swung a fist at her face.

Abruptly, Elena appeared behind Tora. She beat him over the head and struck at his eyes with the bow. Tora dropped Morwena and lunged at Elena, but she dodged away. He came after her and was met by an enraged Freyja. The dolphin rammed him in his midsection, knocking him off his feet, and then bit a chunk out of his arm. The Samoan seized his spike and tried to stab Freyja again with it.

"Run," Morwena managed to say. "Save yourself." Her throat hurt so that she could hardly speak. "Call the guards!"

Elena helped her to her feet, got an arm around her, and helped her to swim back toward the gate.

"My bow," Morwena whispered hoarsely. "Give me the bow!" Her quiver hung by a broken strap. Most of the shafts were broken, but she pulled one intact arrow from the case.

Elena plucked the arrow from Morwena's hands, notched it in the bowstring, and let fly the arrow.

Tora howled as the missile pierced the back of his left thigh. He turned back toward the two of them, his face a mask of rage, and snapped the arrow shaft in two.

Freyja circled and charged Tora again. The Samoan backed against the wall and raised the spike. Morwena shouted a warning, but Freyja was beyond caution. The dolphin twisted, barely avoiding the Samoan's thrust and snapped at his face. Both man and dolphin were trailing blood. Freyja rolled, her dorsal fin quivering with fury. The man lunged at the dolphin, stabbing with the wicked spike.

"Freyja!" Morwena cried. "Come." She pointed to the gate.

"Go on!" Elena shouted. She grabbed a broken arrow,

put it to the string and released it. The shortened shaft hit the man low in the throat. It didn't go in deep, but it was enough to distract him. The dolphin passed over his head and swam toward the gate.

"Grab the harness," Morwena ordered.

Elena seized hold of one side and Morwena the other. The big dolphin crashed through the gate, pulling both women with her into the courtyard. Two guards, several young warriors, and a martial arts instructor burst out of the library door and swam toward Morwena and Elena, weapons ready. Morwena gestured toward the shattered gate.

"A man tried to kill her!" Elena shouted.

"No," Morwena corrected. "He didn't want to kill me. It was a kidnap attempt. It was Tora, the Samoan. Prince Caddoc's man. He attacked my dolphin. It won't be hard to recognize him, if you catch him. He has no tongue. And"—Morwena pointed at Elena—"she put an arrow in his thigh."

"The human?" the instructor asked. She was a tall woman with short-cropped black hair, ivory wrist guards, and the short tunic and studded belt that proclaimed her expertise.

"My friend," Morwena said. "She fought for me. She saved me."

"He won't get far!" said one of the guards. The men rushed out in search of the assailant.

"Are you hurt, Princess?" the woman asked.

"Just roughed up." Morwena swallowed and rubbed her throat. "My dolphin needs medical aid."

More people were coming down the stairs from the library. Elena moved closer to Morwena, and the princess saw that she was shaken by the experience.

"You're sure you're all right?" Elena asked her.

One of the guards returned. "He's gone. We'll keep searching. Are you certain the human hit him?"

"Twice." Morwena nodded. She suddenly felt tired. "Neither were killing shots," she said, "but he's hurt. He'll need a physician." She repeated Tora's name and description.

"And you have no idea why you were attacked?"

"No." She turned away from the guard, her concern now for Freyja. The dolphin bore several deep lacerations which might need to be stitched. "I need to have someone tend Freyja. I want to take her to healers at the temple."

The guard nodded. "Let me send an escort with you." He eyed Elena. "I doubt they'll permit her to enter the temple."

"She goes where I go," Morwena said. "And any who wish to prevent her will have to take it up with my father the king."

# CHAPTER 24

"I was going to take you to meet my mother," Morwena said as she and Elena walked out of the healing center, where they'd left Freyja to rest in the company of other dolphins recovering from illness or accidents. "But with war imminent, I'm afraid she'll be too busy to give you a proper welcome. We'll go to my brother's wife's apartments. You'll like Rhiannon, and the two of you will have much in common."

"Why is that?" Elena asked. She'd passed the point of being astonished by all she saw around her in the city of Atlantis. Now, she was almost numb from senses overload. She'd felt the same way after spending hours in the Cairo museum the first time she'd visited. *How many objects of beauty could you see and process mentally, before it all began to run together?*

In the short time since Orion had left her in Morwena's company, she'd seen a library that might have existed in ancient Athens or Alexandria before the time of Christ. She'd witnessed a vicious attack on her new friend Morwena by a monstrous man or creature, whatever Tora was, and walked through the marble halls of a crowded edifice that seemed a combination of med school, university, and place of worship combined. She'd seen lecture halls and science labs that made Harvard or Cambridge seem like rough country schoolhouses, and she witnessed medicine practiced in ways she'd not believed possible by elderly women in Greek garb. If this was a dream, and that possibility was becoming ever more unlikely, her imagination was far more powerful than she'd ever realized.

Everywhere Morwena had taken her, Elena had been treated with the utmost courtesy, and if she was an object of curiosity, her new acquaintances had taken pains to hide it. What she saw and heard around her was beyond the realm of belief, and yet, it seemed believable. Freyja, Morwena's dolphin friend, had been injured badly—had been bleeding from several deep wounds. Yet, a few minutes of attention from those Morwena referred to as gifted healers and the gashes on the dolphin's flesh had closed without stitching. The same healers had stopped the dolphin's blood loss and eased her pain, and they had done it by touch and mind power.

"Rhiannon is closer to your age," Morwena said, pulling Elena back into the moment. "She and my brother Morgan are but newly married, and they're expecting their first child."

"So Morgan is Orion's brother as well?"

Morwena laughed. "Yes. But we have many brothers. Our father is fond of women; unfortunately, his choices are not always the best. Morgan, Orion, and Alexandros, Orion's twin, are actually my half-brothers, but they've always seemed much closer. My mother gave birth to me, to Paris, to Marcos, and Lucas, who are all younger than I am, and she's expecting again."

"I didn't know that you . . . that your people had such large families."

"We don't usually, but our father is Poseidon. He is the exception to the rule."

"Poseidon." Elena tried to take that in. "As in the Greek god of the sea?"

Morwena laughed merrily. "Our father isn't a god, although Mother often accuses him of thinking he is. I'm sure it would flatter him to hear you say so. He's high king of Atlantis, and as such, he is expected to have many wives and as many children as he can sire."

"Sounds like something out of the dark ages."

Morwena shrugged. "I think it's to prove the king's virility. It's an old custom for the king to have many wives and concubines, but my mother doesn't mind. She's the only queen with real power. She and our father go head to head at times, and he's often put out by it."

"She confronts him?"

"And usually gets her way. Mother has many tricks up her sleeve. If arguing won't work, she sweet-talks him."

"They . . . some of those people in the library . . . and afterwards . . . after the attack, they called you *princess*."

Morwena nodded. "Yes."

"And if Orion is your brother, he's . . . he's a prince?"

Morwena smiled. "He is, but don't be intimidated. He's only second or third in line to the throne. Morgan, Rhiannon's husband, is crown prince. He comes first. And then it would be either Alexandros or Orion, depending on which one my father is least angry with that day."

"A prince of Atlantis." Elena took a deep breath. You had to give it to her—if she was concocting a fantasy, this was a class-A one. "No chance Orion could turn into a frog if I kissed him, is there?"

"I doubt it," Morwena answered. "Hasn't happened yet, has it? And I suspect the two of you have been up to more than a kiss or two."

Elena shrugged. "I'll never tell."

"You don't have to. I know my brother Orion." Chuckling, Morwena led the way into a series of rooms filled with garments, a sort of dressing area where women of all ages were trying on clothes, applying makeup, and styling their hair. There, in a private closet off the main area, Morwena discarded her torn clothing, found a replacement tunic and sandals, and brushed and braided her hair.

"As Mother would say, I'm more presentable, now." Morwena smiled. "I've always been a bit lax on personal attire." She studied Elena carefully. "I think we need to find something new for you to wear as well."

Morwena called to an attendant who hurried out and returned shortly with an armload of clothing. Morwena examined the dresses and chose a shapeless garment. "Try this one," she suggested to Elena.

Dubious, Elena stripped off her clothing and dropped the tunic over her head. It fit as though it had been tailored especially for her. "Lovely," she said, fingering the silken material that fell to her ankles. "What's it made of?"

"I'm not sure," Morwena said, brushing a fingertip across the material. "Probably zuryilon skin. That's a sort of fish from the deepest part of the mid-Atlantic trench. The skin is nearly transparent and takes a gold wash beautifully. See the minute scale pattern when you hold it up to the light."

"Fish skin?" The sides of the graceful skirt were slit to allow free movement, and the color was a pale gold. The styling was classic and Grecian, and Elena, who rarely took trouble with her own choice of dress, was astonished at how attractive and feminine the gown made her feel.

"It suits you," Morwena said as she slid a heavy gold bracelet onto Elena's arm. "And you should have earrings." She produced crystals set in gold that looked very Indian. "Perfect," she said as Elena slipped them into her ears.

"I can't believe I'm wearing fish skin," Elena said. She sniffed the material and smelled nothing but the clean scent of salt water with the faintest hint of lime. "Are you certain that no one will mind if I borrow these things?"

"We don't think of that," Morwena said. "The tunic is yours for so long as you want it. You can have as many as you like. They're here for any who want them. I wear them all the time. The seamstresses weave blessings into the material to ease fatigue and aid in learning. They would be very happy to know you take pleasure from their handiwork."

"But the jewelry must be very expensive. It looks old."

"The sea gives us much, and what good are earrings if no one wears them?"

"So you don't have your own personal clothing or possessions? You take from general stock such as—"

"I do have my own garments, mostly hunting clothes and attire for court functions. And enough chests of jewelry to satisfy a king's daughter. Those I keep in my private apartments in the palace, but I wear something from the temple stores, more often than not." She chuckled. "I tend to be rough on my clothing, and I need a lot of replacements."

Dressed and adorned, they left the area and took another hallway and a flight of wide stone steps to a smaller chamber where weapons were stored. There, Morwena found another bow and quiver of arrows and a slender dagger with an ivory handle. "Would you like something?" she asked Elena.

"No, no, thank you. I'm generally opposed to violence."

"For a peacemaker, you did well enough. Without your interference, Tora might have succeeded in kidnapping me, or worse." She selected a small belt and sheath and found a delicate knife with a curved blade to fit the case. "Take this one, to appease me," Morwena urged. "You might come upon a contrary shark or a moray eel that doesn't want to be your friend."

"All right." Elena chuckled and gave in gracefully. "Just don't expect me to fight off any big Samoans," she warned as she strapped on the belt. The knife fell just below her hip and, after a short while, as they walked on through the temple corridors and courtyards, filled with students, teachers, and visitors, Elena could almost forget that it was there.

As they passed through a magnificent atrium filled with statuary, two men, deep in conversation, came down a curving flight of stairs to the left. Elena stopped short and stared. Only a few yards and a particularly beautiful column of pink marble separated them. The older of the two men, a distinguished gray-haired person of obvious importance drew her attention. She stared at him in disbelief, her heart hammering against her ribs. "It can't be . . ." Elena whispered.

"What is it?" Morwena asked. "What's wrong?"

Elena opened her mouth to speak, but her throat clenched. Was it . . . It was impossible . . . yet . . . Tears sprang to her eyes, clouding her vision. "There," she managed, gesturing in the direction of the man.

He paused to scan the atrium as though he was searching for an acquaintance. For an instant, Elena's gaze locked with his, and the man's eyes widened in surprise. Abruptly, he turned away. His erect, almost military, posture stiffened. Ignoring the obvious confusion of his companion, he retraced his steps, hurrying back up the staircase and vanishing around the first corner at the landing. After a moment's hesitation, the younger man followed.

Elena's voice cracked. "Who . . . was that?"

"Lord Mikhail and his steward. I don't know the steward's name but—"

"Mikhail? Are you sure?" She was trembling. *How could it be him? He was dead—lost at sea when she was eleven.*

"Positive. He's head of . . ." Morwena hesitated. "National security." She smiled. "He's my aunt's consort, practically my uncle. He will be if they marry as court gossip says they might." She took Elena's arm. "Are you all right? Your face is as white as a *czastek.*"

"He looked like . . . for a moment, I thought . . ." Elena took a deep breath. "I just mistook him for someone I . . . someone I used to know." She swallowed. "Sorry, I'm afraid I wasn't thinking clearly."

"Understandable. Orion said the two of you came from the fairy kingdom not long ago. Time travel can upset your system for days, especially if you've never experienced it before."

"That must be it," Elena said, attempting to cover her shock. *Time travel? That was one more unexplainable question to add to the others.* She forced a smile. "I'm fine, really." Her heart still raced. *How was it possible that Lord Mikhail had such an uncanny resemblance to her father?*

"Not far to go," Morwena said. "You probably haven't had anything proper to eat, either. Orion has the constitution of a shark, and he forgets others may not be as resilient as he is." She squeezed Elena's hand. "But, since we're passing this way, I thought you might like to take a quick look into this hall." She turned right, followed a wider passageway and then led Elena under a magnificent marble archway into a round amphitheatre that featured displays around its rim. The arched roof seemed made of glass or some other transparent material; above her, Elena saw a living kaleidoscope of fish, dolphins, and other sea life.

"Wonderful," she said, still trying to shake off what had just happened. Maybe Morwena was right. Maybe she was just hungry, overtired, and disoriented.

"This hall is a children's museum of human archeological treasures," Morwena explained. "Miniature reproductions of structures and sites which were once on dry land that the sea has reclaimed." She motioned to a diorama of a hillside and a circle of standing stones. In the center was a flat stone with the carving of a large and elaborate sword cut into the rock. "You may be familiar with this tomb," Morwena said. "It's fairly recent."

Elena nodded. "The pattern is similar to Stonehenge in England," she said, attempting to make her voice sound as normal as possible.

"Yes, the site is much older than the purpose for which it was adapted. One of your hero-kings was buried here. Arthur Pendragon. The burial place lies perhaps a half mile off the coast of Cornwall."

"This is a copy of something that once existed?"

"Of something that exists today."

Thoughts of the stranger who'd so unnerved her receded. "Really?" Elena could hardly contain her excitement. "King Arthur's grave?" Such a find would prove once and for all that he wasn't myth but a flesh-and-blood man.

"You're familiar with him?"

"Yes. Arthur would have lived and died in about the sixth century, A.D."

"Practically yesterday, as I said." Morwena nodded. "It looks exactly like this. I was there only a few moons . . .

months ago. Maybe a little more seaweed and some oil sludge, but that's everywhere around the British Isles."

"Do you think he's really buried there? Arthur?" *Was this any stranger than thinking she'd seen her dead father in Atlantis?*

"I don't know why he shouldn't be," Morwena said. "Not that there would be much left, other than his grave goods. He was buried with quite a few gold objects, I understand. I didn't witness the funeral, but a friend of mine did, and she said that there were close to a thousand humans on rafts and boats around the island."

"But you say it's underwater now?"

"Yes." Morwena nodded. "Ice is continually melting at the poles, and the sea level rises. Not that the island was very high to begin with."

"What's this one?" Elena asked, pointing to the next exhibit. The display appeared to be Greek or Etruscan in style. There were columns and a domed crystal object in the center.

"Another of your kings, I'm afraid. Alexander."

"Alexander's tomb? Alexander the Great?" Elena's eyes widened and she pressed her face against the glass case. It was all she could do to breathe. "Archeologists have been searching for this for centuries."

"We could have told them where it is, if anyone had bothered to ask," Morwena said.

Tears filled Elena's eyes as she drank in the golden figures of horses, chariots, and mythological creatures carved around the crystal crypt. In the center, she could clearly see the image of a man's body. "This really exists?" she asked. "Why haven't his remains vanished?"

"It's no secret," Morwena confided. "The casket is filled with honey, and that's preserved the body. His hair is undamaged and the color remains as yellow as ever. He's as beautiful as your legends claim. Not a big man, but well formed with muscular arms and broad shoulders."

"Most archeologists I know would give their right arms to see it."

"I don't know that it's worth losing an arm, but I'm certain Orion would take you if you ask him—once he returns, that is."

"Where is he again?" Elena's memories of Orion's whereabouts were fuzzy, and she wondered if Morwena possessed the ability to put her into some sort of trance. Orion's sister seemed so likeable, so normal. How could she be an Atlantean princess, and would she be capable of clouding Elena's reasoning capabilities? And if she could, should she be trusted?

Morwena gave her a shrewd glance, almost as if she could read her mind. "I think we should go," she said. "It would take hours for you to look at all of the displays, and I'm hungry. Rhiannon will have something delicious to eat. She always does. I can bring you back to see the museum another time, if you like."

"I would," Elena agreed. "But I'd like it even better if Orion could take me to Alexander's real tomb." She felt a vague sense of unease. "Is Orion in danger? What was it that he had to do that was so important?"

"Orion is well. You have nothing to worry about."

Immediately, Elena felt a rush of warm reassurance, almost as if Orion's arms were holding her. *I love him*, she thought. *I love him, and nothing else matters. I don't care how crazy all this is. And if I'm dreaming, I never want to wake up.*

She shook off her discontent. "And you're certain Rhiannon will receive me?" she asked. "If she's the crown prince's wife, won't she have duties that—"

"Rhiannon will be thrilled to meet you. She's been urging Orion to find a partner for ages. And wait until you meet Danu. She's five going on fifty. You'll adore her."

"Who is Danu?"

"Rhiannon and Morgan's adopted daughter." The sound of a brass gong echoed down the corridor. "There's a function in the great hall," Morwena said. "We have to hurry or I'll have to attend." She grinned mischievously. "Even in Atlantis, there are affairs that are more bother than worthwhile. And if we're lucky, we'll arrive at Rhiannon's in time to share her meal. She has the best cook, and I love her desserts."

Orion and Alexandros walked out of the ocean onto the beach at Rethymo minutes before the arrival of the tidal wave. Alexandros assumed the appearance of a local police officer and began to order people off the beach at once. Orion raced to the harbor. Few fishermen were there, but he saw at least two American tourists as well as the Greek captain of Elena's charter boat. Two women from her archeological team stood on the dock watching as the captain prepared to take his undamaged vessel out away from the fires that were raging on shore.

Since the older woman of the two was obviously American, Orion conjured an illusion, which portrayed him to the humans as an English-speaking naval officer.

"How fast can you get out of the harbor?" Orion shouted to the captain. "Cast off and head out to sea as fast as it will go or abandon the boat and head for higher ground. We've picked up a tidal wave on our radar. It's heading toward the island."

"Tidal wave?" the captain asked. He shook his head. "This boat is all I own. I won't leave her."

"Then take these people aboard and get out of here. You should be safe in deep water."

"Are you certain?" the younger woman asked.

Orion looked out to sea. He could see no sign of the rogue wave, but the sea birds were circling frantically. There was no time for the women and the two tourists to reach high ground. "Take these people onboard!" Orion shouted. "Otherwise, their deaths are on your head."

The two tourists ran down the dock, and after a moment's hesitation, the women followed. The captain swore in Greek, but he waited until they scrambled onto the deck before he yanked his lines free. "Aren't you coming?" he called to Orion.

"No. I'll be all right. A speedboat is coming for me. Godspeed." As the captain steered away from the dock, Orion continued his sweep of the harbor. He could sense the coming of the wave, not the largest he'd ever seen, but lethal enough. He found Alexandros and together they continued warning all the locals and visitors they could find.

Some were amiable to good advice; others refused to listen. Again, he and his brother split up. There was something Orion needed to do before the wave hit. He remembered the address of the house Elena had been renting, and he hurried through the twisting streets toward it.

"Elena!" he called as he pushed open the kitchen door. He knew she wasn't here, knew exactly where she was, but if the house was occupied, being a friend seeking her would make a good alibi.

He had reached the staircase leading to the second floor when a tiny Greek woman came rushing down. Immediately, he cast a net of illusion over her. "A wave is coming, Grandmother," he said. "Go up to the roof and wait there. You'll be safe there."

"Who are you? Why are you in this house?"

"I'm an angel," he said in her native Greek. "I've come to help you. Do as I say and you'll be safe from the coming wave."

"I smell smoke," the old woman said. "I don't want to burn."

"The fires won't come here. Go to the roof and wait for help to come."

"If you're an angel, what is your name?"

"Who do you think I am?"

She mumbled a name, and Orion smiled. He waited until she had vanished up the steps to the roof balcony, and then he followed her up. Elena had left something in this house, something evil, and he had to have it. He knew where she'd hidden it. He'd read her mind when they'd last discussed the coin that she'd recovered from Melqart's ship.

A quick search of Elena's bedroom proved his memory correct. He removed both the coin and a diamond ring from the box. He wasn't certain what he would do with either one, but leaving the ring here might prove fatal to the old woman. The diamond might have absorbed some of the same evil energy. Orion took that as well.

He'd taken the first steps onto the street when he felt the rush of wind and heard the first screams of the terrified citizens of Rethymo.

# CHAPTER 25

As Orion started toward the harbor, he nearly bumped into Elena's graduate student Stefanos racing toward Elena's house with a small boy in his arms. A terrified Greek woman, carrying a screaming toddler and dragging a girl of about nine or ten by the hand, ran after him. "Go!" Orion shouted. "To the top floor. Hurry!"

The woman stumbled and nearly lost her balance as Stefanos and the boy reached the front door. Screams of the flood victims from the shoreline echoed above the grinding of wood and the groan of metal. Seconds. They had only seconds and all three might be swept away.

Although the wave was still a block away from them, Orion could feel the vibrations of the rushing water and the tons of debris washed along by it against his sensitive skin. The cries of the humans and animals crushed by the force of the tidal wave, fueled his rage toward Melqart. Senseless bloodshed! And for what? A single gold coin? Someone must put an end to Melqart's reign of terror.

Orion seized the woman's hand and wrested the red-faced and wailing baby from her arms. "Run!" he shouted to the woman in Greek. Scooping the girl up in his free arm, he carried the children through the ground floor of the house and up the stairs to the first landing.

"To the top floor," he ordered, setting the girl down. She stared at him with fear in her eyes, then turned and fled after Stefanos. Orion thrust the still-shrieking baby into the woman's embrace. "The house is strong," Orion said. "The water may flood the downstairs, but the structure will stand."

Orion knew as he left the house for the second time that the children saw him as he really was, not as the adults or even Stefanos saw him. It was a risk he had to take. Human children were not so easily deceived by illusion, and casting a spell over more than two humans at one time was always tricky. Luckily for him and his kind, adults rarely believed children when they claimed to see *monsters*. Being seen for what he was broke all the rules, but saving lives had to come first. If he had to face retribution for defying the law, he would pay the penalty.

He headed out again. This was an old part of town, some houses built by wealthy Venetian merchants. The streets were narrow and twisting, houses and shops crowded shoulder to shoulder. Everywhere panic-stricken people ran screaming—parents seeking little ones, husbands and wives calling out for each other. Animals feared the sea's anger as well. A tame parrot flew squawking over his head. Barking dogs, a wheezing goat, and even a braying donkey pulling a cartful of vegetables fled past him up the cobbled street, instinctively seeking higher ground.

As Orion rounded a corner, a wall of water three feet high roared up the alley toward him. He snatched a half-drowned tabby cat from a floating door and tossed the creature onto a flight of stairs that ran up the outside of a stone building. The cat landed on its feet and leaped the wooden steps two at a time until it reached the top, where it perched on a post and meowed pitifully. The cat was plump and wore a rhinestone collar. Orion wondered if the cat's owner had been equally lucky. He hoped so.

The rescue had cost him only a few seconds and several deep scratches on his right hand, but the injuries were nothing. Orion had always had a weakness for cats; he admired their independence and resilience. It was a pity they were poor swimmers and avoided the water whenever possible.

Orion felt pity for the humans, but above everything, he was grateful that Elena was safe among his people in Atlantis. It was for her sake that he'd interfered in Melqart's attempt at mass murder. It would be impossible for him to have her know what had happened and to tell her that he'd done nothing to help. In truth, he had to admit that perhaps he'd been wrong about humans. If Elena was any example of her race, they were not nearly the villains that most Atlanteans believed them to be.

When this was over, if he survived the battle against Melqart's forces, he'd summon the courage to ask Elena to stay in Atlantis with him. And if she agreed and his father objected, he'd go away somewhere with her. He loved his family and he'd spent his life as a soldier, but Elena was more important. If she'd have him, he would put her first above all others.

No matter what happened between them, if she chose to return to her own world or remain in his, it was imperative to protect her, to shield her from harm. If that was love, then he loved her as he'd never loved another. It wasn't enough to have her sexually or to satisfy his own needs as it had always been for him before when it came to a beautiful woman—Elena's happiness must come first.

Those feelings were a new experience for Orion, a little frightening, but one he welcomed with an open heart. He'd resisted telling Poseidon how he felt, not to avoid censure, but because this was all too new to share yet. First, he had to know how Elena felt about him; then he could deal with his father and the High Council.

Strange that he, who'd been so cynical about his brother Morgan's choice of a human woman as his life's mate, should come to the same fate. But Elena wasn't Rhiannon, and he didn't think that winning her over would be as easy. Theirs had been an unusual courtship, to say the least. Few men would seek to impress a woman by nearly allowing her to be devoured by a giant squid on their first date.

Straightening his shoulders, Orion turned his mind to the task at hand. He hoped that there were other victims he could save closer to the shore, and that he, his brothers, and their fellow Atlanteans could make some small difference in this crisis. He would do what he could. Whatever the chasm between his kind and the world of men, it mattered little today.

Reaching the area of the greatest need would be easier if the water were deeper so he could swim, but the deeper the water, the less the chance of survivors. Walking, even running, seemed such a primitive method of getting from one place to another, and despite his gift of being able to exist on land longer than most Atlanteans, gravity and the constant barrage of poisons from the atmosphere made the process difficult.

"Help me! Help me!" came a woman's shout from the interior of a tiny shop.

The water was deeper on this street, still incoming and rising, treacherous with broken glass, jagged metal, nail-studded boards, and all manner of flotsam. Orion struggled toward the frantic cries and assumed the disguise of a rugged Greek peasant with thick neck, bald head, and muscular arms and legs.

"Help us!" the woman called. "My brother! A display case has fallen on Ari! I can't get him out, and the water will soon be over his head."

A torrent of water, as high as Orion's chest, poured in through the open door and the broken front window pushing furniture and all else before it. He saw the woman standing on a counter, soaked to the waist, and pounding futilely at a large glass-and-wood cabinet. The small man, pinned beneath it, strained to keep his face above the churning water.

"How bad are you hurt?" Orion demanded in a rough countryman's dialect as he made his way to Ari's side. "If I can raise the case, will you be able to crawl out from under it?"

"Yes, I know I can! Thank God you've come! I thought I was done for. My legs are trapped, but I don't think they're broken." Water sloshed into the man's mouth and he choked and spat. His sister began to cry.

A drowned rat bobbed up in the filthy water and bumped against his face. The sister screamed, but the man knocked it away from him and took another gulp of air. "You'll have to get help." He gasped and choked again. "It's too heavy for you to lift."

"Please!" the woman begged. "He's all I have. You must help us."

Orion glanced at the sister. She was a plain woman with acne scars on her cheeks and bad teeth, but obviously brave enough to remain with her beloved brother when she could have sought safety for herself. Her eyes were red from weeping and her graying hair loose around her shoulders. "I'll free him for you," Orion promised. "Calm yourself."

"Go into the street and find others!" she insisted. "No

man is strong enough to lift this case alone. I'll do what I can, but—"

"Don't worry," Orion assured her. "I will lift it off him. I'm stronger than I look."

As Morwena had promised, Princess Rhiannon welcomed them into her home with open arms. "I've been waiting to meet the human who twisted Tora's tail and saved our sister's life," Rhiannon said as she kissed Elena on both cheeks and ushered them into her private sitting room off a beautiful courtyard. She was a lovely woman with short blond hair that curled around her face, freckles on her nose, and a warm smile, not at all the regal crown prince's wife that Elena had expected.

"You've heard already?" Morwena asked.

Rhiannon laughed. "You know how fast gossip travels in the palace. Has Tora been found?"

"No," Morwena said. "A pity I didn't put another arrow through his slimy heart. He's probably still running, his tail between his legs. He tried to kill Freyja, as well. For that alone, I should have finished him off."

"Killing is never as easy as you think, not even in the heat of anger," Rhiannon said. "Not even trash like Tora." She glanced at Elena with open curiosity. "Please, sit down. Make yourselves comfortable. Let me have the girls bring you something to eat."

Rhiannon clapped her hands, and the servant who'd shown them into the princess's presence, a shy brunette with a bouncy step and a heart-shaped face, curtsied and left the room.

"I was hoping we hadn't missed lunch," Morwena said. "I'm starving. I don't know when Elena ate last. You know Orion. He thinks the rest of us can go as long without sustenance as he can."

"It's kind of you," Elena said. She was hungry and tired. She wished she could curl up somewhere and sleep around the clock.

"Orion wanted me to take her to Mother," Morwena said. "But I thought she'd be better off here. You have a better grasp on the difficulties Elena is facing. Besides, Mother's apartments are close to Father's." She pulled a face. "And you know how unreasonable he is where humans are concerned."

"Orion?" Elena rubbed her eyes. "Where is he?" When she tried to think of him, to summon his image in her mind, her thoughts were fuzzy. Why couldn't she remember the man who'd brought her to this strange and wonderful place? Was this all an illusion?

And if she wasn't dreaming, what would come next? She'd already seen someone who looked so much like her father that it boggled her mind, yet Morwena had insisted that his name was Lord Melvin, or something or other. The thought that she might not be able to trust Morwena troubled her. She liked Orion's sister immensely, and she thought she would like Rhiannon, too. She glanced around the room. This place, like everything she'd seen in Atlantis, was vaguely familiar, and yet alien. Could it all be a product of a deranged mind? Hers?

"Orion had pressing business," Morwena said, answering Elena's question.

"As did Morgan," Rhiannon added. "Otherwise, I know he'd like to thank you, too. He adores Morwena, and anyone who saves her life has made a fast friend in him forever. You are very brave."

"No." Elena shrugged. "Not brave, at all. I think I'm impulsive. I saw this creep hurting Morwena, and . . ." She settled back into a high-backed, cushioned chair that appeared to be fashioned from a very large cream-and-blue conch shell. "Who was he? And why did he want to kidnap her?"

Rhiannon and Morwena exchanged glances. "Tora is my half-brother Caddoc's stooge," Morwena explained. "And both of them are monsters. My half-brother is my father's eldest son, but his mother was Halimeda, a witch if there ever was one."

"Your stepmother?"

"Ex, I suppose." Morwena wrinkled her nose. "As monstrous as her offspring, but clever and very beautiful. As, I suppose you might say Caddoc is. My father's sons are all handsome."

"As his daughters are beautiful," Rhiannon said.

"But if this Caddoc is the oldest, why isn't he crown prince?" Elena asked. "Or is that rude of me to ask?"

"Hardly rude," Rhiannon said. "Morgan is the son of a high queen, now deceased. Caddoc's mother was a base-born concubine before he was born. Poseidon elevated her to a minor queen position, but nothing could make her babe eligible to inherit."

"She ensorcelled my father," Morwena said, stretching out on her back on a couch and resting her head on her hands. "She wanted Caddoc to be crown prince. She even tried to poison the king. She's evil and so is Caddoc, but he's no real threat. He's an empty bag of wind, all talk without the bollocks to back it up."

"So Morgan thinks," Rhiannon said, "but I wonder. He makes me nervous."

"He's stupid, nearly as stupid as the Samoan. They're lovers, you know. Cladda told me. She caught them behind the—"

"Enough of such talk," Rhiannon chided mildly. "What

will our guest think if we indulge in the same gossip we joked about earlier? Whatever Caddoc and Tora do together is their own business. They're adults."

Morwena chuckled "And nothing is forbidden to willing adults in their search for pleasure so long as . . ."

"No one else is harmed or embarrassed," Rhiannon finished. "I'm afraid we're a sensual race," she said to Elena. "As you know all too well if you keep company with Orion."

Elena felt her cheeks grow warm. "Keep company?" She forced a chuckle. "That sounds so old-fashioned."

"You're lovers," Morwena supplied. "Direct enough for you?"

Rhiannon rose. "I think we could all use some wine. Morgan got a shipment of Malbec from Argentina. It's wonderful, but I have to keep the wine cellar locked. My maids are all crosses, and you know how they are. They'd be too intoxicated to do their jobs if they had access to alcohol."

"Crosses?" Elena asked. "I don't understand. What are crosses?"

"A particular species," Morwena answered. "Not exceptionally bright, but very loyal. Unfortunately, they have no resistance to wine."

"That sounds racist," Elena said. "Surely, that pretty girl who showed us in isn't stupid."

"I'm sorry if we appear uncaring," Rhiannon said. "But it's true. Some people believe they aren't capable of gainful employment. It's why we hire so many in the palace at fair wages. There is prejudice against crosses, partly because speech is so difficult for them." She smiled. "And they are wonderful with children, so patient. Danu loves them."

Morwena looked around. "Where is Danu? Usually she comes running the minute I step through the door."

"Danu's spending the afternoon with Lady Athena. But they should be back soon. She spoils the child almost as much as you do."

"And why shouldn't I?" Morwena asked. "She's my only niece, and she's adorable. She has such a wonderful sense of humor, and she's so inquisitive."

"We're blessed to have her," Rhiannon agreed. "She brings such joy to our home. I can't imagine our lives without her. Danu's adopted," she explained to Elena. "Her life before she came to us was an unhappy one, and we're doing everything we can to make up for it."

"I'm looking forward to meeting her," Elena said. The remarks about the maids had disturbed her. How could Atlantis be the paradise it was supposed to be if some classes of Atlanteans were treated as inferiors? *Shades of apartheid.*

She wished Orion would come back. Again, she wondered where he was and why the explanations Morwena and Rhiannon gave sounded more and more like excuses. Surely, he wouldn't just abandon her here.

"I can't imagine what's happened to the girls with our food," Rhiannon said. "I'll go and get that wine, if you'll excuse me. I won't be long."

For the first time since they'd arrived, Elena felt a sense of awkwardness between them. Rhiannon's smile didn't reach her eyes. And Morwena seemed too relaxed. Were they hiding something from her?

"You mustn't judge us too quickly," Morwena said when the two of them were alone again. "We mean no disrespect to the crosses. On the contrary, my mother has always insisted we treat them with kindness."

"The maid seemed competent enough to me," Elena said.

Morwena got up and stared past her into the courtyard.

It was lovely, a peaceful spot with fountain, white shell paths, and rows of sea grass and greenery, interspersed with marble statuary and benches, and surrounded on all sides by columned porticos. Under other circumstances, Elena would have liked to explore the mazes and walkways.

"Stay here!" Morwena went to the doorway.

Elena followed anyway and was shocked to see three of the soldiers, who'd stood on guard at the entrance to Rhiannon's home, on the ground. One rolled and beat at his head with both fists. Another knelt, howling like a dog and drooling from the mouth. The third man clutched his stomach and cried.

"What's happened to them?" Elena asked.

Morwena pointed to a figure standing in the shadow of the statue of a leaping porpoise. "It's Halimeda, Caddoc's mother, the one I told you about. She's bewitched the soldiers. Go back inside." Morwena ripped down a piece of filmy curtain from the wall and tore it into pieces. "Put these in your ears. If she casts a spell over you, you could end up on the ground like the guards."

"What are you talking about?" Elena asked. "Cast a spell on me? That's superstitious nonsense."

"Just do as I say! You've heard of the sirens, haven't you—the women who lured sailors to their deaths on the rocks with their singing? Trust me." Morwena seized her bow, set an arrow to her bowstring, and stepped out into the courtyard. "Go away!" she shouted at the old woman who walked toward them. "Go back, or I'll shoot."

Elena dropped the wads of material to the floor and followed Morwena back out to the courtyard. Had Orion's sister lost her wits to be afraid of this pathetic creature? Surely Halimeda, if this was who it was, was more to be pitied than feared. Wisps of gray hair sprang from a scarred, nearly bald skull that loomed over grotesque features blotched and misshapen as a burn victim's.

It was hard for Elena not to stare. This was the king's beautiful wife who'd tried to murder him? If she wasn't so tragic in appearance, she would have been comical.

A jeweled coronet balanced precariously on her oversized, bald head, and her ragged garment, consisting of nothing more than lengths of rotting seaweed, fell to her bony ankles. With every hobbling step, Halimeda's twisted legs flashed obscenely to the thigh through gaps in the gown. She was so frail and ill looking that Elena wondered how the poor woman managed to stand upright, let alone walk.

By no standard of any society could this woman be described as beautiful. She was a nightmarish caricature of a queen, weighed down with gold rings and necklaces set with gems too large to be real. Pearls the size of eggs drooped from elongated and ragged earlobes, and a scarlet mouth showed only blackened stubs where teeth should be.

Senseless words spewed from Halimeda's blistered lips, words in no language that Elena had ever heard. Growing more agitated with every passing second, the woman pointed a trembling hand in Morwena's direction and began to chant even more bizarre gibberish. Even Halimeda's fingers were a horror, a series of bones held together with shreds of rotting flesh and tipped with yellowed nails so long that they curled into talons.

"Go back or I'll shoot!" Morwena warned again. "You have no right to be here! If my father sees you, you'll be put to death!"

The young guard on the ground by the woman's feet began to convulse.

Morwena let fly the arrow. It plunged into Halimeda's

hand, and blood welled up and dripped down the front of her garment. She clutched the injured appendage to her withered breasts and shrieked in pain.

"Go back!" Elena cried as she moved toward the old woman. "She means it. She will shoot you."

"I'll put the next arrow through your slimy heart!" Morwena shouted.

"Stop!" Elena turned to her friend. "You can't kill her. She's no threat. She's pitiful."

For the first time, Halimeda seemed to notice Elena. "Pitiful? You dare to call me pitiful? Don't you know who I am, human? Don't you know that I can turn you into a sea slug with a single glance? That I can rip out your lungs with the force of my gaze?"

Elena couldn't help it. She burst into laughter. She tried to stop, but couldn't hold it back. This was utterly ridiculous. Not even the Mad Hatter's tea party had been this crazy. "I'm sorry," she said, covering her mouth in an attempt to stifle her outburst.

"Sorry," Halimeda whimpered. "You'll be sorry."

"No, sorry for you," Elena said. "You poor thing. Is there someone who takes care of you, someone who could . . ."

She broke off, staring again as the weird became even weirder. Halimeda began to turn round and round, faster and faster. Sand churned around and around her in a gray column, and then, in an instant, she vanished before Elena's eyes.

# CHAPTER 26

Rhiannon came running from the house. "What happened? There's something wrong with my servants. They're all vexed!" She stared at the guards who shook their heads as they climbed unsteadily to their feet, looking dazed and disoriented.

"Halimeda." Morwena glanced at Elena and then her sister-in-law. "She tried to bewitch us, but I stuffed my ears so I couldn't hear her sorcery. Elena . . ." She grinned. "Elena just faced her down. I tried to tell her to protect herself, but she didn't. I don't know what happened. Maybe Halimeda's magic doesn't work on humans. She tried to put a spell on Elena, but Elena wasn't fazed."

"How did you do it?" Rhiannon asked Elena.

"I don't know. None of this makes sense to me." Elena glanced at the soldiers as they hurried away, presumably back to their posts at the gate. "I saw a demented old woman, nothing more. I saw Morwena shoot her with an arrow, and then . . ." *She vanished before my eyes. It was impossible to say the words out loud, but it was what happened. Halimeda had spun like a top and disappeared— just like the Cheshire Cat in* Alice in Wonderland. "I saw her standing in the garden. Then she wasn't there anymore."

"Elena laughed at her." Morwena reached out to clasp Elena's hand. "You didn't see Halimeda as I did, did you?"

Elena shook her head. "I didn't see a beautiful woman. I saw an aging woman who'd been in a terrible accident or who suffered from some loathsome disease. She was scarred and deformed, bald as an egg, and dressed in rags and jewels."

Rhiannon shook her head in astonishment. "Illusion."

"But whose?" Morwena asked. "Elena's or mine?" She squeezed Elena's hand tightly. "Why would she appear differently to us?"

"You saw her as beautiful?" Elena asked.

Morwena nodded. "Richly gowned, with curling black hair that fell nearly to her knees. As young as Rhiannon. And fair beyond belief."

"But you shot her," Elena repeated. "I couldn't believe you'd do such a thing? Why?"

"To keep her from entering Rhiannon's house. I don't know why she came, but she meant to do her harm. Don't forget, she tried to poison my father and would have succeeded if he hadn't switched cups with her. Instead, she poisoned herself."

"But she didn't die, so maybe it wasn't a potent poison," Elena argued.

"It was potent enough. Witchcraft saved her, and we suspect it was Melqart's doing."

Rhiannon motioned them to follow her into the sitting room. "I'll send for Mother," she said. "She'll bring her guardsmen. Some of them have earned priestly ranks and are more experienced than Morgan's soldiers—or, at least the ones he left here. No one expected Halimeda to attack me in my own home."

"But it wasn't an attack," Elena said. "She didn't do anything other than babble gibberish."

"No?" Morwena's eyes narrowed. "What about what she did to Rhiannon's guards? Did that look harmless? Those men were in pain and clearly terrified."

"If she wasn't demented, if Halimeda was in her right mind, why would she come here?" Elena asked.

"It had to be for something important," Rhiannon said. "The king has signed her death warrant. She knows that if she's captured, it will be execution, not prison."

"It's clear she didn't come here to find me or Elena," Morwena said. "She seemed shocked to see me, and Elena was a complete surprise to her."

"Maybe she wanted to hurt Prince Morgan," Elena suggested.

"No." Morwena shook her head. "Everyone knows that Morgan and his brothers are away."

"Everyone but me," Elena said. "Away where? What aren't you telling me?"

"There's been an earthquake off Crete," Rhiannon said. "The princes are leading a rescue operation, to save as many humans as possible."

"From the earthquake?" Memories of being in the sea with Orion swept over Elena, overwhelming her senses. She remembered fish and dolphins rushing by, trying to escape some disaster. The memory had been buried, but now she recalled it all. *But that had been hours ago . . . or days. She wasn't sure. Time didn't seem to add up right down here.*

"Worse," Morwena said. "Our far seers tell us that Melqart is sending a tidal wave to destroy Crete and the people on the island."

Elena's brow furrowed. "Melqart?"

"I'll explain later," Morwena said. "It's complicated."

"But why didn't Orion tell me where he was going?" Elena demanded. *Her crew! She should be there with the members of her expedition, not here. All those lives in danger . . . The people and historical treasures on Crete could be lost. And the Phoenician shipwreck . . . her shipwreck . . . What if the earthquake destroyed the site? Priceless knowledge could be lost forever, along with her one chance to prove herself.* "Orion swore he wouldn't deceive me again." Rising anger made Elena's tone sharp. "He lied."

"Not a lie," Rhiannon said. "An omission—to protect you. You're only human, Elena. You have courage and a good heart, but in the midst of a tsunami, if you'd insisted on going, you'd have been a danger to him and to his mission."

"Let me go to your maids," Morwena said. "They may need assistance to recover. Crosses are susceptible to witchcraft," she explained. "They'll be weak and—"

"We may as well all go," Rhiannon said. "If Elena's faced down Halimeda at her worst, a few puking girls won't upset her. And you seem good in an emergency. I'd appreciate your help, Elena. If you would?"

"Of course," she agreed, "but I'm still not convinced that Halimeda is anything but a disturbed old woman."

"Princess Rhiannon!" A distressed male voice echoed through the room. Seconds later, one of the soldiers from the gate appeared in the archway, his face pale and anxious. "Forgive me for intruding, Princess. It's Lady Athena. She's been hurt! She's calling for you."

"What happened to her?" Rhiannon asked. "Danu was with her. Is she unharmed?"

The guard stood numbly, unwilling or unable to speak.

"Where's Danu?" Morwena demanded.

The soldier looked as if he would burst into tears. "She's gone, Princess. Our Danu is gone. The witch Halimeda struck down Lady Athena and stole your daughter!"

*   *   *

"Let go of me!" Danu cried. "I don't like you. You hurt Lady Athena."

"Quiet, brat, or it will be the worse for you!" Halimeda kept walking through the dank tunnel, dragging the child after her. Nothing had gone as she'd planned today, and now she'd be forced to substitute this nasty little wretch for Morwena. When she got her hands on the Samoan, Caddoc would feel her wrath. She'd serve him Tora's balls and staff in an oyster shell with lobster sauce.

A simple thing she'd asked of the two of them. Snatch Morwena and bring her to Melqart's temple for sacrifice. It should have been easy—two warriors against a junior priestess. But, no, they had to mess that up. Since he'd been a boy, Caddoc had disappointed her. She'd kept hoping that with Melqart's help he would act like the prince he'd been born, but so far, he was laughable.

This brat was a princess, and that should satisfy Melqart and his priests as a respectable sacrifice, but it gave her little satisfaction. Halimeda had wanted to strike at Poseidon's heart. This Danu wasn't the grandchild of his loins. She'd once been human. Not only inferior, but disgusting. Luckily, Melqart's priests, humans themselves, wouldn't care.

She was still providing an Atlantean princess for the fires, and that was what was important. But the loss of Poseidon's favorite daughter—that bitch Korinna's whelp—burned like gall in Halimeda's throat. How could Caddoc have been so lazy as to send Tora to carry out her orders? Why had she trusted him? And now neither the Samoan nor her son were to be found, not in Atlantis, and not in range of Melqart's vision, which meant they were either dead or beyond his reach. They'd fled far away, but Caddoc always returned. And if he came, Tora would follow.

And when they did show their faces again, she'd make them both regret their bumbling.

Caddoc couldn't manage without her, and wherever he went, Tora came sniffing after him like a dogfish. The big Samoan could be ferocious in battle, but he didn't have the brains of a sponge and a cuttlefish combined—not that cuttlefish were known for their intelligence. Halimeda had always considered cuttlefish rather dense, however tasty they might be in a chowder. Too bad Melqart didn't fancy oversized and tattooed warriors of the male gender, but his tastes tended to be ordinary, run-of-the-mill. Melqart preferred nubile, screaming, and virgin females as fuel for his fires. Virgins, in Halimeda's opinion, were vastly overrated.

The passageway grew ever lower and narrower. Moisture dripped from the ceiling and the floor choked in rotting seaweed and tidal mud. Fish bones and decaying mollusks jutted out of the sludge. The stench clogged Halimeda's sinuses and formed a palatable and cloying cloud at the back of her throat. She hoped she hadn't taken a wrong turn in the temple maze. The tunnels were cursed with dead ends, pitfalls, and lakes full of flesh-eating plants.

Poor Melqart. History had ignored him, and his wonderful maze had been falsely abducted by something known as a Minotaur. Greek legend told of maidens and young men sacrificed to the bull god of Crete, obviously the fantasies of some hack writer or bard who ran out of material in the middle of an important gig.

Virgins were taken as offerings from Crete as well as Carthage, mainland Greece, the islands, Thrace, and the area where Troy had once stood. They'd been gathered by the dozens from Tyre, Ashkelon, Cyprus, and the lands which would one day come under Roman rule, not for a bone-headed Minotaur, but for Melqart, himself. True, he did possess the ability to assume the form of a bull-headed man, but that was a minor apparition. And Crete had never been important. Crete was a backwater nothing, certainly not the center of his worship.

With the passing of centuries, the civilized world had moved on to newer gods and newer superstitions, but at the cost of Melqart's power. He'd held on for eons, remaining formidable long after the cults of Jupiter and Artemis had withered and been abandoned. Deities such as Zeus, Mars, and Diana required worshipers. Without believers, they gradually lost power and faded away. Melqart stood in danger of such a fate—not yet, but within the realm of possibility. He needed priests and sacrificial lambs and living beings to praise his name. He needed *her* to give him some backbone.

"My daddy will come and get me," Danu said, interrupting Halimeda's thoughts.

"Shut up!" She scowled at Danu. What kind of a sacrifice didn't weep and scream and beg for mercy? The brat was unnatural. No wonder, having been born a lower species. *Once a human, always a human,* she thought. But she'd have to do. There were other female offspring of Poseidon's, but this one, at least, was young enough to be certain she was a virgin.

"You're going to die," Halimeda said slyly.

Danu thrust out a stubborn chin. "Nope. You're telling lies. And when my daddy and Uncle Alex come, you'll be sorry you were mean to me."

A frisson of icy water dripped onto the nape of Halimeda's neck. "I'm a witch," she said. "I could turn you into a sea slug."

"No," Danu said. "You can't." She pulled her hand out of Halimeda's grasp. "You're a big stinker."

Halimeda drew back and began to whisper incantations. Danu stuck out her tongue. "Stinker!"

"What is this you've brought to me?" boomed Melqart's toad voice.

Halimeda turned and peered into the darkness. There wasn't enough water here to swim and she hated being on solid ground, even if it was a muddy and disgusting tunnel that led to a rundown and second-rate temple. Atlanteans would scorn such an edifice. Still, Melqart retained enough power to cause an earthquake and tidal wave, so she needed to tread carefully on his ego.

She forced her tone to a properly submissive one. "Great one, my son, Prince Caddoc sends you a rare prize. The offering of an unblemished princess of the royal house of Atlantis to honor you. A worthy offering for your altar."

"A puny-sized offering," he rumbled. "Hardly worth the trouble."

"The granddaughter of Poseidon."

The child stared wide-eyed.

"Show yourself, lord of blood and fire," Halimeda urged. That would make the brat piss her tunic. The sight of Melqart would strike her deaf and dumb.

A light flickered and hot wind blasted from the spot. The toad image flashed, driving a foul stench before it. Halimeda glanced at the child. Danu's eyes were clenched shut and she was whispering a strange, frightening chant.

> *"Hey diddle diddle,*
> *The cat and the fiddle,*
> *The cow jumped over the moon . . ."*

Halimeda swallowed against the tightening constriction in her throat. "See him," she croaked. "See Lord Melqart's face!"

"My daddy is coming for me. You'll see. And you and the fat frog will be sorry." The girl smiled and began the chant again. "Hey diddle diddle . . ."

The Rethymo harbor had become a bloodbath. Orion threw himself into the waves, sword drawn. Everywhere the humans who'd been washed into the sea by the receding tidal wave were being decimated by shades.

"Sharks!" a woman on the debris-cluttered shore screamed. "Sharks!" As usual, Orion thought, sharks were being blamed for the massacre.

Alexandros and Morgan were in the water ahead of him, along with twenty or more of their companions. They cut and slashed at the shades, trying in vain to save the drowning victims. A few they were able to surround and drag back to shore, all the while casting an illusion over the poor humans so they'd remember nothing of what had happened in the water. But for most, it was too late.

Human flesh is easily ripped and savaged. And humans possess none of the resilience of Atlanteans. Once mortally wounded, they died. So frenzied was Melqart's horde by the loss of life and the masses of energy rising off the dead bodies that they paid no heed to the warriors. The fanged creatures died in the hundreds on the prongs of razor-sharp tridents and whirling blades.

Not all the dead were humans or Melqart's minions. Once, Morgan fell and a half-dozen shades swarmed over him, biting and clawing. Orion and Alexandros cut their way to his side, heedless of their own safety, and both suffered terrible wounds. Three Atlanteans warriors lost their lives in the quarter of an hour that the battle raged, but in the end, the pack was decimated. A few fled, but not far enough. Steely-eyed Atlanteans hotly pursued, hunting them down with ruthless efficiency. None were spared.

"What now?" Alexandros asked, once the last of Melqart's host had ceased to exist.

Morgan clasped a deep wound in his thigh together as Orion wrapped it with a length torn from his cape. "We've done what we can. We go home."

Alex gazed around at the blood-tinged water. "Three of our own lost, and most of the humans who were unlucky enough to end up in the ocean. Was it worth it?"

"We helped some on land, didn't we?" Orion asked him. His own injuries were bleeding heavily and he was keeping a sharp lookout for real sharks. If they came, his band might be hard-pressed to protect themselves.

Alex shrugged. "Three good men dead, men I've known and fought beside for centuries. Hardly a fair trade."

"But, we won." Their younger half-brother Paris had conducted himself well. He'd shown consistent bravery, tempered with sufficient caution to keep him alive, and Orion was proud of him. Paris bore a gash down one leg and his right hand was badly bitten, but he was grinning. "We killed them all. Not one escaped."

Alexandros threw him a hard look. "You've faced shades before."

Paris nodded. "Not this many, but yes, we fought them at my first—"

"But there were more of them today, and the odds were not so good for us?"

Paris glanced at Orion and then back at Alex. "True, but—"

Alexandros rubbed at the deep bite on his neck. He was bleeding from a dozen places, and his sword was stained black. "How many of them do you think we killed?"

Paris considered. "Two, three hundred, maybe more."

"Closer to five hundred, little brother," Morgan said quietly. "And how many more can Melqart command?"

"A lot more."

There was no humor in Alex's brusque laugh. "We lost three men against five hundred. But Melqart will send thousands more, maybe tens of thousands. And he has the ability to create more at will. They could easily overwhelm us, destroy our army, and leave Atlantis and our colonies helpless."

"Our women and children, our priests and priestesses . . . our farmers and scientists and mathematicians," Morgan said.

"So we won't fight?" Paris asked.

"We'll fight," Orion assured him. "We will fight so long as any of us can stand and wield a sword. Whether there will be enough of us to matter—that's the question."


"Father, you must do something," Morwena pleaded. "How can you allow your own grandchild to be snatched away by that evil woman and do nothing?"

"Danu is so small. And she is precious to me and to your son," Rhiannon added. "You must send a scouting party to—"

Poseidon rose and embraced his daughter-in-law. "Don't tell me what I must do. I know my duty as king. Don't you think my heart is equally torn by this treachery?"

The family was gathered in Korinna's private sitting room: the king and queen, Lady Athena, Lord Mikhail, and Princess Eudora, as well as other women that Morwena had whispered to Elena were minor wives or concubines. Dozens of children milled around, climbing on Korinna's lap, being fed grapes and shrimp by their mothers or rocked by nurses.

It was the first time that Elena had met the high queen and Orion's stepmother had greeted her with warmth and affection. But, clearly, everyone was shocked by Danu's abduction and Halimeda's invasion of Rhiannon and Morgan's apartments, not to mention the attack on Lady Athena.

"You can't just stand by and see—" Morwena began.

"I do what I must!" Poseidon insisted. "Morgan, Orion, and Alexandros will be back soon. The other groups that went out to assist the humans returned as well . . . most of them. Our count of dead is over thirty, and another six are sorely wounded."

Queen Korinna's face whitened. "Paris?"

"Safe," the king assured her. "By the grace of the Creator. None in this room have lost brothers or sons, but others will mourn in our city. And I can't mount a rescue mission until I have consulted Morgan and my generals. It may be a trap, a lure to destroy more of our soldiers. As much as I care for Danu, I must think like a king and not a grandfather. She is one. I must balance her well-being against that of many."

"But it's Danu!" Morwena said. "If you won't, I'll—"

Her mother raised a hand and touched her lips. "Peace, daughter. Have faith in your father's wisdom. If Halimeda took our Danu, she took her for a reason. We must know that reason before we rush blindly in to save her."

"Acting without thought could bring about her death," Lord Mikhail said. "I've sent out scouts to find where Halimeda took her. We should know more shortly."

Elena's gaze returned to linger on the nobleman. Tonight, he didn't look as much like her father as he had when she'd first seen him on the staircase, but there was something . . . something that drew her to him. Tonight, he seemed sterner, more distant and reserved, and his appearance seemed different. But was she seeing him as he truly was? Orion's tricks of illusion had made her suspicious.

Knowledge that he was returning soon was a relief, but worry about Rhiannon's little girl chilled her. This place Atlantis was more complicated than she'd ever imagined, just as her feelings for Orion were complicated. He'd given her his word, and then deceived her again. Could she ever trust him? Had what they'd shared been only an infatuation? Maybe this was all a dream and the man she'd believed she was in love with was as much an illusion as her attempts to succeed in her chosen field of archeology.

# CHAPTER 27

"Elena?"

She opened her eyes. Had someone called her name? Or had she been dreaming? She lay in a heap of sweet-smelling comforters in an enormous bed in the guest wing of Rhiannon and Morgan's apartments—more palace than a suite of rooms. How long she'd been asleep, Elena wasn't sure, but she felt rested. She stretched like a lazy cat and gazed around at the elegant bedchamber, still not sure what had awakened her out of such a deep sleep.

This chamber, richly but tastefully furnished, boasted crystal domes along one entire wall in place of windows. Beyond the domes stretched the garden court with its ever-changing view of a coral reef inhabited by hundreds of exotic species of fish, plants, reptiles, and mammals. The room was softly lit, both from artificial stars set into the high ceiling and from the blue-green light streaming in from the garden.

Elena stretched, realizing how much better she felt for the solitude and rest she'd enjoyed in this comfortable bed. A tray of delicious-smelling food and drink waited at a bedside table, and fresh clothing lay draped across a marble bench. She yawned and rolled her head, easing the kinks out of her neck. She hated to admit it, but she could get used to this luxury, to the smiling servants, and the beautiful garments that appeared out of nowhere without lifting a hand.

The guest chamber offered other delights that she'd sampled before she'd slept. A panel of different colored and shaped shells stood close to the bed, and touching the various shells brought forth a myriad of strange and peaceful music. Some were whale songs; others the cries of seals and seabirds, or crashing surf. What intrigued her most were the instruments that poured forth notes touching chords deep inside her.

A sunken bath filled one corner of the room. Warm mineral water with a light, refreshing scent bubbled up from the bottom of a marble pool surrounded by decorative tiles which might have been excavated from a Roman villa. The wall facing the foot of the bed contained dozens of cubby-holes filled with scrolls, a library arranged much like the one Morwena had shown her when she'd first arrived.

In these unique books, all translated into English, she'd found histories of ancient civilizations, works of poetry, mathematics, science, and medicine. One scroll she'd read until she could no longer keep her eyes open, was a fantastic first-person account of the arrival of a fleet of starships from a distant solar system.

"Elena."

She sat up and turned toward the voice, hoping that Orion was really there. Grinning, he crossed the distance between them in four strides and gathered her in his arms.

"Orion." He kissed her, and she wrapped her arms around his neck. He had much to answer for, and she'd been prepared to be angry with him when he appeared, but at this moment, she relished the joy of his lips on hers and his hands touching her. "I've missed you."

"And I you," he answered huskily.

She looked at him. He looked much the worse for wear. His eyes were bloodshot and his cuirass marred by slashes and tooth marks. Healing cuts and bruises covered every inch of his skin. "You're hurt," she said.

"Nothing to concern yourself with." He hugged her tightly and kissed her again. "I can't stay. The troops have been called up. We're going into battle, but I couldn't leave without seeing you."

"Battle? I don't understand. And why didn't you tell me where you were going when you left?" She swallowed the lump in her throat and cupped his face between her palms. "Morwena said that there was a tidal wave that hit Crete. What of my crew? Are they safe?"

"The captain of your charter boat took the two women out to sea. They had time to get away. They should be all right. Vessels not at anchor and away from the shore are usually unharmed. Stefanos was at the house with an older woman. Is she a servant?"

Elena nodded. "Our cook. You're sure the wave didn't reach the house?"

"The lower floors may have been flooded, but the house is strong. It will stand." He pressed something into her hand.

Elena looked down to see the diamond ring that Greg had given her.

"It's yours, isn't it? It must be valuable," Orion said.

"How did you get it?"

"I wanted to retrieve the gold coin that you took from the Phoenician ship. It's evil, and it needs to go back to its rightful owner. It might save lives if I return it. Alex and I looked for the site, Elena, but we couldn't find it. I think it was buried again in the earthquake."

Her heart raced. The ship that she'd put all her hopes on was gone, as lost to the world as it had been for twenty-five hundred years. She waited, expecting to feel crushing disappointment. But, oddly, it didn't come. All she felt was a sense of relief. "Did you find the coin? It was in the box with the ring."

"Yes. I have it, but I won't give it to you. It's too dangerous."

"I don't want it, and I don't want the ring either. It was given to me by a man I thought I might want to marry. But I was wrong. He was wrong."

"I don't want your ring, at least not that one. It's yours. Do with it what you want."

"I will." The image of another ring suddenly rose in her mind. "Wait . . . there *was* a ring . . ." she began. "An old ring that . . ."

Orion smiled at her. "This ring?" He took her left hand and slid the gold ring on her finger. It fit perfectly.

"How . . . Why?" She looked down at the ring. This felt right. Warmth bloomed in her chest. "I don't understand," she said. "I found it in an old wooden boat, and then it came back to me at . . ."

"It's very old and very precious," he said. "And it was always meant to be yours."

Her throat tightened. "I love you, Orion. I do, but there's so much about you that I don't . . ."

"Trust me."

"How can I? Whatever I see, whatever . . ." She sighed in exasperation. "What am I supposed to think? You promised me that you wouldn't lie to me anymore, that there'd be no more deceit between us."

"If this is about not telling you where I was going, I couldn't. I couldn't take you to the rescue operation any more than I can take you to war." He gazed at her with those haunting green eyes, and she had to steel herself to remain firm.

"I don't know what kind of women you're used to, Orion, but I've never been the subservient type. I won't be controlled. I won't be ordered around and *taken care of,* and I won't be lied to."

A hint of a smile passed over his sensual lips. "You've spent time with Morwena and Rhiannon. Do they seem subservient to you?"

"No, but nothing here is as it seems. It's worse than the fairy kingdom or whatever that place was. There was an old woman that they called a witch. Halimeda, they said her name was. Morwena is convinced she tried to cast a spell over her, and she shot her with an arrow." She shook her head. "This isn't normal behavior. Not by any stretch."

"You're right. I've brought you here, dumped all this on you, and you don't know what's real and what's not."

"Rhiannon and Morgan's daughter, Danu, is missing. They believe that Halimeda took her. Is that possible?"

His jaw tightened. "Yes, it is."

"Are you going to do something about it? Aren't you going to try to get her back?"

Orion swallowed. "I wish I could, but I can't. Not now. My command is waiting. We're going into battle against Melqart's forces. When I come back—if I come back, I'm going to ask you a question."

She gripped his hand. "But what about little Danu?"

"If we win the war, the chances are that we'll get her back safely. For now, Poseidon has to balance her life against that of hundreds—maybe thousands. If Halimeda took her, Danu could be anywhere. Lord Mikhail's spies are searching for her. Once we have proof where she is, there may be—"

"Lord Mikhail? I've seen him, Orion. Do you know him?"

"He's my Aunt Eudora's consort."

"How long have you known him?"

"Does that matter?"

"It does to me. He's not who he says he is." She hesitated. "You'll think I've lost my wits, but I could swear . . . His voice . . . something about him." She took a deep breath. "I think he's my father."

"Mikhail? A human?"

"I'm a human. I'm here, aren't I? Logically, it's not possible, but I'm here, under the sea with you, and I have to accept that. So, why couldn't the same thing happen to someone else? My father vanished at sea. Maybe he was captured by Atlanteans, turned into one of you by illusion or magic or whatever you do. I've tried to speak to him, but he won't talk to me. Tell me that I'm crazy, Orion. Or is it possible?"

"You're telling me that you believe that Mikhail was once human?"

"I don't know what I'm telling you, but I have to know the truth, and you're the only one I can turn to. Morwena wouldn't believe me. And if he is my father, he must be brainwashed or something, because he's avoiding me."

He hugged her again. "Mikhail can't be who you think he was. If he was, I'd know it."

"Will you ask your father—someone who'd know for certain?"

"There's no time, Elena, not before I leave. But I promise I'll find the truth for you."

"And you'll tell me? No more secrets?" When Orion was away from her, she could make sensible choices, but when he was here, she wanted nothing more than to make wild, passionate love to him. She wanted to hold him and never let him go. Everything she'd worked for all her life was nothing compared to this man. It was impossible, but it was true. "Don't leave me," she begged him.

"I don't want to, Elena. But I have to do this. I'm a soldier. This is what I do, what I was born to do. If I don't fight to defend you—to defend all I love—I'm useless. I couldn't look at my image in a mirror. I couldn't live with myself."

Tears gathered in the corners of her eyes. "If you keep leaving me, there's no future for us."

"Be patient, just a little while longer. Wait for me. When I return, I promise things will be different." He turned and walked away from the bed. She slid down and followed him. "I have to go now, but there's one thing I can share with you."

Her eyes widened. "Yes."

He took both of her hands. "Close your eyes. And when I tell you, open them."

"Why? What . . ."

"Trust me. I'm giving you what you want. I'm showing you who and what I am—what I really look like. No more illusions between us."

She began to tremble, frightened of what she didn't understand, afraid that the truth she wanted so badly would destroy everything.

"Open your eyes."

Slowly, she did. And what she saw nearly knocked her off her feet. The man in front of her was Orion, but more than the Orion she'd come to know and love. Not exactly human, but beautiful all the same. His body was covered with a pattern of tiny scales, and his skin, if it was skin, had a faint blue tinge. His golden hair fell long and curling around his impossibly wide and powerful shoulders. He looked like a Greek statue of a god come to life.

"Ohhh." It came out of her mouth as a long sigh. "You're . . . you're . . ."

"Atlantean," he answered. "Not human, but another species of humanoid."

Tiny webs joined the base of his fingers and toes, but the sight of them didn't repulse her. Rather, she stared in awe. "You're wonderful," she whispered. The Grecian armor remained, glittering gold and silver. He carried the same sword that she'd seen, black and shiny, huge and frightening. But most of all, she was struck by the perfection of his face and form. "A superhero," she said.

He chuckled. "Hardly that. But we do possess strength beyond that of your kind."

*Apollo,* she thought. *I've been sleeping with Apollo. No wonder he's such a fantastic lover. He isn't human.*

"I don't frighten you in this state?"

She smiled. "Hardly," she teased. "But why did you hide from me all this time? Or, is this an illusion, too, and you actually look like an oversized squid?"

He laughed. "This is it, Elena. And I take no credit for my appearance. Eons of superior genes and an attractive mother."

"And your brother Alex. Is he this beautiful?"

"He's my twin. He'd tell you that he's the sexier of the two of us, but don't believe him. Alexandros likes to exaggerate, especially about the size of his . . . his attributes."

"I suppose Morwena is some kind of superhero, as well? And Rhiannon?" She didn't want Orion to go. If she could just keep him talking, delay him, perhaps . . .

"Just Atlanteans, all of us. Once you accept what I look like, the others won't seem so unusual."

"So if you look like you do, why were you attracted to me? I'm nothing special. And, as you like to remind me, I'm only human."

He lowered his head and kissed her tenderly. "You're not only anything, Elena. You're special. And, in time, I'll prove just how special."

"And what if there isn't time?" Elena whispered, looking into his eyes, seeing him in a new way, beyond the foreign surface of his skin and the webbing between his toes. "What if there is no more time for us?" She drew her hand over his high cheekbone, feeling the slight ridges of his scales. "What if our time has passed and this is . . . the end?"

"Elena—"

"What if we've found something, only to lose it, something special?"

"I must go, my precious. No matter how much I want to be here with you, I have to, but I swear I'll come back to . . ."

A tiny sob rose in her throat and she covered his mouth with hers, silencing his words, words he could not possibly guarantee. "Orion," she whispered, out of breath when she pulled away.

He hesitated.

"Love me," she said softly. "Make love to me this one last time."

She felt his arms around her relax as he pulled her against him. "And if it isn't our last?"

She slipped her arms around his neck, molding her body to his, to this new body she didn't know and yet did not seem so foreign. "Then what harm will it do?" she whispered seductively.

As she lifted on her toes to kiss him again, he began to change form, back to the human form she knew. "No, don't . . . I want . . ." She gazed into his eyes hesitantly. "Will you hurt me . . . as you are now?"

"Not if we go slowly."

She smiled, took his hand and led him back to the seashell bed. "Then we'll have to go slowly, won't we, my glorious merman?"

"I'm not a merman. You're going to have to get that right, Elena. We're entirely different species."

She lay down on the bed of soft seaweed and put her arms out to him. "Kiss me then, Atlantean, and stop arguing.

"I never argue with a beautiful woman." He knelt in front of her on the bed and she parted her legs, the flimsy fabric of her clothing fluttering as he leaned over her to take her mouth with his again.

Orion seemed larger now than he had before, and as she felt his tongue push into her mouth, she couldn't help wondering what else was bigger. She felt her body flush with heat as he stretched out beside her, still thrusting his tongue into her mouth, now caressing her breast with one big hand, with its thin webs between his fingers.

Elena pushed the sleeveless tunic off his bulging shoulders, suddenly eager to touch every part of his body. Feel it with her hands. Taste it with her tongue . . . know him as he truly was. As he stroked her breasts, then her stomach, she ran her hands over his body, exploring. The scales were not rough, more like tiny ridges under her fingertips. And though his body was different, larger, harder, more sensitive, it responded in the same way it always had to her caresses.

She felt Orion's hand skim over her bare thigh and then lower. Her breath was already coming too fast. Too fast! She wanted this time—what might be their last—to be painfully, beautifully slow, but she was already throbbing in want of him. Need.

His finger brushed the cleft between her thighs and she opened her legs, arching her back, threading her fingers through his long, beautiful blond hair. He lowered his mouth to that sweet place, and she closed her eyes, moaning as the waves of pleasure washed over her. She didn't want to surrender; she wanted to savor the moment, but she couldn't hold back and she cried out as she reached orgasm.

Orion rested his cheek on her thigh and caressed her hip, giving her a moment to catch her breath. His motion remained constant, though. Stroking her . . . then more kisses: first between her breasts, then her abdomen, then lower again.

"Orion, please. I want to feel you inside me."

"We cannot rush this, my love. You must be ready."

"I'm ready," she moaned, already feeling herself building again.

But still, he denied her. He kissed and stroked and then thrust his fingers inside her. She bucked against him, coming again almost at once. Only then, when she had caught her breath once more, did he finally strip off his garment.

Elena lay back on the bed and stared at his engorged shaft, more a wonder than his exotic, scaled blue body. It was so big . . . surely too big. But then Orion kissed her again, first her mouth, then one nipple and then the other and she could not bear the thought of not finishing what she had started.

When at last Orion drew his body over hers, she reached down and closed her fingers over him. His murmur of pleasure encouraged her to stroke his full length and breadth, and then, certain she could wait no longer, she guided him inside her.

There was no pain, thanks to Orion's tender care. She opened up to him, taken him fully, consumed by him and the love she felt for him at this moment, no matter what of God's creatures he was.

He gave her a moment catch her breath, to acclimate, and then he began to move inside her. Slowly, at first, then faster to match the pounding of her heart. She tightened her legs around him, meeting each thrust, dragging her nails over his scaly back. She came quick and hard, but demonstrating great control, he teased her upward again . . . then again.

Tears slid down Elena's cheeks as one last time she achieved an unbelievable orgasm, this time going hand in hand with Orion's.

"I didn't hurt you, did I?" he murmured in her ear as he fell beside her.

"No." She gave a little laugh, brushing the tears from her cheeks, a little embarrassed. "You didn't hurt me. That was . . . it was incredible. "

He kissed the tip of her nose. "I'm glad you were able to find pleasure in my body as it is in true form. I feared—"

A metallic gong sounded from somewhere in the distance, followed by the deep resounding peal of a horn, and Orion quickly sat up, reaching for his clothing.

"What is that?"

"That's the signal," Orion said. "I must leave now. Wait for me. I'll come back to you, if I can, and then we'll make plans."

"Will we?"

He embraced her a final time, brushed her lips with his, and then strode out of the room, leaving her more confused than before. *What had he meant by they'd make plans? And would he find out if the man who called himself Lord Mikhail was really Randal Carter, her father?*

Orion nearly collided with Mikhail in the secret passageway that led to Poseidon's small throne room. The older man carried an armload of scrolls, and seemed deep in thought. "Prince Orion," he said. "I've just come from a final consultation with your father."

"He's going into battle with us."

Mikhail nodded. "I know. I tried to talk him out of it."

"In his place, I'd do the same. Good men will die today. He wants to be with them."

"He's appointed Queen Korinna to stand as regent in his place, with me to assist her. And the High Council, of course. In case . . ."

"In case Poseidon should be one of those good men."

"I'm afraid so." Mikhail shifted his weight, obviously in a hurry to end the conversation.

Orion hadn't intended to confront his aunt's consort before he went into battle, but the hallway was deserted except for the two of them, and there might be no better chance to keep his promise to Elena.

"Is it true?" he asked the older man. "Did Halimeda kidnap Morgan's daughter?"

Mikhail nodded. "I'm afraid so."

"Do you know where Danu is?"

Mikhail shook his head. "My contacts are working on that. I have my suspicions, but I'd rather not say until I'm certain."

"She's a child, a little girl. What kind of monster would take her?"

"You know what kind." Mikhail looked grim. "I'm afraid she took Danu to Melqart's lair. If she did, we'll be hard-pressed to get her back."

"Alive, you mean."

Mikhail nodded. "It's not a mission that can be done openly. If Halimeda suspects we know where Danu is, she may kill her out of spite."

"But why would Melqart want an Atlantean child? Not as a hostage. He's never—"

Mikhail's expression hardened. "Danu is a royal princess. She would make Melqart's slimy priests shit in their kilts for joy."

Orion's heart skipped a beat. "They couldn't mean to . . ."

"Sacrifice her on the altar. Yes, they could. And it wouldn't be the first time one of Melqart's followers has done something like this. Not to us, but I know for a fact that three fairy queens have burned in his fires over the centuries. And one was younger than Danu."

"I'll strangle the bastard with his foreskin if he so much as breathes on her."

"I'll do what I can," Mikhail promised. He shifted the scrolls into his right arm and laid his left hand on Orion's shoulder. "My operatives are very good at what they do. Sometimes mer folk or silkies can get into areas an Atlantean couldn't. As you are well aware, our illusions don't work with Halimeda or with Melqart."

"If I find Halimeda, I'll part her head from her neck."

"May it come to pass." A scroll slipped from his grasp. Mikhail caught it and tucked it back into the pile. "Now, we both have places to be. Take care of yourself. You've always been dear to Eudora."

"One more question before you go."

"Yes?"

"Elena, the woman I brought from Crete."

"I'm aware of her. A human is difficult to miss in Atlantis."

Orion looked into Mikhail's eyes. "Elena believes that you're her father. That you were once human. Is there any truth to that?"

# CHAPTER 28

For an instant, Mikhail's stern mask slipped, and Orion glimpsed the troubled man beneath the façade. Orion studied him intently. *Was there some resemblance to Elena? The eyes, maybe? Mikhail's coloring was different, not simply the skin variation between humans and Atlanteans, but his natural complexion was fairer than Elena's warm olive complexion. But if Mikhail had been human, it was possible that he could be her father. If so, it was a secret that had been well kept in a palace where few secrets were.*

Orion couldn't have been more stunned if Caddoc's man, Tora, had jumped out from behind the granite statue of the centaur that stood only an arm's length away and struck him over the head with a Samoan war club. "You were human, Mikhail? How is that possible? Aunt Eudora . . ."

"Don't blame her. She knows, of course. She's the one who found me, who returned me to life when my ship went down. Not the same kind of life, but life. It's no secret to Poseidon, but few others were aware that I wasn't born to the Kingdom."

Orion swore.

"It's something that I'd naturally prefer not be known,

considering the key position I hold in government. Some Atlanteans might hold it against me and be suspicious of my actions."

Orion tried to come to terms with what he'd just heard. "I suppose Elena will be ecstatic," he said finally.

"You can't tell her."

"Why not? Doesn't she have a right to know? She's your flesh and blood. She worships the memory of you."

"The memory of who I was," Mikhail said.

"She said you refused to talk to her when she saw you. Why?"

"It's not a question that I care to answer. Not to you."

"She loved you. Loves you. Doesn't that count for anything? Don't you care about her, you heartless bastard?"

Mikhail drew himself up to his full height, which brought him within several inches of Orion's. "I care more than you could possibly know or understand," Mikhail said. "Elena and I were always very close. Losing her was one of the hardest things I had to come to terms with when I went through . . . my transformation. Which is precisely why you can't tell her who I am."

"What's to stop me? I promised her that I'd find out, and that I'd share the information with her," Orion said.

"She's human. You can't reveal the truth. She might decide to stay here, simply to be near me. And that would be terribly wrong."

"She's not a child! Elena has the right to make that decision."

"You're wrong, Prince Orion. This is between a father and a daughter. It's not your decision to make."

Orion knotted his hands into fists and clamped them to his sides to keep from striking the man. "So you'd deny your own daughter? Have me lie to her?"

"As if you hadn't already. Otherwise, how would you

have gotten her here in the first place?" He met Orion's gaze. "Isn't this a little late to play the noble prince?"

"What I did," Orion said, "was for her protection."

"And my intentions are the same. She's human. I'm Atlantean. As you are. I can see that you're infatuated with her, but you have no idea how wide the chasm is between our worlds."

"But it should be Elena's choice," Orion repeated.

"And if she makes the wrong choice, there's no going back. If she stays here, she gives up her humanity forever."

"Was it such a bad decision for you?"

"I didn't have a choice. I had drowned. Eudora made the choice to revive me in another form. It's different for Elena. She has a life in front of her, possibilities, the opportunity to rise to the top of her academic career field, to show up the fools who laughed at me."

"I love her, and I think she loves me. Doesn't that count for anything?"

"It does, but love is inconstant. What Elena is—what she can become—that may be more important to her happiness. She could do so much to advance knowledge of the ancient worlds. Perhaps even open a dialogue between Atlanteans and humans."

"She couldn't do that if she were to become one of us?"

"Absolutely not. Humans would regard her as a freak. She is more likely to be stoned by a crazed mob than to be treated with the respect she deserves. Any message she might give would be utterly buried in a tide of fear and superstition."

"Are humans so backward?"

Mikhail scoffed. "What happened when the last interplanetary visitor landed in the western part of the United States? The ambassadors were murdered and the government denied that they ever existed."

"I'm aware of what happened, but that doesn't mean—"

Mikhail cut him off curtly. "Whether my daughter remains here or returns to earth, she must decide for herself. I refuse to interfere with that choice. And you are honor bound to keep my secret."

"Why should I be?" Anger made Orion's voice harsh.

"Because I ask it of you. A father's rights come before that of a lover."

"I won't tell her now, and—for Elena's sake, I'll give you the courtesy of considering your opinion. But, if I survive the coming war, I mean to ask her to be my wife. If she agrees, will you tell her the truth?"

Mikhail rubbed his chin thoughtfully. "We'll see when that time comes. It may be that she'll refuse you, and then the question will be moot."

"Did you ever love her?" Orion asked.

"I did. I do. I always will. But that was another life, another time. She was nine years old when we met last. And we all change. She may not like the person I've become. I'd not have her decide the rest of her existence based on a child's memories of a doting parent."

Hours later, Elena stood at one of the crystal domes in her bedroom, staring out at a dolphin and her calf. The two dolphins were playing together and showed such obvious affection for each other that it seemed to Elena that—except for shape and color—they could have been a human mother and child.

She sensed rather than heard someone in the room and turned to see Morwena. "I never realized that dolphins possessed a sense of humor," Elena said.

"Oh, they do," Morwena said. "In many ways, they feel things more intensely than we do. Laughter, anger, sorrow.

Never underestimate a dolphin. They possess the highest intelligence."

Elena glanced up at her. Morwena's face was pale, her eyes red. She'd obviously been weeping. "You saw Orion?" Elena asked.

This was still Morwena, the same, but different. The illusion that she was human no longer existed. Morwena, princess of Atlantis, could have been a shining, larger-than-life superheroine. And, she, too, was beautiful in form and features, too beautiful for words. At any other time, in any other place, her friend's transformation from human to alien species would have been impossible to assimilate, but at this moment, all that mattered was Morwena's obvious distress.

"And Alexander and Paris." Her eyes glistened with tears. "Morgan's being treated for the injuries he received off Rethymo." She came to stand at the crystal dome beside Elena and reached for her hand.

Elena took the offered hand and squeezed it tightly.

"This ring—where did you get it?" Morwena asked.

"Orion gave it to me before he left. I think he's given it to me three times, now. Maybe it's time I wore it."

Morwena nodded. "Maybe it is."

"I love him."

"Enough?"

"For what?

"To trust him."

Elena shook her head. "I don't know."

"Make certain you are sure before you make any commitment."

"I will."

Morwena was silent for a long time, and they stood and stared out the window at the reef together. Finally, Morwena broke the silence. "Rhiannon says that Morgan's in a rage. Not only has Poseidon refused to allow him to mount a rescue effort to find Danu, but the healers have declared him unfit to go into battle. Our father the king has forbidden Morgan to leave Atlantis."

"I didn't know Prince Morgan was badly hurt. Was he injured trying to rescue the tidal wave victims?"

"In a manner of speaking. You saw Orion's injuries, didn't you?"

Elena nodded.

"Did you see the bite marks?"

"Yes, but I thought . . ." Elena didn't know what she'd thought. She'd wanted to ask him, but once he'd kissed her . . . once he'd given her the ring and she'd seen him as he truly was, the moment had passed. All that mattered was keeping him in the circle of her arms as long as possible. "Sharks?"

Morwena shook her head. "Not sharks. Something worse. Shades."

"What are shades?"

"Soulless creatures, all teeth and claws. Melqart's horde. They're big, taller than I am, and they hunt in packs, sometimes in waves of hundreds. They feed on flesh and bone. Melqart is an ancient Phoenician god of war. They're his minions. Every life the shades extinguish adds to his power. The shades drink blood. Melqart exists on the life forces of those he destroys. It's the shades our men and women have gone to do battle against."

"You're telling me that some kind of supernatural *things* made those wounds on Orion? Something called a shade? It's hard for me to believe, Morwena. I don't doubt you believe what you say, but you called that old woman a witch, too. And I didn't see witchcraft."

"Didn't see witchcraft, or didn't believe it?" Morwena asked. There was no anger in her gaze, only sadness. "Life is more than what you see and hear and touch, Elena. We are spiritual beings as well as physical. Magic is real, and not believing in it doesn't make it go away."

"If these things, these *shades*, exist, why haven't we . . . Why has there been no evidence of them? Why haven't my people—humans—ever seen them?"

"They hunt mostly at night. They pull down lone swimmers. Sometimes they just suck the blood out of the victims, and sometimes, if they're hungry, they tear them to shreds and devour everything but hair and bone. For centuries, for thousands of years, humans have blamed sharks. The bite marks are similar. The teeth and jaws on shades are out of proportion to their size. You've probably read about such attacks all your life and believed that it was a killer shark. And how many humans have supposedly drowned in the ocean and their bodies never found?"

Elena shuddered. "If what you say is true . . . and I say *if*, then why are the Atlanteans going to war against them? It seems an unfair fight."

"It is," Morwena admitted. "Melqart can field untold numbers. And there have never been many of us. Not like the human race. Our warriors number in the thousands, not tens of thousands. And we're going to war against Melqart. He's behind the attacks. Shades think like . . . like a hive of insects. They don't possess individual intelligence, but they have a pack mentality. Without Melqart to give orders, they'll cease to exist."

"So why aren't they going right to the source? Why aren't your people attacking this Melqart?"

"He's very powerful and elusive. He takes many forms. I'm not certain that he even has a solid existence that could be killed. For thousands of years, men worshiped him. There were many other evil gods of war and violence in the dawn of time, but most have vanished from the minds of men. Without adulation, they wither and die. In time, even the memory of their power is forgotten."

"So the Atlanteans go out to fight monsters with swords and tridents."

"Yes." Morwena nodded her head. "If we can destroy Melqart's power source, we destroy him, or at least drive him into hibernation. It's happened before. Once, he didn't surface for hundreds of human years."

"Can these shades be killed?"

"Actually, swords are pretty effective. Tridents, not so much. If you cut them in two, they die, and when they die, they turn to a black oily smoke. Unfortunately, Melqart can create more."

"Where does the witch come in to all of this?" Elena asked. It was crazy, impossible, but was it any more impossible than the fact that she was walking around under the sea and in love with an Atlantean? Was it any more ridiculous than her suspicion that her father was still alive and had become one of them?

"Morwena!"

Elena turned at the sound of Rhiannon's voice.

"You've got to come and see this. You, too, Elena. A newscaster just showed your photograph. They think you drowned in the tidal wave that hit Crete."

"Newscaster? Don't tell me you have television?" Elena said.

"Not exactly." Rhiannon chuckled. "We do pick up your transmissions. How else would we know so much about your world?"

Elena and Morwena hurried after Rhiannon into a small library. In the center of the room, someone had mounted half of a large seashell on a marble pedestal. The shell held clear liquid of some kind, and an image flickered on the surface. Elena heard a man with a British accent say, ". . . live from the island of Crete . . ."

"Look." Rhiannon pointed to the screen. The picture was wavy, but Elena could make out the reporter and several people standing at the edge of a harbor. Behind and around them shattered remains of boats, shops, and homes lay on a flattened beach.

". . . An American hero," the reporter said, thrusting a microphone at a man in cut-off shorts and a ball cap that read RETHYMO IS FOR LOVERS in Greek.

Elena stared. It was Greg Hamilton. And standing beside him were her associates, Irene and Hilary, and a blond woman that she didn't recognize.

"Yes, well, it was pretty evident that people would die if someone didn't take charge," Greg said. "And . . . when the earthquake hit . . . I . . . I . . ."

The blonde slipped neatly in front of Greg and addressed the camera. "My husband was magnificent," she cooed.

"Her husband?" Elena echoed.

"Shh," Morwena hushed her. "Listen to what they're saying."

"People were panicked, running, screaming," the blonde exclaimed.

The cameraman zoomed in on her pretty American face and revealing T-shirt as, clutching Greg's hand, she continued her dramatic tale.

"The hotel was coming apart around us. Walls were falling, and fire had broken out below us. Some guests and employees tried to take the elevator, and Greg stopped them. Greg led them all out, everyone from our floor. He saved my life as well as all of theirs."

The reporter tried to resume control of his news spot, but the well-endowed blond woman flashed a smile at the camera and kept talking. "He's Greg Hamilton from Texas in the United States. We were married just before the earthquake struck and on our honeymoon."

"Were you acquainted with Dr. Elena Carter, head of the expedition . . ." Static rippled the images and garbled the words, but Elena saw her own smiling face flash across the screen again. The photo was a couple of years old, but not bad.

"Dr. Elena Carter, respected academic and underwater archeologist, led the team to Crete where they were investigating a . . ." More interference marred the reception and broke off the reporter's words. A few seconds later, the picture firmed and they heard him say, "With Dr. Carter missing and presumed dead, the university has canceled the project and . . ."

There was static, an erratic picture, and then Greg and his new wife appeared again. She was speaking. ". . . understandably saddened by Dr. Carter's death. My husband has generously offered to fly Dr. Hilary Walden back to Texas with us on his private jet."

More scenes of the destruction on Crete and several other locations followed, as well as an estimated death toll. Elena felt numb. Greg had given her an engagement ring and then—within hours—had married some woman that Elena hadn't known existed.

It was all she could do not to laugh. Not only had she survived an earthquake and a tidal wave, she'd barely escaped being the wife of the biggest ass in Texas. Not that she would have agreed to marry him. She wouldn't have. Orion or no Orion, she'd made that decision while Greg had walked away from her at the harbor.

"They think you're dead," Morwena said.

"Maybe I am." Elena gazed at her. "Maybe I died and this is all some sort of dream . . . or another dimension."

"Hardly a dream to us," Rhiannon said. "My daughter is missing, our army is about to face an overwhelming force and might not come home, and my husband is acting like a madman."

"Poseidon named him co-ruler," Morwena explained. "The king wanted Mother to act as regent with Lord Mikhail to assist her, but apparently he's gone to join the fight, as well."

Elena's breath caught in her throat. "Lord Mikhail went with them? But he's not a soldier."

"No," Rhiannon agreed. "He isn't, but he's an Atlantean. Many went this day who weren't trained as warriors."

*Lord Mikhail.* Elena's heart raced. *If Mikhail was who she thought he was* . . . She shook her head. *She might have found him again, only to lose him a second time.* It was all too much to take in.

"I wanted to go with my brothers. There are women warriors in the ranks. But I decided I had something more important I needed to do."

"More important?" Rhiannon asked.

"Yes," Morwena said. "I'm going after Danu." She looked at Elena. "And you may as well come with me. You've nothing to lose. You're already dead, aren't you?"

# CHAPTER 29

Orion cut and hacked his way to his father's side. Poseidon and a crack force of seasoned fighters had positioned themselves in the shelter of a wall. The huge stone blocks, which had once formed the outer defenses for a city older than Troy, had been covered by the Aegean Sea for three thousand years. Now the wall protected Atlanteans from a merciless enemy.

With their backs protected, the king and his battalion could stand, men four deep, rotating when the front line became fatigued. That way, fresh fighters met each new onslaught of shades. They'd been killing and dying for half a day, yet the horde came on in endless numbers.

The king had just shifted to the rear position after half an hour in the first row. He was winded, breathing hard, and covered in his own blood, but grinning. Fighting beside his troops had kindled a fire in Poseidon's eyes. When he saw Orion, he nodded and sighed heavily. "Too long I've sat in the throne room and let others win my battles for me," he said. "It's good to know that I haven't lost the old skills with a sword."

Orion nodded. His own mood was grim. He'd seen dozens of his own elite Blue-Shields go down under overwhelming numbers. So decimated was his command that he and Alexandros had joined their men. Orion had taken advantage of a lull in the fighting to seek out his father.

Poseidon grasped his arm. "You look well enough for a general. You don't have enough wounds to be out of the fight, and you've shed enough of your own blood to prove your valor. Never ask a man to do what you can't, that's the code I've lived by."

"And so you taught me and my brothers." Orion stepped close to the king, dropping his voice so that the men on his left and in front of him couldn't hear. "I needed to tell you something."

"Make it quick," his father said. "The scales on the back of my neck are twitching." Poseidon wiped blood from his brow with a bare forearm. "Unless I miss my guess, we're about to be hit hard by about a thousand fresh shades."

"I agree, but this can't wait. I wanted you to know, so that . . . if anything happens to me . . ."

"Enough of that talk. Out with it. You've had enough of fighting and decided to enter the priesthood?" The king let out a burst of raucous laughter. "You've gotten a mermaid with child? Or is it that human woman? Is she pregnant?"

"Not that I know of," Orion said. "I took every precaution to make sure it wouldn't happen."

Poseidon scowled at him from under a plumed helmet. "Not enough precaution, if there's a chance she might be with child. I've bedded my share of willing partners, male, female, and otherwise. Once I tried a . . ." He laughed again. "But . . ." His gaze grew hard. "It would turn my stomach to bed with a human, even one as comely as that wench of yours."

Orion forced himself to contain his growing anger. Nothing would be gained by incurring his father's wrath. What was important was Elena's future, and Poseidon held the power to add to her happiness or destroy it. "I intend to ask Elena to be my wife—to remain at my side."

"In Atlantis? By Hades, you will!" his father roared. "Not so long as I draw breath. One in the family is enough. I'll not have a second!"

"You don't know her," Orion argued. "Elena is—"

"Beneath you. It's bad enough that your brother went against me and won the right to keep his human. But at least, she was half-Atlantean. I forbid you to keep her. Send this creature back to where she came from, or I'll make certain she doesn't live long enough to bear a halfbreed abomination."

Orion gritted his teeth. There was no time to try to persuade him, and he knew his father all too well. Set in his ways and stubborn as a moray eel. "If she'd have me, I'll make her my wife," he said quietly. "And if you wish to harm her, you'll have to kill me first."

A warning shout rippled down the line. "They're coming!" a warrior shouted. "Steady! Form up! Give them fire and blades, boys!"

"You forget who I am," the king said. "Swive her all you want, but she'll be no daughter-in-law of mine. I've plenty of brave sons and the means to make more. I'll see you banished for life, as I've done Caddoc, before I tolerate any more—"

"So be it," Orion interrupted. "Do what you must, sire." He turned and started back toward where he'd left Alex and the remaining Blue-Shields. Then he stopped and glanced back over his shoulder. Despite everything, he loved his father.

"Guard your back," Orion murmured, but he knew as he spoke that the words wouldn't carry to Poseidon's ears. And then, softly, almost to himself, he said, "Good-bye, Father." Drawing his sword from its scabbard, he pushed everything but the image of Elena's face from his consciousness and returned to take his place with his men.

Danu stared through the cage bars as the funny-looking men with the fat bellies dragged out the screaming girls, one after another, from their cells. The men were only two cages away, and Danu's heart was beating so fast that it sounded like a drum in her ears. This was not a good place.

Danu hadn't seen the witch Halimeda since the men had locked her in here, and no one had come to bring her food or anything to drink. She was thirsty and her belly ached. Her skin hurt when she touched it. It almost felt like her scales were falling out. She found it harder and harder to breathe because of the black, oily smoke seeping down through the ceiling. Even her hands were drying out and cracking. Danu didn't like being out of the water. She missed the ocean, and she didn't like it in this scary place at all. She wanted her mother, and she wished her daddy would hurry and come for her.

A girl, bigger than her, but not as big as Morwena, screamed as two men dragged her past Danu's cage. The men were laughing. Danu wanted to call out to the girl, but she was afraid. Maybe, if she was very quiet, the bad people would forget that she was here. Behind her, Cymry, her new friend, huffed and snorted, shifting restlessly, so that her silver hooves made hard clicking noises against the stone. "Shh," Danu whispered. "We're hiding."

It was easier for Danu to be brave, now that she wasn't alone. At first, when they'd thrown her in this bad place, Danu had been so scared she almost cried. Then, *poof*, the tiny blue seahorse had appeared! Cymry glowed in the dark, and nobody but Danu could see her. Having her very own magic seahorse made everything better.

"Hide behind me," her friend said. "And think of the reef outside your bedroom window at home. Think about the mother dolphin and her baby and how you like to watch them. Picture it in your mind, and don't think of anything else. And don't make a sound, no matter what you see or hear. Hurry!"

She did as Cymry said, and no sooner was she behind her, than the blue sea horse grew bigger and bigger. Her mane and tail grew longer and thicker until Cymry filled the whole cage, leaving only a small cubby hole in the corner for Danu to hide in. It would have been scary, but Danu knew that Cymry would never hurt her.

There was a scrape and a *clunk*. The metal door creaked open. Danu bit her bottom lip and held her breath.

"Get that one!" one of the bad men said. "That's the special one. She goes into the pit first."

Guided by two mermen, Tadeu and Moises, Elena and Morwena ran through the pitch-dark caves that snaked under the island of Cyprus. Elena had lost track of time since they left the kingdom of Atlantis in the deepest part of the Atlantic and traveled to the bowels of Melqart's temple. The mermen had warned them that most of the temple lay above sea level, foreign territory for them and for Morwena.

Had the distance been shorter and time not so critical, Morwena said that they could have brought young recruits from the military academy and fighting dolphins, but under these conditions, they were on their own. No one knew that they had come to rescue Danu, no one but Rhiannon, and she'd sworn not to tell anyone, not even her husband. Whatever they faced here, they would have to rely on their own wits and Morwena's skill with a bow.

As Elena understood it, the mermen were spies in Lord

Mikhail's network, rather than being warriors, but Morwena assured her that they were more than capable of defending themselves. Certainly she and Morwena would never have known where to look for Danu if it wasn't for Moises and Tadeu. Both claimed to have a vendetta against Melqart, but refused to elaborate.

The journey hadn't been an easy one. Elena shuddered as she thought of the frightening experience of going down into not one seraphim transit system, but four separate ones. She and Morwena and the mermen had endured storms and an encounter with the largest school of sharks Elena had ever seen. Finally, the four of them had nearly been run down and shredded by a Soviet submarine just outside the entrance to the underwater caves that led to Melqart's temple.

*What am I doing here?* Elena thought, trudging behind the mermen. *I don't believe in witches. I certainly don't believe in Phoenician gods, and I've come to the conclusion that this isn't a dream. The man I love is off somewhere fighting cannibalistic creatures with vampire teeth and long claws, and I'm playing Indiana Jones with a female Atlantean archer and two seal-men. I'd better be crazy,* she thought, *because if this is real, I'm in big trouble.*

One of the mermen stopped short. Elena bumped into him and would have fallen if the other one hadn't caught her. "Shh," Morwena said. "Listen."

Elena listened, but heard nothing but her own breathing. The darkness around her was awful, blacker than the darkest night. The cave floor was wet, oozing mud, slippery, and stinking. Cobwebs or something else as sticky and stringy dangled from the low roof. She would not think about the size of the spiders that must have spun webs this large.

Someone tapped her arm, and the small party moved

cautiously forward. In a short while, Elena began to hear singing, something like the chanting of Benedictine monks. And she definitely smelled smoke. *Could a cave burn?*

"Are you sure that Danu is here?" she whispered.

"They're certain," Morwena said. "They followed Halimeda and Danu here."

Elena couldn't imagine a five-year-old child in this dark cave, let alone an Atlantean child. The thought was too horrible to contemplate. She wished that Orion was here with her. Somehow, no matter how bad things had gotten before, she'd always felt safe when he was with her. Almost . . .

The first hint of light was so faint that Elena thought she might be imagining it. She heard Morwena stop, and then she heard the hiss as Morwena drew an arrow from her quiver.

"We have to move faster," Morwena said. "Can't you feel it?"

"Feel what?" Elena asked.

"Something bad is going to happen. Soon."

Heart in her throat, Elena followed the merman ahead of her until the light grew larger and brighter. The sound of chanting had increased as well. "We must be getting closer." But to what, she didn't know.

As screams rose above the chanting, the four broke into a dead run.

Halimeda, garbed in her richest gown and jewels, stood at the base of the thirty-foot-high statue of Melqart. It was a very old likeness, carved crudely of stone. The bull head on the naked man's body was disproportionate. The horns and the phallus and testicles would have been too large and unwieldy for even a god of war to carry around. The feet, in particular, were ridiculous, small and flat, poorly carved, and stained black from centuries of sacrificed goats, chickens, and pigeons. The feet with its stubby toes made Melqart look like a small boy who'd been playing in the mud, rather than an awe-inspiring god.

Halimeda didn't feel the features of the face did her master credit either. The nose was too large, the eyes bulging, and the mouth too small. She hoped that the stone-cutters who'd created this masterpiece had been the first to go into the fiery pit as offerings.

These human priests who served him here seemed equally inadequate. They were too fat, proving that they had grown greedy and lazy, keeping back too many of the goats and platters of sweets brought for Lord Melqart. In addition, it appeared to Halimeda that the priests had failed to secure proper girls for sacrifice. The first slut that had gone into the fire was no prize. Halimeda doubted that the she was even a virgin. She had a well-used look about her, and she was missing several front teeth, a sure sign of inferior stock. The only good thing you could say about her was that she had good lungs and a talent for screaming.

Halimeda studied the face of the bull man statue, hoping to see some spark of life. If Melqart made an appearance in the flesh tonight, it would be a show that these poor excuses for priests would remember for the rest of their short, pitiful lives. Caddoc should have been here at her side. She'd given him the credit for producing Poseidon's granddaughter, and here she was standing alone. It was a total waste. Lord Melqart had looked hard for her son. Since Caddoc was apparently nowhere to be found, she supposed he must have fled to the far oceans of the world—probably to Samoa with his stupid crony Tora.

Another victim was dragged kicking and wailing toward the crack in the earth. The ever-burning fires below were the remains of an old volcano, thousands of feet below. She wondered how many of the humans who resided on Cyprus realized that their homes and places of business perched on top of a festering time bomb.

The priests began chanting again, off key as usual. It was all Halimeda could do not to cancel the entire production. Lord Melqart should allow her to bring mermaids into the temple. Their voices would put those of these puny humans to shame. She prepared herself for the prospect that nothing would go as she'd so carefully planned. With her luck, Halimeda thought, Poseidon wouldn't even notice that his grandchild was missing. One girl child more or less, especially such a troublesome one, probably meant nothing to him.

This second sacrifice was a joke as well. Not a girl, but a woman. Halimeda never could guess the age of humans, especially the females. But she would venture the squalling bitch, presented to Melqart's image by the two grinning priests, was at least forty. She was so skinny that the priests must have been gobbling her rations, rather than fattening her on sugary treats and fat meats, as they were supposed to do.

Back in the day, a real god like Artemis or Ares would have blasted the entire temple with a thunder bolt and started anew with a fresh batch of dedicated priests. No, to put it in human vernacular, in spite of his tricks with the earthquake and the tidal wave, Melqart wasn't quite up to par. It was past time that she took the reins of power into her own capable hands and set him straight.

"Bring out the princess!" she ordered. "Lord Melqart demands the Atlantean king's daughter." *Daughter, granddaughter, what did it matter to him? Not being a humanoid, Melqart would have little grasp of personal relationships anyway. One was as good as the other.*

The two priests by the edge of the pit stopped and stared at her as if unsure what to do with the shrieking woman.

"Throw her in!" Halimeda commanded. *What else would they do with her? Crown her with flowers and carry her back to her cage on their shoulders?*

In an amazing burst of energy, the woman wiggled out of their grasp, fell face down on the floor, and began crawling away. The priests, forgetting all dignity, ran after her. One grabbed a handful of her dirty hair and the other a dirty bare foot. The woman continued to squeal so loudly that the chanters stopped singing and gaped fish-mouthed at her audacity. The bald priest, the one who had the victim by the foot, began dragging her back toward the hole. She howled and scratched at the floor in a most undignified manner.

Halimeda covered her eyes with her hands in exasperation. When she summoned nerve to look again, she saw the priest closest to the pit had let go of the woman and was clutching a handful of feathers that had appeared in the center of his bare chest. The second priest, too concerned with his squirming offering to see what his companion was doing, had thrown the woman over his shoulder and was attempting to carry the bitch to the edge of the hole.

But then, as Halimeda stared at the fiasco the sacrifice had become, an arrow flew from the darkness at the back of the sanctuary and struck the second priest in the throat. He dropped the woman, staggered toward the pit, and toppled in. He screamed louder than the first sacrifice on his way down.

The female offering leaped to her feet, arms flailing, and took off like a shark after a bucket of chum. Bare-assed and tits bouncing, she fled past Halimeda, past the chorus of chanters, toward the front of the temple.

The humans who'd been singing dissolved into utter panic. Some ran one way, some fled another. At least two followed the first priest into the pit, one aided by another feathered shaft, and the third because he'd apparently lost his mind and sought the nearest way out. Two mermen dashed in among the throng and were happily slashing and stabbing anyone they could with wicked looking knives.

Halimeda didn't know whether she should pursue the escapee and bring the sacrifice back to finish her performance or simply to make herself absent. Lord Melqart would be heartily displeased by this display of total incompetence, and she didn't want his vengeance to fall on her. Tidal waves would be child's play compared to what he might do when he realized what a debacle this worship service had become. And anyone his gaze fell on would be fair game.

As she turned to make a safe exit, an arrow buried itself in her thigh. The pain nearly drove her off her feet. "You!" she screamed as Morwena stepped from the shadows, bow in hand. "You've killed me!" Halimeda howled.

"Not yet!" Morwena drove a second shaft into Halimeda's stomach.

A second figure ran toward Halimeda as she struggled to pull loose the arrow in her thigh. A priest fell into her, his blood soaking her beautiful gown. As he went down, he clutched at her, caught a necklace of priceless rubies and broke the string. A Hindu king's ransom in gems rained over his thrashing body and mingled with the gore.

"Where is she?" Morwena demanded.

Halimeda looked up to see Poseidon's daughter standing over her, the wicked bow drawn, an arrow only inches from Halimeda's head. Blood was running down her leg and pooling on the floor. The pain in her gut was excruciating. Halimeda knew that if she didn't get back to the salt water soon, she would bleed to death before she could have a chance to regenerate.

Morwena's expression was frightening. "You have three seconds," she said. "One, two—"

"There! There!" Halimeda pointed toward the passageway leading to the crypt where the sacrifices were housed. "The brat is there."

Morwena turned away, but before Halimeda could run back down the tunnel to the sea, the great statue of Lord Melqart began to crumble. Jagged pieces of stone fell around her, striking her flesh and destroying the remains of her lovely gown. And as she watched, the stone cracked and Melqart emerged. Not so much emerged as appeared, this time in the form of the life-destroying, bull-headed man.

"How dare you invade my temple?" he bellowed, his voice as powerful as the roar of an enraged bull. He threw up a hand, and a bolt of lightning flew from his open palm, blasting the nearest priest to eternity.

Morwena froze, eyes wide, mouth open. Even the two mermen ceased their harvest and stood staring in terror at the incarnation of Lord Melqart.

"Do you know who I am? Do you know what power I possess?" Melqart demanded.

Morwena dropped to her knees, her face ashen. The bow fell from her fingers.

"What are you? You're nothing but a child's nightmare!" came another woman's voice. This one was human, Halimeda was certain of it. "You don't exist. You've never existed." There was laughter. "You're nothing but an empty sack of lies."

# CHAPTER 30

Alexandros climbed the rise where Orion and the remaining troops of the Blue-Shields had drawn up in a circle. Waves of shades surrounded them on all sides except the west, the direction Alex had just come from. That side was all rocks and thick outcrops of sea grass which had grown up around the remains of a sunken ferry from the early twentieth century. It wasn't the best protection, but better than none, and there weren't enough able-bodied soldiers left to defend the entire perimeter.

"How bad?" Orion asked when he saw the warrior Alex carried in his arms. It was their younger half-brother Paris, so drenched in blood that Orion wouldn't have known him if it hadn't been for the blue tattoo of a trident—the mark of a king's son—on his right bicep.

Alexandros's eyes revealed the emotion he'd never admit. "Paris needs the healers. If we could get him to the temple . . ." The rest went unspoken as he laid the unconscious boy down on a bed of seaweed. Atlantis lay far away to the west in the depths of the Atlantic Ocean. If there were men free to transport Paris, he would never have survived the journey through the seraphim's gut. Alex shrugged. "His chances are as good as the rest of ours."

Orion nodded. "We could have used his sword. There

are few enough of us left to hold . . ." He trailed off. Fatigue and blood loss had made him slow-witted. "Poseidon? Wasn't Paris—"

"At our father's side?" Alex knelt in the sand and scrubbed his sword blade clean. "The horde swept over the wall. All who fought there died but Paris and a standard bearer, Klemenis. But Klemenis was too far gone. He told me where to find Paris." Again, pain flashed in Alex's green eyes. "I had to fight my way back. I could only carry one of them." His voice cracked. "As it was, the shades were on Klemenis before I'd gone ten yards."

"All died?" Orion repeated numbly. "All?"

His twin rose and laid a hand on Orion's shoulder. "The king is dead. Long live the king."

"Morgan . . ."

". . . Is the new Poseidon," Alex finished. "He died well, our father. As he wished. May the bards say the same of us."

"Here they come!" a sergeant shouted. "Atlanteans to arms! The bastards come!"

"Are you some sort of child's joke?" Elena shouted at Melqart. "You're as pitiful as she is." She pointed at Halimeda who was creeping away toward the tunnel entrance. "Maybe more." Elena scowled and made a shooing motion with her hands, as you might do to clear the water of a bad smell. "Go away! Back to whatever hole you crawled out of."

Melqart attempted a bull's roar, but it came out more of a bleat.

Morwena raised her head and stared at the god of war.

Melqart's face fell, and he looked as though he was about to burst into tears. One horn had sagged, and as they watched, he was visibly growing smaller.

Elena snickered, hands now resting on her hips. "This is what you are? *This* is what frightens people? Broken horns and a saggy gut?"

Melqart's other horn cracked off at his head and fell onto the floor.

Elena paused for breath, and Melqart's eyes narrowed.

"Keep it up!" Morwena cried. "He is ridiculous, isn't he? Laugh at him, Elena."

Elena chuckled. "You really are nothing, aren't you?" She glanced around at the wailing priests who'd managed to evade the knives of the two mermen. "This is what you committed murder for? This is what you've damned your souls for? This . . . this nothing?"

Melqart threw up his right arm. With a sizzle and pop, both arm and hand shrank and dissolved before their eyes. This revelation sent another priest careering over the crack in the floor. He didn't make it. His screams could barely be heard above Melqart's howling.

Elena's voice had become a whisper. "No one believes in you, Melqart. No one ever did."

The howling became a shriek as the rest of Melqart crumbled into a heap of dust. Morwena leaped to her feet, scooped up her bow, and ran to Elena's side.

"Be gone!" Elena shouted at Melqart's crumbled remains. "You're nothing."

The dust settled. The temple grew silent as a tomb. And then, from the pile of dust, came a faint rustling. Morwena held her breath as a fat and loathsome toad wiggled out and hopped away. In the blink of an eye, the gray toad gave a giant leap and vanished into the pit.

Morwena inhaled sharply as she remembered her old enemy, but when she looked at where Halimeda had crouched only a minute before, the witch was gone. "Halimeda's escaping!"

"Danu," Elena said. "We've got to find Danu."

"This way." Morwena hurried in the direction that Halimeda had pointed out. Elena followed, leaving Tadeu and Moises to keep watch in case Melqart returned in a more lethal form.

"How did you do that?" Morwena asked. "How did you know the magic that would destroy Melqart."

"I didn't," Elena admitted. "But it worked with Halimeda, didn't it? I was making it up as I went along." Elena grinned. "But I really don't believe in monsters or in witches."

"Danu!" Morwena called. "Where are you?" A flight of stone steps loomed ahead of them. She glanced at Elena. "Down there, do you suppose?"

Tadeu came up behind them, the point of his knife under a priest's Adam's apple.

The priest was shaking and pleading for his life. "I just get paid to sing," he cried. "I never hurt anybody. I just sing."

"Where is the princess?" the merman asked softly. "Danu."

"I don't know. I just sing."

Tadeu pressed the point harder. A bead of blood appeared on the knife tip.

"They keep the offerings in cages down there!" the priest squealed. "But they couldn't find her when they went to get her. She must have got away. I heard Moris say that her cell was empty."

Morwena vaulted down the steps. The narrow room cut in rock was low ceilinged and dingy. The atmosphere here was one of pure evil. Morwena could almost taste the fear trapped in the stone-walled space.

Small cubicles with iron gates lined both walls. Elena

ran from cage to cage searching, but the only thing that stirred was a scabby brown rat. It bared its teeth at her, squealed, and scurried away.

"Danu!" Elena shouted.

"Danu, come out!" Terror filled Morwena's throat and distorted her voice. *Had they come too late? Had little Danu already been tossed into the pit?*

Tadeu came soundlessly down the stairs.

"Ask him again," Morwena said. "Ask that priest if he knows anything else."

The merman shrugged. "Can't."

"Why not?"

Tadeu looked as rueful as was possible for one of his kind. "He had an accident. He fell."

"On your knife?" Morwena asked, knowing the answer.

The merman nodded.

"But he said he was only a paid singer."

"He watched. For that he deserved to die."

"They're empty," Elena said, throwing her arms out. "The cages are all empty. I looked in every one."

"Shh," Cymry whispered in Danu's head. "Someone is out there. Stay still. They can't see you if you're behind me."

"It's Morwena," Danu said, pushing at the sea horse's rump. "She's good."

"Are you sure?" Cymry asked.

"Yes, I'm sure. She's my daddy's sister. She's come to get me."

"All right, if you're absolutely certain," Cymry said. "But don't tell them about me. And don't tell them I made you invisible."

"In what?"

"*Invisible*. It means that I made a wall of blue light, but it was solid. The bad people couldn't see through it."

"Oh. Am I *im-viss-ble* now?"

The sea horse shook her head. "Not if you don't want to be."

"Why can't I tell anybody about you? You're my friend. My best friend."

"Yes, and you're my best friend now, too. But this is our secret."

"I can't tell anybody, not even Mommy or Grandmother?"

"Nope. Someday, Danu, but not now." Cymry was growing smaller. Danu could see Morwena's face over the top of Cymry's withers.

"Are you going away? Don't go," Danu begged, catching hold of the sea horse's mane. "I don't want you to go away."

"I have to," Cymry whispered. "But I'll be back. When you're older."

"Promise?"

"I promise."

And then, as Danu tried to hold on, the sea horse shimmered, melted into a shower of blue and gold stars and disappeared. "Cymry! Come back!" she cried.

"Danu?" A strange woman's face appeared at the front of the cage. "Morwena! She's here! She's in here!"

"And she's alive!" Morwena cried.

"Of course, I'm alive," Danu exclaimed as she wiggled forward and put up her arms to her Aunt Morwena. "I was here all the time. Hiding. Is my daddy here? I've been waiting a long time for him to come and get me."

\*   \*   \*

Orion came to Elena in the coral garden outside her bedroom in Rhiannon's house after Elena had almost given up hope. . . .

She, Morwena, and Danu had returned to Atlantis, and with the others, waited anxiously for news from the battle-field. First reports, which had come hours after they'd arrived in the city, had been both heartening and terrifying. Poseidon was lost. The king had met his death fighting Melqart's horde. Many had died with him, but there was no word of the safety of the royal princes. What was known was that when all hope was lost, the myriads of shades had inexplicably stopped in mid-assault and dissolved in a frenzy of smoke, stench, and black, oily steam.

"When Elena destroyed Melqart, his shades were destroyed as well," was Morwena's explanation.

But nothing had eased the pain in Elena's heart as she waited and prayed for Orion to return to her. Even now, as she saw him walking toward her, her knees went weak and she rubbed her eyes to make certain that she was really seeing him.

"Orion? Are you *really* alive?" she called. "Or are you just another illusion?"

His answer was to enfold her in his arms and hold her so tightly that she could feel the beating of his heart next to hers. She laid her head on his shoulder and wept for joy. "I was so afraid for you," she whispered. "When I heard that your father . . ." She broke down and sobbed. "I'm so sorry. The king . . ."

"Died a hero's death, as he would like to be remembered."

"Alex?"

"Barely a scratch on him. He has the luck of Apollo."

"No," she whispered. "You're Apollo, my Apollo."

He covered her face with kisses. "I couldn't believe it when Morgan told me what you and Morwena did . . . that you followed Halimeda to Melqart's temple and saved Danu."

"Rescuing her was a lot easier than getting there. I hate the seraphim."

"The seraphim serve us well." He tilted her chin up and kissed her lips tenderly. "Rhiannon sent Lady Athena and teams of healers to the battle site by way of the seraphim transport system. Many good men, including my brother Paris, were saved because she and the other priestesses came."

Elena couldn't stop trembling. "I love you so much," she said, touching him to make certain in her mind that he was real and solid and not her imagination. "I was so afraid that I'd lost you."

"Do you remember that I told you I had something to ask you, something important?"

"Yes, the answer is yes!"

He laughed. "You don't even know what I'm going to ask."

She thumped his shoulder, and he groaned. "Oh, I'm so sorry. Did I hurt you? Are you wounded?" She kissed the spot that she'd just hit with her fist. "Where does it—"

"I hurt everywhere, but it doesn't matter. Pound me all you like, so long as you never leave me." He kissed her again. "Now, what did you just agree to?"

"To become your wife. To stay with you always. To become one of you."

He pushed her away just far enough to gaze into her eyes. "But how did you know that was what I wanted to ask?"

"Rhiannon and Morwena. They told me. Explained all the rules—how, if you asked me to join you under the sea and I accepted, I could be transformed, and we could be married." She smiled up at him. "Morwena said it would save precious time . . . time we should spend together. And if I did the asking, you wouldn't have to worry about me refusing and you being condemned to be frozen in coral for all eternity."

"Woman . . . you are . . ." He stopped. "You will? You agree? You'll become an Atlantean? You'll give up being human to be my wife?"

She laughed. "What did I just say? What did you think? After what we've been through together? Did you think I'd start all over with another man, someone like Greg Hamilton when I can have Apollo?"

Orion gathered her up in his arms and swung her around. "Elena, Elena, Elena, what am I going to do with you?"

"Take me somewhere we can be alone and make love to me."

"Granted. Your wish is my command. Always."

Suddenly, her giddiness dissolved. "But, Rhiannon told me that there would be a six-month period of mourning for Poseidon."

Orion nodded. "That's true. If you want a royal wedding with all the trimmings, we'll have to wait until that's passed and Morgan is crowned."

"What if we took our honeymoon first?" she suggested. "A long one?"

He laughed. "A woman after my own heart. We could do that, Elena, or we could have Lady Athena marry us now, quietly. Whatever you want."

"I think . . ." She smiled at him. "I think I'll hold out for the fairy-tale wedding, with or without the actual fairies." She stroked his cheek, reassuring herself that this was really happening, that she hadn't lost him.

"I warn you," he cautioned. "Atlantean marriages last a long time."

"I wouldn't have it any other way." She chuckled. "There are a lot of underwater sites I can't wait to excavate. If that's allowed . . ."

"Allowed and encouraged. Once you're transformed, you'll be invited to join the royal scientific society, probably given more projects than you'll have time for. We value scholars, Elena. If you want to continue your archeological work . . ."

"I do, I do. My work means everything to me." She laughed. "At least it did before you came along."

His gaze grew serious. "There's something else, Elena, something you need to know. Lord Mikhail . . ."

Fear chilled her. "He didn't die, too?"

"No, he's very much alive. But he isn't here. He's gone on a diplomatic mission to visit all of our colonies and carry the official news of Poseidon's death and prepare them for our new king. He may be gone some months."

"I see."

"You will. You were right, Elena. Mikhail was once human, and he . . . he was your father . . . Is your father."

"But why did he leave before telling me? Doesn't he want me here? Or doesn't he love me anymore?"

Orion cupped her face in his hands and kissed her lips. "Mikhail loves you very much. He asked me to tell you that he would come to you when he returns."

"But why didn't he tell me himself? How could he just go away?"

Orion kissed the top of her head and cradled her against him. "He has to come to terms with his own existence and yours as an adult and as an Atlantean. All these years, you've remained a child in his eyes. That—out of all the human women in the world—I would find you, fall in love with you, and bring you here to Atlantis, is almost more than he can comprehend. Remember, your father is an academic, a scientist. It can be hard for such people to accept fate, and even more difficult to believe in the magic of love."

"Not for me," she said. "Not anymore. I'm sold. Turn me into a mermaid."

"Atlantean woman," he corrected. "Definitely not a mermaid."

"You can really do that? Transform me? Is it painful?"

"We can, and I promise it won't hurt at all."

"How long will it take?"

"A few weeks. Normally it would be sooner, but we'll have to obtain permission from the High Council and from my brother Morgan."

"He's already given it." She chuckled. "Or he will. Rhiannon said that since Morwena and I brought back Danu, we can choose our rewards."

"And have you picked one? A reward?"

"I have. I want you to take me to every historical site featured in the children's museum, starting with Alexander's tomb. It would make the best honeymoon destination . . . destinations." She laughed again.

"We can do that," he promised. "But first, we have some minor housekeeping to tidy up. The coin from Melqart's treasure ship. We can't keep it. It has to be returned. It's not something you should have. Not something safe to have in Atlantis."

"But he's dead, Melqart's dead," she assured him. "He turned into a warty toad and went down into the fire pit in the floor of his temple."

"Maybe he is," Orion said. "But I've found that evil

isn't always easy to destroy. Alexander's tomb lies off the coast of Alexandria, in fifty fathoms of water. We could drop the coin near the site of the shipwreck on our way."

"All right, and . . . I've been thinking about the ring you brought me."

"Which one?"

"The diamond engagement ring that Greg gave me. It seems to me that the best thing to do with that would be to donate it to the tsunami relief fund, if you wouldn't mind doing just a little illusion to deliver it. Greg Hamilton has become somewhat of a hero on Crete. I'm sure he'd be pleased to have his ring go to a good cause."

"Are you certain you want to part with it?"

"Absolutely."

"And the one I gave you?" Orion asked.

"I want that to be my wedding ring."

He kissed her again. "That's what it is, darling. It was my great-grandmother's wedding ring . . . and my mother's. I know she would have wanted you to have it."

Elena felt a new surge of emotion, and her eyes clouded with tears of happiness. "Your mother's wedding ring? And you gave it to me? When you hardly knew me?"

"I love you, Elena Carter. You're the only woman I'll ever want, the only wife I'll ever take."

"Then start by keeping your promise," she said, looking deep into his beautiful green eyes.

"And which promise is that?" he asked.

"To take me somewhere we can be alone and make love to me."

"As I already told you, your wish is my command."

And that's exactly what he did.